HOUSE OF SIGHS

AND ITS SEQUEL

THE SOUND OF HIS BONES BREAKING

AARON DRIES

Let the world know:
#IGotMyCLPBook!

Crystal Lake Publishing
www.CrystalLakePub.com

ISBN: 978-1-64316-675-9

Cover art:
Ben Baldwin—www.benbaldwin.co.uk

Layout:
Lori Michelle—www.theauthorsalley.com

Proofread by:
Paula Limbaugh

House of Sighs was originally published in a limited edition hardcover in 2011 by ChiZine Publications (Canada), and in 2012 by Samhain Horror.

WELCOME TO ANOTHER CRYSTAL LAKE PUBLISHING CREATION.

Thank you for supporting independent publishing and small presses. You rock, and hopefully you'll quickly realize why we've become one of the world's leading publishers of Dark and Speculative Fiction. We have some of the world's best fans for a reason, and hopefully we'll be able to add you to that list really soon. Be sure to sign up for our newsletter to receive two free eBooks, as well as info on new releases, special offers, and so much more.

Welcome to Crystal Lake Publishing—Tales from the Darkest Depths.

OTHER TITLES BY AARON DRIES

The Fallen Boys

Where the Dead Go to Die (co-authored with Mark Allan Gunnells)

A Place for Sinners

And the Night Growled Back (a novella)

OTHER NOVELS BY CRYSTAL LAKE PUBLISHING

Beyond Night by Eric S. Brown and Steven L. Shrewsbury

The Third Twin: A Dark Psychological Thriller by Darren Speegle

Aletheia: A Supernatural Thriller by J.S. Breukelaar

Beatrice Beecham's Cryptic Crypt: A Supernatural Adventure/Mystery Novel by Dave Jeffery

Where the Dead Go to Die by Mark Allan Gunnells and Aaron Dries

Sarah Killian: Serial Killer (For Hire!) by Mark Sheldon

The Final Cut by Jasper Bark

Blackwater Val by William Gorman

Pretty Little Dead Girls: A Novel of Murder and Whimsy by Mercedes M. Yardley

Nameless: The Darkness Comes by Mercedes M. Yardley

OTHER NOVELLAS BY CRYSTAL LAKE PUBLISHING

Quiet Places: A Novella of Cosmic Folk Horror by Jasper Bark

The Final Reconciliation by Todd Keisling

Run to Ground by Jasper Bark

Devourer of Souls by Kevin Lucia

Apocalyptic Montessa and Nuclear Lulu: A Tale of Atomic Love by Mercedes M. Yardley

Wind Chill by Patrick Rutigliano

Little Dead Red by Mercedes M. Yardley

Sleeper(s) by Paul Kane

Stuck On You by Jasper Bark

ACKNOWLEDGEMENTS

Heartfelt thanks go out to Don D'Auria, Brett Savory, and the fine folks at *ChiZine* and *Rue Morgue Magazine*. To Nate Kenyon for the ongoing encouragement. Also, Halli Villegas, your keen eye made this novel so much better.

No book is written, edited, marketed, or given a second life alone.

I could not have done this without Jian Vun, Simon Anlezark, Emma Pandeleon, Amy Neat, Adam Neeves, Belinda Smith, Ben Brock, Lou Smith, or my family—Anne, Warwick, Brent and Kyle Dries.

And of course, Joe Mynhardt.

HOUSE OF SIGHS

PROLOGUE:
IT BEGINS

"There is only one Evil: Disunity."
—Pierre Teilhard de Chardin

ONE HUNDRED AND FOUR

SUZIE MARTEN WAS ten years old when she died.

She lived to dance. Spinning herself sick in search of rhythm, pirouetting until her toes hurt in the ballet shoes her father bought. They were a perfect fit—and let's not forget the pink ribbon laces. She scuffed and broke the soles of those shoes with a knife spirited from the kitchen drawer, just don't tell Mum. Yes, Suzie adored them with the pure love only children can muster, or sustain, for inanimate things. And she was wearing them the day she came unsewn.

November 12th, 1995.

To Suzie, Sunday mornings were the final love-hate pit stop between freedom and being a 'big girl'. Suzie despised school and feared her raven-faced teacher, a man who sometimes got so mad he threw things. She imagined he spent his Sundays alone, watching the clock, eager for Monday to roll around so he could overturn yet another desk. He did this to her best friend. Books and pencils crashed to the floor, an eraser bouncing up to clip one boy's ear. Suzie sat beside her humiliated friend at recess and draped an arm over his shoulder—a brave move considering his sex, because as any ten-year-old girl knows, where there be boys, there be a whole lot of germs.

"It's okay," she whispered in his ear. "I saw on the telly that teachers can't hurt kids. We can sue if we want. He's such a dirty shit."

They looked at each other, shocked. *Dirty shit.*

"Suzie Marten, you can't say that. If they hear you, they'll send a letter home to your ma and she'll wash your mouth out with soap. I saw that on the telly, too."

"Na-uh she won't. My ma's too tired for that. Always in bed. Besides, she says words like that. She works the dogwatch at the hospital—whatever that means. She gets home from work when everyone else is getting up. I don't know what the dog has to do with it. I once saw this boring black-and-white movie about a vampire who only ever came out at night. He could turn into a bat and flew 'round eating people, and during the day he slept in a box. Did'ja ever see that one?"

Suzie once teased her mother's mouth open with a spoon while she slept to see if she had fangs. Donna Marten bolted awake, grabbed her daughter by the wrist and pulled her under the sheets. They laughed and had Fruit Loops for dinner.

On the morning of the ninth, Donna fell into bed after a ten-hour shift. Knees ached, the stink of disinfectant and cigarettes sweating from her pores, too tired to shower. Suzie pulled the blankets up to her mother's chin.

"Mum," Suzie said, voice drawn out and meek.

"What is it, honey? I'm dead on my feet."

"Well."

"Come on, out with it. I'm two ticks from dreaming."

"Well, I was just wondering. How come on television mums don't get old? How come Julia Roberts never gets wrinkles or anything, but you're starting to look like an old lady? A bit of an old rag."

Mother stared into daughter's innocent eyes.

Innocent, Donna reminded herself. *Innocent. Forgive her, for she knows not what she says.*

It was an expression her own mother had been fond of using, and often. Donna never really understood its meaning—its weight—until that moment, there in her bedroom with her daughter by her side. For the last time.

"Count yourself lucky I love you, Suzie," she said, wishing her little girl were old enough to start lying like everyone else. Despite this, they kissed each other bye-bye and all was forgiven, as it should be. Donna watched her daughter pull the door shut, taking with her the smell of Strawberry Shortcake, of pre-teen sweat.

Suzie passed a cabinet of her gymnastics trophies in the hallway, glass planes shaking as she bounced along. Her reflection twittered from one family photo to another. Leaping into the kitchen in her socks, she slid to the refrigerator; it was covered in drawings and magnets, school reports, and shopping receipts.

Alone at last.

Her father was away on another one of his business trips. Where he went she didn't quite know, but she was always glad to see him go because he never came back empty-handed. Once he brought a packet of windup crayons home—and the good kind, unlike those her friends owned, crayons that had to be tossed if twisted too far.

Another time, the ballet shoes.

Watched *Sailor Moon* over cereal. Pulled her hair into a ponytail. Brushed her teeth, bristles frayed as the wheat stalks on her uncle's farm after a storm. Suzie didn't see much of her extended family anymore, not with her father always traveling and her mother sleeping day after day.

Donna Marten would find dried toothpaste splashes on the bathroom mirror a week later. She licked them off and fell to the floor, mouth tasting of mint and the briny tang of tears.

Suzie put on her headphones even though the padding itched her ears, and slipped into a pink leotard and tutu. Thumbed PLAY on the Walkman so music filled her ears. She went into the yard, front door clapping shut behind her.

Meanwhile, within the house, a mechanic hum escaped the freezer. The grandfather clock ticked away. Gentle draughts tickled the wind chimes near the window until they laughed. Through it all Donna Marten snored.

The little girl danced to *Mister Boombastic* ("say me fan-tas-*tic*!") on the front lawn. In her opinion, she lived on the most boring street in all of James Bridge, maybe even all of Australia: a rarely traveled stretch of road on the outskirts of town. They had no neighbors, but should a car come along she liked the idea of being seen. This was why she danced, and why she danced so well. She didn't twirl and fall for herself, but for everything. There was simply nothing else to do.

Autumn was hot that year, her house surrounded by matchstick grass. The valley hissed when the wind blew through the dead trees, a desperate, lonely sound.

Suzie spun and curtsied, laughing. *I could do this all day. And I just might, too. Go on, try to stop me.*

Dirty shit. Dirty shit!

She loved watching her shadow on the lawn, the way it was a part of her, except for those times when she leapt into the air and they separated. These moments, which seemed so much longer than they were, left her floating and sad. The kind of sad not even *Mister Boombastic* ("say me fan-tas-*tic*!") could mend.

I wish I could fly forever, only I'd miss my shadow. I really would.

That would be a little like losing a friend.

Four hours after falling asleep, panic reached into the dark and ripped Donna from her bed. Her stomach knotted, brow flecked with sweat. It hadn't been the screeching tires or muted gunshot that woke her—fatigue muted both. It was that her mind fled her body and the flesh had no choice but to follow.

She threw the door open and ran from room to room. Nothing.

"Suzie!" Voice feral and unrecognizable.

Something burned within her chest, fueling dread. The house was empty.

Donna stumbled outside, squinting against sunlight. Pain thudded in her head and shot down her spine. Suzie wasn't in the backyard. As she rounded the house and neared the front gate, heat waves coming off the brick wall to her right. She fumbled with the latch. Next to her were the trashcans, their stench reaching out to make her feel ill. The latch opened and the gate swung wide—a sharp cry of metal grinding metal.

Donna ran onto the front lawn and stopped.

Her daughter's shattered Walkman near the gutter, ribbons of gray tape fluttering in the wind. Suzie Marten was strewn in pieces across the road.

Crows fluttered over intestines, disturbing the stillness. One hopped onto the little girl's head, spread its bloodied wings and squawked. It lowered its beak and ate the tongue cooking against the tar.

A pink ballet shoe. The foot still inside.

Donna screamed. Breath ran short as her nostrils filled with the stink; a putrid mix of chemicals and sugarcane, shit and salt. She would never forget it.

Darkness flittered over Donna's vision as she ran to her child, lashing at the birds. They twirled and cawed, sprinkling blood drops over her face. "Get away from my baby!" she screamed, arms thrashing. But the beaks returned to meat, to gorge.

Delicate, soft stabbing sounds.

Another crow settled on Donna's shoulder and its feathers brushed her cheek. Her world emptied. She clambered over gravel. *This isn't happening. It can't be. I'm dreaming—that's it! I'm still sleeping, my baby isn't torn to pieces*. Donna giggled. Parents weren't equipped to see these sights; to smell such insane, bitter scents.

She fought the birds again, kicked, punched. Donna didn't comprehend what she was doing until she held one of the animals in her hand. Its scream mingled with her own, formed a single high-pitched mewl that echoed across the fields. She let it drop, wings broken.

Donna fell to her knees and attempted to scoop up as much of her daughter as she could. Arms swept wide in manic, possessive hugs, pulling the larger chunks closer. Tears slipped down her face. She gave in and settled on the largest intact fragment: Suzie's head, neck, collarbone, and left arm, which held on by a thinly stretched tendon and little more. Only the birds were hungry and selfish and wouldn't let their bounty escape without a fight. They swooped, black-on-black eyes both empty and cold.

The chunk of Suzie was only a quarter of her corpse, but it felt heavier than her daughter had ever been intact. She turned her back to the crows, deflecting swoops and scratches. The weight in her arms lessened and something slapped against her shins, something warm and wet.

Donna was a nurse and assisted doctors in surgery. What she saw now was unlike anything she had ever seen at work. It was small and childlike.

A child's healthy heart with many years of beating left to do.

Donna collapsed amid a flurry of dark wings, dark shadows.

PART ONE:
BOARDING

"Men's courses will foreshadow certain ends, to
which,
if persevered in, they must lead . . . "
—Charles Dickens

ONE HUNDRED AND THREE: JAMES BRIDGE

"WE HAVE TWO cemeteries and no hospitals—so drive carefully", read the sign coming into James Bridge. The population at the time was marked at a firm 2022.

Outsiders built homes in its vacant lots, leaving neighbors scratching their heads, wondering what spell The Bridge cast over those not born there. Surrounded by vineyards and two hours northwest of Sydney, it was a highway town passed through on the way to somewhere better.

Bobby Deakins, the local mail carrier, laughed when he read books about people in small communities knowing everyone and their business. "Not true of The Bridge," he often said to his son, a boy defined by naivety. Their town was its own schoolyard—with cliques and bullies, princesses and nerds. People didn't mingle much. It seemed it was only he who knew what postcards were sent where, whose magazine subscriptions were to be slipped under the Welcome mat and not left face-up on the veranda.

On Sunday, the twelfth of November, he attended a morning service at St. Joseph's with his wife.

Watched the Australian Grand Prix on his old Panasonic television, despite reception so shitty it looked like the cars were racing their eighty-one laps in snow. He listened to a football game on a transistor radio forever tuned to 2HD—*none of that young'un shit, thank you!* After all this, an afternoon nap with a damp cloth over his eyes. By Monday the town changed, word having spread.

The editor of the *Bridge Bugle* failed to get his cover story completed in time for the early printing, so it came out in Tuesday's paper instead. When Bobby saddled his motorcycle that morning, he did so with a heavy heart. The *Bugle's* front page listed the names of the dead, and he delivered those names door to door. The editor stood at the threshold to his office, cigarette in hand, face as white as the pages his namesake was printed upon.

Bobby Deakins looked at the sign on the way into town and hated it for its cheeriness.

Drive carefully!

"Fuck me," he said.

That Tuesday morning, he also wanted to add, *We have an unmanned police station and nobody really knows anyone and we're grieving and why don't you take your cameras and fuck off.*

Bobby always assumed the worst killer on those streets were the streets themselves. *In Memoriam* wreaths were pinned to telephone poles all over town. When the roads were wet, they could be murder. He believed this before what happened, before Liz Frost.

Over the next three weeks, Bobby Deakins attended more funerals than he had ever been to in his life.

ONE HUNDRED AND TWO: LIZ

"THE GIRL'S NOTHING but skin and bone." Laughter, the electric crackle of the wicker chair under his weight. "I've seen scarecrows with more stuffing." Liz shied away, dug her toes into the lawn and closed her eyes. In the dark—the smell of grass and cooked onions, the wind growling until her father's voice faded away.

Safe.

At fourteen, her mother measured Liz at five feet against the kitchen doorframe. "God's stretching you like taffy," Reggie said, tucking the permanent marker into her blouse pocket. "I'm going to have to put a brick on your head to slow you down." A shy smile on Liz's face as her mother ruffled her bangs. "Out you go." She gestured towards the back door, a hand on the seat of her daughter's overalls to get her moving, and within seconds Liz was outside with two tennis rackets in hand. She gave one to her younger brother.

"Here you go, weed."

"That ain't my name," he spat back. "It's Jed and you know it."

"Yeah well, 'ain't' isn't a real word, so why should I call you anything when you can't speak any proper

English? Don't they teach you anything at school?" The two siblings glared at each other, their slight shadows long across the ground.

"Yeah well, you're skinny. So how's about we just do this, okay?"

They spent the afternoon playing tennis with mandarins plucked straight from the tree. Exhausted, they lay surrounded by a litter of exploded orange grenades, each wearing beards of citrus and dirt. Liz was happy.

Her father threw the back door open, picked a dripping racket up off the grass, and smashed it across her face. It made a hollow *boing*-ing sound, like something from a cartoon. "God damn it, Liz," he said. "Look what you did to that bloody tree!"

Jed leapt to his feet and stumbled across the yard on shaking legs, unaware of his screams. He disappeared among the trees and continued to run, hating himself for not staying to defend his sister. Hidden in twilight and the branches of a dying eucalyptus, Jed collapsed, crying, and wondered why Liz had been punished and he had not.

Summer, 1979. Liz fumbled with the fly of her boyfriend's denims in the front seat of his Mercury Cougar. The Knack's *My Sharona* whispered through veils of static on the radio. She noticed his faint smile, green in the glow from the dash. Her body tingled, the hair on her arms dancing. In his smile, she saw a chance for happiness with someone who maybe loved her. Maybe was enough.

He leaned forward, imitation leather seats whining

as he kissed her. When their lips drew apart, Liz could still taste his tongue. Juicy Fruit and sour lemonade.

The following day she found her father weeping into his hands, bent double in his favorite chair. "Daddy?"

Wes turned to study his daughter. "You break me, Liz." The bones in his neck cracked. He sat upright, not looking at her, and said she would never see that boy again. She didn't.

The notches on the kitchen doorframe scaled higher and higher.

Friends came and went. Liz was a good student, nothing extraordinary. She got top marks when it came to hiding bruises from teachers' prying eyes.

The Frost residence was a two-storied house on an open property in the Hunter Valley. The nearest neighbors were a mile and a half away. Oven-hot in summer, freezing come the colder months, Liz knew every creak of the staircase, each loose floorboard its own alarm bell. She couldn't step onto the veranda without her father, Wes, grabbing her by the wrist and yanking her back inside.

"Why won't you let me go, Dad? I'm nineteen. I'm not an idiot."

He stood over her, pushed in close. His breath smelled of dead mice. Somewhere in him she knew there was sadness, could hear it in his warnings. "I want you to go, but you know you can't. It's not you I don't trust."

She bought her first car at twenty-two and that grip on her wrist loosened. Wes aged overnight. Liz drove for the sake of driving. She had nowhere to go.

All roads led home.

Liz eyed the mirror on the rear of her bedroom door.

Yeah, I'm skinny. Too tall? Hell, maybe.

Then again, she could be all the things people said she was. If she gave in to it.

Sparse clearings behind the thicket of trees at the end of their yard. She walked through them some early mornings, watched frost melt from the branches and dropping onto her nose. Into her mouth. Cool on her tongue.

Here she lay with ghosts.

The ghost of a girl who refused to let herself grow into something she didn't want to be; the ghost of the teenager who hoped for happiness holding hands with a woman who also never existed and was only aspired to. Liz was happy in the clearing. But each morning brought with it spiders waiting to spin fresh webs, ushered snakes out of hibernation. The scrub came with risks, and not even her ghosts could keep Liz safe. Here, among trees that resembled piled skeletons, watched by kangaroos foraging for berries, next to the remains of a dead fox with a tawny pelt writhing with maggots, Liz's ghosts took her by the hand. Time to leave this place. She walked to the house with pangs of dread in her gut and twigs in her hair. Nothing lasted.

Liz Frost was born on the sixteenth of August, 1963, with her umbilical cord tight around her neck. She fought from the start. On November 12th, 1995, at seven forty in the morning, she sat on her bed, put a gun in her mouth and closed her eyes.

The day began.

ONE HUNDRED AND ONE: SARAH

SARAH CARR RAN down her hallway and stopped before a mirror to check her cropped, spiked hair. "Pushing sixty-three but I don't look a day over forty-five." Her laughter was a sad, husky sound in this house. Self-affirmations like these got her through the day.

Flat shoes thumped the floorboards as she searched for the keys. Sarah considered herself, and with a certain amount of pride, as a hip nanna in high-waisted jeans. The kind of nanna her grandchildren could approach with anything. Nobody would deny her open-mindedness, maybe even calling her a little *different* by Bridge standards—yet still she wore those shoes. Always. Those sensible flats, as reliable and well-worn as her wisdom.

"Do unto others as you would have them do unto yourself," she told her grandkids, their round, innocent faces staring up at her. "And those aren't my words." It was one of her recycled lines, one that left her feeling a little flat, a little well-worn herself. Though she sometimes spoke His words, she didn't give a flying fuck about God anymore.

Still, a large, garish crucifix hung around her neck.

"Every nanna needs her bling," she once said to fellow parishioners after a Palm Sunday luncheon, face still streaked with ash. They glared at her, shocked. "Oh, come now, Madame here isn't fading into the background. How else are the young going to know who to turn to if us old biddies are invisible?"

Hot air blew through the house. Unusual for autumn.

She doubled back to the mirror and snarled, checking for lipstick smears; were she to see them on someone else, all conversation must cease until the affected person rectified the matter. "Don't be bashful, Joan. If a bird shat on my shoulder and I hadn't noticed, wouldn't you hand me a Kleenex?" Mitigate your humiliation, that was her policy. Relieved, lips drew shut, shielding smear-free teeth.

A heavy voice floated up the hall. "Sarah!"

"What do you want?"

"I'm dy-*iiinnnggg.*"

"Oh, jump in the lake." She picked up her over-the-shoulder purse and went to her husband. She found Bill Carr upright in bed with tissues stuffed in his nose.

"I thought you'd left and left me for the crows."

"No, sorry, sweetie. I'm not having any dirty birds flying around inside, thank you very much. When you're a hairsbreadth away from meeting our maker, I'll ever so gently throw you on the lawn. Got to keep clean house."

"Your kindness knows no bounds." He chuckled, coughed, a wet rattle in his throat.

"Love, I'd fix you another batch of warm lemon tea if I had the time."

"No, it's okay. I like sounding this way. I sound all gangster."

"Ah, posh *Gangstah!*" She waved him off and returned to the hall. "Have you seen the thingies?"

"The what?"

"You know, the thingies?"

"What thingies, you silly old bat?"

"The doo-en-acky. Oh, shit."

"English, woman, for Heaven's sakes. And swear jar, please. I may be bedridden and dying but I'm not deaf. Dollar to the fat lady, thank you muchly."

Sarah went to the mantelpiece and found her husband's wallet. She took a dollar coin and ran to the hallway table. Upon it was a wooden moneybox in the shape of a female Islander. The coin slipped through her breasts and disappeared with a clink.

"Done." Then resumed her search. "Now where is it? If I keep this up, I'll miss the bus to town."

"I'm a sick man. Enough with the badgering, you coot."

In the living room, she lifted a lounge cushion, revealing keys bound to a ring with a thumb-sized photograph of her grandkids in a silver frame dangling from it. "Found them, Bill, you can stop searching."

Sarah glanced around the room. Small. Neat. Theirs. She opened both the front and back doors each Saturday to let the breeze flow through, sitting in the airflow with her eyes closed. Bill often found her there, silhouetted against the sun, cursing. The crucifix about her neck reminded them of who betrayed whom. Sarah never forgot those who had crossed her.

Congratulations, ma'am. You've won our annual sweepstakes. And your prize—yep, that's right, your husband has cancer!

Sarah thought it a terrible injustice to witness her

husband's slow death, day after day, and feared living on once he was gone.

"Did you find what you were looking for?" Bill asked, the last word dropping as Sarah emerged in the doorway, straightening her collar. She showed him the keys.

"Ah, keys! *Keys* they are called. You're losing it, old woman."

She buckled her cowboy belt. For years, she'd been trying to lose weight. Now she couldn't keep it on. Stress took its toll. "This old gray Dane, she ain't what she used to be."

"What do you need them for anyway?" Bill coughed again. "I'm not going anywhere so you don't need to lock up."

"Bill, you never know these days. Anyone could just waltz on in and rob us blind. God only knows you're not going to get up off your throne and defend our telly, right?" She ran to the foot of the bed. "And don't forget, our darling daughter is coming by with Madame Five to see her pa-pa after lunch, so don't go and, like, die or anything before they get here, 'kay?"

"Begone, foul hob!" He threw his arms at her. "The power of Christ compels you!"

"Jump in the lake. Bye-bye, baby-luv."

"See you later, Peggy-Sue," he said.

Sarah ran out the door and slammed it shut. Silence descended over the house, disturbed only by the occasional shuffle as the near-dead man wrangled with his bed sheets.

ONE HUNDRED: PETER

AS FAR AS Peter Ditton was concerned, a little sun was always a little sun too much, so he settled for whatever shade the **STOP HERE** sign granted. His fair features were burning already. Australian sunshine knew no mercy, and although clouds would come, the sky above remained a clear bowl of hot blue for now.

Peter shielded his eyes from the red cloud of dust stirred by a passing truck, the first vehicle to swish past in over an hour. He'd mistaken the weekly route for the weekend's and had expected the 243 bus to Maitland earlier than this. Oh, well.

A notebook in hand. The spine cracked and a sliver of twine marking his page.

The plan: skip church, visit a friend, together go to a creative writing and poetry class at the Rotary club in town, and pour out their souls to the laughter of slot machines chewing pensions in the adjoining room. The room stank of beer and old paper. Sometimes the organizers provided tea. Nice in a way.

Embarrassment almost always overcame Peter as he stood before the group. *I'm a joke to them because I'm only eighteen.* On his last visit, the head mentor urged him to write something real. This time, Peter felt he'd done just that. Up to now, his poems concerned girls, echoing the rhythmic timing of pop ballads. Peter wrote to calm himself, and he found he needed calming after his mother finished with him. She was furious that he was missing another Sunday sermon, and as such, refused to drive him. And so, the pen scratched hard and fast that morning, words spilling onto the page.

He felt better afterwards, a little less like punching someone.

On the bus stop sign, someone had written the words "die aids breedin faggets". He turned away, bothered, and fiddled with his notebook, the end of the scarlet twine like a cut in his palm. He couldn't imagine why someone would choose to be homosexual—didn't they know what they were condemning themselves to? He'd read that one out of every ten men was or had the possibility of being gay. If that were true, then the graffiti might be directed at someone he went to school with.

He experienced nightmares about AIDS. In one, a man whose flesh had been eaten away came for him. When he spoke, corn-kernel teeth fell from his mouth, clattering on the floor. The man put his palsied hand on Peter's shoulder, and then he understood—*He's got the disease!*

Awaking, he still felt that clammy touch.

Peter held the notebook so hard his fingertips turned milky. He cocked his head at the sound of crunching gravel, the shadow of a man mingling with his own.

NINETY-NINE: STEVE

STEVE BROWN WANTED to scream.

Instead, he focused on catching his breath. The skinny kid next to him at the bus stop—who looked like he'd been too busy doodling his notebook instead of some schoolgirl like other normal kids his age—hadn't reacted. Good. His cool was in check.

Poor shit, Steve thought. *He's better off.*

Or maybe he knows something about women that I don't.

Although he doubted that.

Steve's thoughts turned back to his wife. She had the wonderful ability of confusing him into anger, which hurt because he loved her like the world was ending. No wonder he wanted to bellow frustrations into the new day.

Bev *appeared* okay with him quitting his job as janitor at the James Bridge Public School. He gave his reasons, citing differences with the principal and harassment in the workplace. Bev nodded along, understanding.

Or so he thought.

In reality, he'd been fired—caught smoking pot

under the year-six dormitory where the kids stored their bicycles. "You can do whatever you damn well want in your own time," yelled the principal, "which, *Charlie* Brown, there is going to be plenty more of. I'll be damned if I'm going to sit here and let you burn the place down. Jesus, there's a fire ban at the moment."

Man, he hated people calling him Charlie.

Fuckers.

Bev stared at him, her look almost feline, and right then he understood why Babylonians sealed cats up in bricks. "Okay," she said. Ice cold. "I guess I'll pick up a couple of extra shifts at the mill. Until things pan out. You'd do the same for me, right?"

A test. "You got it, babe."

Two days passed and over a dinner of mashed potatoes and homemade rissoles, Bev snapped. "Would you eat with your trap shut! Watchin' all that meat there going in and out of you is making me wanna puke, you lying cockroach."

She pronounced it *cock-a-roach*, like a sing-song.

He swallowed, hard and slow.

"Nope, don't say anything! Don't say a single bloody word. I don't want to hear it." She stood and left the table. From the next room, he listened to her bang plates, to mutterings loud enough for him to hear—an aggravating, deliberate move. "I work so hard. I work so hard and *he* does this to us."

Steve didn't get it. *I try to do right and hold back on the details so she doesn't have to worry, because she's the one making the dinner and buying the food as well, and look where it gets me?*

He hated the entire situation, especially now that every time he laid money on the dogs down at the

James Bridge Federal, guilt near crippled him. It didn't stop him from laying that spectacular 'winning' bet, though. And losing. He loved his wife, but he didn't think that was enough anymore. Not by a long shot.

Bev blew her top when he told her he was thinking of going to the Maitland golf club with mates that morning. "It's okay, babe. Eddie's gonna pay for it and you know it's only a couple of bucks. They're going to be showing the Grand Prix on those big screens they just put up near the bar, and I read in the Saturday papers that Bon Jovi's going to sing afterwards. Bon Jovi! Come on, Bev, it's a Sunday."

"Sunday? Jesus, Steve, you're on the dole!" She shook her head and banged a hand against the kitchen countertop. He grabbed his wallet out of Saturday's football shorts, traded flip-flops for running shoes—club regulation required closed footwear on the course at all times—and pulled a jersey over his bare chest.

"If you're going, don't even think about taking the car."

"Oh, come on, babe. There's never police on the road. Not here."

Her look silenced him. *Babylon had it right,* he thought.

"Shaping up to be a hot one, eh?" Steve asked the kid.

"Excuse me?"

"Hot one, don't you reckon?"

"Oh, right. Sure is." A moment passed. "Aren't you burning up in that jersey?"

Steve laughed. "This ain't no jumper, mate." He

puffed his chest out, chin rising. "This here's a second skin. You follow the Newcastle Knights, then?"

The kid looked at his pigeon-toed feet, straightened them out. "I don't really follow League all that much."

"Shit a brick. Don't tell me you're a Union fan?"

"Yeah, don't really follow Union either. Soccer's all right. I play it at school every now and then."

Steve snorted. "Soccer. *Ha.*"

The kid snatched his backpack off the ground. "Looks like the bus is going to show after all."

Steve studied the horizon and saw the gilded reflection of sun against glass up ahead. Heard the whine of an approaching vehicle. A dull, lifeless sound.

"Better late than never," Steve said.

NINETY-EIGHT:
DIANA AND JULIA

NOT SO LONG AGO, nothing more than a worn patch of grass by the road signaled the stop. Two people sat on the new bus bench now, quiet and unmoving, handbags clutched in their laps.

Diana Savage appeared younger than her twenty-six years. Hair pulled back in a bun, face covered in a film of sunscreen lotion. She despised putting it on—it felt like chicken grease. Nevertheless, burning was worse. She would happily trade this moment, her job, her future in Australia, for one more look at Astoria, Oregon. Home. She wanted to fish the Colombia River and laugh at the tourists walking up the private driveway, cameras clicking, to where *The Goonies* had been filmed. She missed sitting near the E. Morning Basin at the end of Thirty-Sixth Street, smoking cigarettes and skipping class.

Home wasn't dead trees and inescapable heat. Hell, Summer was still nigh.

In her world, yellow fire hydrants crouched on every corner. Pastel chalet houses. Pontiacs and GMC trucks. Watching the Fighting Fishermen at the LCB Bowling Alley. An American accent.

Her mother's grave.

Susanne Savage wrapped her car around a Douglas fir, ripping herself apart in the process. Diana was thirteen at the time and had been at summer camp when the news got to her. No more advice or discipline from that great woman. No more Christmas presents signed, *Luv Mom*. Diana faced womanhood alone. Memories bobbed like scattered debris in the ocean, some sinking one by one.

Her mother taking her to the Haystack rocks on Cannon Beach, making sandcastles and waving to the joggers.

Diana's first taste of olives. Holding the little green marble in her fingertips, a bead of oil slipping into her palm. She put it in her mouth and spat it out just as quick.

That girl with a mother bore little relation to the one tossing roses on the casket, or the young woman who stood by and watched as her father met a new woman—the Australian tourist with a child of her own.

Her stepsister sat next to her on the bench.

Julia Belfry, sixteen, her narrow face hidden under a black bob. Her shoulders were slight and cheeks freckled.

My God, she's like porcelain, Diana thought. *And so stupid.*

Their secret hung heavy between them.

Diana suggested the movie. *Clueless* was playing at Reading Cinemas in Maitland. Afterwards, they could prowl the shelves at K-Mart, seeking distractions in the budget bins near the wraith-like woman at the front who checked your bags with the ferocity of an airport customs officer. If Diana's car hadn't chosen to sputter and die that morning, they very well may be at the theater by now, chewing on their stripy Coke straws and still trying to avoid what needed to be said.

Instead, they sat there with their heels crossed and clutching their belongings on that brand-new bus bench. Waiting. Wooden palings hard against their backs, yet neither voiced discomfort. Even speaking was a kind of defeat.

Diana burned. And remained no closer to home.

NINETY-SEVEN: MICHAEL

MICHAEL DELANEY USED to be fat. Not puppy-padding fat—bursting-frankfurts-in-a-boiling-pot *fat*. He remembered gym class and swimming lessons. All the thin guys could be divided into one of two groups: those who looked but didn't comment, and those who looked and commented with enthusiasm.

Tubby Bitch.

Fat Mumma.

Fanny Tits.

The silent ones were the worst. They just stared.

Fat kids are like alcoholics, he now knew. They always have excuses.

"I'm not big, just big boned," he said. Michael could fool himself but he couldn't fool the skinny kids. "I'm fat. Butterball fat," he would tell the person staring back at him in the mirror, smart enough to know that no fat kid ever got thin unless they started calling themselves what they really were.

"I'm Santa-Claus fat. I'm I-make-you-sick fat. I'm I-make-myself-sick fat."

He was something else also, but that was harder to say.

Another memory: crying after swimming class,

hating having to strip down to his Speedos in front of the other guys. He tickled himself to tighten his chest but the indoor pool was heated, and soon his nipples turned to marshmallows again. He once made a girdle out of *Glad Wrap* and wore it to school. It worked, even though it made breathing difficult. Come twelve thirty in the middle of Mrs. Montgomery's Legal Studies class, he started sweating. *Sweating bad.* Every time he moved, plastic screeched. It dug into his skin and refused to tear when he tried to rip it off in the washroom. He had to slide the girdle up to his midsection, the top edge wedged into the cleft of his breasts. He cried in the shower that night so his parents wouldn't know.

Michael wanted what the other guys had—sculptured bodies. For the longest time, he mistook attraction for admiration. Eventually, he realized he liked looking at the bodies because he liked the bodies. *I guess I'm gay. The last thing I fucking need.*

So Michael started to walk. Walks turned into jogs. Pounds fell away with surprising speed, and people noticed. He liked that they looked, especially guys, even though he felt dirty for enjoying the attention.

Halved meals. Occasional purging. Instant lightness was heaven. He broke himself of that addiction when he read that continuous self-induced vomiting increased the chance of throat cancer, teeth rot, and of course, bad breath.

Cancer.

He knew the word meant death, but even that word 'death' was alien. It was the concept of his teeth falling out that made him pull the bile-coated fingers from his throat.

The last of his fat disappeared over the course of

one six-week Christmas break. When he went back for his final year of school, people didn't recognize him. His parents sent him to the doctor, fearing some terminal disease, only he wasn't dying. No, Michael lived, as did the ugliness in the mirrored reflection, the skinny somebody who hadn't built muscle to accommodate the rapid loss. Breasts were empty sacks covered in stretch marks, just another something to hate and be embarrassed by. It was likely his need for validation that drove him to what came next.

On the twelfth of November, 1995, he stood outside a house in James Bridge.

The house.

Within those walls, Michael said fuck you to the lies, a decision cast the night before, under the sheets. The house belonged to Clive, a man who as far as Michael knew, bore no last name. He found this as sad and depressing as anything he'd ever experienced in his life—that so much could hinge on the warrant of a man he didn't know.

Michael exhaled, the stink of *Old Spice* and engine grease on his skin. Clive's smell. He wanted to be back in the house, with this stranger, wanted to slip his tongue in Clive's ear again and taste the bitterness of those lonely thoughts.

No more lies or sadness. Michael *liked* last night—and this morning. Loved it. He could outrun fat, but he couldn't outrun this.

Gay. Fag. Poofter.

Sure, Michael believed he'd suffer. When his parents found out, their slaughtered expectations would change everything. Because this was the way things went—wasn't it?

Clive's half-obscured silhouette in the window, a knot of shadows and curtain.

Michael could still taste toothpaste from an undignified morning after finger-wash. Clive's bathroom was small and smelled of cigarettes. A wedding ring on the basin, catching morning light like a coin at the bottom of a wishing well. The minty flavor lingering in Michael's mouth made him feel like a man. It confirmed reality. His new now. That turned him on.

Warm wind sent the trees into shivers about him. Michael's cowlick fell over his eyes. His reflection illustrated the window, ugliness turning away. He walked at first, but those strides evolved into a run. The world rushed up to meet his feet.

Michael ran to the bus stop with the exact change for the 243 back to Maitland in his pocket. He looked up the street and noticed the vehicle approaching. It grew larger and larger, rolling to a stop before him, blocking out the sun. In its shadow lurked a chill. The door hissed as it opened. A murder of crows shot into the sky nearby. Flapping wings like distant schoolyard giggles.

He climbed the steps into the maw of the bus. Stopped. Waited for his eyes to adjust. Out of the dim swam the driver, all pale and sweaty. Michael offered her his palm—sunlight turning money into embers.

"The ride's free today," she said.

Michael was shocked by the melancholy in the driver's eyes—and shocked, too, by how easily he identified it. This was his language, as though they were kindred. Breath abandoned him. Her face was a landscape seen from a distance, with the slow-moving shadows of clouds snaking across impassive rises and falls. The dunes of her cheeks, the river of her mouth, it all felt *elemental*, something older than it actually was, something fated to be. She was a mystery to him, a place of secrets. Michael could see this now because he was ready to see. And through her landscape, he saw a road he wasn't sure he wanted to travel.

Doors clattered shut behind him.

The driver shifted the 243 into gear, and then they were gone.

PART TWO: ON THE BUS

" . . . there are no accidents. Nothing happens unless someone wills it to happen."
—William S. Burroughs

NINETY-SIX

TREES ALONG THE highway like the skeletons of contortionists hired to distract commuters from the rising temperature outside. Bushfires devastated coastal New South Wales earlier that year, resulting in the death of four people. Over three hundred houses were lost. Many thought it nothing but blind luck that James Bridge escaped damage. Its townsfolk sat drinking beer on their front lawns, watching the skies roll brown as others less fortunate burned to death. Denial was the best distraction because bad things didn't happen in places like this. Not in The Bridge.

Airwaves still brimmed with news of Anna Wood, the Sydney girl who died in October from water intoxication after taking Ecstasy. There was a sense that something bad was seething in the cities, something which was yet to touch these country suburbs.

Jed Frost, Liz's brother, begged to differ. Anna's death gave pills some press and as a result, business was a-boomin'.

On television were ongoing memorials for New South Wales State MP John Newman, shot outside his home in Cabramatta, the first political assassination in Australian history since the seventies. People changed the channel and watched *Full House* instead.

NINETY-FIVE:
THE GUN

7:40 AM, NOVEMBER 12TH, 1995

A FEW HOURS before picking up her final passenger, Liz put a gun in her mouth with hands so sweaty the handle went slick. She gagged and forced vomit down. Throat aflame. Teeth clattered against the barrel of the Kel-Tec P11 9 mm pistol, a sound telling her brain, *Wait a minute—I'm not dead.*

Yet.

White noise. Liz tried to blink the noise away but every time her eyes closed, her vision worsened.

Outside, her father, Wes, tended to his garden. His trowel stabbed the earth and sliced a worm in two, matching halves arcing in silent agony amongst the weeds.

Her brother in the shed plowed at the punching bag strung from the rafters on a chain. Jed's knuckles started to bleed.

Reggie, her mother, was in the living room of their house. A half-finished bundle of crochet sat at her feet. Needles imbedded in red yarn.

On the other side of James Bridge, ten-year-old Suzie Marten woke to the sound of her mother coming home after a dogwatch shift at the hospital.

I'm going to die. I'm going to be meat.

Liz's head was a television set, the wiring all wrong and flashes of reason fighting against the dark like ghosts longing to be heard. *If I could only just disappear, I could win.*

No, don't give in.

Don't.

She'd been doing this her entire life, eyes closed and ears blocked. Walking through the clearings on winter mornings. Avoiding it all.

No, this wasn't the first time Liz contemplated killing herself.

Four years ago: a knife. She wanted to kill It. *The Beast.* Even if it killed her in the process. The Beast both fed and fueled her loneliness. Still, Liz put the knife away, defeated. Later that night her mother used the same blade to chop up vegetables for their dinner.

Her second contemplation came two years later. Again, the lure of the knife—but the concept of pain terrified her. Death wasn't orgasmic. It would be the ultimate snap, a pain so extreme it undid you. Liz decided she didn't want to bleed into oblivion and returned the knife to its rightful place in the drawer.

Liz rarely visited the shed out back because she was put off by its humid sweatbox nature. There, tools hung from the walls, the ugly half-finished car. Scary stuff. This particular visit proved worth the discomfort.

She slipped her father's gun off the rack and brought it back inside the house.

The sport of fingering that trigger. Nothing made you appreciate what you had like glaring down the barrel of a pistol. Releasing the trigger set off a release in her that was next to none, amplified, too, by the PCP in her veins. When you were high, you assimilated with death.

Pull it.

(pain)

Do it now.

(peace)

Now.

(pain!)

Today, Liz drew the weapon out of her mouth. Her jaw ached. She threw herself against the wall, dropping the gun. Her old wooden doll's house next to her, its façade open to reveal all the dusty Barbies and Kens, their arms and legs pulled off and rearranged into new people. Little chairs and little lives within a little house that wasn't real.

Coward.

She scrambled to the window and threw it open.

Two levels below, her father looked up from the garden.

Wes Frost took in his daughter's pallid looks. Her messy, shoulder-length hair dangled in a lifeless mess. He noticed sweat dripping off her nose.

Sick eyes.

He'd seen that stare in cattle soon to be slaughtered.

She moved her lips. One word. It sounded like 'today', though he could have been wrong.

"You okay up there, Liz?"

Wes knew something was off. Therefore, it wasn't surprising when no answer came, the awkwardness of the moment forcing him to speak again.

"Shaping up to be another horror of a day. Who knows, it might boil into a storm." Wind blew dead leaves about his ankles. "You can't tell."

Liz closed her eyes and breathed clean oxygen into her body. Alive.

"Bye-bye, Dad."

Closed the window.

She relit the joint and pulled smoke into her lungs. Sound drifted away, numbness settling in. There was a lunchbox with two vials of powdered PCP tucked away in her wardrobe.

Liz climbed into her work uniform: short-sleeved blue shirt, ironed collar and crested front pocket, knee-length navy shorts with the creases down the front. An oversized hat perched on her head.

"Today."

I'm gonna do it. I'm beyond caring. Past help. I don't know when but it'll be today. My god, the relief.

I really can't wait.

She left her room and walked down the steps to the kitchen. No feeling in her feet. Flickering shapes in her peripheral vision, evoking twitches twitch. Floating, floating, all motions dictated by this wonderful drug, everything flowing so nice and smooth. She transitioned from one place to another, one role to the next.

Room to room; daughter to driver.

As far as Liz knew, she was rostered onto Route 243 today. She would make her way to work and step onto her bus and accelerate when needed and brake when the time came, and this would go on and on and on for as long as it needed to.

NINETY-FOUR: REGGIE AND JED

HEAVY BONES WRAPPED in fifty-five years of worry. Reggie Frost clutched at her nightgown, startled. "Shit, Liz! Do you have to sneak around like that? You scared a decade off my life."

She smiled, making for the kitchen where her daughter stood. "You're a bit blurry. I just put my eye drops in." She stopped at the sink and watched the mess come into focus. "That bloody father of yours. He never washes his dishes." A sausage finger scratched at the plates. "He knows I hate having to scrub itty-bitty pieces of cornflakes off with the steel wool."

Reggie threw a dishtowel over the edge of the sink and turned, intercepted by her daughter who crossed the room to kiss her on the cheek. A surge of warmth on Reggie's skin, gone as quick as it came.

"Bye, Mum," Liz said, voice soft.

A smile played at the corners of Reggie's mouth as she watched her daughter stop near the open window and glance outside. The family dog, a large, black Rottweiler named Dog, yapped at the end of its chain, eager to be fed.

Reggie knew that Liz hated Dog and his muscular

hind legs and slobbering jowls. Dog bit her once years before and she had never forgiven it.

"We have got to do something about those Christmas decorations," Reggie said. "I know it's going on close to the season now, but those damn things have been up since last year. It's embarrassing. The lights are still in the trees—God only knows how many of the bulbs have busted." Vague hope in Reggie's eyes. "Want to help me with them when you knock off?"

Liz stood silhouetted against window light, holding her breath.

A ticking clock. The gurgle of dirty water running down the sink.

"Well the damn things aren't going to take themselves down!" Reggie snapped.

Liz, embarrassed, came outside and found her father troweling the flowerbed near the porch, the burial ground of many unloved dolls so many years ago. Her cheeks burned and whatever words she wanted to say turned to sand in her mouth. She felt icy hands clutch at her bowels.

Under her father's kneecap were the remains of tiny plastic people, their hair eaten away and eye sockets full of grit. Liz walked away.

Wes wiped sweat from his brow, giving himself a war-paint streak of dirt. Were those tears he'd seen glimmering in Liz's eyes? He wanted to stand and reach out for her but she was already halfway across the front yard, having passed her car and Jed's battered pickup truck.

The knapsack looked heavy on her shoulder.

He sighed, dug the trowel into the earth again and tilted his head to the faraway perimeter trees. "Damn," he said.

His girl broke him in a special way, a way only daughters could.

Grass crunched underfoot. Liz's backpack swung on her shoulder. It bore extra weight today, though she couldn't remember why. She slipped through the shed door and her shadow fell over her brother's tattooed back, Jed's ornate rendering of an eagle spread from shoulder to shoulder.

Eagles always fascinated him. The species escaped extinction because of their tenacity and could carry four times their own weight. She knew Jed admired the eagle's speed and loyalty to its young, he'd said so many times over. He got the tattoo two years ago when he was twenty-three in a cheap Melbourne parlor, and when he came home from his trip, their father said how much he hated it, said it made him look like a thug. However, the eagle was Jed's baby; the needle and its sting sew them together forever.

Sweat beaded from the bird's wings. Jed faced his sister. Their eyes locked, shared the same look.

A punching bag strung from the moaning rafters.

It swung on its chain like a corpse at the end of a noose.

Jed moved to the unfinished Volkswagen in the corner of the room and sat on the hood. The car had been their father's pet project for years. Jed tinkered with it every now and then, a passing hobby. It kept the grease under his fingernails, an issue of pride between father and son.

Tools covered one wall, and on the opposite, were guns upon racks crafted from the antlers and tusks of dead game. Underneath the twisted rack of metal and tooth, a titanium chest of drawers full of nails, bullets, and beetles gathered dust.

Liz stepped forward and watched her brother raise a hand. Even in the dim, she saw the awkward alignment of his knuckles, the blood.

"I caned my hand something shocking, Sis."

Sis. She loved the word because it was hers and hers alone. Special to them both. This twinge of familiarity pierced deep. She knew he would miss her most.

"You off to work then?" His shiny face, dust in his buzz cut. He twitched and clenched his jaw. His long arms flexed, muscles rolled into prominence.

"Maybe," Liz said, voice cracking. "You should see a doctor or something." She fought the urge to tell him everything, to tell him about The Beast and about how much she wanted to run away with him and make new lives, to piece themselves together as new people like the Barbies and Kens in her room. "Y-y-you should come with me, and I, well I can drop you off at the depot and you can leg it in from there and I'll spot you enough money to catch a bus back and Mum and Dad aren't working so they can pick you up from The Bridge—"

Liz said anything that came to mind so long as it wasn't truthful.

Jed laughed. "It's not that bad."

Silence fell. His comment forced her into uselessness again.

"Well." Liz tapered off.

"Yeah?"

"Well, I came in to say—" She searched for the right word. "Goodbye."

He snorted again, shaking his head.

"Ah, Sis, you're—" He was going to say 'weird' and stopped, jumped off the hood and bounded over to her, radiating energy and heat. "You want me to get you more stuff?"

"What?"

"You know, *stuff*." That's what he called the powder in the white vials. Phencyclidine, 'angel dust', PCP. Jed bought it and cut it with ether. He would roll himself a joint, slice fifty-twenty hash and tobacco, and dip it in the solution. Jed called it 'getting wet'. PCP numbed the senses, punctuated with fireworks of high-energy bouts. Some users, but not all, turned violent whilst high on the drug. Liz had read about it.

"No." She almost laughed. "I'm okay for now."

"All right. Just don't say I didn't try."

"You're sure about not going to the doctor? I don't mind, I got the time—"

"Really, let it go." Jed stepped closer. "I may have busted my knuckles but it's okay. I've got brother bones. They grow back strong when they need to."

Their gazes latched together again, twin sets of stars—at once dead and alive.

Jed was nine years old, his hands covered in blood. He stood at the bottom of the stairs in the shadow of the man who had cut him. Each gash a drooling, puckered mouth. Too shocked to cry.

Liz saw Jed's vacant expression from the living room floor where she lay covered in bruises, the left buckle of her suspenders broken at her side. Rage ripped through her.

"You hurt *him," she screeched, pulling herself up. "You hurt my brother."*

The man turned to see the girl launch at him and snatch the knife from his grip. She dropped it and the tip of the blade impaled carpet they had walked across for years, carrying meals to the living room, carting presents to sit under the Christmas tree. Liz glared through the shadow, through memories, and saw the man.

His tears terrified her.

Jed never forgot his sister's defiance. Like scars, his love and respect for her never faded.

Liz's '89 Mitsubishi Colt pulled into the bus depot parking lot in Maitland. She only had a vague recollection of the twenty-five-minute trip from James Bridge to work. Flashes of images—passing trees and recollections. A gray blur.

The highway out of James Bridge.

Gray.

Her mother opening the living room door as Liz edged towards the kitchen, her father on his knees in the dirt, her brother.

Gray.

The bus had a distinct smell before a shift, one that would recede as the day progressed. Disinfectant and shoe polish. Light beamed through the windows in shafts, struck the railings and handlebars. Fifty plush seats awaiting passengers.

As Liz guessed, she was on Route 243. The Sunday 'back-road' valley transit, with two rarely frequented stops along Wollombi Road to James Bridge, followed by the same return trip, an outskirt detour designed specifically for The Bridge Folk. "Easy money, little dice," her boss often said about the shift. Liz suspected that given time, the route would go the way of the Tasmanian tiger.

Gray.

The bus roared to life. Vibrations ran through her body. From her pocket she took a small glass diamond strung on a chain. She bought it for two dollars at a flea market. Liz slipped the trinket over the rearview mirror, movements robotic and sluggish. The diamond hung just above her eye line. She wound the Route and Destination signage into place with a manual crank.

Next to the diamond, on the same silver thread, a second twinkle caught the sun, this one old yet polished. Her mother gifted her the Saint Christopher medallion on her first day of work. To keep her safe.

NINETY-THREE:
THE LAST PASSENGER

TEN MINUTES PAST ELEVEN.

"No charge today," the driver told Michael. "Everyone's riding free." She avoided his stare, knuckles tight on the wheel.

"Thank you," he replied before continuing up the aisle. Loose change jingled in the pocket of his jeans from squirreling it away. He became very aware of how little oxygen was inside the bus. Everything struck him as *thick*. The metal handlebars he grabbed to keep his balance were almost too hot to touch. No air-conditioning, just a caged fan above the driver—no use to anyone, really.

As Michael was about to drop into a seat in the first half of the bus, he made eye contact with two young women further up the aisle on the opposite side. The older one smiled at him.

"Our lucky day, see?" she said.

"Sure is," he replied, caught off guard by her American accent.

Diana's smile faded. Next to her, sixteen-year-old Julia shied away and watched her reflection in the window.

Sarah Carr toyed with the spikes of her hair, and understood two things straight away. The women were goodly. *And they're sisters. Though I don't see the resemblance.*

Six seats ahead of her, Peter Ditton sat upright, notebook across his kneecaps.

Steve Brown fanned himself, heat building within the heavy fabric of his football jersey. He sat behind the skinny kid who had been at the bus stop with him.

Steve had been that young and fit once. He wiped his hands on his shorts—his old hands. The years left him soft and pudgy, not that he cared; a lot of that bullshit lost its glean once you married, a time in your life when impressing others dropped on your priority scale. Bev, on the other hand, kept her figure and that was great for her. Steve was proud of his little gym-bunny, but still, the awkwardness between them increased. She was beautiful and he wasn't the movie-star type, as she would put it. When they made love these days, he tended to tire quicker and sometimes didn't orgasm at all. Steve even faked it once.

I'm sure she saw straight through that as well. Bev always does.

All around him, Steve's fellow passengers sat in

silence. No music issued from the old speakers that day. He stared ahead and saw the driver slump in her seat, a deflating gesture. A crackle from the two-way radio corrected her posturing.

Don't you go nodding off on us, love.

Sarah placed her hands on the handlebar and felt the tarmac rumbling through it. She studied the driver and could have sworn the woman almost fell asleep. The first lick of panic flirted with her skin. Hairs stood in attention.

"Hey!" yelled the young, porcelain-looking girl across the aisle, the one with the older sister. Sarah, like all the passengers, reeled at this outburst.

She clutched her chest.

All eyes landed on Julie. She chose to ignore those intimidating looks and pushed up off the seat. A wintry sickness ran through her, cold and deep.

"What are you yelling about?" Diana said.

"Driver, stop!"

NINETY-TWO

THE VOICE OF the teenager dripped into Liz Frost's mind, a splattering of acid. Somewhere inside, the wet nose of The Beast turned towards its host, ruffling leathery wings. She slammed the brakes.

"You went straight past that stop," called the older of the two girls in the same seat.

"There's a—" started the young man close to her. He held a book in the air.

Liz could tell he was about to say "a guy there" because she could see him out there on the path in the rear-vision mirror, approaching the bus.

This new passenger appeared strong and athletic, lost in his early thirties perhaps, it was difficult to tell. Close cut hair, and a goatee masking someone younger. The wind plastered his plain gray shirt against the pad of his belly.

Liz opened the door with hands that wouldn't stop shaking.

NINETY-ONE

JACK BARKER HATED going unnoticed. In fact, there were few things on this planet that fueled his anger more.

The bloody driver went straight past my stop. What am I invisible?

He forced himself to calm down, pushing the heat back with each stride towards the bus. By the time the door opened, Jack almost had control of himself again. Almost.

Once inside, he reached into his denims for change, wishing he'd worn shorts; it was too hot for pants like these. The veins in his forearms filled with blood, rising up through his skin like a string of cursive letters, reading, *You need to get fit again, buddy*. He gasped.

Jack lifted his gaze to meet the driver's.

'Death' was the only word he could think to describe her.

Like she hasn't slept in years. Jesus.

"What's the rush, luv? You in the Grand Prix, too?" he said, shaking his head. Jack's voice was a deep drawl. "It's all right though." He paused and glanced down the length of the bus to find everyone looking at him, clay pigeons in a shooting gallery. "I'm here now, so all's good."

"I didn't—I went so—" she said, words failing her. "It's free." Her words came out too loud, too abrasive.

Jack smirked. "Free? You sure? It's okay that you missed me. It happens. Water off a duck's back."

"I'm sorry."

"Really, it's fine."

Her face darted to his. *She moves like a bird,* he thought.

"You're. Riding for. Free. Today. That's the way it's going. To be. You go have a seat. And just pull the wire when you want to get off."

Somewhere in Jack's head, an alarm went off, an alarm silenced by the shaky contortion of her half smile. He thought the driver had the potential to be pretty, assuming she tried. With this in mind, he gave her one of his thousand-watt grins, an easy task because that initial anger was nearly gone now. Not flirting required more effort. "Well thanks, luv. I won't say no to that."

Jack had lived in James Bridge his entire life and to his surprise, recognized no one else on the bus, though the older fella in the football jersey seemed familiar. Perhaps they shared a beer once at one of the town's watering holes, giving each other cursory nods over the lip of frosted pints, conversing in grunts as a game played out on a television behind the bar. But familiarity wasn't the same as knowing someone, no matter how many cold ones had been downed, regardless of the games they cheered on, and to some degree, Jack liked it that way. That was why he passed the man—who could have been anyone, really—and dropped onto the backseat without offering acknowledgment.

Fingers curled the handlebar.

Just like school days. Jack recalled water fights on the bus ride home, laughing children throwing balled-up pieces of paper. Their driver back then had been a big Maori guy named Sao. *Man, he was the best.*

He let us get away with anything.

For a moment, it looked as though the driver might speed off without closing the door. It clanged shut and Michael felt a wave of relief tide over him; this struck him peculiar because he hadn't even realized his tension. He watched the woman's smile melt away as the vehicle accelerated into the day and listened to her struggle with a gear change. The engine shrieked bloody murder.

Ahead of Michael, the young guy with neatly combed hair and a notebook glanced around.

"If you can't find it, grind it, right?" Michael said.

NINETY

PERSPIRATION WELLED IN the folds of Steve's gut. The bus was fitted with large, inoperable side windows; above each were sliding glass panels a child might get a head through if they were dumb enough. They were all open however, and whatever air could get in the vehicle was in already.

Steve imagined sitting at the Maitland Golf Club bar, a schooner in hand, talking to mates over the whirr of Formula One cars. "I can feel a XXXX comin' on," was the catchphrase from the advertisements—and the old line had never been more inviting.

The fantasy dissipated as his gaze passed over the emergency escape window near the kid from the stop. Next to the window was a small box where a BREAK IN CASE OF EMERGENCY hammer should have be tied. Yet was not.

Tears in the seating, scuffs on the handlebars. Alert wires sagged in long, thin smiles. Graffiti scratched into the glass on Steve's right. Peeling warning stickers covered the walls, a faded cardboard advertisement for Wrigley's Extra Sugar-Free Gum.

"Stop looking at me like that, you're really annoying me," Julia said to her stepsister, Diana, who sighed in way of reply. Julia flicked the hair from her eyes, tucked it behind her ear—a trademark move. Diana found these small habits endearing. She wanted to take Julia in her arms and hug her until all the bad things evaporated.

In the tiniest of voices: "I wish I'd never told you."

Each word was a bee-sting. Julia continued. "I mean—oh god. I just wish I never *had to tell you*."

Diana touched her leg, pushed in close.

"I know you're trying to get my mind off it all, but I just can't," Julia said. "This thing isn't growing in me. It's eating me up. It won't be much longer and Mum and Dad will be able to tell." Her lower lip started to quiver. Another strand of hair fell across her upturned button nose and this time Diana slipped it behind her ear for her.

"Everything will be okay," Diana said. "Please, don't think about it. I know that's easier said than done. But just empty your head. Let it all just disappear. Look out the window and watch things go by. Think about those things. I'm here, Jules. Think about the movie, okay? *Clueless* will rock. We love funny stuff, right? Do you remember when we saw *Mrs. Doubtfire?* That movie was hilarious. Oh, what was that line? Ah . . . 'Layla, get back in your cage! Don't make me get the hose!'"

Julia couldn't help it. She giggled.

"Or what about that part when he's pretending to be Spanish? Remember?"

"'I. Am. Job,'" Julia recited, laughing now.

"'Ah, do you speak English?'"

"'I. Am. *Job*. Ha. Ha.'"

"'I'm sorry, the position has been filled.' SLAM!" Diana nudged her sister in the arm, drawing a smile. Julia nudged her back and turned to the window, skin glowing white in the glare.

EIGHTY-NINE

THE OUTSIDE WORLD shrunk to a pinpoint and Liz pushed the bus towards it. Nothing else existed, just a vanishing point that she longed to vanish into. She chased the dot, pushing her foot against the accelerator. If she lost sight of it, then it all would have been for nothing.

Sounds grew louder and louder. The hum and inner workings of the bus. Her dot of light brightened.

Wheels spun faster, kicking dirt.

A mother pushing a baby carriage with two additional children at her side threw her hands into the air, cursing, as the bus roared past her stop at the entrance to Combi-Chance Road.

Three days later, Bobby Deakins will leave a copy of the *Bridge Bugle* in the mother's mailbox. She will read about what happened, about who died and on what bus it all occurred. The woman will cry for four continuous hours.

In the cloudless sky, five black crows circled.

Jack Barker tracked the angry people on the roadside until their yells bled away, forms lost in a cloud of dust. He stood to look through the back window and realized the bus had no back window, just a metal plate covered in stickers.

"Oi, driver!" he called.

Peter turned towards Michael as though their initial eye contact had made them partners. "Geez, she's gone and done it again."

The driver didn't respond.

Diana caught Sarah's surreptitious glance. Shrugged. "Whoopsie-daisy."

"Whoopsie-daisy my bloody big toe is more like it," Sarah said, chortling. Her thick crucifix bobbed against her breasts. "That poor mum. And with three little ones in tow. I've got half a mind to go up and give this young lady a piece of my mind."

The rumbling of road under wheels, the force of the engine in Liz's fingertips. A high-pitched metal-on-metal screech made her nipples harden.

Oh, to be in that light, to live in this sound forever, she thought.

She drove on.

The speedometer climbed, trees skimming the windows faster than they should. The houses were sparse and their lawns wide as open fields, but acceleration drew them all together. A great uniting.

"We need to stop," Michael said. He watched the driver pitch to the left again, tilting like a building before the inevitable collapse. And *collapse* was an appropriate word here he thought, as though the woman with whom they entrusted their lives had been slated for demolition. If she went down, so would they all, together crushed by debris. His gaze shifted to the window again. They drifted closer to the curb.

Hot air shot past Michael, twirling specks of grit that carried to Sarah. They speckled the lenses of her glasses. "We're going awfully fast," she said to nobody in particular.

"What?" asked Julia from across the aisle. That wind ruffled her bangs.

"She's right," Diana said. "Something's wrong."

Jack was the first of the passengers to rise. As he did, he stepped into the flow of rushing hot air. It made him squint and his mouth turned dry. Dust on his teeth, grinding between molars. "Hey, driver-lady!" He whistled at her. "You tryin' to kill us?"

Outside, the curb loomed. The tread of wheels blurred into a wave.

Inside, Steve stood as well.

Peter slouched in his seat, eyes even with the sill of the side window. Panic coursed from his neck to his toes.

At the back of the bus, Jack took a first step. His sweaty hand slipped on the handlebar of the seat in front of him and he stumbled.

Julia's heartbeat quickened and in turn, deep inside, another heartbeat raced to keep up.

Closer to the dot—
(it's so bright!)
—closer—
(it's beautiful!)
—closer.
(oh god)

Liz bathed in the white. It encompassed everything, burned everything else away. "Yes," she said, her gentle whisper like a breeze through reeds.

This light was the sun reflected in her diamond trinket, radiating from the face of Saint Christopher. Together they waltzed back and forth on the end of a silver chain.

Screams as the wheels on the left-hand side of the bus collided with the curb.

EIGHTY-EIGHT: SHADOW

LIZ ON THE ground of her parents' shed. An exposed light bulb swung back and forth in a lethargic arc.

Shadow. Light. Shadow. Light.

A leather belt tied around her left bicep, the skin bruised. On the floor next to her was the syringe. From a hole in her arm a single line of blood oozed free.

The Beast hid in the dark. She opened her eyes. Teeth chattered. A shadow that remained even when the bulb swung the world into illumination. A person so tall and far away. In the middle of this shadow, she noted the winking red eye of a cigarette.

She felt so good and she wanted more.

"Please—"

The shadow fell over her.

"Please don't leave me."

The shadow withdrew. Where Liz's face had been, there was now a spluttering pulp. Blood erupted from her nose and flooded the wells of her eye sockets. Limp hands swiped numbly at the red. Screaming, followed by silence.

The shadow was fearful of what it had done. Its

wet cigarette fell to the floor where the night continued to breathe in its bitter calligraphy. This figure stumbled around the room, looking down at the crooked nose on Liz's face, and without thinking, grabbed the loose cartilage to snap it back into place. Pause, then: "Thank you."

In reply, the shadow spoke. "I'm so sorry—"

(light)

"—I will never hurt you. Oh, god."

(dark)

"I'm so sorry, Liz."

(light)

"I'll never leave you."

The shadow moved away.

Through the red, Liz watched the eagle flap its wings as it sailed out between the corrugated doors astride her brother's shoulders. Soon there were only stars.

EIGHTY-SEVEN: IMPACT

THE TWINKLING OF the Saint Christopher medallion blinded Liz. She couldn't tell how long she'd stared at it, hypnotized.

Where am I again?

Tingles ignited in her fingers, forcing them to squeeze around the steering wheel. It was hard and real, a realness that made her fog dissipate, focus blooming outwards to encompass the dashboard, and beyond, the windscreen of the bus she was employed to charter, though the world on the other side of the glass remained too glary to discern. Just yet.

Oh, Christ.

Liz swerved the vehicle—eighteen tons of paid responsibility—away from the curb, and as she did so, caught a suggestion of the world past her medallion. A land of blur, which now Liz was back in her body, she forced into focus. Something floated towards her at an unimaginable speed.

A cherub swathed in pink light.

Ten-year-old Suzie Marten spun in her leotard to the

music from her Walkman, knowing only the happiness of the moment. Behind closed eyes, her future played out.

They cheer. They laugh. A spotlight lands on her face, tracing the length of her legs. She pirouettes and is beautiful.

Her parents are there, and they are so very proud.

No slowing. Just the hard thump. A millisecond before impact, fear drew Liz's next breath for her. The first victim of the James Bridge massacre died instantly.

Blood splattered across the windshield in a fountain of red. Liz jammed both feet onto the brake.

Peter slammed into the seat in front of him, busting his lip. Julia and Diana held on to each other as they fell into the aisle; Sarah reached out to them. Michael saw the accident, heard the lightning crack of the bus hitting the child and every muscle in his body cramped up, an instinctual need to be whole. Steve saw it happen, too—he was closest to the driver, after all. Jack held himself steady in the backseat, grabbed the nearest handlebar, veins rising through toned flesh once again.

The bus screeched to a halt but the engine still ran; Liz hit the clutch, threw the gears into neutral. The airy *ding-ding* of the Requested Stop sign went off.

Liz's vision bruised, dark threatening to swallow her up. She fought through it and looked at the exterior left mirror, angled with perfection so she could best see what death looked like.

Nobody on the street. Nobody to come running at the sound. No rubberneckers peering from windows, as there were no neighbors in the first place. Inside the Marten residence, Donna slept undisturbed and would continue to do so for another forty dreamless minutes. The nearest house to where her daughter lay in pieces was the size of a fingernail on the horizon, a single-story structure reduced to quicksilver by the day's heat waves.

Above, the caw of a crow.

Within the bus, Liz *assumed* she was hearing words, but it all sounded like underwater reverberations in the deep end of the James Bridge pool as a child, pressure bearing down on her lungs, eyes stinging from the chlorine, curling into a weightless ball as kids bombed into her private stillness. The pool was a rare summer treat, and many good times were shared there with her brother, the two of them safe below the surface, tempting death by trying to see who could hold their breath the longest. Jed always won.

Only this wasn't the pool.

These were not kids at play.

Her brother wasn't here, either.

"What the fuck?"

"Oh, my god!"

"Jesus!"

Liz turned to look at her passengers. They huddled close to the windows like flies.

Steve forced himself into the aisle. His red and blue jersey stained with dark sweat patches.

Julia held her stomach. She saw two things at once—an exploded ballerina on the road, and a set of familiar, terrified eyes: her reflection in the window. Diana's hands gripped her shoulder so tight it started to hurt. Julia didn't shoo her away, and they both watched the man approach their driver instead, palms outstretched—not—in surrender but as a shield.

Jack fell into his seat. "You didn't see her, you didn't see her," he said over and over again, his voice another random noise in the sweaty air.

Shakes gripped Sarah. She pushed her face against the glass, leaving behind a small smudge of lipstick. *That was a little* girl; the revelation chimed in her head like a bell. A death knell.

Tutu blew in the wind.

Steve continued towards the front of the bus, wondering why everyone wasn't doing the same. Didn't they want to get out of here as quickly as possible? Surely, that was the only option. Or maybe they felt it, too. *It*. That heat radiating from the driver. He watched her stand, a silhouette against the red windshield. Her burn was just for him now.

"Open the fucking door," Steve said, unsure if he was whispering or yelling. "I'm getting off. We all are."

Liz held the back of her seat for balance. "No," she said. And then louder, so much stronger: "FOR GOD'S SAKE PLEASE DON'T GO!"

Steve stopped, unsure.

Something clicked in Liz's brain, a click that felt good.

They're all so alive, so human. It's beautiful. In each of them there's a bit of me. One of them will hold me and never let go. They aren't scared of me. Why would they be scared? I brought them together. They need to love me as much as I need their love.

This is meant to be.

"Please don't leave me."

Diana called to her sister who didn't respond. She grabbed her by the chin and pulled her close. "We're getting off. Get up, get up—*now*!"

"Girls," said the old woman across from them. "Sit down!" Her crucifix dangled from the folds of her shirt. A finger rose to her lips, hushing them. "Wait."

Liz wiped her face. She held eye contact with the man in the sweat-stained jersey who had come to save her. He was the one. She felt honored. Liz couldn't remember the last time she'd been this wanted.

"Move or I'm gonna throw you to the fuckin' floor, woman!"

Why are you saying this to me? This rejection encompassed all; the Beast swallowed all memories of the dead child.

Steve watched the driver's expression shift from happiness to sorrow and back again, its unpredictability as dangerous and fickle as a bushfire. Years before as a volunteer for the State Emergency Service, Steve witnessed a winter backburn get out of control and turn against the wind to chew through three houses. Those flames frightened him then; the flame in driver frightened him now. She seared him deep. She seared them all.

"No," Liz said. "Why? Why are you going? I need you to stay."

Jack stood. He felt pathetic, useless and ignorant. His hands didn't move, frozen fingers threaded with small white scars.

"Fuck this shit," Steve yelled. "Get outta my way!"

The passengers flinched as he dodged for the door. They also caught the movement of the driver as she reached behind her seat. She yanked herself upright and there were screams from everyone—except Steve.

He stared.

Confused, unafraid.

How could he be afraid of something this unreal? The driver wasn't the bogeyman under the bed; she wasn't even his wife on a bad day. She was just some skinny nobody who had driven herself into a world of lawsuits and television cameras and, most likely, a stretch of prison-induced labor.

So why did she hold a gun?

Why was she pointing it at him?

Julia, Diana, and Sarah dropped low. "This isn't happening," Julia whispered.

Peter and Michael forced themselves against the floor. Cramped and bent double, they chanced a look down the aisle. Michael tried to swallow. Dry.

"W-what?" Steve said. He didn't move.

All was still, a tableau broken by the driver's quick look at the mirror. Saw the dead child in the concave surface. Understanding's blade pierced her chest. The girl would never again draw breath. *Gone forever*, Liz thought. *And it's my fault.*

This blame couldn't be attributed to her parents. Not the drugs in her system. Not even to The Beast.

Just her.

Why are they looking at me like that? A weight in her hand: her father's gun pointed at the man in front of her. Again, that awoken-sleepwalker sensation filled her, dreaming shattered by the fully loaded pistol.

They don't love me. They hate me. It's all my fault. My fault.

The solution came simply. Natural, really. She knew it would end like this. Liz slipped the gun into her mouth, so far she gagged.

A scream from the back of the bus. "*No*!"

It came from Sarah. Her hands were against her cheeks, head shaking. "Don't do it," she said.

The voice echoed inside Liz's head, taking on a life of its own.

Steve watched the driver pull the gun from her mouth. Its barrel was so small and he, as a man, was so big. How could something so tiny damage a human being of his size? The weight of that absurdity pushed him for the door. Nothing mattered but getting off, and he was willing to take a gamble even if the others weren't brave enough to play along. Laying high-priced bets was something Steve was familiar with.

Three steps and then the bang. Bullets didn't hesitate. It slit the air.

The left-hand side of Steve's face no longer existed.

Arterial explosions threw red draperies over the ceiling. There they clung, before slopping to the floor.

"Stay with me," Liz said.

EIGHTY-SIX

WHAT ONCE WAS Steve but was now merely meat, arced backward. He hit the ground hard. A splinter of skull landed near Michael's hand.

Liz watched the corpse dance. Soon the spasms died, but the blood continued to gush.

This is what I would have looked like if I'd shot myself this morning. Or all those other times, she thought. *Doing a little tap dance to music nobody else can hear. Going to pulp. Making a darn mess over the carpet that Mum would hate to clean.*

"L-l-look wh-what you all d-did," she sputtered. A line of spittle between her upper and lower lips shook with every word, threatening to snap.

The sounds of her passengers were tortures she could no longer stand, so when she screamed at them to "Stop it," the words drained her person. Liz could have collapsed, a skeleton without substance. But no, she held true. To Liz's surprise, the passengers went silent. Still. This power over them kept her flame burning, a glimmer in the skull's eye socket, flickering movement within the window of what once had been a home.

Julia shook her head as her sister reached across

the aisle to grab Sarah by the crook of the arm, pulling her towards them. Sarah felt the little hand on her flesh, watched the world turn sideways. She landed on the seat in front of them; her glasses fell to the floor.

Jack wanted to get up and run but didn't want to end up like the poor bastard on the floor. Another part of him wanted to pound at the windows and shout for help. Did he dare make a run at her? Dare try to knock the gun from her? He could always drop his shoulder against the emergency exit window near the back of the driver's hub and escape that way. Instead, he remained where he was.

"D-don't any of y-you move," Liz yelled. Then to herself, "Oh gosh-oh gosh-oh gosh, it's all messy—" The gun dropped. It was so heavy. She snapped it back up. These creatures brought all this hell down on her. This wasn't how things were supposed to go. *Death was peace and the end to all that was horrible and unfair*. The Beast pretended so well, years of trickery under its belt. She recognized its smell, a secretion that stunk of hatred. Liz sighed, knowing what must be done.

The passengers watched their driver stumble back to her seat, heard the gun clicking in her grasp.

We're all going to die, Peter realized. On the floor in front of him, he found his notebook. Grabbed it. Dragged it to his nose. It smelled of his bedroom, safety. *I'm eighteen,* he thought. *I can't die. It's not possible.*

Liz fell into her seat, the gun landing in her lap. The Beast was in the mirror, divided into small parts among them all. They continued to watch. *I've got to get out of here.* Her hands found the steering wheel again. Vibrations.

I will beat you.

I do not want to die anymore.

The bus moved, a calm acceleration. Smoke drifted from the dented grill. Windshield wipers sprung to life and cut upturned Christmas trees in the blood.

PART THREE:
ON THE ROAD

"There are no foreign lands. It is the traveler only who is foreign."
—Robert Louis Stevenson

EIGHTY-FIVE

PETER PRAYED ON the floor, notebook in hand. *I'll never fight with Mum again if I get out of this alive.* This had changed him, made him see the value in her spite. All he wanted to do was write, but he would give it up to see her face again. He smiled, knowing that when the police found the dead girl rescue wouldn't be far away.

What Peter didn't know was that Suzie Marten's body wouldn't be found by police for almost two hours. A haystack-toting pickup will stumble upon mother and daughter on the road. It will take another hour and a half for the police to arrive, the farmer constructing a makeshift barricade around the body from his cargo. He would spend his time comforting the woman, throwing rocks to keep the crows away, and at one point chasing a guinea fowl with a torn-off finger in its mouth through a thicket. The James Bridge police station was unmanned as per usual. The single unit came from Muswellbrook, the ambulance from Maitland. When the kind Samaritan saw the authorities arrive, he dropped to his knees and wept. A second unit arrived forty-five minutes later, the mother already taken to the hospital. The police wouldn't connect the hit-and-run with the reports of the missing bus until sunset.

Sarah emerged from her cloud of shock. *We're trapped in a bus with a psychopath*, she told herself. *There's only one door and it's near her. There is only one emergency exit and it's near her too. The psychopath has a gun.*

She touched her crucifix.

If life were a falling series of dominoes, she thought, *then when was this chain reaction put into place?* Sarah could trace the evil back to birth if she wanted to. She longed for her husband, longed to lie in bed and kiss him.

Bill, now I understand.

Death could come at any moment. She got that now.

He lives with this every day, every waking moment.

The sisters held each other, speaking in whispers. "I'm so sorry, I'm so-so sorry, I'm so sorry—" Diana said, blubbering. Julia's reply only shushed pleas for quiet. There were two heartbeats inside her now.

With Diana clinging to her and the bitter stink of blood and brains in the air, Julia hated herself for wishing away her child's life. Even if her parents kicked her out home, she *knew* she had to live long enough to tell them the truth about why she had been missing so much school, about the sickness that came at dawn.

Her death's oath.

Michael watched Peter genuflect and wanted to yell at him, telling him he was speaking to nothing, that he might as well pray to the floor underneath them.

Instead, Michael pulled himself up off the ground, and with tenacious delicacy, eased back into the seat. He'd never seen a dead body before, only in movies. He struggled to understand how anything, even the spirit of someone searching for heavens that didn't exist, could survive that mess of bone and bullet. Prayers had no place here.

Jack watched in rage. Since the bus lurched into motion, he'd kept his eyes on the driver. The flickers of movement in her shoulders reminded him of dogs trying to run in their sleep. He felt safe for the moment, understanding it wouldn't last.

How long are we going to sit here and let this woman take over our lives?

Not me, not Jack Barker.

The bus gently ebbed the stream of blood down the aisle. A red sliver ran against Jack's shoe. He wished he could remember where he'd seen the dead man before, connect the dots that drew them together. Out of respect, if nothing else.

That bullet could have been for any one of us but he was the one who took it.

Jack was an only child, unmarried and without children. Nobody would miss him. It used to make him sad. Now, it just made him angry. He led a small, insignificant life—but it was *his* life. And the driver threatened to take even that away from him, just as she'd taken everything from the little girl and the dead maybe-stranger.

Honesty amid the growing heat: The passengers infuriated him, too. There wasn't a respectable Aussie amongst the lot. None would stand and fight. Jack wasn't the type to carry a gun; he lived in James

Bridge, not Detroit. But what he would give to be that type today.

Wish all you want, Jack-o, said the voice in his head. *You ain't got a pot to piss in or a window to throw it out of.*

You got shit.

EIGHTY-FOUR

THE EMPTY FROST family kitchen.

Water dripped from a faucet. The refrigerator hummed. Danish figurines lined the top of the kitchen door architrave, collecting dust. A pair of long-bladed scissors hung from a hook by the sink.

Wes was upstairs in the bathroom. The Kinks and *Waterloo Sunset* lilted down the hallway from the record player. His wife loitered in the living room watching television, a magazine across her lap. Daytime soap operas mingled with the music.

There was a filing cabinet in the study full of tax reports, and Liz's and Jed's old school papers—Reggie held on to it all. Every drawing, every Easter card, all kept and forgotten in that tiny room.

Outside, last year's Christmas cutouts flanked the house. Dead fairy lights in the trees swung low over Santa and his reindeer, a shepherd leading his donkey. It embarrassed Reggie that they were still up, though she couldn't find the energy to take them down now.

The shed: thirty feet from the front door on the left, facing the driveway leading up a hill and out of their private valley. The driveway disappeared into a hollow of trees, crows loitering in the branches. Reggie considered it an eyesore having a garage in the front yard. "Anyone can see what a shit heap it is if they come to visit."

"Love, who ever comes down our driveway except us anyway?" Wes would say, waving her away.

Jed Frost wore his knuckles away in the shed as he wrestled with the punching bag. The eagle tattoo danced across his back. Jed lived at home, paid no rent. His boyish looks collided with the buzz cut; when he wasn't smiling, he came across as threatening. It made him the perfect go-to guy. Three days a week, he stacked shelves at the Maitland K-Mart. There, girls and co-workers flirted with him and sometimes he flirted back.

The other days Jed sold pot for his friend Brody, who had a hydroponic set up in his living room.

Brody the perfectionist. He grew plants in alternating rooms on a four-month rotation, the time it took to develop buds for harvest. Once the living room crop had been bagged, the hydro unit would be shifted to the next room, which Jed coated with seventy-five percent reflective paint. Sometimes they used Mylar if they had the spare cash. Jed babysat the stash whenever Brody left town, which was often.

Selling drugs paid well and Jed had no girlfriend to blow it on. His money went into pleasures that wouldn't be outgrown, unlike women. He had a delicacy of choice.

Getting wet.

PCP was a cheap and easy high, though dangerous. A friend had slipped into a coma at a party once after overindulging. The thought of being implicated in someone's death frightened him. Jed left the party and ran outside. In a field, he watched the stars turn to welts that vomited pus and glitter over the landscape.

Another time when he and Brody got high, Jed found his mate in his bedroom, jeans around his ankles, belt tied to his genitals, attempting autofellatio. Brody's head was at an unhealthy angle, eyes rolled back to expose the whites. Jed closed the door, went downstairs and did sit-ups while watching *Married with Children*.

The bitterness of the drug lingered in his mouth. He spat onto the shed floor, flakes of weed in his spit. His world shimmered. Punched the bag. Over and over with his injured hand. No pain, only hollow thumping sounds.

The shed was hotter than usual. Corrugated roofing groaned under the sun.

He only sold PCP to a select few. These transactions were more about trust than money. His most loyal customer was his sister.

EIGHTY-THREE

JULIA AWOKE WITH a start, relieved to be in her own bed. Her face tattooed with pillowcase creases. The room bathed in blue light. Her lips were chaffed and bleeding.

A nightmare.

In it, she'd been hovering on the ceiling of her room, looking down at her sleeping form on the bed. She enjoyed the sensation of weightlessness as she hung in the air. But when she tried to move, her arms remained in place. She floated crucified, damned to scrutinize her own body forever. She started to panic, tried to talk.

Nothing.

The bedroom door opened. A sliver of light across her sleeping face. A man with long, gray hair tiptoed into the room like a Punch and Judy doll on jerking strings. She wanted to scream a warning at her other self. No luck. The man had come for her. He stopped at the head of the bed and bent over. She heard him sniffing, the sound of his pebbled tongue running over her skin. Then, with a robotic slowness reserved for nightmares, the intruder lifted his head to see her floating.

Shark eyes.

"Did you have a bad dream?" asked the boy lying next to her. His eyes gazed at her, morning glow on his pimpled face.

"Yeah."

He stroked her cheek. Julia nuzzled against his touch. She was safe but scared and guilty as well. *I'm only sixteen,* she told herself. *So I guess it's okay to be scared.*

I didn't do anything wrong.

The Grays sang to her from the cassette player on the dresser.

She rolled away, unable to look into his face. He wrapped his arms around her, penis hard against her back. He'd been gentle the night before but it still hurt. The sheets were lightly freckled with blood. Pleasure too, somewhere among his red-hot thrusts.

Sometimes, all Julia had was music.

The walls of her room were covered with posters. Her friends gave her weird looks when they saw them. "Who are these people, why can't you listen to normal music like everyone else?" She pushed the hurt aside until she was alone and then cried, ashamed for loving what she did. When the other girls in class were worshipping The Backstreet Boys and Boys II Men, she listened to Grant Lee Buffalo. Sang along to Jellyfish with the lights out.

The morning Julia found out she was pregnant, she searched through her cassettes until she found a song that soothed her panic.

Diana introduced her to this music. When she arrived in Australia, tanned and gaunt after an extended Greek holiday, Diana handed her a mix-tape. That cassette changed Julia's life.

Julia opened her eyes. The drone of the bus had lulled her to sleep. She gasped, remembering. The smell: *Copper and shit.*

"Oh God."

Diana's fingers shot over Julia's mouth, one slipped inside. "Shhh."

Bent double in the seat, her older sister's tightly bound hair fell out in curled ringlets. Julia wondered how it was possible to appear beautiful at a time like this, and yet she somehow did.

"Please, be quiet," Diana said.

"I think it's safe to speak," came a voice from across the aisle.

The old woman on the floor.

"The driver's out of it," Sarah said. She sat on her haunches, bones cracking. *Old gray mare, she ain't what she used to be,* she sang to herself whilst reaching out to the girls. Her crooked fingers shook. That hand had seen a lot of hard work over the years, had been bleached and bitten and burnt, and had dealt out its fair share of comforts and discipline, but all of that didn't compare to the simple act of reaching out to these two young women. Nothing did.

"No, don't," Diana said, pressing close to her sister. "She'll see."

"*She* won't." Sarah gestured toward the front of the bus. "Trust me."

Julia found honesty in the woman's face.

Their fingers stretched across no man's land and intertwined.

Squeezed.

A sting of envy in Diana then. The small betrayal on behalf of her sister, whom she'd always been there for, didn't go unnoticed. *Why not me?* she couldn't help wondering.

Sarah saw her husband in them: shattered yet feigning composure. It felt good to tell them that things were going to be okay, even if it was a lie. They had to know they weren't alone. That above all else.

"It's going to be okay, you get me?" Sarah smiled.

Julia nodded.

"What's your names, then?"

Julia answered for them both, a quick rat-a-tat-tat of syllables.

"Sisters?"

They answered yes together, bringing a thin smile to Sarah's face. "I'm so sorry you kids had to be here for this. You two have to stay with it. Be strong, like this, you hear?" Sarah intertwined her fingers with Julia's. After a moment, the two hands, each laced with the other's sweat, parted and returned to their respective owners.

Julia bit down on her lower lip and kicked the floor—a definitive *why us?* gesture that made her seem all the more childlike.

"Hey, don't you go thinkin' like that," Sarah said. She had raised enough children to recognize the frustrated stomp, and although she thought it warranted and was, in fact, asking herself the exact same question, she knew nothing good could come from it. Not all questions were answered; life wasn't always fair. "I know it's hard. My name is Sarah, Sarah Carr. And we're all in this together. Now tell me what you two have in your purses?"

"I don't have one," Julia said, flummoxed. "What? Why?"

Diana scrambled through her clutch, understanding at once what she was scouting for. Weapons. *Anything*. "Shit, I don't have much."

"No nail file? Those little scissors? Nothing?" Sarah asked, desperate—a fissure in the veneer of her calm.

Scissors.

Scissors.

Scissors.

The word cut the air and stabbed Jack's ears.

EIGHTY-TWO: SCISSORS

TEN YEAR OLD *Jack stood in the backyard. His parents were gone. The smell of evening barbecue: oily and rich. Next to him was the apple tree. Beetles flew in its shadows.*

Sunset. An orange sky raked with purples, and high above, an airplane. It left a long silk thread in the ozone, like a spider web when it catches the light. Jack could just make out the Boeing's drone.

Another sound. Closer.

Screaming.

EIGHTY-ONE: NOISE

THE MEMORY ROSE from somewhere deep inside, a bubble from the bottom of a lake. Pop. It made Jack dizzy. Sweat dripped into his eyes. Crunching thirst.

A fly buzzed by his head, its whine like the roar of chainsaws at dawn. He tried to ignore it and focus on the scene in front of him, on the shape and texture of that one word, on *the* word.

Scissors.

If someone wanted or had scissors, it meant that someone was willing to *fight,* willing to bring those twin blades down in a shimmering arc—over and over—into the driver's face until she was dead and someone else took control of the bus. That person would be him. Jack always knew he was hero material. It silently thrilled him.

He stared through the Perspex hub at the back of the driver's head—little life there. She reminded him of a toy whose batteries were winding down.

If only the emergency escape window was closer, he thought, *then I could just make a run at it. Or if we all decided to take her down together, the bitch wouldn't stand a chance.*

There were six of them and one of her. It paid to remember that.

If they rampaged, the bitch would no doubt react, would jerk the wheel and steer them off the road and into an accident. She might even grab the gun. But then again, maybe she wouldn't. Maybe she wouldn't see them coming. Maybe. Maybe.

"Fuck," he said.

Scissors.

He had to know.

Jack lowered his foot into the aisle, stepping into gummy blood. His hand grabbed the seat in front of him. Joining the women was a risk, a risk he was willing to take. He scanned for movement, looked in the concave mirror above the windshield; it appeared so small from where he sat—a silver eye. The longer he waited, the closer the driver was to checking on them. He was quite sure whatever mental capacity she had left was focused on getting them to wherever they were headed.

It had to be now. Quick and quiet.

Jack bound into the aisle and slipped. His palm landed on a seat, a loud clap cutting through the silence. Too late to turn back now.

Sarah shot her head in his direction, chest seized.

Michael noted this flurry of excitement in the mirror above the driver and spun around. He couldn't believe what he was seeing: the man with the goatee, running towards the others. *How could he be so stupid?*

Jack skidded to a stop behind Julia and Diana, a soldier diving for cover in an old World War Two film, his movements trailed by snipers—though safe all the while because he was just an actor directed by someone beyond the camera's view, someone who pulled the strings without hesitation. The girls recoiled as he slipped into the seat behind them. *The Eagle has landed,* Jack thought, giddy. *And cut!* "Someone say they got scissors?"

Nobody answered at first. Jack saw the chicken-shit kid at the front peering his way in the mirror. From here he could just make out the driver's face, too, her expression a dead and unmoving thing. *Good, stay that way.*

Relief swelled in Jack. He hadn't been seen, as he knew he wouldn't be. This soldier wasn't going down any time soon.

"Someone's got scissors?" Jack asked again, stronger this time.

Sarah cursed the man for his selfishness. He'd gambled with their lives. But despite her fury, Sarah understood that if she didn't answer his question, he would only ask again, and the more noise he made increased the chances of breaking through whatever emotional wall separated them from the driver.

"They don't," Sarah told him. "Neither do I."

"Shit!" Jack lowered his head.

"I've only got credit cards and receipts," Diana added.

Jack snagged on her accent. *Nasal and whiny—a Yank. What the hell is she doing in James Bridge?* Jack hated Americans; they were all the same. Spoke too loud; never had enough; they all thought they owned the world. *Girl even* looks *like a Yank.*

"You got anything?" Sarah asked Jack.

"Nope."

"Wait—" Sarah's hands flew to her bag and she pulled out her house keys. "Is this any good to us?" The thumb-sized picture of her grandchildren swung on the hook, catching the sun.

"Look, we're just going to make things worse," Diana said. "Let's wait this out. It's the only way."

Jack looked at Sarah, who he assumed would understand.

"I'm not saying we do anything about it," Sarah explained, "but I think we should have whatever we've got on standby should things go that way. Though I hope to Jesus on the cross that it doesn't."

"I'll be fucked if I'm going to sit here and let that happen." Jack swiped at another fly.

"Look," Sarah said, "I've got keys—" She shifted them in her hand so the jagged metal spikes faced outwards through her fingers. "And a couple of ballpoint pens."

The veins in Jack's neck drew tight as guitar strings.

Keys? Pens? scoffed the voice in his head. *The cunt has a gun!*

His eyes were wide, teeth clenched. "We can't let her do this."

"What's your name?" Sarah asked, her voice different from anything the sisters had heard from her so far. "Well?"

"It's Jack." He glared at her, taken aback. Without warning, his director fled the scene, leaving his lead actor to fend for himself under hot lights.

"Well right, Jack-o," Sarah said. "We can't Rambo our way through this. God gave you a brain, why don't you use it?"

"Please, shhh," Diana moaned.

Michael could hear their words catapulting around. Every sound made him flinch; they were unexploded hand grenades falling at his feet.

We're going to get caught.

We're going to get caught.

We're going to get caught.

EIGHTY

JULIA DIPPED LOW in her seat again, drawing a ragged breath. The driver hadn't moved after all. It struck her as almost impossible that the woman could be both *there* and *not there* at the same time. Though then again, possibly not. Because when Julia closed her eyes, she could see the posters in her bedroom far away, could hear music crooning from the cassette player on her dresser.

Pulling something close to her chest, assuming it was one of her teddy bears. Only it wasn't. The baby in her arms was a viscera-coated, half-dead creature clambering for breath.

She clenched her fists as hard as she could, refusing to resign to the worlds of hurt on either side of her blink. Two places at once, and neither of them safe.

"Look," Jack started again, his voice like a shake in the dark. Julia didn't know why she feared him so, yet fear him she did. She watched the way he held up his large strong hands, both as big as trashcan lids, and shivered. "I've got these. I can—" he mimed a kind of strangling, "—from behind."

"And lose control of the bus, killing us all in the

process?" Sarah tapped her forehead in a *think, man* gesture. "Not in this life, Jack. You grab her and she'll jerk the wheel. We flip, who knows?"

"But if we all go at her together," Jack said, cracking his knuckles.

"*Kids,* Jack. This is a bus of *kids*. Those guys up the front are terrified, and I don't blame them. I'm scared, too. We're not an army."

"She's right," Diana said. "We wait. The driver will stop eventually and when she does she'll let us go. It's simple. Either that, or the police will come. Whichever happens first. A dead girl in the middle of the road doesn't go unnoticed, you know. Not even in James-a-fuckin'-Bridge."

"She has a gun, woman! What you think she's gonna do when the police show? Jesus."

"We should fight," said a voice.

They turned to the speaker.

Julia.

SEVENTY-NINE

JULIA'S HEAD PRESSED against the seat. Skin clung to the leather. Its grip drew her face into a deformed jester's smile.

"See!" Jack pointed at her.

She closed her eyes again. Something dark and primal pounded in her, a second heartbeat that couldn't be ignored. "Who knows when there will be police?" she said. "You're right, Di. This *is* James Bridge, and there's never any cops at the station. If they come, they'll come from half an hour away in any given direction. God only knows where *we* are. Any idea?"

"Trees and more trees," Jack said. "I can't see a thing."

At the front of the bus, Michael tried to imagine what the others were talking about. He longed to be with them—safety in numbers, as they say—and not here at the mouth of the lion's den. Or lioness. Either way, if the driver moved, he and the prayer-happy teenager would be the first to know. The first to die. Michael's urge to join the others grew and pulsed.

If you join them, you will be seen, he told himself.

You won't get away with it like the big dude with the goatee did.

Guys like him always get away with their risks, and you *know it. You really do. You're too slow, too clumsy, and too bloody unlucky.*

Michael remained where he was, biting his knuckles.

SEVENTY-EIGHT

"This isn't the road that takes us into town and it isn't the one taking us to Maitland or Cessnock, either," Sarah said. "We're in a hollow. The road is narrow. If we were on the main stretch out of town, we'd be seeing fields, right? She's driving us further and further into scrub."

Julia sat up. "We have pens, keys." She balled her shaking hands into fists. "Together we can take her down. One of us just has to grab the wheel. All or nothing, though."

"And there's a big old gun right there in front of her just waiting to tear through us," Sarah said. "You're brave—" She paused, choosing her words carefully. "But you're a bub. This lady won't do anything to us unless we make her—"

Jack moved forward, a sudden realization upon him. "We're fucking hostages here."

Julia spun on them. "I don't want to die."

Diana flinched.

The bus filled with crashing; it drowned out their screams. Windows rattled in their frames.

Liz Frost snapped back into reality, her pupils dilated. Everything burned bright.

SEVENTY-SEVEN

REGGIE FROST CLIMBED out of her well-loved recliner and decided to make herself useful, something she'd long ago thought she ever could be. Yet she kept trying, kept on climbing. There were things that needed to be done after all, and hate it though she did, nothing ever found its way back to its rightful place unless Reggie did it herself.

The Christmas cutouts for example. She'd forgotten how many times she'd asked any one of her family members to take them down. The seasons had rolled on by and it was somehow November again; almost time to put the damn things back out again.

She knew she was invisible, an extension of the furniture in some ways. *I'm being worn away, eroded.* Reggie daydreamed of meeting someone who made her feel young, someone who maybe—just maybe—knew how to love her. Where there was no love there was no life, and this nothingness left her with two simple conclusions: she was over being a mother and wife.

Tired of trying.

On those few and far between days when Reggie thought about leaving this place, guilt wracked her body. Her existence was interwoven too far into the fabric of the family to ever consider being apart from it. Such a great overdue unsewing would, no doubt, leave her beyond repair.

"You're a silly, fat fool for thinking like that," Reggie told herself as she shuffled into the kitchen. She wore a loose-fitting one-piece dress covered in faded flower-print. How long had it been since she'd gone out and bought new clothes—or anything for that matter? Too long.

Poured herself a glass of cloudy water. Tipped it down the drain. Went to the refrigerator, opened the door and looked inside. Closed it. Left the room.

Upstairs, Wes played his records. She hated the music more than she hated his silence.

Reggie entered the study, pulled bags full of tinsel and handmade decorations from the shelves. Thoughts turned to her daughter. It would be hard to leave her. In whispers, Wes and Reggie agreed that forcing their daughter out of home might not be the best thing for her. Her husband was a tough and often unfair man, but there was a loyalty in him that she still respected. Liz was a lamb.

At fifty-five Reggie felt the time had almost come for her to be alone again.

"Oh, well."

Dust filled her nose. Sneezed. Blessed herself. She found the box of fairy lights—a cardboard corner eaten away by mice—and placed it on the floor, neat and straight, an illusion of rightfulness and order. Ignorance wasn't bliss—not by a long shot—but it was better than giving in to everything. Reggie's love for her children had gone misty.

Without having things spoon-fed to her, Liz floundered. Pathetic, really. That her daughter was going to be a bus driver came as little surprise. Routes and routine; hell—it may even be good for her. And even better, Liz managed to hold on to the position. In her own quiet way, Reggie felt pride at this—not that she knew how to express it. Once upon a time, maybe. Not anymore.

A small, gray mouse crouched in the corner of the room. Its fur was matted, eyes dark and fearful. Reggie grabbed an old shoebox to sweep it into. Family photos tumbled out and wisped onto the carpet. She studied those faces for a beat and then stepped over them. Her giant shadow fell across the mouse.

A cool wind blew through the house when she threw the front door open. Reggie hobbled across the veranda where the wind chimes tinkled and sat on the steps as she used to back in the days when it was okay to smoke. Wes silenced her habit, though interestingly, not their son's. Her legs spread wide to show off the varicose veins. Reggie lowered the shoebox to the grass and upturned it. Her mouse scurried away.

Escaped.

SEVENTY-SIX

THE CRASHING SOUNDS of metal on metal.

Jack launched himself onto the seat behind Sarah. Julia and Diana screamed. Sarah, however, fell. Her hands shot into the air and grabbed at nothing, only to land on the floor, limbs peddling like a beetle on its back.

The sound continued. An intense rattle and pound.

It consumed all.

Peter knew that at some point he must have fallen asleep. Yes, the nightmare was vivid, but it was a nightmare nonetheless. Things like this didn't happen to people like him—simple, really. His life had intertwined with his fiction. The notebook flew out of his hand and clapped onto the floor; a corner soaking up the dead man's blood. Peter couldn't help it; he wept. Jagged vibrations bulleted through him. His already busted lip cracked again.

The bus shook.

To Michael it felt like they were driving into the sky. The strobe of sun through the passing trees disappeared. He squinted against this blinding light, slammed his eyes shut and saw red.

The noise. The driver placed it in his head. *I hate*

you, he thought. *I hate you as much as you seem to hate me for some reason.* He was afraid to look in the mirror just in case she looked back, in case she knew.

Liz was also shocked by the noise. Her hands flew in the air and landed hard against the wheel with a slap—

—a hand against her face. Pain. A child needed to be disciplined, that was what she had always been told. He pulled away then, her father's face full of sadness—

The bus jolted to the right, not much, but enough to throw Michael off balance and into the aisle. An endless second where he had no control. He watched, unbelieving, as his hands drew closer and closer to the floor, to the black ooze of blood and brain.

Bang!

His nose slammed the floor, gore filling his eyes. He cried out and inhaled the mess into his mouth. From behind him, he heard the driver yell. Her shrill voice cut through him. Michael tried to crawl, hands and knees slipping.

The bus lurched again.

Metal screeching, sparks fanned in the left-hand side windows. Endless thunder. It was too much for Sarah, who screamed.

Michael moved but didn't appear to be going anywhere. He sometimes had dreams where dark entities chased him down his street in Maitland, a pursuit he endured in painful slow motion. In these dreams, he grabbed fence posts, the doors of cars, all in the desperate hope of propelling himself along faster. That same desperation was upon him now.

Closer.

And closer.

He studied the long abattoir floor. His blood-streaked hands grabbed on to the nearest handlebar, and he forced himself forward.

Sarah reached out to him. "Come on!"

Michael missed her hand, arced forward, and his own sunk wrist-deep into the gaping hole of the corpse's head. He pulled free of the mess with a sickening *schlop*, stood, ran. Wet heat squished between his fingers—it seemed to spread up his arm like quick-moving vines, strangling the life from his person. Within moments he was surrounded by the others, and after so long, felt safe in their number. It was then he experienced the virgin ebb of claustrophobia, those vines drawing tight.

Jack went to the window and at first, saw nothing but his reflection glaring back at him. He pushed through this image and beyond, to see sky, to see water. "What?"

A spark of recognition. Things fell into place. The thunder they heard was the sound of the bus crossing Flagman's Bridge. It linked the roads on either side of the Hunter River. The metal-on-metal was the bus grinding against the railing. It alone had stopped them from plummeting over a hundred foot drop into the dry riverbed below.

Thunder ceased.

They made it across the bridge.

Jack went to tell the others that they were at the far end of town, heading west, but stopped. Shadow crossed the bus again like the giant wing of some threatening bird blocking out the sun. His eyes returned to the window. The bird swallowed up the last of the blue sky, or so it appeared.

They re-entered the hollow of trees on the other side.

The driver shrieked at them to sit. Her passengers did as they were told. A steady quiet descended over them.

Michael's blood-smeared face met the driver's. She was looking straight into him through the mirror and knew all his secrets.

I see you, fat faggot.

He bent over, face touching the artificial leather.

Jack intercepted the driver's look: she lowered her eyes and watched the road with an obvious, newfound concentration. She slipped the oversized hat from her head, dropped it on the floor. Life in the bitch yet. Going over the bridge had snapped her from her fugue state, just as the death of the girl had done beforehand. This brought a glimmer of hope to Jack. If the driver went 'under' twice, then it stood to reason she may do so again.

And that felt a little like hope.

No more whispering or talking, Jack thought. The bus was an extension of this mad woman's arm, and they were in her grip. *She's running scared and those who died just got in her way.*

He bit his tongue; the old woman was right. They had to wait it out, no matter how much it frustrated him to do so.

Somewhere between screech and murmur, a voice broke the silence.

"Hey come in, Lizzie, come in."

Jack punched at the seat in front of him. *Holy shit.*

At no point had they considered the two-way radio.

SEVENTY-FIVE:
RADIO

"REPORT BACK, TWO-FOUR."

The handset sat on its hook, DC cable swinging in an arc, ticking the dash.

Static crunched. "You there, Liz?"

The voice on the radio belonged to Bridget Sargent. Bridget was overweight and loving, her messy hair tamed by bands and pencils. She greeted Liz every morning by tapping her garish fingernails against the window of her cubicle. Bridget was their Lead Fleet Correspondent. She alerted employees to changed traffic conditions and radioed drivers concerning route punctuality. Liz knew this was why Bridget was calling. A commuter must have tired of waiting for the bus to arrive and called the transit hotline to file a complaint. It was Bridget's duty to find out the reason for the delay.

Liz imagined her co-worker's plump face washed in the lights from her switchboard, could almost hear fingernails drumming against the desk. Brow furrowed, the first twinge of concern.

A wasp slammed against the windshield and splattered.

The bus carved through the humid day. Nobody dared move.

They waited.

White noise, *click*, and Bridget's voice came again. Firmer: "Come in, two-four."

Liz felt the passengers staring. She saw them in the mirror above her head, their red eyes blinking in shadows that wouldn't sit still.

When she reached for the microphone, it rattled in its bracket like something alive and anxious. At any moment she expected it to jump right into the palm of her hand.

Sarah watched the driver's head dodge from the road to the radio and back again. *If she picks it up and talks into it—should we yell for help? Will they hear? Will she turn around and go for the gun? Do we charge? Is this the perfect distraction? Will we crash? Will we burn alive in an explosion as the bus wraps itself around a tree?* Sarah wished Bill were here—he would know what to do.

Meanwhile, half-finished sentences and empty excuses flashed through Liz's mind. Another bug detonated in her line of sight; a bloodied star.

Bridget's voice crackled through the radio a final time.

Liz snatched the microphone and yanked it towards her. The coiled DC cord pulled taut and tore from the unit. It snapped, flung upwards and slashed her cheek. She fought for control of the wheel and tossed the microphone out the window.

It shattered against the tarmac.

Watching, Sarah's heart emptied out.

The wheels crunched over gravel, a kind of lullaby

to Liz, especially after such chaos. Blood trickled down her cheek from where the cord whipped her raw, yet she experienced no sting, it being lost to adrenalin, to the remaining angel dust in her system. Only sorrow here. In her time with the company, Bridget had never been anything but kind to her. Liz wondered if her co-worker would weep if she learned that Liz was dead, had shot herself in the privacy of her bedroom, with no note or explanation left behind, just the echo of a bang nobody cared enough to listen to within the walls of her own home. Would it be Bridget who cleaned out her locker, Liz wondered, who tied together her final pay stubs and sent them to her mother?

Likely, yes.

Liz didn't want that to happen. She wanted to live. Everything had changed. Now she had friends—an entire busload of them, believe it or not. With time, with a little tenderness, they would grow to see her in ways her family had forgotten. The two young men could be the sons she never had, and Liz couldn't wait to fill their lives with happiness and loving. They would never feel loneliness measuring her own.

And the oldest person on the bus: her new mother. So much to learn from her.

The two girls: people to gossip and share stories with.

Liz imagined the goatee of the man tickling her nose as she nuzzled close to him. He loved her and told her everything that was bad was behind them now. Nobody had died, no blood, no carnage. Just forgiveness and a future worth living for.

A twinkle on the horizon broke these thoughts. An oncoming car.

SEVENTY-FOUR

ARTHRITIS THROBBED AS Wes Frost sifted feed among the chickens. The birds looked up at him between their frantic pecking with absent, dispassionate eyes.

Food, those black peepers said. Nothing else. *Food.*

He rounded up their eggs, placed them in a basket and whisked them inside. He returned with a butcher's knife.

The Rottweiler growled and barked at the end of its chain, furthered its arc in the dirt as it skidded back and forth. "Shut up, dog," he said.

Wes set his eye on one of the fatter hens and upended her. A single brown feather lodged under the collar of his shirt. He stretched her neck against the cinderblock and envied the bird its simple thoughts, its lack of fear.

Severed the head. Set the bird to run blind. Watched it fall.

Wes plucked it bare.

He cleaned his hands in the upstairs bathroom, whilst listening to the record playing down the hall. Wes looked at himself in the mirror, drew a single feather from his collar and set it beside his razor.

Downstairs, his wife rifled through the study and prepared to take the Christmas decorations down.

He shaved and wiped the mirror clean.

In his bedroom from under the bed, he took out a footlocker, opened it and took out a worn copy of *Hustler*. The women admired him with fake smiles.

Getting old there, babe.

Struggling to get it up? It's okay, we're here to help you.

Come on, big boy, work it for me.

He loved the ladies. He hated the ladies. They spread their legs for him but never let him in. He missed the touch of others. Wes and Reggie hadn't made love in two and a half years, and even then, they had been short-lived interludes. On the page, there was a woman who looked like Reggie maybe twenty years ago. Upturned nose and freckled cheeks framed by burnt honey hair. Wes smiled. His fingertip traced the line of her torso.

"I miss that," he said, speaking as much of his youth as her flesh.

I miss you too.

Wes stroked himself hard, eyes closed. He saw himself at twenty in the rain, a black umbrella in hand. The woman, pretty in her own quiet way, ahead of him with the bags of groceries and water in her eyes. He ran, introduced himself and opened his umbrella. Her name was Reggie and a year and a half later they were married.

Wes spilled himself into a rolled-up piece of toilet paper. He opened his eyes and looked at the woman on the page.

Her left eye was welted black. Blood poured from her nose, ran down her breasts in a threaded, ruby necklace.

That's the last time you ever lay a hand on me, Reggie said.

And she'd spoken the truth, too.

Dog barked outside, the chickens clucked, and somewhere his daughter shot a man she didn't know in the face. He died as Wes came.

Weakened, he closed the magazine, put away the mess. The footlocker returned to its place under the bed, slipped into the heavy indentation in the carpet. Wes showered and washed his false teeth. He'd lost his own to sugar and a bar brawl five years prior. He flexed his muscles to remind himself those at least were still there.

Dried and dressed he went to the window and threw it open. The sun sucked the moisture from his skin and spat it back at his face as humidity. He knew the day would end in thunder and lightning.

Dog continued to bark.

SEVENTY-THREE

IT WASN'T A well-traveled road they pummeled down; the stretch grew more treacherous with each proceeding turn. As though to spite danger, their speed didn't decrease—if anything, the odometer climbed. Yes, the 243 to town had strayed far from its route and wound deep into the valley.

Within the bus, Jack bit his thumb, a habit he'd had since school, biting his nails down to the quick as he waited for a teacher to ask him questions he didn't know the answers to. Not much had changed since then; there were few solutions within reach now, either.

Peter saw the oncoming car. Perhaps his prayers had been answered. He swore to himself that he would get out of this alive and trusted his God to shield him. Sitting there in the heat, he knew that when the time came to run, there would be a fleet of angels protecting him. Their strong, white wings would be his armor.

His mother's voice in his ear. *I'm proud of you*, she said, breath thick with the stench of liquor. *This is a test of faith. And you* will *have faith. You'll have faith or I'll put my cigarette out on your arm again. You know that, don't you?* Peter sometimes wondered if his mother was using religion as an excuse to hurt him. *The discipline of the Lord.* It was more warning than doctrine; words as vicious as the blows that followed.

A childhood memory came back to him.

The wooden spoon at the top of the spice rack.

He'd dubbed the utensil Mr. Cranky. Into its moon-face was drawn an angry expression in permanent marker. When Peter was bad, his mother made him get the spoon and bring it to her. This hurt the most, the endless walk from kitchen to living room where his mother always had soap operas playing too loud and obnoxious, a room that always smelled of tobacco. Afterwards, once she was done, young Peter would limp as he returned Mr. Cranky to his home and then go to his room without having to be told. He would kneel and pray, not for forgiveness but for his mother to die. And now, after all this time, Peter realized his mother was right to do what she'd done, to slap and pinch him. He would be tested, and her advice and the pain she inflicted had crafted him into the man he was now—faithful, resilient, and ready.

He missed her. He missed her most of all.

Michael watched the car approach, lightheaded. His movement caught Diana's attention. The bus shifted to the left and right, as though correcting itself. Julia grabbed her sister and they found balance together.

"Don't! Please don't!" Liz yelled.

Diana fought the urge to bang at the windows. If there was ever an opportune time, this was it.

"W-what is it? What is it?!" Julia asked, panicking.

Jack wanted to scream for help—and more. He wanted to run at the glass. Drop his shoulder against it. He had power in him to break it, too. Fear fueled power like little else. His life was on the line. *I'm too young to die,* he thought. *I'll smash that window to fucking smithereens. Sure, I'm going to fall out and tear myself to almighty shit, but by God, I'm going to live.*

The car drew closer.

Don't do it, Jack-o, said the other voice in his head. *You won't break the glass. You'll end up stuck in it, stuck like a cow on a hook, squirming half in and half out, guts spilling every which way.*

Do it, Jack-o, and you're a dead man.

"I can't," he said aloud. Thoughts of quickly writing a letter and tossing it out the window were extinguished by the fact that they had no paper. Even if they did manage to get a note written in time, who stopped their car to pick up discarded litter thrown from a public bus? This was one question he had utter confidence in answering: Nobody, that's who.

They might see the dented grill, though. *See it and flash their headlights to signal to us that hope is not lost. What about the blood, for Christ's sakes?*

Diana looked at the sliding planes of glass above the windows. If only she could find some sort of *Alice in Wonderland* potion that would shrink her to a size small enough to wiggle through. Her Disney-inspired escape would lead her not outside, but all the way to Astoria. Tumbling onto soft green grass, rolling to a stop, towered over by Douglas Firs so tall they seemed to scratch the sky. And lying there, panting, she would hear the distant toot of a boat on the bay.

Reality: the howling bus as it accelerated.

"Now, now, now," Sarah said. *Whoever's driving*

that car is going to see the blood. It's impossible not to. We're saved.

It came at them faster and faster.

But unknown to the passengers, the water from the windshield wipers had filtered down and washed away much of that blood. There were still long slivers of gore decorating the grill, only much of it had dried and gone sticky, covered now in a blanket of dust. Nobody would see it. Not at that speed. Not on a day like this, when it everything conspired against those on Route 243.

The car drove past.

As deep down they all knew it would.

Peter slumped. He knew truths the others did not. He could hear his mother again, took comfort in her words. *Should the car pass by and nothing come of it, it means it wasn't preordained to stop. There's always a plan in place, Peter.*

It's your lot to accept it.

Heads turned and saw nothing. No brake lights, no car at all; nothing except the end of the bus. It glared back at them, dark and bleak.

Liz hit the brakes hard. Her new family zipped through the air, screams cut short by collisions with the seats and each other.

SEVENTY-TWO

THE BUS CAME to a stop.

Jack pulled himself up off the floor. *This is it*, the voice in his head told him. He poised himself to run.

Sarah wanted to grab this hot-headed young man and hold him. She pitied him for his machismo. They weren't going to survive if one of them made a martyr of themselves. With every death, the group would come more unhinged. They were welded together now by tragedy, and a risk by one was a risk to all. *Why can't he see that?* she wondered. *Oh, Bill, please make him stop.*

The bus shifted into reverse. "What the fuck?" Jack said.

Michael glanced up at the ceiling escape hatch, which was open a crack to allow airflow into the bus. He imagined himself getting up and forcing it open the rest of the way, but he was frozen in place. Terrified. The driver was *alert* now. Were he to attempt escape there would be the eventual *bang!* And in a flash his entire history would be wiped clean, all the problems, hopes and dreams that stitched him together—ripped apart in a bloody spray.

The bus crashed into a post box, knocking it to the

ground. They swung outwards, extending the length of the road, blocking non-existent traffic in both directions.

Diana dragged her sister away from the window. There were multiple versions of Julia now. One she'd seen so many times slumped over the edge of her bed, talking to boys on the landline telephone, tucking strands of hair behind her ears. Another was this shattered girl before her. The division hurt. It hurt *real* bad. Diana hoped there was a third incarnation someday, a Julia who was happy and knew her worth. A Julia who had managed to put this whole nightmare behind her.

The bus jumped, throwing them again. Sarah snapped her hip against the edge of a seat.

Darkness swallowed light as the road slid lengthways from view. Impenetrable clouds of dirt blocked the windows. They drove off the road and into a second, narrower hollow. A side street, perhaps, or a driveway.

Peter no longer prayed in silence. He recited the words out loud. New vibrations filled the hub as the bus drove over loose ground. "Our Father, who art in *Heaven*!" He saw his mother beside him, screaming the words along with him. Every stab of pain she'd inflicted was worth it to have her here. To think that he'd spent so much time pouring energy into wordplay when prayer was the only verse he'd ever need.

Julia dropped onto her side. She put her fingers in her mouth, bit down. Her left hand cradled her stomach.

Sarah stood, blood from the aisle sticking to her shirt in gory patches. "Can you see up ahead?" she asked anyone.

Diana leant over her sister, squinting through the windshield. “No.”

The hollow narrowed.

Trees flanking the road scraped hard against the sides of the bus. Knotted limbs of dead gum trees scratched like the hands of a thousand psychopaths trying to get in.

“Stop this, you crazy bitch!” Jack yelled. “Stop and let us out!” Self-control fled the scene. His yells were more noises in a world of noises, and because of this they went ignored. This was the way it had always been for Jack.

Needlepoint scratching sounds drove into their ears, fingernails on a chalkboard.

Light.

SEVENTY-ONE

AND THAT LIGHT was brilliantly white, warm. Trees unclasped their knots, peeling away on either side of the windshield as they entered a wide-open space.

Hands fell from ears and eyes opened. The passengers took in their surroundings.

They were in a large yard. In front and to the left stood a huge, decrepit shed, a pickup truck parked next to it. The bus drew closer to a house flanked by faded Christmas cutouts. The property sat in the middle of this clearing, and beyond it, Sarah noted trees standing guard, the flash of a clothesline. The words slipped out of her: "No neighbors."

Julia stepped away from the window. Dread filled her. "This is it," she said. "This is it this is it. This is it."

She's about to kill us.

Diana went to her sister and eased her into their original seat, and whilst the grip on her arm remained relaxed, her shouts to shut the hell up were nothing short of intense.

"YOU ALL BE *QUIET*!" the driver said. She glared them all. Her shoulders rose and fell, breath coming harsh and shallow.

Michael put his head in his hand and cried. Even

now, he felt self-conscious about this. *They will think you're girly*, he thought.

Oh, don't be so fucking stupid.

They're not thinking that.

You're not that important to them.

SEVENTY: HOME

SARAH WATCHED THE peak of the house grow taller through the windshield. Jack stepped up next to her and whispered, “Whatever’s going to happen is going to happen fast.”

She didn’t reply, just continued staring. Never in her life had she known what it felt like to be paralyzed, rooted to the spot with fear. Did terror numb her body or was her body numbing itself to the terror? Sarah didn’t know. And perhaps she didn’t want to, either.

The bus rolled over crunching earth.

Julia apologized to her sister, who now rubbed her back and held her close. “It’s okay. It’s a-a-all right. Once she s-stops the bus s-she’ll let us off.”

Diana shut her eyes.

Astoria, Oregon. Her mother’s funeral.

She opened them. There was still the dark house out there, so she pinched her eyes again—that same reflex was the one that said yank your hand out from under the water for fear of being scolded; distrust that man walking behind you on the empty street. Pure elemental instinct. Survive when you can, always survive, and sometimes denial is the best sort of survival. Sometimes, it's all we've got.

Santorini, the Greek Islands. A blue sky, white houses covered with splashes of colorful paint. She had walked these streets on a vacation before arriving in Australia. Lost herself in the streets to shake the bitterness she felt towards her father for uprooting her life in the first place.

Diana heard Jack's voice to her left. His grating tone brought her back to the bus. "When she stops, the bitch will want to get out and—"

"—that's when we run at her," Diana finished for him. She had no idea where the words came from, only that they were spoken without regret. Without hesitation. Survival of another kind.

The bus crept forward. Nice and slow.

A wheel dropped into a deep pothole in the lawn. The sound was an explosion. Nobody screamed, but every heart seized within every single chest.

"We take her quick," Diana said.

Sarah knew the young woman wasn't the same person she'd been when boarding that morning. In her hands, Sarah clutched those keys, the teeth sticking out in spikes, and it occurred to her that she, too, wasn't the same person she had been earlier that morning. And that was why Sarah handed Diana and Julia the two ballpoint pens from her handbag without hesitation. You must change in order to live. The girls, sensing this too, snatched those pens up—almost greedily—but soon felt the weight of this realization settle over them.

It looks like a pen, Julia thought. *Like the ones I use in school, like the ones I write letters to my friends with.*

Can I really do this?

The bus rolled to a stop.

Yes. Yes, I think I can.

"We push her out. Anything," Sarah said. "We do whatever we have to do."

Julia nodded, her head held high.

SIXTY-NINE

THEY PARKED IN the middle of the front yard. Positioned at the intersection between house, shed, and driveway. Nothing moved except for the thick towers of clouds upon clouds above them.

Inside the bus, the passengers watched their driver stand and look through the windshield. Searching.

Sarah and Diana poised for action. Jack took Julia's pen and gripped it tight, ready to stab.

The engine ticked.

Liz's eyes moved from the shed she associated with her brother to her home. Stillness there. She leaned forward and took the gun from its place on the seat cover.

The fan blades spun a final time, and then came to a grating halt.

Jack didn't breathe. Couldn't. *She'll open the door,* he predicted, taking pride in his calculation, *and when she does, we'll pounce. But we have to wait until she's down the first step.*

Catch the cunt on uneven ground.

Liz flicked the door release switch. It clattered open. Heat rolled into the cabin, up over her exposed legs, drafted through her ill-fitting shorts. She took her first step towards the stairs leading outside.

Sarah grimaced, ready.

Liz took her second step. Then hovered. She took half a step backward. Her foot lingered above the blood-splattered floor.

The front screen door of the house swung open, banging against the jamb. A young man in a blue wife-beater stepped into the sunlight. He was tanned and had a buzz cut like Jack's, Sarah noted.

The arrival of the man shattered all thoughts of attack. The pacing was off, things skewered. The possibility of outside help. The tattooed twenty-something brought with him the anticipation of rescue.

Comprehension clicked inside Julia. "Oh, shit. She brought us home."

Liz spun on her heel, the gun spinning with her—she underestimated its weight and her aim went wide. Straightened. "Y-you all stay here."

They knew the driver was beyond reason. Whatever illness she'd lived with had now taken over.

Liz ran down the steps, hair billowing in the wind.

Jed hurried to his sister but stopped short when he saw the gun. The sight scrambled his thoughts. "Fuck, what—fuck-fuck—what?"

Her arms reached out for him, shaking. The gun slipped from an outstretched fingertip and landed in the dust with a *thunk*.

Jed looked at Liz and took in her scrawny legs, her urine-stained pants, the sweaty shirt clinging to her breasts, her face. Those eyes staring back at him with desperation.

The hot sun on his shoulders. Jed flexed the muscles in his back and the tattooed eagle appeared to fly. He caught his sister just as she collapsed in a dead weight that drove the wind from him.

"Sis," Jed wheezed.

She howled into his collarbone, her voice tearing through his body. Jed wasn't sure if he'd ever heard anything quite so awful. Confused, he absorbed the sight of the bus parked in his front yard and shuddered. Jed was aware that inside him there was a switch, as he assumed there was in everyone on the planet. The power behind that switch grew over the years, charging, and it became harder to keep in the OFF position. As he held his sister in his arms, he reached into the dark and flicked that switch without hesitation. Electricity flowed through him.

He was positive the hatred he felt for whoever had reduced her to this sodden mess had never been matched. The yelling from the bus made Liz flinch. From its open doorway, without stopping to look left or right, a teenager ran.

Jed pushed Liz aside. Something inside told him to pick up the gun.

SIXTY-EIGHT

IT WAS BRIGHT outside, just like it must have been in the beginning. Born again. Peter felt grateful. So scared he almost forgot what he was running for or towards. No direction. Every direction. The important thing was just to run. He was born to do this, not to write. His pounding feet against the dust were the only poetic rhythms in his life now. He trusted the light around him.

SIXTY-SEVEN

MICHAEL JUMPED ACROSS the aisle to the opposite window. He passed Jack as he dropped his pen. It rolled across the floor.

The passengers scrambled from side to side, confused.

Should they run or should they stay?

Jack stumbled to the dead body between him and the door. A small blowfly landed on the nose of the corpse. He didn't know why it scared him but it did. In his ear, someone quiet grew loud.

Kill the fly, said the voice. It was the voice of a familiar man.

If you run to that door, Jack-o, you will die and you know it.

Jack shook his head.

Stay here and kill the fly.

The insect rubbed its dirty legs together. Jack brought the heel of his foot down on the nose of the corpse. An atrocious crack. A splash across his face.

Good boy, Jack-o.

SIXTY-SIX

THE KID RAN for the trees closest to the house near the Christmas cutouts. Jed followed every foolish movement with the gun. These people had destroyed his sister, and worse, invaded his private property. His home. They must have forced Liz to drive them here. It was unforgivable; he had every right to pull the trigger.

SIXTY-FIVE

A TIN-CAN WHISTLE near his ear. Around him, a landmine of dirt blew into the sky. Peter breathed it in and coughed hard. He continued running.

To the right.

To the left.

Straight.

Trees.

Another sound. It wasn't him, but *in* him. Wetness in his ear, sloshing around. Peter touched the place where his ear should have been. Blood ran down his neck, the fibers of his shirt soaking it up.

Sarah screamed at the boy. "Run and never stop!"

She squinted; saw the blood running down his head in spurting jets. "Oh my God, he's been shot." Her hand went to her mouth. "Oh, sweet Jesus."

"Do we run? Do we go for it?" Julia asked her sister. "Do we go now?"

Michael toppled back into his seat. "Shut up! Shut up!"

In the aisle, Jack stepped over the body, his heel covered in brain matter. He watched the stupid kid running in circles dodging bullets. It was like a cartoon. Jack laughed, veins sticking out of his forehead. He'd planned on using the kid as a distraction for his own escape, but it was too late. All too late. Now he watched, unmoving.

SIXTY-FOUR

I'M BLEEDING! *Oh God. Oh God. Mum! It's okay. It's okay. I'm running. Just keep running. It's all I need to do. Every step is bringing me closer to—*

Impact. It was as though an asteroid fell from the sky and landed in his chest. Peter tumbled through the air. Time slowed to a crawl. His spinal cord severed by the time he hit the ground. He rolled onto his back and could feel nothing from the neck down. Unattainable breaths. Blood drained out of him. It was like being burned alive—a small glimpse of life in Hell. Wetness around him. A baptism. Peter began to drown.

It's not meant to be like this. It shouldn't hurt.

His eyes rolled up into his head; the white grew larger. He caught a glimpse of the upturned Christmas cutouts.

Blood-streaked angels.

The last thing Peter did was smile.

SIXTY-THREE

WES KNEW A little something about fear. Or at least he thought he knew.

Before age forced him off the field, he'd played half-back for a local football team. And he was good, too, real front-page-of-the-*Bugle* material. Everyone came to watch those games, and he was proud the members of his family were among their number.

One winter, six-year-old Jed taught his father a lesson. Wes hadn't been playing that day, a recurring knee injury having pulled him off the field. He cheered in the stands with the others. If there was something else Wes was learning about, albeit slowly, it was the fine art of being patient. More than anything, he wanted to be out there playing with his mates, to smell the churned grass and sweat.

Reggie held his shoulder, her idea of comfort. He knew she pitied him and he loved her for it. Loved her too for her loyalty to the team. Football sparked something in her. When she got angry or excited as someone scored, or a referee made a imbecilic call, it reminded him of the girl he married and prized.

His children paid little attention to the game. They would wander with friends, which was fine enough.

But they knew the rules: when the final siren wailed they had to be waiting by the food stands, ready to be collected. If they disobeyed, well kids, expect a spanking. Wes was, as he saw it, a tough but fair father—just as his old man had been. On that particular day, as the game drew to a close, siren echoing across the field, Jed put that firm fairness to the test. The boy was nowhere to be seen, and as a result, Wes saw red.

Reggie asked Liz if she'd seen her brother.

"Nup."

Wes went to look for him, dragging his bad leg behind him, already rehearsing what he was going to say.

If I've told you once, I've told you a million times.

Jed, get your behind over here now.

You had me and your mother worried sick.

Next to the field, there was a children's playground. At the sandpit, he found the open belly of the jam sandwich Reggie made Jed that morning. This sight didn't scare him. No. It made him angrier. *Kid never stays put when I tell him to.* He kicked sand over the remains, buried sport for the cats.

Ten minutes passed. Irritation turned to worry. Images of men in cars holding bouquets of two-cent candy out to his son filled his head.

Wes walked through a small thicket of trees and saw his son's bare back.

Jed's soiled shirt was thrown over the arm of a collapsed tree. He stood on a mound of upraised dirt: the spout of an ant nest. The hive thrummed with swarming black and yellow pinpricks. Wes called to his son. Jed slowly turned. His arms were lathered in jam, smeared over his cheeks. His pale skin was covered in a frenzy of ants. Thousands of them. On his lips, through his hair.

This was Wes's lesson in fear.

Jed's mouth moved. No sound.

My son is going to die, Wes now understood. *He will die if I stand here and do nothing. Move your feet now, old man! You're as useless as tits on a bull if you just stay put.*

He rushed forward and tackled his son to the ground, rolled him around in the grass until the insects were gone. Jed lay in his arms, unbitten and safe.

Fear. But Wes was wrong. That day after the football game was nothing compared to this.

Fear was the sound of a gunshot and realizing that the person who pulled the trigger was that same boy.

Wes blinked. It turned out fear had a smell to it, too. Jam. Dirt.

Gun smoke.

He couldn't understand why the bus was in his front yard, or who the people were aboard. He stopped in his tracks—behind him Reggie stepped out of the house and screamed. She'd seen what he'd seen: a dead boy on their yard, a bloodied fountain shooting red into the sky.

The gun fell from Jed's hand. Wes gazed at the bus and the passengers running its length. He could see the bus door, a slit into darkness.

Reggie's bare feet hit the dirt. She yelled to her daughter who now writhed on the ground. Dazed, Wes reached for her. Their fingertips almost touched.

No, he told himself. *Get the gun.*

SIXTY-TWO

Hollow wind.

Reggie collapsed onto Liz, pulling at her. "Get up," she yelled. "Into the house now!" Her fingers around Liz's sweaty arms. Jed watched them fall over each other and thought of that old show his dad used to make them watch when they were kids, *The Three Stooges*. In his mind, he heard kazoos and a crackling laugh track. He could still remember laying on his stomach in front of the television watching monochrome images play out through a scrim of dust. Liz next to him on the shag, cross-legged, chin cupped in her hands. This tableau felt like another life from another world, idealized statuettes in a dry snow globe. Now, as Jed watched his mother and sister struggle out the front of their house, his face impassive and cold, he wondered if this memory was even real. Their snow globe was most certainly cracked.

Wes picked up the gun and something snapped in him.

Something in the dark.

The weapon was his.

Wes was never one to theorize about fate. He didn't believe in all that astro-hoo-ha-tabloid bullshit. But he did believe in retribution. What could he have done to deserve this? His private answer lay in the question itself.

Movement on the bus broke his daze; the door slammed from the inside with the ferocity of a bear trap. Wes only became aware of the numbness in his body once he started to shake it off, when he realized the gun had dropped from his hands.

Trespassers. They had no right to be on his property any more than they had the right to bring harm to his family. *Get off your high horse, hypocrite*, he told himself. *After everything* you've *done?*

You're a monster, remember?

Now go back to your garden, you fucking joke.

Wes ground his false teeth together.

No. No, I won't.

Regret and shame softened him, but he smiled anyway. He'd been waiting for this moment to come, waiting for a reason to become a man again. A man defended what was his—even though the family were failures.

But they were *his* failures.

Nobody had the right to touch them.

Except me.

His anger ignited a familiar flame, one he thought had gone out for forever. He strengthened, years peeling back to reveal the harder man beneath, a man devoid of mercy.

Wes watched his son moving away from him with the gun now, saw the wings of the great eagle fly through Jed's wife-beater.

"Nobody," Wes said.

Jed shot at the bus, holes punching into its side.

One wayward bullet blew out the front left tire—hissing as it deflated. Wes ran to his son and threw his arms around him, pulling him towards the house by the midsection. The final bullet before the click-click of empty chambers went wide and speared the dirt.

"Don't fight me, Jed."

"Let me go! Jesus-fuckin'-Christ!"

Jed wormed free, stumbling at the bus with the empty gun raised. Wes followed, bolts of pain in his knee, grabbing Jed's arm. Jed turned and thumped the gun against the side of his father's face. Instant pain flared in Wes's forehead; warmth ran down his cheek.

Wes saw the terror in his boy. It wasn't dissimilar to the expressions he'd witnessed on a hundred television newscasts over the years: the face of the captured assassinator as he screamed, "They made me do it!"

He punched his son in the chest.

Winded, Jed bowed to the ground and scrambled, the gun forgotten. Another blow stopped him short and he felt himself being dragged in lunges towards the house. Wes had him by the waist of his jeans.

The building looming above them was the place Jed had been raised, a place that was so much a part of his being it might as well have been a structure of meat and skin, an organic being which, like him, flinched when scalded at, which knew of things like sorrow and hope. It wasn't simple brick and iron. No. This was the place where brother bones grew strong when they needed to. This place, it breathed, and its whispers carried through the quiet. Yet despite the kinship evoked as Jed passed into its shadow, he rejected it just the same. *Don't take me back*, he longed to scream—if only he were brave enough. He needed to be in the yard, outside of himself. Detached as he defended his family.

As he defended Sis.

Reggie pulled her daughter's thin frame up the stairs and onto the verandah. The mother caught her reflection in one of the windows—face flushed, messy hair sticking to her skin. Reggie didn't think she could possibly be the same woman who only minutes before placed a chicken in the refrigerator to marinate for dinner that night. They usually ate around six o'clock, the kids flying off with plates to their respective corners of the house, and her and Wes retiring to the living room to chow down as the game shows droned on. That was the way it always had been, and always would be.

Jed looked up at his father from the bottom step. *You're not a man,* he thought. *How can you* not *feel the anger I feel now? These people have done something to our Liz. They have done something to* me. *They've made a murderer of me.* Dizzy from the punches, Jed whispered aloud, "I did the right thing."

To his shock, Wes put out his hand and helped him up. "I know you did, son. But we got to be careful, we've got to move slow. Those people on the bus, they're—" Wes searched for the right word. "—Animals."

SIXTY-ONE

SAID ANIMALS WERE on the floor, huddled behind seats like chickens complacent within the confines of their cages. The bus stunk. They breathed into the crooks of their arms. The air twirled with upholstery dust and sheet metal rust from the bullets.

Sarah moved.

Staying put and dummying up struck her as the smarter option, but the situation *had* to be assessed. Every second counted. If they waited too long the cleaver would fall and off would come their heads.

"Get down," came a voice. She couldn't tell from whom. A man. Jack. He ran forward and closed the bus doors. She knew he was scared, his confidence impotent in the face of this chaos. No more heroes or escapees here. And he seemed to sense this as he joined her, clicking his tongue. Together, they searched the driver's hub for her keys.

"Are they there?" she asked.

Jack's face was white. The driver must have put them into her pocket before stepping outside. Sarah watched him scramble with the radio, bang it in frustration. Nothing.

She crouched by the side window. "I need to see."

"What are they doing?" Jack asked the old woman. They listened to the sounds of a scuffle and muffled yells out there.

"They're fighting," Sarah said—not just to Jack but to them all. "The old guy and the one who shot at us."

"Fighting?" Michael said as he joined them only to have Jack spin about and grab him by the arm. Skin slapped skin, an almost comical sound. Michael snapped his arm back as Jack stared, eyes screaming, *Don't screw with the big boys, kid.*

Sarah's hand cupped the window. The younger man pushed the older man away, and she understood: *father and son.* Their dynamic was clear as day; the way the son stood, chest puffed out and arms wide—it spoke of bottled-up rebelliousness. His father knocked him down.

Her Bill loved nature documentaries. Once they watched a late-night program in which territorial stags locked horns until one claimed the land as his. The parallel between that memory and these two men wasn't lost on Sarah. Then, weirdly, the father helped the son to his feet—some sort of agreement now reached. What, though, she couldn't guess. They ran side by side to the woman at the threshold of the house, the one who beckoned in loud hoots, and they forced her into the house.

The door closed.

Sarah bit her lip hard enough to stain her teeth red. Waited. This wasn't over. Not yet. And likely not by a long shot, either.

The door opened as she knew it would.

Sarah's focal point remained the size of a thumbprint, but she could see him easy. The son. He stood on the verandah looking straight at her.

SIXTY

SARAH CRIED OUT—the glare from the son like a punch to her throat—and fell back into one of the seats. Nearby, Michael and Julia flinched. "Stay down," Sarah told them.

"What is—" Julia began. Stopped.

Footsteps outside. Slow and deliberate.

Wind blew across the bullet holes, whistling breath over the mouths of Coke bottles.

Michael imagined running out the door and into the trees beyond the shed; and before he knew what he was doing, turned toward the front of the bus. Jack pounced out of nowhere and threw him to the ground.

"Stay the fuck down," Jack said, a fist raised.

Michael blinked, confused, and felt a shadow crawl over his face. They both turned their panic-stricken faces to the window on their left.

Julia screamed.

The son peered in at them, a dark silhouette with burning, murderous eyes. The bus rocked. *He must be standing on the wheel*, Jack thought, rolling off the faggot beneath him until he could see the man outside. Jack had never seen eyes so crazy.

Diana put her hand over Julia's mouth. The man

moved away from the window, arms outstretched as though crucified against the glass. His sinewy muscles, the matted hair of his armpits.

A beat of silence.

The son banged his forehead against the glass. A blister of blood popped on his face.

Sarah thought of those late-night documentaries again, this time of monkeys wrestling with the bars that kept them captive, and she could almost feel Bill's hand holding her own.

"One day we should just get up and go see this stuff. What you think, baby-luv? The world is big and wide and it's a-waitin' for us."

The young man roared, and Bill's hand evaporated away, her fingers clutching at the empty space his future death would no doubt leave in her life. The voice from outside was fire, almost darkening the glass. He spat on the window and dropped from sight.

FIFTY-NINE

I'VE SEEN YOU. *I've seen all your faces, you fucks. I've seen your sharp teeth. You've all got ants for eyes.*

Half of his world was red. Jed wiped blood from his brow.

Look what you did to me. You cut me.

His scarlet fingers were the hands of someone who had shot and murdered. Past the fingers, he saw his sister. He'd never seen somebody so scared. All Jed wanted to do was get wet, to take a drag and dull the reality of the situation, but he knew this shouldn't be diluted. No. A busload of strangers had turned Liz into a wreck, and he'd never felt more alert. He scanned the lawn to the dead teenager sprawled near last year's Christmas cut-outs.

Who are you? Why would you run if you'd done nothing wrong? I did the right thing. You ran because you were guilty, because you were a ringleader in Liz's torture. And I've got no doubt the others had sat back and laughed as you did your thing. Now look where it got you? Dead. You first, and them next. I'm going to rip out their teeth and shove them into their eyes, stick them in deep until they scream apologies.

Until they beg.

"No."

I'm not a murderer.

The world spun.

Yes. Yes, you are. You killed that boy.

He ran to the corpse and stopped short, swaying.

"Get up," he told the body. "Get up, I said."

It didn't move, so he kicked it. Again and again.

"No. It wasn't me. I-I-I didn't do it."

No, you didn't.

"That's right, I didn't." He smiled, relieved.

They did it.

"Yeah. Them." He could even hear their giggles from where he stood.

They're laughing. Can you hear that?

"Yeah, I can hear it. Jesus."

They're laughing at you. At Sis.

He took another step closer. Mincing little girl giggles. Without thinking twice, Jed ran at the silver monolith on the dead grass. His mouth was open but no sound came out. He slammed against its side and within, laughter turned to screeching. He lurched to the door and peered through the glass. A small face peered out at him, or maybe it was just a reflection—he wasn't all that sure. Lifeless white skin, hair falling from its scalp; its eyes were hives full of ants and running jam.

Frightened, Jed stumbled.

"You won't beat me," he said to the creature.

Jed launched at the door. His fingers struggled to find a grip.

FIFTY-EIGHT

"HELP ME! Get over here now!" Jack screamed to the others.

Michael couldn't move. It was as though all the weight he had lost had been piled back on his bones and it was pinning him to the floor. He couldn't even muster words. All of it, gone.

Jack had a hold on the door. The accordion opened inwards and he propped his knee against the vertical hinge. Every muscle in his body rioted against him—as did the young man on the other side of the glass. Jack held firm; he had to. Their lives depended on it, on his strength, on muscles he'd worked hard to sculpt. Pride would keep them safe. Sure, there was a significant part of him that was afraid of the madman getting into the bus, but his adrenalin numbed that emotion's jagged edge. Jack's real fire was for the kid on *his* side of the door. Despite all the chaos and confusion, there was something about that dark haired, pale skinned fella that bristled his nerves. The air of pussy on him—and not the good kind of pussy, mind you. The kind of pussy real men sense a mile off, the whiff of faggot like rot on the wind.

Michael knew he'd been spotted.

His true self. A person who had woken up in another man's house and cleaned his pearly whites with a toothpaste-lathered finger.

Michael rose up off the floor, a movement which coincided with the man ceasing his assault against the bus and stepping away. Judging. An artist approving his masterwork.

Jack stared through the blood-smeared glass of the door to see a presence on the verandah of the house across the lot. The parents called to their son.

Thank God, Jack thought. *Go to the house. Then mum and dad will call the police—because that's what sane people do.*

Or maybe they won't, Jack-o. Maybe they ain't sane.

Jack's mind connected the dots. It was the family unit they were dealing with now, not just one person. Because the driver had run home to her kin. Jack didn't have any kids, hell—he didn't think he *ever* wanted them—but it wasn't a stretch to imagine how protective he would be should he ever fall into said trap. And family *was* a trap. It locked you up for life. It hooked you into the lives of others in threads of co-dependency that even death struggled to splice, and that wasn't living as Jack saw it. Living was a selfish thing; it had to be.

He watched the house.

An open door, swinging in the wind. The son stopped at the bottom step, fumbling with his pockets to retrieve something shiny, something that caught the sunlight just so. That starburst took form.

Keys.

Jack swallowed dry.

Bastard's got the bus keys. But how? When? He's going to come and open the door. No. Wait! YES! That's good. We want him to come and open the door. Then we can take him. Hell, I could take him alone. Take him and the keys and get the fuck out of here.

The son walked back in their direction—it coincided with a buzzing near Jack's ear. It was the fly again.

But I killed it. I know I did.

Only you didn't, replied the other voice.

These thoughts were shattered by the sound of a closing door. The young man hadn't been approaching the bus at all. He'd crossed the lot to a pickup truck near the shed.

The fly shot past his ear. Jack swatted at nothing.

"What's going on?" Diana asked.

Jack faced her. The woman was a nothing. Without hope. He sighed, pitying her for those scrawny arms, and that ugly, twisted hair.

The pickup sat idling outside.

Michael crossed his arms, covering his chest, a gesture of anxiety. This habit had started at the pool when he was fat with low-hanging boy-breasts, at a time when it was imperative that he cover up as much of his body as possible. Even now as an adult, he struggled to shake the comfort it stoked.

Sarah stepped away from the window. Her right hand grabbed the handlebar closest to Julia's face.

The teenager's eyes widened. A vein pulsed in Sarah's index finger.

Pound.

"Oh no," Sarah said.
"What is it?"
Pound.
"He's in the car."
Pound.
"Do we run now?" Julia asked.
Pound.
"Oh, shit. No." On "no" the front door of the house swung open and the father emerged. He ran to the truck.

"What the bloody hell do you think you're up to?" they heard him yell.

The blank face behind the wheel didn't answer. He gunned the engine by way of reply.

Pound.

The truck leapt forward. Wheels spun. The father lunged at the hood and missed.

"He's coming at us!" Jack yelled.

FIFTY-SEVEN

THE PICKUP CAME at them.

Such speed. Such precision.

The sisters shot to their feet and joined the others, climbing over seats and cramming against the right-hand side wall. From inside the bus, the incoming vehicle appeared gargantuan. Logic dictated there was nowhere they *wouldn't* be hit.

Julia panicked, slipped, grabbed the "stop now" wire for balance. It snapped, recoiled like a broken rubber band and whipped the side of Michael's face. He shied away, hand raised. Gasped.

The pickup swerved to the left at the last moment and crashed into the front of the bus. Chewed metal drowned their yells. The entire hub rose off the ground, throwing the passengers against the windows. A seat at the front dislodged. The dead body jolted in a horrific pantomime of life. The bus skewered again as the truck fought to dislodge itself. One of the windows split but held true. Like a blade from between ribs, the pickup slinked in retreat, its front bumper ripped loose and dragging through the dirt.

"Again!" Michael yelled in warning.

The pickup lunged through a cloud of dust.

They were stunned, yes, but the passengers were also quick. In the time it took for the truck to cross the lawn, they grabbed the nearest handrails and braced for impact. The second collision proved harder than the first.

Diana tumbled. Julia landed on her shoulder and shielded her belly. The others moved with the weight of the bus and somehow remained on their feet.

The bus angled in a permanent slant to the left and the front door buckled inwards. Sunlight hit the cracked windshield, painting the hub in a spectrum of delicate spider-web shadows.

FIFTY-SIX

JED LIFTED HIS face from the steering wheel, loose teeth on the tip of tongue. He wanted to look at himself in the rearview mirror, only the mirror wasn't there because the front of his pickup was partially inside the bus.

No pain, not really. Only shock. And when he saw blood fanned across the twisted console, Jed wondered where it came from.

The door next to him opened from the outside. Bewildered, Jed registered the sensation of sunlight spilling over flesh. He bathed in the warmth for half a moment, and in its fleetingness felt wonderful.

"No," was all he managed to utter before his father pulled him from the truck. Jed hadn't been wearing a seatbelt. Pulled free, he became aware of the erection tented in his jeans. He thumped on the ground as his father's face loomed overhead.

"Stupid boy!"

Wes stared down at his son: face a welt with slits for eyes. A part of him wanted to flog him like a child for being so foolish, whilst another longed to drag Jed into his arms and grease him with kisses. And just perhaps—though stronger than a mere maybe—there was admiration in his mix, too.

"I'm sorry, Dad."

Something throbbed in the old man's chest. They were family, and family stuck together, even when things were bad. Even when the members of that family went bad themselves. Hadn't they always? Wes begged forgiveness from his children in so many ways, so many times over, though mostly through silences. Silences could be powerful things, indeed. Sure, Wes had been too tough on them, maybe even cruel at times, but he'd only ever done what his own father had taught and done to him. Now, with his boy bleeding all over his shoes, it pained Wes to think Jed felt he had anything to be sorry for. In so many ways it was Wes who had brought them to this day, a day he'd sensed from the very beginning would end in thunder. The throb in the old man's chest was self-inflicted, of that he was sure now.

Wes dragged Jed across the lawn. He told Reggie to stay with Liz, who was in the throes of a fit. But Reggie left her daughter's side.

She stood in the doorway now, skirt billowing, hands inside her mouth. She swung her upper half in wide arcs. Head thumped the doorframe.

Insanity. Insanity everywhere.

There was no time to hate himself. Hating *them* was easier.

Jed opened his eyes. Bright, electric waves of energy coursed through his muscles from head to toes, to the tip of his cock. He shook off his father's grasp and stood, back cracking. He pulled the blue wife-beater over his head. It came away red. Jed ran across the lot and threw the shirt at the bus from a distance. The faces inside recoiled as it slopped against a window. Slid from their sights.

He laughed. A tooth fell from his mouth. Jed smiled because he knew their refuge was a prison. He wasn't the kind to appreciate irony, perhaps lacking the smarts to identify it in the first place, but he knew when the doors of favor were swinging your way. Such times were worthy of a smile, even if it came at the cost of teeth.

Stop, a part of him said. *Who are you?*

The voice belonged to a small boy. He forced it aside.

A hand on Jed's shoulder. His father. They considered each other's eyes and found themselves equals for the very first time.

"Jed, stop it, mate," was all Wes could say.

Pound.

"Ah, fuck it," Jed told the ground. He pointed at the bus, fingers splayed, looking like a man with magical powers about to deliver a curse. "Don't move, don't fucking leave and if you do, you'll fucking die!"

Wes took in the vehicle once more. It was welded shut by the remains of the pickup. He had no idea what to do next. His feet banged up the verandah steps as he followed his son into their house.

Inside, Reggie embraced Jed. Rocked him, kissed his forehead. Her face was finger-painted with snot and blood.

Another hot gust of wind blew through the valley. It made the trees applaud and the old, broken Christmas lights twinkle. It blew through the house and drew the door shut.

PART FOUR: SCISSORS

"The leaves of memory seemed to make
A mournful rustling in the dark"
—Henry Wadsworth Longfellow, *The Burning of the Drift-Wood*

FIFTY-FIVE

FLIES SWARMED PETER'S BODY.

A spider in a tree ran the length of its web to catch its prey; it usually hunted at night but couldn't pass a prize as sweet as this. The spider wrestled the butterfly until its web broke and both fell to the ground. A martyr to hunger.

Beads of sweat clung to Diana's upper lip. Musk wafted from her armpits. A ping of self-consciousness. As a teenager, she suffered from acne and spent innumerable hours scrubbing at her face with ivory bars, squeezing blackheads. Wherever she went one could smell her perfume, always spring flavors, citrus, and pink sugar. They now mixed with sweat in an odor that almost sickened her. She blinked and watched the house for movement. *Prioritize, girl,* she thought. *Do you think anyone here is worrying about how you smell?*

It had been an hour since the family retreated inside.

Broken glass from the battered door covered the bus floor, every shard its own tiny sun eliciting warmth. Peter's notebook remained under a seat.

Sarah scanned the windows of the house. Every so

often curtains shifted, a shadow looking out. Shivers wracked her body every time this happened.

Michael's eyes closed.

In his mind, he sat on a beach, the sound of waves pounding the shoreline. There was nothing in the water that could hurt him. He was alone and not embarrassed to be naked; nobody to laugh at his stretch marks or flaccid skin.

Funny.

He never really liked the beach, hated finding sand in every crevice, the constant sunburn.

But right at that moment, Michael would have given anything to be there, so very alone and far from threat.

Julia curled up in shadow. She wondered if fear could kill a baby.

Sarah stood at the window and wrestled with a series of ifs.

If I'd only missed the bus.

If I'd only overslept.

If I had stayed with Bill, I'd—

She stopped, knowing that blame and consequence could be traced back through history until she was exhausted, and it still wouldn't change the facts. She was here, not at home. People were dying, and she had to be strong.

Jack surveyed the damage. The pickup was wedged into the bus—the door had buckled inwards but still held firm, exposing a diamond of space ten inches wide. Like a man tugging at the bars of his cell, he tried prying the doors apart. They wouldn't budge and he was far too big to squeeze through. Jack could see the house through the gap, its façade a mocking face. He slumped to the floor. *We're not going anywhere*. God, Jack hated enclosed spaces.

They made him anxious.

He crouched low and made his way up the aisle, trying to avoid stray shards of glass. When he passed the corpse, he remembered the sensation of its face giving way beneath his foot. The smell of shit and ammonia hung heavy in the air. More than one fly now. They clogged the dead man's mouth. Jack slumped into a seat near the two young women, distancing himself from the young kid with the faggoty hair. *If he wants to wear his do like that, he should just move to Sydney*. His distaste went deeper though. Jack hated cowards, and a coward was what he saw when he looked at Michael, among other things of course.

"Does anyone have any water?"

"Sorry, Jack-o, I don't," Sarah said.

He spun. "Don't call me that, okay?"

Sarah clenched her jaw. She wanted to tell him to grow up, to let it go. Another part told her to apologize and just humor the boy. *And that's really what he is, a boy*. She'd noticed the expression he gave her on the faces of her own children: the defensive teen starved for control. Sarah imagined telling him: *Don't talk to me like that. I'm your elder, and more than that, right now, I'm all you got. Don't turn me or anyone else here into your enemy. If you were my kid, I'd have smacked that spite right out of you.*

Instead, she remained silent.

Jack cracked his knuckles.

The sound of snapping cartilage made Julia flinch. *You can really tell a lot about a person by the way they do their hair,* Jack thought, smirking. *Old bird looks like one of those dykes. Just my luck to be stuck here with a bunch like this.*

"None of us have any water," Sarah said.

FIFTY-FOUR

Diana rubbed the back of her sister's neck. "That nice?"

"Mm-mm."

Sarah dropped her head and slapped her thighs. "I'm tired of that damn house. It's like staring at the sun."

"Sit with us," Diana said. "What difference does it make if they are checking on us or not? We're still stuck."

Jack sparked up as though he'd been waiting for someone to say that very thing just so he could refute it. "But we should try to get out, right? See that?" He pointed at the window closest to the driver's hub on the left-hand side, a large crack running its length. "That's the emergency exit window. It's the only one on this bus and it's already broken. All we got to do is push on it—"

"We can't do that," Sarah said, stern. "We push it out and it shatters on the ground and they'll come running."

"Pfft." Jack's eyes turned cold—old bird had a point after all. "Okay, fine. Whatever. So what about that?" He pointed at the escape exit above their heads, the wind whistling through it. "We're not stuck here. We're not in jail. The only thing keeping us here is us."

"We're being watched," Sarah said. "People are dying, Jack."

"I'm not blind, lady."

"Look. Take it down a notch, okay? We have to wait this out."

"What the fuck do you mean, 'wait this out'? We push out the window or we bust through the ceiling. We fucking run full tilt for the trees. They can't catch us all."

"But they *will* catch some of us. We can't risk that. They have guns. They're scared. We've seen what happens when we panic, when *they* panic. If we draw attention to ourselves the game is up." Sarah pointed at him, brow furrowing. "Pardon my French but we cannot fuck with these people. Now, I know you're smart, Jack. So why are you acting like this? Now's not the time to be willfully thick."

Jack smiled.

Ha.

He would never let a woman talk to him like this in the real world.

"I'm not being thick, lady. I'm—Aughh." But Jack gave up, waved her away.

And that angered Sarah. It seemed so silly to be aggravated by such childish behavior in the midst of what was happening, but his was such an atypically male dismissal. She hated it.

"You're what, Jack?" Eyebrow raised. "Come on. You're what?"

"Fine. I'll bite," he said. "It looks like I'm the only one here with an ounce of brains. We're stuck, so let's escape! Bam. Problem solved. You think they'll chase us? Well, here's a solution for you: we run. Am I speaking Australian here or what? Have I woken up in the *Twilight Zone*? Am I blabbering ching-chong-Chinaman noises and just don't realize it? See, I know you're smart, lady. So, you tell me, what's so hard about this to get?"

She sighed. "Jack, we're going to get out of here. Just not that way. Don't forget that they haven't forgotten about us. This is the hardest thing you'll ever have to do. We got to support each other. Let's not fight. We're all in the same boat."

He moved as though preparing to defend himself.

"Just breathe, Jack. The longer we wait and do nothing, the longer we don't piss them off, the longer we keep out of danger. We're buying time. Soon the police will be here. There's a dead girl in the middle of a road back there, God rest her soul. She's someone's daughter, someone's neighbor. She'll be found. A busload of people is missing. The bus company tried to get through and the driver didn't reply. The driver's family is panicking, so they might not have called the police. But someone somewhere has. So now we wait, okay?"

"Oh, quit your preaching, woman," he said.

Sarah smiled, wry and sad, and unlocked her horns from his.

Just a boy.

FIFTY-THREE

SUNDAY HEAT INTENSIFIED as clouds brooded in the sky. The ozone remained heavy, burdened, appropriate. Every time a face peered from the house, it stabbed the passengers' collective consciousness, a series of small defeats that confirmed where those on route 243 were and what they had been reduced to.

Jack was in the backseat with Sarah not too far away. Diana's need to urinate overwhelming her; she closed her eyes and tried to distract herself with rocking, rocking. Julia fought the urge to suck her thumb, imagining that she was in her bedroom writing in her diary, an entry that read: *nothing much happened today*. Michael was closest to the dead body with his hands over his mouth to keep the stink at bay, a stink so thick he was sure he could feel it on his skin.

Every window had been closed to stop more flies from getting in. They watched them congregate on the other side of the glass in writhing patches.

In the steamy silence, Julia whispered, "It's a girl."

Diana lifted her head, hair stuck to her face. "What's that, bub?"

"You heard me."

Julia closed her eyes, choking on tears. "I've got a

psychic streak to me, I guess. And I know it's a girl. I can feel it." She pinched at her brow and wiped her eyes. "I don't want to die. I don't care if Mum and Dad find out about the baby. I don't care anymore. I want to tell them. Really. I just want this to be over."

"We all do, bub."

"Yeah, I know." She sighed. "Some psychic streak though, hey? If it was so good, I should have seen this coming."

"Julia, it doesn't work like that."

"I know it's like, stupid to feel this way, but I can't help it. I feel like I'm being punished."

"Oh, sweetie. That's not it at all." Diana held her sister tight, whispered in her ear. "Bad things happen to good people. That's the way it goes. You just never think it'll happen to you. Never. Someone does a good thing, that doesn't mean good comes to them. Same with all our mistakes. Nobody's being punished. Luck isn't credit. Gee, I don't even know if luck even exists." Guilt settled in. "Besides, it's my fault we're here."

"No, it's not your fault. It's not." They cried together.

Diana placed a hand on the slight curve of her sister's stomach.

FIFTY-TWO: INSIDE

FLUCTUATIONS OF MOVEMENT. Her parents, her brother. Their faces sometimes grimacing; other times, still. Liz heard her heartbeat, and it terrified her because it was so slow. *I'm fading, shrinking down to nothing.*

Overhead the ceiling appeared miles away.

Her mind separated from her body. No thought or feeling ran its proper course; neurons fired only to have nothing eventuate. Paralyzed. Her mother grabbed Liz's head and begged her to speak, but the words refused to form. Liz wanted to scream at her parents and tell them that the passengers weren't the enemy—*they're my new friends!* They were put into her life just to show her love and for her to love them back, and for that reason alone, they shouldn't be corrected. To be honest, Liz was scared for them. She knew her father had a terrible temper, had seen it in action so many times over. Liz longed to forgive him, but that was impossible when he wanted to hurt these new people in her life.

She watched her father yank the phone from the wall. Listening to her parents argue, random words flew around her head, trapped in imaginary bubbles. They shimmered and she was fascinated.

Jed kept on going to the windows. She wondered why. Was there some sort of threat behind that glass? Liz knew that couldn't be the case because they were her buddies out there, nothing more, and they sure must be getting hot by now. If anything, Jed should be running water out to them. Or maybe she should invite them in, tell them they can be part of the family. Invite them all to sit around the kitchen dining table.

The image of a shot man in a football jersey. The hole in his face was an exploding balloon filled with red cordial. Liz furrowed her brow. Maybe this was a scene from some gory, B-grade horror movie she'd watched on television late one night. It was strange though that it should pop into her head right now.

Another image floated by—she reached out for it, disappointed that such beauty could not be held. In the bubble a little girl twirled in the middle of a road. It made her smile; Liz hoped to see something that pretty one day.

Yes, there were reasons to live.

The *slap* was sharp and loud.

Wes walked away from his wife, who fell to her knees, holding her face. He still had the useless telephone receiver gripped in one hand.

What's the matter? Liz wondered. *Why did he hit Mum like that?*

Phantom pains in her arms and legs; the memory of her own beatings. Liz's gaze flittered to the staircase and the sensation passed. She watched her brother disappear upstairs, listened to his feet banging across the floor.

The ceiling fan spun in slow cycles.

FIFTY-ONE

TEN-YEAR-OLD JACK in his backyard. An airplane carved a long, white streak through the orange sky. His senses were alive with the smells of barbecue and the apple tree.

He heard a scream. It echoed across the yard.

It came from inside his house, which towered above him, its mass a jagged silhouette against the sunset. The back door opened. He remembered the sound of it crashing against the wall. Kimba, the family cat, ran ahead of his father's feet and scuttled under the stairs. His dad was a hulking, whiskered mammoth lurching and wheezing as he ran.

The screams belonged to a boy, although the wails were high-pitched. It made him laugh, despite the fire in his father's eyes as he approached.

Jack felt the heaviness in his hand.

He looked down. The sky, the airplane, the house and his dad tilted away until he saw his shaking fingers, and what he held in his grasp.

Scissors.

FIFTY:
OUTSIDE

THE MEMORY LEFT Jack spent, weak. His hands were covered in blue blotches, and tingled. *Fuck me,* he thought, *where did that come from?*

Jack felt the eyes of the passengers on him, and in a flash, he was back in the classroom, his teacher towering over him. Spitting questions.

"But I don't know the answer," he mumbled.

"What?" Sarah asked, leaning in close. "You okay there, Jack?" The others huddled behind her. Even Michael turned.

He couldn't handle the silence anymore, or their eyes burning into him.

"Don't," he said.

"What?" Sarah was holding on to a handlebar to keep herself steady.

Say something, cunt, Jack told himself. *Say something, you dumb shit. Open your mouth and make some fucking noise!*

He took a breath and focused. "What if we busted out one of the windows on the right-hand side and got out and ran?"

A gust of wind shook the bus. Dust pelted the windows and the hub filled with a soft, quiet hiss.

Anger crept up on Sarah, and she had to hold herself back from reaching out and slapping this guy. "Jesus-Mary-and-Joseph, would you stop it?" she said. "Just sit there and don't say a word."

"You don't quiet me, old duck."

"Please, Jack—"

"Please, what? What? Please make this shit better? That's what I'm trying to do. Don't any of you want to get out of here? We got legs so we should use them. We take something hard and we bash out that fucking window and take our chances."

Michael leaped forward—he couldn't hold himself back. "Just stop it for God's sake! Just stop, all of you!" Face flushed red.

"He speaks!" Jack laughed. "Well fuck me Freddy, I better drop everything and—" He lost the momentum of his words. "Oh, just fuck off, kid."

Michael realized it felt good to speak, to have his opinion heard. A minor victory. His elation faded when Jack turned his back to him. Michael stood alone in the aisle, an exposed figure on a stage.

His spotlight brightened, illuminating memories.

FORTY-NINE: BANGKOK

BANGKOK WAS EVERYTHING the travel agent said it would be. Michael fought through congested traffic, laughed at the total disregard for rules and the polite sensibilities of the Western world. Going to Thailand was the best thing he'd ever done, perhaps an even greater achievement than losing weight.

Nobody knew him there. He could swish when he wanted to and nobody called him names. Michael didn't mind the looks he got from some of the guys in the streets. In fact, it excited him.

He saw a live sex show in the red-light district. Watched a woman tug a birdcage from her vagina, then live birds. Another pulled a transistor radio out. *Hotel California* played through the speakers.

Later in the week, he stumbled into the gay district. Effeminate staff beckoned to him as he passed.

"Sexy white boy, where you from? Want to see cabaret show?"

Flashing lights inside and bland, though not entirely unappealing music. Rows of chairs faced a stage where velvet curtains were drawn, stirred. Michael's seat was central but six rows back, which suited him fine.

Two drag queens stepped out onto the stage with an appropriate amount of flourish. Together they welcomed their audience. Their accents were heavy but retained all the fling and fancy of what Michael considered the stereotypical gay man—as in the men he saw in movies and on late night current affairs programs. Michael wondered if gay men acted gayer when they were around like men, just as straight guys acted more masculine when around their mates.

Is this how I'm supposed to be?

Am I like that?

The crowd went wild. Michael's Singapore Sling arrived at his table.

Lady-boys in elaborate costumes flooded the stage. Kylie Minogue routines. A Liza Minnelli revue.

The night started to wind up. "Oh. Don't you leave yet! Da best is comin'!" One of the hosts stepped into the crowd, wove her way through the tables scouting for a volunteer. She chose Michael; somehow, he just knew it would be him. The spotlight blinded him. Glitter floated in the air and settled on his nose.

They whisked him backstage. A gaggle of gay men in tiny, revealing shorts and punk haircuts unbuttoned his shirt. He forced them away. "What are you doing? What's going on?"

A tall man dressed in a kimono stepped forward, armed with lipstick. Red. "Oh, you shy, it's okay. We going to take off ya shirt and put kisses on you-uuu and it okay and it just a little joke and fun and no prob'." Michael's shirt fell away and revealed were his sagging breasts, the patchwork of stretch marks.

Silence. Someone laughed.

Another man, more masculine and for whom he

felt a twinge of attraction, tweaked his nipple. "I think it's hot, white boy. I like softies."

One of them kissed his stomach, a red smear on his sweaty skin. "I'm not going out there without my shirt."

In the crowd, mouths opened and closed, and he heard nothing. They had their laugh and gave him a drink, then finally his shirt. It smelled of perfume and make-up. In the bathroom, Michael wiped at the red kisses. Water spilled down the front of his jeans, growing damp and cold. He did up his shirt and stared at himself in the mirror. He swore he would gain back every pound if someone could take this humiliation away.

Shaking, he pulled at the paper dispenser. The sheets turned to mush but he fumbled for more. Damp shreds stuck to his palms. Useless.

Michael cried. They didn't understand what he'd been through to be this weird person in this weird country on this weird night, how long it took to build up his confidence. With a joke and a free drink, it all vanished.

FORTY-EIGHT

LIZ STOOD. *When did I take my shoes off? I don't remember doing that.*

She didn't remember a lot of things anymore. It was good to be numb—it was like "getting wet".

Her mother rifled through bags in the study.

Where am I? Liz glanced around. *If that's the study, then I must be in the living room. I know I've seen that sofa before. It's comfy. I've wrapped my legs over the arm of that chair before.*

Reggie doubled over in the small room, surrounded by torn-open garbage bags bleeding Christmas tinsel. In her hands were two handmade tree ornaments. Little, worn Santas, their faces bent inwards.

A memory of the family at Christmastime. It was one of the years that her father hadn't been there. He came and went. Sometimes he said he needed a holiday from them. In this memory, Liz and Jed put those ornaments on the plastic tree. Everything smelled of mothballs. They weren't happy, but at least they weren't crying or bleeding. This was the children's barometer: the yardstick between laughter and locking themselves in their rooms out of fear.

The memory floated past. She let it go by.

FORTY-SEVEN: BLED WHITE

SANTORINI WAS WHITE, *as though an artist scraped away Fira's colors to rediscover the canvas underneath. Empty streets and not even the sea made a sound.*

Diana fell in love with the city on her travels before landing in Australia. It soothed her, made her whole again after her mother's death. Now, she felt like Dorothy coming back to the Emerald City only to find it home to vandals and all her friends turned to stone. There was no queen with a hundred heads here though. Only silence.

She wove through the narrow streets. At the bottom of an incline, she turned and looked up a thin, cobblestone street. Diana saw him then.

Him.

The brother.

The one with the eagle tattoo on his back.

He walked towards her, his pace steady. Face contorted. She couldn't tell if he smiled or screamed. Terror gripped her.

The ground underneath their feet shook and the brother stopped.

Behind him, there came a gigantic tide of blood,

meat, and paint. It rushed towards her. He became a part of the wave and together they thundered downhill, splattering the white walls in fans of red.

Over the roar of the wave, she heard a laugh.

She turned at the sound. An inch from her face was the bus driver. She wore a tattered leotard; one bruised breast hung loose of the costume, the nipple hard and bitten at. Blood beads in the tutu filaments.

Diana opened her mouth to shriek and half-eaten olives fell out.

FORTY-SIX

DIANA OPENED HER EYES. The smell awoke her. Next to her Michael pressed his face towards the sliding window, sucking air into his lungs.

"Ooof. He's getting bad," Julia said.

Michael closed the window again.

"Why don't you leave it open?" Diana asked, sitting upright. Her body ached, bones cracked. Her bladder felt at bursting point.

Sarah held a handkerchief to her nose and inhaled the eucalyptus oil in its fibers. The scent reminded her of home. "There's about a billion fucking flies wanting to get in here, best to keep them shut, methinks."

"You know, for an old woman you swear like a sailor," Julia said. They smiled at each other.

"Oh, my God!" Michael said.

Everyone whipped their heads to the house.

The father stood in the side yard, having come out the back door without them noticing. His stillness sent a universal chill through their bodies. They waited for him to move, or to maybe draw an axe from the shadows and run at them. But there was none of that, just his gaze, cold and steady. The tableau broke when the passengers backed against the opposite wall.

It made Jack want to laugh.

"You really think moving like that is going to make you any safer?" he asked them.

Every muscle in Julia's body grew so tense it hurt. She looked at the man. Sunburn reddened his forehead, the upper rims of his ears. He had a crooked nose that flared into two large, twitching nostrils. Julia had never seen such a look in real life, only in documentary footage in school about soldiers returning from war, the haggard men, their features deformed by the weight of guilt, by their own individual dread.

Behind the father: rows of dead trees. In their branches, crows ruffled their wings and sharpened beaks against the thorns.

Wes watched them for some time. Their small faces through the windows. All white-faced, all squinting against the sun.

Once, there had been a large spider in the corner of his bedroom. Reggie was next to him, asleep at the time—and that was for the best. Had she seen it there would've been screams and melodrama, and that he couldn't stand at the best of times. The spider nestled above the door, a Woodsman, an insignificant and harmless thing, but an insignificant and harmless thing that he didn't like having in his bedroom.

The bastard was big.

Wes propped up in bed, a hardcover copy of Ira Levin's *The Boys from Brazil*, spine-snapped over his knees. It was darker at the spider's end of the room. He felt it staring at him, waiting for him to go to sleep so it could scurry around and make its web, or worse.

He turned off the bedside lamp. Quietness except for the crickets singing outside. Then came the soft patter of eight crawling legs. He switched the light back on and wasn't surprised to see that the spider wasn't where it had been before. It was, in fact, a good foot and a half closer.

It waited for darkness.

He watched it watch him and then gave it what it wanted: darkness once more. The same thing happened. Crickets. Quiet. *Scratch-scratch-scratch* as it pulled its thick abdomen across the ceiling.

"Sneaky bugger," he said, flicking the light back on. The spider was a foot closer. Wes didn't turn the light off again. He reached into his lap and picked up his book, pulled it so close to his face he could smell the old, yellowed pages.

"I've got all night," he said. "Do you?"

But Wes didn't have all night—soon his eyes grew heavy and within an hour he was asleep. The book sat on the end of his nose until he rolled over and Ira Levin ended up on the floor by his slippers. Reggie woke him with her soft snoring at dawn. He rolled onto his back, wiped his eyes and remembered the silent duel from the night before. The ceiling swam into focus and he saw that it was bare. Instead of crickets, there was now birdsong; a sweet sound. He wet his gums and cleared his throat, rolled over and reached for the lamp, bed-springs squeaking. The light had been on all night. His fingers touched something warm and bristled—maybe one of Reggie's frayed hairbrushes. Wes stretched his neck, looked at his hand and saw the giant spider under his palm. Before he knew what he was doing he brought his fist down and felt it explode.

"Got you, little bitch."

The people on the bus stared at him the same way. He knew they would move as soon as his back was turned, just like the insignificant and harmless Woodsman. Only these monsters were malevolent; he need only look at the mangled corpse in his front yard to know that. They were dangerous.

And that was why he watched them.

They invaded his home as the spider had done, and he thought it best to crush them under his touch. He forced the thought away for the time being.

"Only if need be," he said. "Only then."

"Go back inside," Diana said. "Please. Please. Please." Her firm whispers were a comfort to the others. But the man didn't move. His head cocked to one side, as though weighing up his options.

"You're going to go back inside now," Diana continued. She thought if she said it enough she might make it true.

The man lifted his head and turned away. He staggered like a drunken man, and as he rounded the rear corner of the house, his shoulder clipped the weatherboards.

He disappeared, though the tension remained.

The crows flapped away, shadows floating over the lawn in circles.

They were hungry, patient, and refused to leave.

FORTY-FIVE

AS MICHAEL NEARED the deformed bus door, he thanked a God he wasn't sure he believed in for air that didn't reek of septic tanks and abattoirs. He sucked in a hot breath and thought, *Man, that feels better.*

He had an issue, and it was a big one considering their circumstances. Michael needed to pee. He'd contemplated using the corner next to the driver's upturned chair. Only no, that wasn't an option. The bus was on a slant and the stream would run across the floor and down the steps. It seemed undignified, like a dog. He almost laughed. *This isn't the time to be coy,* he said to himself. *You're not a prisoner by choice, you know?* A shake of the head, decided. The corner just wasn't going to cut it; he would piss out the door instead.

Before going to the front of the bus, he told the others what he was going to do. They tried to talk him out of it, explaining the risks of being seen. He convinced them that he could manage to do it without drawing any attention.

"Can't you just hold it in?" Diana asked. "I need to go like a racehorse but you don't see me dropping my pants, do you?"

"It's easier for me. I'm a guy. I can do it quick.

Diana, I don't care if you need to go and you end up doing it in a backseat. I don't mind. But I'm sorry, I just don't want to. If I don't go now, I'm going to pee all over myself. Please don't make me do that."

He slid down the stairs and crouched low, placed a palm on the bent doorframe. It wouldn't budge. Over the hood of the pickup, he could see the house. If he stood, he would be seen, but that was only if the family looked out at the same time, of course. The only way to do it was to urinate while kneeling, hips forced against the jaws of the door, with his upper half twisted almost parallel to the truck roof. Awkward, yes; but it could—and would—be done.

The pressure intensified, a large blackness in his mind, distracting him from everything else. Michael tried to remember what he'd drunk that morning; it hadn't seemed like much at the time. After blowing Clive, he'd had two glasses of water because his throat was sore and dry.

Two glasses too many.

Sunlight twinkled in the broken glass littered across the hood. He swallowed.

Maybe this isn't such a good idea after all.

"Oh, shit-shit-shit."

Michael pushed himself up onto the top step and looked back at the other passengers. They all sat in their respective seats. He saw them all caught in the act of spying—and watched them twist their heads away with awkward swiftness. "Yeah, whatever. I'm more entertaining than an in-flight movie," he said under his breath, brushing diamonds of glass off the steps with his foot. "If you're going to do this, Michael, you've got to do it now."

He lowered himself back on to the bottom step, twisted his legs up underneath him and brought his weight down upon his knees. A nerve pinched between his shoulder blades as he pressed his pelvis flat against the doorframe, torso contorted so it bent to the right. Leaned his face against the glass of the door.

The house.

Michael raised both hands and wormed them towards his crotch. He didn't realize how much his fingers were shaking until he attempted to grasp his zipper. The glass warmed against his cheek. It fogged with every breath. *Come on, man. Just do it.*

He opened his fly, felt the tiny teeth parting. Movements slow and deliberate. The house continued to stare. From his twisted position, Michael could see the roof and one upstairs window, and in it was a curtain.

The curtain pulled back.

The zipper jammed.

Michael hadn't realized that he'd closed his eyes. He heard his lashes brushing against the glass.

The curtain was still.

Your mind's playing tricks on you, Michael. Keep it together.

But his zipper *was* stuck—that had been no invention.

The waistband of his jeans dug into his bladder, making the pressure worse. His eyes shot to the house again. He'd imagined seeing a face there before, but it was only a matter of time until that vision became a reality.

Whispers from the other passengers reached his ears.

Michael reached into his jeans and curled his fingers around the top of his boxer shorts. When he pulled them down, the skin under his sweaty pubic hair prickled in goosebumps. *Okay, the job's half-done. Just do what you got to do and get the hell out of here.*

The angle of his arm dictated how far down his underwear would slide, and for things to work smoothly, he needed an extra inch or two.

The bones in his spine cracked and popped.

Do it now! Jesus Christ, Michael.

He pulled his underwear down another inch and with his free hand, slipped his fingers inside and pulled out his cock. Michael aimed downwards so the stream wouldn't arc onto the hood of the truck. In the end, he couldn't see what he was going to urinate on and simply hoped it wouldn't splash back on him.

The door of the house.

At any moment it was going to spring open and the driver was going to come running out, screaming. Would they come with more guns, he wondered? Or maybe it would be knives this time.

Eyes eased shut, pushing the thought away. Focused on the mission at hand.

Nothing came.

"Come on."

A small dribble. The pressure was agony—it burned through his torso and upper chest. His eyes closed again and soon numbers ran through his head; large, purple numerals floating by as though proudly featured on *Sesame Street* in his mind.

Today is brought to you by . . .

"One, two, three."

Another drop.

The house continued to stare.

Try counting backwards, he thought. *That sometimes works.*

"Three, two, one—"

The stream came, urine orange. Lightheadedness as the pressure drained away.

A huge black mass dropped onto the hood of the truck.

He clammed up mid-flow. A bullet of pain shot through his abdomen. His legs were wedged between the gap and the second step. He couldn't escape.

A crow.

Unafraid, it hopped on the hot surface of the pickup. Its clawed feet scratched at the paint, small head twisting from side to side, curious and hungry.

"Shoo," Michael hissed. "Bugger off."

The bird would not move.

Piss hammered metal, louder than he would have liked.

I'm gonna jump down there and eat your pecker, he imagined the crow saying. *I'm gonna grab it in my beak and tear it right off!*

The house. Still no movement.

I'm gonna throw my head back and let it slide down my gullet like an oyster.

"Stop it, go away."

The upstairs window. The curtain. Nothing. But for how much longer, though?

Gonna rip and tear and scratch and bite and—

Michael finished. He whipped his penis back into his jeans and flung himself sideways, allowing enough space to free his right knee. He collapsed onto the stairs, head thumping against the bloodied aisle. Soon the stench of meat returned. It disturbed him that inhaling these horrors now signaled some kind of safety.

The crow flew away.

FORTY-FOUR

JULIA'S HEARTBEAT QUICKENED. "The things we've seen today," she whispered. "The things we've seen." Flicked hair behind an ear.

Diana didn't reply, deciding instead to let the observation fester in the air.

They held each other for a long time. Their humming soothed those about them like icy water on a burn. It eased into melody.

Sarah lifted her haggard face.

The sound of the ocean withdrew from Michael's ears, replaced now by that soft, sweet singing. A sigh fled his mouth with mocking ease. He listened to the women and rocked along in his seat. It wasn't a song, rather undulations of pitch similar to trees blowing in the wind, sometimes in sync, sometimes creaking together, but beautiful all the while. Oh, to be outside, Michael couldn't help thinking. To be free from this fucking place. Running happily through the bush he loved yet which refused to love him back. The Australian scrub was like that, he knew—as they all did. You could chart it, photograph it, romanticize it; but the damn thing would eat you alive if given half a chance. Michael stopped rocking, and let the girls sing.

He wished for the ocean again, because yes, that was better, and soon felt the tickle of its froth on his shins, briny salt catching in his stubble. His tongue ran over his lips and was safe for now.

Jack refused to look at them. Doing so would admit defeat. He kept his eyes on the body in the aisle. On the flies making homes of the poor bastard's ears and eyes.

FORTY-THREE

JED JUMPED UP and down in his bedroom. Shook his head from side to side. He turned to the wall and drove his fists through the plasterboard. Over and over and over, not feeling a thing. Plaster fell onto his mattress in clumps.

His bloodied hands.

"Murderer."

FORTY-TWO

HEAVY SILENCE FOLLOWED the song's slow death.

Michael said the one thing they all were thinking but nobody wanted to give in to. "I wish we weren't here."

Jack glanced up from the corpse for the first time in ten minutes. For a moment when he saw the limp-wristed kid, he saw nothing but meat and gristle superimposed over a scrawny body. A moving wet mouth spilling wishes Jack refused to acknowledge.

"Oh, would you shut up, mate?"

Michael tensed. Threat emanated from the man. "I'll say what I want." He knew he was being challenged, and knew that it was imperative he not back down.

"Yeah, that's right. You're all talk, aren't you?" Jack smiled. Putting someone in their place always felt good.

"Stop it," Sarah said.

Jack turned to Michael, pointing. "You and me. Let's move the body to the front of the bus. Get it as far away from us as we can."

"I don't want to touch him."

"Come on, kid. I'm sure it's not the first time you've grabbed a dude."

"Jack, please," Sarah said.

"No, come on. It's Michael, right? Huh? What, you don't speak anymore? Yeah, thought so. Maybe the old bird should follow your lead and keep her own mouth shut, too. So come on, kid. Come on, *Michael.* You and I are going to move this body."

"I said no, Jack."

Diana stood. "I'll help." She'd do it herself if it meant the end of all this bickering.

Jack laughed. They hated him, despised him for his logic. It was only natural to hate what they didn't want to hear and could not face. For once in his life, his message appeared to be getting through. "Nah, toots. You sit back down." He jabbed his thumb at the kid again. "How about we let the Queen of Sheba get his hands dirty?"

"Frigging stop it," Sarah said. "Can't you see it's just too much for him, Jack? And there's nothing wrong with that. Nothing at all. Getting the body to the front is a good idea, though. Let's do it together. I know how to cart weight—I've done my fair share and you don't get to my age without having a strong stomach."

"I tip my hat to you for your balls, old duck, but it's about time we saw some from the lad."

"Fuck you," Michael said.

Jack's eyes widened. "What did you say to me?"

Michael had been waiting for him to say it. It was the one line he wouldn't let anyone cross, a deliberate prod at conflict, and yes, a part of him *did* want to fight back. He steeled himself and repeated the words. Only they were shakier the second time 'round. "I said fuck you."

"Yeah, you'd love that!" Jack readied himself to charge, stopped by Sarah.

"Enough's enough." She felt old and desperate, sensing that apart from Jack, their characters were blurring into one. "This stops now. Jack, pull your head in. I'm not your mother but I know she'd say the same thing to you."

"Back off."

Sarah chuckled and shook her head, hands on hips. "Hear the way he talks to me? Hate to burst your bubble but you're not the first person to think I'm a high-flying bitch. Now sit yourself down and we—"

"I wouldn't get too close, luv. The kid'll sneeze and cover you with the fag disease."

The words pierced Michael deep.

Will I have to put up with this for the rest of my life?

Is it worth it? Really?

Maybe dead is better.

Sarah had seen Jack's type before and understood that brute strength was only worth its weight if it muscled something good into the world. And it only took a single glance at Jack to know where he'd come from, and where he would one day end up. This made her sad.

"You got daggers for me, old duck?" Now it was Jack's turn to smile. "Trust you to side with him. Should've known, you with your stupid haircut. You look like a dyke—"

Sarah slapped him across the face.

FORTY-ONE: THE CRYING

JACK WAS TEN years old again, there in his backyard.

He dropped the bloodied scissors and the blades pierced the lawn in a V. Glanced away from his father. Saw the white slash left behind in the sky by the airplane.

Jack's dad had him by the collar of his shirt. A cooking apron covered the old man's chest; it was smeared with fingerprints of grease and barbecue sauce.

"I can't believe it, I can't believe it," his father said. "You look at me when I'm talking to you. Don't you blubber on me, boy. March yourself in that house now!"

Jack propelled through the air as a thick finger jabbed into the back of his neck. "Did you do it? DID YOU?"

In the memory, Jack couldn't recall if he answered yes or no.

Kimba the cat ran underneath his feet and Jack almost fell again, caught by his father, who proceeded to slap him around the ears. "Did you do it? Did you do it? Jesus, boy."

They stepped inside the house and the stench of cooked onions wrapped around them. It made Jack feel sick. The floor was covered in linoleum, and in the darkest corner of the room, an air-conditioning unit growled. His gray-faced mother grabbed Jack by the hair. Blood on her shirt. She drew him through the doorway, her face stricken.

Something wrapped around his ankle. Jack lifted his foot, frightened. His mother pulled him into her bedroom, where the smells of barbecue were replaced by the stench of cigarette smoke. He was relieved when he saw that the thing around his ankle wasn't a decomposed hand as he'd imagined, but rather, a blood-stained towel.

The far window was open—a brilliant portrait of framed sunlight. In its glow, he saw the small figure of a boy near the bed. A skinny kid with no shirt on, his hands wrapped in curtains and dishcloths. When he saw Jack, his cries turned to screams.

FORTY

THE SHOCK OF Sarah's slap knocked the anger out of him, leaving Jack empty for a few seconds. Soon his anger swooped back in, filling him up, relieving him. The memories vanished.

He smiled.

Sarah slapped him once more.

Finished now, she clenched her fist and realigned her knuckles.

Click-crunch.

His smile was gone.

Sarah didn't let her pain show. "I get it," she said. "Things are bad and this is how you get through. Now, I'm not saying you're a bad guy. I'm saying it's okay to be shit scared. But picking fights is feeble, Jack. You know what that means, don't you? Feeble?" She looked him up and down. "And calling the kid names. Ha. And as for me? Newsflash, Jack: sticks and stones and all that jazz. From the dropped-pie look of you, you're in no position to be calling anybody anything. And there ain't nothing wrong with my hair!" Sarah raised a crooked finger in his direction. "So suck my dick and call me madam, 'cause I'd sooner *let you* than watch you kick a kid when he's down."

Jack searched their faces for an ally and found none.

Sarah went to the corpse and threw her handkerchief over the busted face.

Michael didn't understand how he could grow to love someone in such a short period of time—yet he had. Sarah became his everything. Nobody had ever stood up for him before.

Not even himself.

THIRTY-NINE

WES LEFT THE HOUSE. All he wanted to do was go to his garden and dig for the sake of digging; there, at least, he was at home. The soil was safe and didn't rebuke when shaken. Only Wes didn't quite make it to the bed where the roses grew. Exhaustion deposited him on the last step at the back of the dwelling instead.

Dog barked at him from the end of his leash near the clothesline.

"Shut up." But the Rottweiler persisted. "Shut the fuck up!" Wes ran to the animal and kicked its head with the heel of his boot. Dog howled louder, charging again. Wes backed off, the world spinning. He fell to his knees and tore at the grass as though scrambling for answers buried beneath.

THIRTY-EIGHT

MICHAEL HEARD THE barking and thought of Mr. Maclachley's junkyard. He used to pass the old man's auto-wreckers every day after school. The chain-link fence stretched the length of the block, it being the only barrier between the eleven-year-old schoolboy in the ill-fitting clothes and the old man's guard dog.

Before boarding the route 243 bus to town, Michael thought the worst fear he would ever experience was that evoked by Mr. Maclachley's Rottweiler. In its bark, young Michael heard screaming, gutted children, laughing maniacs—noises that stalked him even into nightmares where he was running past the fence as fast as he could, the black monster leaping at the mesh through clouds of dust.

One day his sports sneakers fell out of his backpack. Michael hadn't dared go back for them. When he got home, his mother yelled at him.

His father went back for the shoes.

Maclachley's dog never attacked him, of course, or any of the other kids who had to run the dreaded junkyard mile. But when he heard the distant barking from outside the bus, that same, childish, and irrational fear of being consumed alive stalked him once more.

"His name was Peter," Sarah announced to the passengers, those both living and dead. She held a notebook in her hands and ran her fingers over the name inscribed on the first page. Her face was drawn, shoulders slumped. "Peter was a writer."

Julia leaned forward and noticed freckled blood on the pages. A flutter of unnerved sickness in her stomach; she had a diary just like it tucked away in the drawer beside her bed. Once upon a time she'd filled her book with lies on the rare chance that someone would come across it, scour the contents, and say, Wow—what a life this gal's livin'! But as things complicated, and reality-based drama proved spectacle enough, her literary lies faded, and not too long after, the journal was abandoned completely. This perhaps revealed truths in Julia that she didn't entirely like admitting to.

"Peter the poet. Poor little rabbit." Sarah focused on the pages as she returned to her seat. "I'd cry if I wasn't so damn dry." She glanced around the hub of the bus, seeking out the gaze of all, her eyes full of need. "This thing he was working on, this poem. I want to read it out loud. Will you all let me?"

Jack dipped from view and rolled onto his side, blood rushing to his head. His anger dissipated. He wracked his brain trying to remember what this Peter looked like.

It don't matter what he looks like in the end, Jack-o, said the voice in his head. *Kid's dead as disco.*

"Please?"

Nobody answered. And that was answer enough.

Sarah began to recite what the young man wrote.

"I saw a man who was becoming more than his reflection. I am him."

She paused. How long had they been trapped within this bus? Two hours, perhaps. Maybe less. It was difficult to tell anymore. In many ways, it felt like a lifetime, or multiple lifetimes strung together like pieces of twine, threads undone from the fabric of their stories knotted here against their wills. There hardly seemed to be any other existence than this, with its carrion stink and swelter, with these people looking back at her with their sad, scared eyes—except Jack, of course.

They weren't family, they weren't even friends.

They were a colony.

"If there's a God—and I do believe—then there's still room to breathe."

Sarah was no English major, but the words had weight. Sure, they were clunky, and the rhythm and intonations were all over the place, but the sentences rung true.

She read on, even though it hurt.

"Today is a graduation and there's no going back. I'm undone by that reflection, my final imperfection—"

Sarah held the page with her fingers and could have sworn the words buzzed beneath her touch, a buzzing that wasn't so much alive as haunted, a brimming voice, youthful and not quite formed, asking Sarah to be heard one final time.

Her voice cracked. She dropped the notebook.

"I'm left behind because I walked, and did not run."

Diana couldn't help it; she started to cry. Licked at her tears, slumped against Julia.

Michael understood and was afraid.

Jack sat upright with his hands in a neat bundle on

his knees. When Julia turned and made eye contact with him, he didn't shy away. Not this time. Things were different.

Even for him.

Sarah knew that reading the poem aloud had changed them. Either Jack had become one of them or they had become one with Jack. She didn't know which. The colony was ready to mobilize.

Julia was the one to say it. "We're dead if we stay here."

PART FIVE: HOUSE OF SIGHS

"A crab was nothing but a carrion-eater . . . He was more the kind of man to shrug
and say life was life; and to suppose that, like anything else,
the crab had found its evil little niche."
—Jack Ketchum, *Off Season*

THIRTY-SEVEN

4:37 PM

JACK WRIGGLED THROUGH the ten-inch gap in the door until he could wiggle through no more. His hand swiped the air and landed on the hood of the pickup. Pebbles of broken glass pinched his palm. He strained, veins sticking out in his forehead, and relented. “It’s too tight.”

Michael, Diana, and Julia watched the house for movement from the back of the bus. The last sighting had been four minutes earlier. Diana kept the time, her watch angled towards the light.

Sarah crouched next to Jack on the warped steps; he held her arm to keep himself steady. From here she could see over the top of the destroyed pickup. The rear was elevated, the nose pinched tight to the ground. This angle gave them enough cover to worm out of the bus and onto the hood and then slide to the ground without being observed.

Assuming one of them could fit through.

It had been discussed: their aim was to get someone to the garage. There, they hoped said person would discover some sort of weaponry and return to the bus armed. Escape wasn't part of the plan—not yet. On a primal level, they understood they needed to defend themselves first, and that the time to do so was a lot more nigh than anyone anticipated, except perhaps for Jack.

Ballpoint pens and prayers were *not* going to cut it.

By Diana's counting, the family glanced out the window once every ten minutes. She was positive the son was their scout; a frantic snap of the curtains, a head bobbing up and down, movements that struck her as juvenile.

Sneaking through the mangled bus door was the only way. Pushing out the emergency window was too high a risk. It would shatter, the noise drawing attention to them. They contemplated escaping through the emergency exit in the ceiling but all agreed throwing open the hatch, crawling across the roof and stumbling to the ground lacked an essential element of stealth.

Sarah's hope fell as she watched a red-faced Jack struggle backwards out of the door. "I can't get through," he said. "My chest is too big."

"Shit-shit-shit." Sarah rubbed her head. Dehydration's dry fingers were stirring a headache behind her eyes.

"What did he say?" Michael asked, his head swiveling between the left-side windows and the silhouetted forms beyond the body.

"He can't fit," Sarah whispered.

"Down!" Julia yelled, ducking in her seat.

Movement at the window.

Sarah lost her balance and hit the floor, landing on her arm. She bit her tongue. Jack pushed himself flat against the stairs. A fly settled on his face. "Stay down."

A minute passed.

Diana took a quick survey again. "It's okay," she said. "The coast is clear."

Jack looked at Sarah, who had tears of pain in her eyes. He wanted to know if she was okay but couldn't bring himself to ask. They approached the corpse, bent, trying to stay out of sight. They climbed over two seats to avoid stepping on the body and then continued up the aisle.

The passengers gathered together, perspiration dripping. A cloud of stench hovered over them all. The interior had grown oven-like over the course of the day, despite the accumulation of clouds in the sky.

Sarah blinked away the image of her handkerchief over the dead man's face; his blood had seeped through in patches. Her fabric was his caul.

"Look, maybe this is a bad idea," Michael said.

"Yeah," Diana added.

"Don't you think help should be here by now?" Jack wiped his face and then rubbed his hands across his shirt. "If they have no plans to call the police, then what are they planning to do to us? They're plotting. I hate to say it but I think they want to kill us. Two of them are murderers now. Just like Sarah said, would you turn in your own kids? I don't think so. If we sit here with nothing to fight back with, we're dead. I thought we all agreed on that."

Sarah grew anxious. "But we can't get through, Jack. There's just not enough space. I don't even think Michael could fit through, or me. Bugger-bugger-bugger!"

Diana touched her arm.

"I'm all right. Swear jar. Pop a dollar in the lady."

"What?" Jack asked.

"Nothing. Back home, me and my hubby, we have a swear jar. It's a joke. I'm sorry."

"It's okay," Diana told her.

Michael crawled across the aisle, dizzy and hungry. He had no idea what emotion he was feeling. Suspense was as good as any other; the nervous trepidation of reaching the highest point of a roller coaster. Only this wasn't fun, this wasn't a ride he could walk away from laughing, high-fiving his friends and saying, "Man, you should've seen your faces!" The door to the shed was ajar and beyond it, only darkness. No, this wasn't a ride at all.

Another gust of wind beat the side of the bus.

Julia stood. She walked past Michael, towards the body.

"Have you tried hotwiring the engine, Jack?" Sarah asked. "Can you even hotwire a bus? I don't know."

"It doesn't matter if he can or can't," Michael told them. "Even if we get the engine running—which we won't—they'll hear and come running. We can't go anywhere. Not when there's a truck *impaled* on us. We're screwed. It's us who have to move, not the bus."

The voices behind Julia faded. She stepped between the dead man's arm and side, a space the exact size of her shoe. A fly landed on her chin. She didn't swat it; it sat there, twitched. Julia reached the end of the bus and stared at the ten-inch gap without fear any more. Dropping low, she crawled down the three steps. It was hard to see the house because of the truck, which was fine, because that meant they couldn't, in turn, see her.

This could work, she thought. *I might be able to do this.*

Julia slid her arm through the gap, found a clearing on the hood, and balanced herself as she started to push through.

The house. The window. The curtains. All was still.

Jack shook his head. "The kid's right, you know? They'd hear everything. It won't work. A family on a property like this has got more than one gun in the drawer, believe-you-me."

Air rushed up over Julia's face and she relished in it, loved the way it dried her sweat into a brittle layer of salt. Her shoulder squeezed through the gap and blood rushed to her head, teeth grinding as she contorted herself to fit through. She was so very close.

"Julia!"

Her sister's voice broke her determination—a lapse that couldn't be afforded right now. Panic bloomed and her hand slipped. Julia heard a struggle from behind, vibrations through the bus, muffled voices.

Diana ran towards the scissoring legs sprawled on the floor. Sarah followed hot on her heels and grabbed the younger woman by the wrist. "Let go of me," Diana yelled, trying to wring herself free. "Julia, get back in here right now!"

"Please don't yell!" Michael implored. Still no movement in the house—but that wouldn't last. "Please."

Diana struggled free and continued down the aisle, stopped. She leapt over the remains of the man.

Sarah closed in on the action, realizing that

desperation wasn't a place you find yourself in; rather, it is a place you can't get out of. That made sense to her now, and the small, brave girl was their only hope of changing it. This broke something in Sarah, something that she'd always assumed was iron-clad, and that hurt made her miss Bill more than ever, even his illness. Suffering had been a part of her life for so long, and really, how was that different to being trapped on the bus? Once her husband was gone, Sarah knew her own life would be over—it was a trap, all of it. Desperation's cage is built one bar at a time and we construct it ourselves without even realizing it. The part of her that was breaking was the part that knew no matter how much she fought Bill's cancer, no matter how much the young girl writhed for the sake of their safety, there is no real release. No real escape. We're born desperate to climb back inside our mothers, and when the end comes rushing at us, we find that not much has changed.

And between this beginning and end?

Suffering, suffering only. No wonder Sarah clung to her faith.

Without it, what was the goddamned point?

"Sweetie," Sarah said to Diana, who by this point had leapt on her sister. "Julia's the only one who can fit through."

"She can't go. She's too young."

Jack approached. "Look, keep it down."

Michael wanted to offer help, voice his concerns, but his thoughts were a mess. "I—ur—ugh."

Jack nudged past him. "Got nothing useful to say, say nothing at all. Got it, mate?"

Gripping Diana's shirt, Sarah looked deep into her

eyes. "It's going to be okay. This young lad here is going to keep watch," she said, gesturing at Michael. "You should go with him. Help us to protect your sister. You love her, don't you? Let's keep her safe."

Diana cried out. Julia pulled her head back inside the bus. "Di, I got to do it." Her hand landed on her sister's arm, fingers pinching at the skin. "I'm going to shotgun it to the shed, look for something. Hammers or whatever. Anything we can use if they come back." She nodded, encouraging Diana to nod with her. "Then I'm running straight back here. It's now or never."

Sarah hugged Diana tighter, locked her in her arms.

"If something happens—" Diana started.

"Jesus, Diana, nothing's going to happen, okay? I've got to do it. You keep watch with—what's your name?"

"It's Michael," he replied, shaking his head. He thought letting the girl go was crazy.

"Help us, sweetie," Sarah asked of Diana.

"I've got to go now."

"She's got to slip through now." Sarah kissed Diana's cheek.

"Sis, you don't have to do this."

Michael watched them lock eyes. He couldn't believe what was happening. A girl younger than him was going out there. He knew he would never be a hero, and was ashamed.

Does knowing you're a coward defeat the cowardice? Is acknowledging your failings enough to cheat the problem, to cheat death?

Michael didn't think so.

He watched Julia turn back to the gap and force

her way through. Michael wanted to say something, anything. Perhaps wish her luck. Only she was likely far beyond hearing.

He watched for movement in the house.

Sarah had her wide, calloused hands on Diana's shoulders. "Breathe for me, sweetie."

"She can't go. She's pregnant."

Julia stopped. The words froze the other passengers.

All eyes turned to Julia, whose blotched face was twisted at an awkward angle so she could meet their stunned gazes.

"I'm going out there *because* I'm pregnant," she said.

With no fanfare, no tears, Julia pushed herself back through the doorway.

Pregnant. Sarah let the word sink in. *How old is she? Thirteen, fourteen?* It all was too hard to comprehend. She'd known the girls for mere hours but thought they had developed a bond of trust, of unity. *You're as naïve as you always were,* Sarah told herself. To know the three of them were, in fact, four altered things. They were just strangers, after all. She knew nothing about them, and though it pained her to do so, Sarah struggled to find acceptance in the child's revelation. The cost of belief made sinners of some angels, and although Sarah often hated herself for it, as she did right now, her life-long prejudices were too deeply founded to uproot now.

"I'll hate you forever and ever and ever if you don't come back," Diana told the shuffling legs. She didn't know if her sister heard her.

A baby, Michael thought, shocked. It wasn't

difficult to imagine a young pregnant girl. In fact, it was common. So no, it wasn't that; it was just inconceivable to him that the stakes could get any higher.

Let her go, you know you have to, a voice whispered in Jack's ear. He turned to address the speaker. Only flies.

THIRTY-SIX

THE GLASS ON the hood stuck into Julia's palms but didn't break the skin. Every muscle in her body tensed. Elbow quivered. Inside, her baby continued to grow, unaware of what was happening, of the world it was fated to be born into.

Hair swished across her eyes. Blew it aside.

You can do this, she said to herself. *You've got no choice.*

The house faded into shadow as clouds filled out overhead. A hot gust of wind rattled fairy lights in the dying trees.

As best as Michael could tell, there wasn't a possibility of Julia being seen until she was off the truck and on the ground, at which point she would be out in the open and visible to all eyes. "Please, please, please, be safe," he said.

Diana moved away from the others. Hatred boiled, rolled to the surface like fleshless bones in a pot. They deserved to die, everyone except Julia, a girl who was too young and stupid to know better. How adults—

including Diana herself—could let something like this happen baffled her.

We're evil, she thought. *All of us.*

The pressure in her bladder tightened. She pushed her face against the window, oil streaks on the glass. Fingers dug at the artificial leather seating until under her nails were black crescent moons.

THIRTY-FIVE

JULIA'S HIPBONES, already beginning to widen in the early stages of motherhood, struggled to fit through the gap. Both hands were on the hood now, her grip sliding due to cuts in her palms—the skin had relented in the end, a reminder that there were no guarantees in this game. She experienced no pain, though; nor was there fear. Adrenalin wiped it all away. Body twisted. Hips slid free of the pinch.

"Come on," Julia said. "Come on."

She pulled her right leg through the door and lowered her kneecap against the hood. A muscle gave way and she fell flat onto her chest, leg slamming against the grillwork. Oxygen emptied from her lungs. So many adult concepts had been forced upon her today that something as natural as breathing seemed a complication, a hiccup in her fight for existence. Breathe! She took a mouthful of air and her mind focused.

"Everyone down!" Michael half-yelled, half-whispered.

The curtain in the window shifted: the mother, not the son this time.

Diana dropped her head and looked at her hands. *They are not my hands. My hands would have held on to my sister. They wouldn't have let her go. They would punch the old bitch and the man with the veins in his arms. They would not let this happen.*

The woman in the window continued to peer.

Diana sympathized with the mother, a woman who had rushed to her daughter when she collapsed on the lawn, dragged her dead weight back into the house. Maternal instinct gave her strength and she wouldn't let her family go to pieces.

They are stronger than me.

Julia lay as still as she could. It was too late to go back now. A smile parted her lips. She hugged her stomach and waited for the all-clear signal.

The shadow in the window scoured the lawn and the bus. Then it disappeared. The curtain eased back into place.

Relief filled the passengers. It wouldn't last for long.

Michael composed himself and told Jack that the woman was gone. Jack informed Sarah, who in turn, pushed her face into the gap and told Julia, "The coast is clear."

Julia looked back at the old woman through the jaws of the door. The wrinkled, kind face instilled faith in her.

Sarah reached through and her hand lighted on Julia's leg, but what she'd intended to be a comforting touch turned into a shivering grip instead. "I'm so sorry," Sarah said.

Julia nodded.

"Be careful."

Shattered glass. Clouds. Lawn. Dirt and dead grass. The barren trees near the house and the jungle vine of Christmas lights in their branches. The blood-speckled cut-outs below them. The corpse of the kid who had made a run for it. A crow nestled on his broken skull. His eyes were gone, all plucked out. One dangled from the beak of the bird like a prize.

Julia feared many things. Namely, the driver and her family—even Jack scared her to some degree. But above all else she feared those crows, including those now perched on the roof of the house up ahead, and that they would come for her before she was dead.

She rolled off the hood and landed on the ground. Hard. Knees curled up towards her stomach.

Hissing.

A snake near the busted tire of the pickup, lured from the bush by the prospect of rain. Horrible thoughts jabbed into her mind: *It's here to bite and kill me.*

This is meant to be.

Too startled to be stilled, Julia crawled around the front of the bus to the opposite side, facing the driveway and not the house.

Sarah and Diana crossed the aisle, tracking her movements. Michael focused on the windows of the building across the yard. Watching it had the effect of an optical illusion, or one of the *Magic Eye* illustrations he enjoyed so much when he was younger. The longer he looked at the house without blinking, the more it seemed to be breathing, that it was alive and hungry.

Though still a distance, the driveway beckoned.

I could just run for it.

She remembered the snake and glared under the bus. It slithered through the wreckage, leaving winding curves in the dirt.

Julia stood. Jack's face was almost unreadable through a series of hand streaks on the windows, fingerprints highlighted like feathers in the sunlight. Sarah kissed a finger and pressed it flush against the glass.

Her sister wept.

They shared a moment and then she motioned for Diana to keep watch. "Go," Julia mouthed. "Help me."

Julia stepped back into shadow. She forced herself against the side of the bus, inching along its length, hands on its warm, metal surface.

It was like playing hide-and-seek as a child with her school friends; some inanimate object or playground feature was "home" and therefore "safe". If you were touching it, you had outplayed the seeker. She felt that same anticipation now. As strange as it was, the bus that had confined them for what seemed like forever was now her "safe" place.

Julia came to the end of the vehicle. Her hands went to her stomach. She longed for more of a bump, something to wrap her fingers around. But it was enough to know that there was life in her. Julia peeked around the rear of the bus, revealing a clear view of the shed. When the time came to sprint for it, there would be no turning.

Scanned the ground for upraised rocks or anything that could trip her—a forgotten cricket bat or Frisbee. Anything. If she sprawled on the grass, Julia knew she would no doubt die.

Every moment she stood there in the shade proved a moment closer to the family taking the time to check on them, and that could not happen. Not now. Not anymore.

Julia was a mother.

She ran.

THIRTY-FOUR:
THE SHED

FEET POUNDED EARTH.

The faces in the bus slid from view, drawn into time-lapse blurs as Julia increased speed. Her hands swung in tight fists, back and forth, hard and fast.

The shed loomed closer.

Julia was a mouse under the eye of an overhead hawk.

She increased her speed but it just didn't feel quick enough. Every step was half a step too short. She faltered, regained her footing, pushed onwards.

Run.

The shed door swallowed her whole.

Darkness. The temperature dropped. A chill rocketed up her back like lightning in reverse, electricity retracing its jagged steps home to the clouds. Breathless, Julia dropped to her haunches. It took some time for her eyes to adjust.

I made it. Her victory was so powerful she almost forgot where she was, and that she was only running from one hell to another.

I did it! I did it!

Her parents would be proud. If only they were here

to witness her bravery. They would smile at her and clap their hands. When she returned to the bus with the weapons, they would take her in their arms and tell her how wonderful she was, how heroic. Australian of the year!

This fantasy didn't last; the sight of the punching bag suspended from a rafter in the middle of the room slaughtered it. The tin roof ticked under the heat. Julia walked around the room, fighting the urge to close the door behind her. The family would notice. *And then I will be dead.*

Just like the others.

Car and hunting magazines covered the floor. Yellowed newspapers littered a workbench; on top were a collection of tools and loose screws. A hammer. She lifted it up, the metal head scraping against the paper and then the cool, satisfying heft of it in her grip.

I could never hit anyone with this.

Would she break someone's skull with a blunt object to save herself? Julia wasn't sure. What if by hurting someone else Julia saved her sister in the process, or her child? Fingers tightened around the handle. *Maybe, oh Jesus, just maybe I could.* Shaking, Julia slid the tool into the deep, rear pocket of her jeans and returned her focus to the table. She had to be swift.

Sifted through the mess, tissues and cigarettes. Ancient tobacco flakes stuck to the gummy blood covering her hands. A clear, empty vial and a roll of gaffer tape. Julia went to the door and surveyed the house.

Nothing.

Only dark clouds moved out there. And the crows.

The headlights of a half-assembled Volkswagen

caught the sun and glowed in the darkness of one shadowy corner. Seeing it there made her stomach constrict. It was like some half-dead monster peering at her with grimy eyes, waiting for the right moment to draw together its old, battered bones and pounce. Julia felt its stare on her back when she turned away.

A toolbox under the bench. She skidded to her knees. Flicked the latches. The snap echoed through the room. *It's okay—just keep moving.* The box held nails, a small ratchet, a couple of loose ball bearings, and a can of WD-40 spray grease. Next to it, there was an X-Acto utility knife. She picked it up and thumbed the blade. It rose from its shallow casing with a rusty squeak. Yeah—now *this* was something they could use. She pocketed the knife, a giddy laugh escaping her, yet another victory in the face of madness. *I'm doing it, I really am. This is going to work.* Julia spun on her heel to face the opposite side of the shed.

Stopped.

On the far wall were rows of guns on antler racks.

A hot gust blew into the shed.

Movement in the corner of her eye. *Right beside her.* Julia stumbled backward.

A punching bag swung in the wind.

Stop it, Jules, you're losing it. Stay together, okay? You've got this.

Determined, she returned to the rack. Underneath the horns and dust-covered guns, there was a metallic chest of drawers. She stood next to it and attempted to grab for the nearest gun.

Julia drew open the bottom drawer of the chest. The metal screeched, reminding her of Freddy Krueger in those *Nightmare on Elm Street* movies and the way his horrible, child-murdering finger-knives scraped against pipes. She'd seen the film with friends and been unable to sleep. Her mother was angry with her for watching such nonsense. "It was fun though," she told her. After all, it was fun to be scared, even if it gave her nightmares because when the nightmare was over she went on with her life, normality returned and she was safe. Standing there in the dank shed, however, Julia wondered if she would ever see her mother again, or if there would ever be another day without this lucid terror coming after her.

She put her left foot on the drawer and hefted herself up. *Careful now, Jules.* Her weight bore down on the chest, rattling objects. Her right hand stretched up to one of the guns. She grabbed the handle and started to twist if off a polished boar tusk.

A tickle on her left hand.

The spider sank its fangs into her skin. Her eyes were on it for only a microsecond. Time enough to register its size—about a centimeter, with a scarlet hourglass on its abdomen. A red-back.

Julia let out a short scream, flicked her hand and lost her balance, taking the chest with her. The contents rushed towards the front of the drawers and it leaned forward, unbalanced. Julia wrestled with its weight, the gun dropping to the ground.

Drawers started to fall open, pushing against her breasts and thighs. With a loud bang and rattle, Julia pushed it back onto its four corners and clawed at her clothes. The spider could still be on her somewhere. She spun on the spot, shaking her arms, slapping at her hair and face. When she stopped, she scoured her flesh and saw nothing.

On the ground next to the gun, the spider crawled back towards the corrugated wall. It didn't make it that far.

Julia crushed it with her foot. Pop.

Red-back spiders could be deadly but she took comfort in knowing people didn't often die from their bites these days. All you had to do was rush to the hospital and—

Venom pumped through her body.

She looked at the small, pink teat of upraised flesh where two tiny fang marks wept clear liquid, and squeezed the bite as though it were nothing more than a pimple she'd awoken to find on her face. Pain. She collapsed to the dirt, crying.

How could I have been so stupid? Sheds are red-back cities, all dark and dusty. Julia had been taught to shake out her shoes before putting them on, just in case a spider had crawled within them during the night, and to never walk under or between trees in the summer for fear of webs. She'd been so diligent, fear acting as the best discipline.

Pain seared again, a second wave. Her memory flashed to lessons at school, blurred advice from science teachers about spider bites. Should she tear strips from her shirt and fashion a tourniquet, or was that for snakes? Was it better to localize the venom or let it spread and dilute? Damn it, she couldn't remember.

What about my baby?

She grabbed at her stomach. Nausea painted her face gray.

"Oh, my God."

She was at the end of the earth and flooded with

the venom from the second-most deadly spider in the fucking country. *Diana will know what to do.*

Julia snatched up the gun and put it in her front pocket. It rested against her hipbone. She ran to the door and looked out.

The sound of the clanging cabinet and her screams hadn't alerted the family. "Thank you, thank you."

She approached the chest of drawers with caution. The fingers on her good hand wrapped around a drawer handle and pulled.

The drawer was full of unlabeled boxes, loose bullets, and shotgun cartridges. She whipped the gun out of her pocket and tried to open the chamber to see if it was loaded. Dull, throbbing aches pounded through her shaking hand. With a gasp of frustration, she jabbed the gun back into her pocket. Julia opened random boxes, shoveled handfuls of bullets—big and small—into her jeans. She backed away from the cabinet, not bothering to close the drawer.

The sound of a barking dog—a deep, rasping noise.

Full of anger.

She halted by the shed door, considering running out into the remaining daylight without checking to see if the coast remained clear. Julia slammed her hand against her forehead, cursed herself for being so hasty. Images filled her head of her minuscule child contorting and screaming inside her womb, strangling, as venom reached its tiny, unformed heart. These images themselves were a kind of poison, a poison that was weakening her.

Somewhere there was another sound.

And it was louder than the dog.

Julia pushed her hair out of her eyes and moved a

little closer to the door. From here she could just see the rear windows of the bus and the faces of the passengers signaling for her to run. Arms waved; a hand stuck out of one of the sliding glass planes, beckoned.

The concept of running across that barren no man's land again was overwhelming. But then there was the sound again.

Crashing.

It came from inside the house. Breaking glass and muted yelling. A woman, the driver perhaps. No— another woman. The mother.

Julia gripped the doorframe until her knuckles turned milky. She took in the bus again, watched the hurried signals for her to break free from the shadows. Her hands touched her stomach once more as she put her head between her knees. Hectic, random words spilled out of her like water from an overfilled bathtub and soon there was a tattered melody lost among the torrent. Julia started singing "Rock-a-bye Baby" to herself, and to her child.

She tugged at her earlobes, something she used to do as a toddler when scared. The lyrics drifted away; only half-hearted humming lingered on.

My baby is a girl. She is going to be beautiful. It will be hard for her to grow up without a dad. But maybe he will come back, maybe he'll answer my calls. It's hard to have an adult life with adults looking down at you. I'm sure my parents think I'm into drugs or something. Ha. Maybe that would be easier . . .

My daughter is going to be so beautiful. She's going to love music and movies, just like me, and she's going to do well in school and meet a nice boy and be married one day, and then have her own kids. She will be happy because she will know she is the happiness her mother fought for.

I love my baby, my tiny, little Tinkerbell, fluttering in the deepest part of me. My bub, she is like light. So beautiful, so wonderful. It's like magic.

My daughter's name is going to be Astoria, after my sister's hometown in America. I want to go there so bad, to see all the places that meant something to her and her own mother, before she died. Together, Diana, my baby and I will sit at the crossroads near the train tracks beside the docks and watch the water.

Astoria.

"—cradle and all."

THIRTY-THREE

LIZ STOOD IN the doorway. Her eyes were deep red scratches in her face. She staggered down the front steps, her sudden appearance making the crows lining the eaves and peaks of the house flap their wings and screech in applause.

Dust devils whirred between the driver and the girl running into the daylight.

A current of terror palsied Julia's legs, but she held true and pushed on. She didn't see a woman rushing across a lawn at her; no, she saw death itself closing in, The Grim Reaper with its scythe held high, black cape billowing.

Her ankle twisted, bullets slipped from her pockets. Julia hit the ground.

Helpless, the passengers screamed at her to get up, the bus rocking. Through the hair hanging over her eyes, Julia saw her sister banging on the windows, screaming her name over and over. Diana's voice hooked under her skin, reeling her to her feet.

Liz lurched forward. "Where are you going?" she yelled. Above, clouds flexed and belched the day's first thunder. "Don't leave me!" Her arms outstretched before her. "Take me with you!"

Jed appeared at the door. "Mum, Dad! She's out—come 'ere!" He rushed down the stairs. Thunder boomed again as he started sprinting.

Wes stepped from the shadows and onto the verandah.

Julia was close to safety. Her aim was for the mangled nose of the bus where the door met the shattered truck. Stealth didn't matter anymore.

But speed did.

Wes watched his son run towards Liz and registered nothing. Things were happening too fast. His wife latched on to his arm. Wes shook her off and headed for the shed.

The passengers continued to scream from the windows. Diana ran down the aisle, not stopping to go around the dead body. Instead, the heel of her foot pushed hard against his chest, springing her forward. Flies scattered and buzzed.

Jack followed Diana, grabbed the metal bars above his head and swung over the corpse.

Spider bite forgotten, and pain lost to panic, Julia dove onto the pickup's mangled hood. Her hands slid over slivers of windshield, embedding themselves in her palms. She lost her grip and snapped forward. Her head slammed the doorframe of the bus, cutting her eyebrow open. The gun and utility knife flew from her pocket and clattered amidst the broken glass. More bullets rolled free and dropped to the ground. Stunned, Julia glanced up, vision running red as blood dripped into her eyes. Her sister screamed at her to hurry.

Dizziness overcame Reggie as she watched her husband disappear into the shed, watched her children rush at the bus. Her eyes were dry, mouth frozen in a gasp as she ran after them. She felt so heavy and was quickly out of breath. The dress she wore flew about her legs.

Jack landed next to Diana and elbowed her out of the way. She fell on her side and for a moment could see nothing but the foot pedals in the driver's hub. A towering gear stick cast a faint shadow over her vision. Jack forced himself down the twisted steps on his belly and extended an arm through the gap, face pushed against the broken door.

"Give me the gun!" he screamed.

Julia's hands were part flesh, part glass, but they still bundled up the loose bullets, the handgun and utility knife with no regard to cuts and venom. She tossed the bounty through the gap and into Jack's calloused palm—he vanished from her sight. Julia lost her balance and her hands slapped against the hood. The broken shards stabbed deeper; one sharpened point scraped the bone.

Jack ran from the door, dropping a shotgun cartridge. Diana pushed past him and threw herself towards the gap.

At the rear of the bus, Michael followed Sarah, whom he grabbed by the collar.

"Please be careful," he called after her.

Liz reached the pickup and wrapped her arms around Julia's kicking legs. Diana had her sister by the arm and pulled, surprised by the ferocity of her strength. "Hold on to me," she heard Julia call through the door.

Jack swooped onto his knees, utility knife beside

his foot, gun in one hand and three remaining bullets of different sizes in the other. He flicked the chamber open and squeezed a bullet between two fingers, lined it up to slip it into the gun. The bullet flew through the air as Sarah bumped him, running to help Diana. It bounced on the floor and pinged out of sight.

"Fuck!" he screamed, spittle flying. "You stupid bitch."

THIRTY-TWO

HALFWAY THROUGH THE GAP, the collar of Julia's shirt tore on a twisted piece of metal. She reached for the hammer in her rear pocket. Gone. Shaken loose when the driver wrestled with her legs. Julia had no air in her lungs with which to scream, just a rattle. She glanced up at her sister who wasn't looking at her, but at the driver in whom they had placed their trust at the beginning of that day, the woman who had hit the girl in the road and brought them to this horrible place, at the driver crawling onto the hood beside her.

"Don't go," Liz pleaded. Julia felt her breath on her skin.

Directly behind the driver's wide, frightened eyes, the brother slid into Diana's line of vision—an angry blur of tanned skin and tattoo.

Julia sensed his presence and kicked, one foot connecting with the driver's jaw. Crack.

Jack tried to push the second bullet into the chamber of the handgun. Sweat dripped from his nose and he wished the faggot would shut up.

Michael screamed at the back of the bus, throwing himself against the windows, battering for escape.

From the mouth of the shed, Wes materialized, a large, loaded shotgun in hand.

Sarah's body intertwined with Diana's; they rolled against one another to keep a hold on the little girl's arm. They butted heads, reeled but didn't let go.

The second, useless bullet landed on the bloodied ground. Jack fingered the third into the chamber. It didn't fit.

Jed scrambled with his sister, trying to drag her backward. "Sis, let her go—" Her hold on the girl's legs was stubborn and Julia spilled back onto the hood when he pulled.

Julia stomach dropped.

Jack searched for the bullet Sarah had knocked from his hands. His finger brushed against it. "I got you, you little shit." He rolled onto his back and held the gun over his head, forced the blunt tip of the bullet against the chamber and pushed. It slid in with an audible crack. "Move, move, move!" He threw himself upwards and rushed at the door. One hard kick drove Sarah to the floor.

Liz scratched at her brother's face.

Jed winced. His gaze settled on a hammer on the ground. He picked it up and again attempted to pull his sister away. She huddled over the young girl.

One of Julia's hands remained inside the bus, fighting to keep hold, and the other lashed out at her attackers.

The driver's skin and bones through Julia's shirt. It disgusted her.

Jed held the hammer in both hands, shocked by how light it felt. He brought it down in a glimmering arc, thunder booming once more.

It connected with Julia's shoulder.

She screamed.

Jack pinned Sarah under him. He stretched, one hand resting on Diana's shoulder. She refused to let go of her sister's hand.

Jack pushed his hand through the gap, aimed, and pulled the trigger.

THIRTY-ONE

THE DRIVER'S HEAD EXPLODED. A spray of blood filled the air. It covered the hood, the broken door. Jack's face became a mask of dripping scarlet. His own skin broke in multiple places where button-sized flakes of skull pierced him.

Reggie witnessed it all. She continued a few steps and then fell. A cloud of dust blew up off the earth and colored her face until she almost seemed a part of the landscape.

Wes, who had been crossing the yard, stopped beside his wife. His mind must be playing tricks on him—this couldn't be real. His limp arm hung by his side, the gun still in hand. "Nope, don't think so," he said to nobody, to the ground, to the green clouds in the sky.

Reggie's wail ended abruptly like a record needle spun off the vinyl. "That wasn't my little girl, Wes," she said. "That wasn't her."

Wes shambled to the bus.

Reggie didn't stand; she crawled, braying her mantra of denial.

The girl who had been in their shed was at Jed's feet now. The one who had run for the bus but hadn't made it. The one who fell off the hood when the bullet had—what? *Killed my sis.*

The explosion echoed in his ears.

Julia rolled onto her back, grit peppering her face. She, too, was lathered in blood, stabbed with bone fragments. A clotted mess clung in her eyelashes. She searched for a gunshot wound, oblivious to the shape towering over her, the shape holding the hammer.

What remained of Liz propped against the broken windshield of the pickup. Her legs buckled underneath her, back arched and two jittering arms upturned like split bellied snakes. Attached to her neck was her lower jaw, broken teeth glimmering, an ear spun on a strand of flesh. The rest? Gone. Where there should have been eyes and scalp and nose and love and sadness, only space and jets of blood. Jed leaned forward and took the now still hand in his own.

No one moved inside the bus. Diana fell backwards, blood in her eyes. Sarah rolled over, cramps burning through her lower back and shoulders, wet, red matter in her short-cropped hair. The force of the gun threw Jack onto his ass and he sat against the driver's chair, blood drip-drip-dripping from the tip of his nose.

You did the right thing, Jack-o, said the sweet, comforting voice.

THIRTY

YOU DID THE right thing, Jack-o, *said a voice he had never heard before.*

"Did I?" he asked.

"Did you bloody what?" roared his father, who still held him by the arm. His other hand latched around the back of his neck, squeezing tight. "I ask the questions around here, got it?"

Jack didn't reply. He couldn't take his eyes off the boy before the window, the boy whose hands were still wrapped in bloodied sheets. This boy was his cousin, Charles; he was six years old.

"You speak to me when I speak to you, you little shit."

"Yes!" Jack yelled back.

"Yes, bloody what?"

"Yes, sir. Dad!"

"Now you own up to me, boy. You own up to me or so help me God you'll get a bigger bloody thrashing than what you already got coming. And trust me, a thrashing's the least I should be doin' to you." His father bent in low, close to his ear. Out of the corner of his eye, Jack saw yellow teeth. "Did you do this to young Charles over there?"

The cousin stopped his screaming, stood and pointed at Jack. As he did, the makeshift bandages of his right hand fell away. Revealed were multiple cuts along the lengths of his fingers, through the curves of his fleshy pink palms. Blood pooled and dripped in bright red leaks.

The smells and sensations of what he had done came back to him. He could feel his mother's sewing scissors—"my good pair" as she often referred to them—in his hand. They had been cold but warmed up the longer and tighter he held them. Heavy too, something he hadn't expected. In his small hands, they appeared enormous.

He and Charles had been playing in the backyard while his parents got dinner ready. He couldn't remember what game they were playing. Cheesecloth memories. Football and Frisbee were cast aside, toy soldiers buried in the soil. It had been Charles who went back into the house, snuck into the kitchen and found the scissors in the drawer nearest to the refrigerator.

"I wonder what it's like to be cut," Charles asked.

Jack had always wondered that, too.

He recalled how easily the blades slit open the fingers, no harder than cutting through a block of room-temperature butter. The blood had not spurted out as much as he'd hoped, just as for Charles there wasn't pain instantly, only a hot sensation that grew with every heartbeat. Neither boy got what he was expecting. Charles pulled away, tears swelling and then exploding in his eyes. He was really starting to bleed. Droplets speckled the grass. Jack reached out and grabbed him by the forearm, pulled him in close and lashed out with the scissors.

He had no idea why. Through the mist of his thoughts, there was a lighthouse, throwing pale light into the gray air. Only it wasn't a lighthouse. It was the scissors in his hand, glinting in the final light of the day, zipping forward and drawing red calligraphy over his cousin's hands.

Jack hadn't felt a thing. Sweet nothingness.

"Uncle, it was him, it was!" Charles screamed. He moved from behind the bed and ran to Jack's mother, wrapping his arms around her waist.

"Jesus, Charles, you're gonna go bleed all over my dress," she said.

"Take him out into the kitchen and wait there for Doc and the boy's mother."

"But—" she began, keeping the weeping child at arm's length. "Oh, now you're bleeding all over the carpet!"

"Take him."

"Want me to take Jack too?"

"No." His father swooped in low again. "Did you do it, son? You admit it and what you got comin' won't hurt half as bad." Even though he asked, he knew the answer already, his heart no doubt breaking.

Jack said nothing.

His mother took the child into the kitchen, closed the door behind her. Charles' screams could still be heard.

He felt his father push him and he landed face first on the bed. Jack smelled his parents in the blanket. Heartbeat raced. He expected to hear the dreaded sound of his father's belt buckle sliding loose as he prepared to tan his hide. Jack even started to push down the back of his shorts to prepare himself for the beating.

"No, boy. Not this time." His voice was a drawl. "This time you got to learn a tougher lesson so you have the bad smashed out of you. Little boys who cut little boys grow up to be bad men. That scares me, mate. And I'd die of shame before having you grow up to be one of those shits."

Jack turned around to face his father. He was so tall, his body cut in two by shadow and sunset. In his hands were the bloodied, soiled scissors. They threw light into his eyes, blinding him. Jack closed his eyes.

Snip-snip.

A fly buzzed within the room. Then came the voice again, soft and kind. He'd been longing to hear it again.

You did the right thing, Jack-o.

TWENTY-NINE

"Did I?" Jack replied, turning to Michael. The faggot had no answer for him.

Drifting gun smoke.

Sarah attempted to get up. Diana watched the brother scoop his sister up in his large, strong hands; one still held the hammer. His gaze honed in on Diana's.

Blood poured onto his shirt from Liz's wound. He dropped the corpse and it hit the hood with an undignified thump. A stunned Julia watched the huge, wet mass tumble towards her. The loose remains of a tongue slid out of the broken head to slap her thigh. The body pinned her to the ground.

His father, who had dropped his gun and rushed to the remains, distracted Jed. Reggie was close enough to see Liz, headless and now being pulled into Wes's arms. Julia covered her face as the body lifted off her chest, leaving behind large, red patches. Then the pain settled in. Her sliced open hands.

The mother screamed.

Wes couldn't believe what he was holding. This couldn't be everything he'd poured his hopes and dreams into, his mistakes and regrets. This eviscerated, headless thing could *not* be the girl he'd disciplined too hard and never loved right. This meat. Slaughterhouse throwaways.

No.

Yes.

He held her to his chest, letting out a deep, guttural sound. Reggie came to his side, reached out with pudgy fingers and touched Liz. Reggie recoiled, hands coming away red.

Somewhere Christmas music began to play.

Julia knew that getting inside the bus wasn't an option. She wanted to cry out to Diana but held herself together. Going to the door equaled murder. Her only chance was to make it to the driveway and hope for the best.

The brother leapt onto Julia. She wasn't sure, but she could have sworn she heard something snap inside her, followed by a pressure where there hadn't been pressure before.

Yes—you deserve it, you do, Jed thought. He wrestled with her, his face was close to hers.

Inside, Diana followed her sister's movement to the front of the bus. Diving to the front windshield to look out, she pushed Sarah out of the way. The old woman landed on the steering wheel and the horn sounded across the landscape.

Michael pulled himself into a ball, wedged between two seats.

Reggie's eyes rolled back in her head. Her knees gave way and she buckled under her own weight, her floral dress rising. A bolt of lightning shot from the sky and split a gum tree in the valley. Reggie landed on her back, fat legs and soiled panties exposed. The sight of her husband easing Liz's body onto the ground had been too much. In her lonely, private dark she saw nothing but Christmas decorations and fairy lights.

Julia raked at the brother's face and arms until her fingernails cracked. She threw her knee into his balls.

A yellow sun of sickening pain exploded in him. He didn't have to move; the girl remained pinned underneath. He looked up at the bus, through the door, back to Diana.

Sisters. They don't look alike, but they are sisters. I know it.

Without hesitation, Jed raised the hammer, held it with both hands, muscles flexing. He glared at the girl—the stupid, murdering, pubescent cunt who had no business being on his lawn, or in his life. And so, he brought the hammer down hard.

Julia's eyes closed before impact.

Bright light in the darkness, and when her eyes flickered, everything blurred. A coppery smell. Another burst of pressure, this time on her nose. Then heat, uncontrollable furnaces roaring. It didn't occur to her that she was being beaten to death until she heard her teeth shattering and felt their spiky dust slitting open her throat. More explosions in the blur and soon she drowned. Sightless. Agony. The fires were too hot. Adrenalin couldn't match the assault. What was happening was an unimaginable thing, and yet she had no choice but comprehend it.

My baby.

Her head filled with noise. A noise that sounded like crow song.

And then silence.

TWENTY-EIGHT:
CAMP

DIANA AWOKE TO the sound of seven gossiping friends. Two older teenagers slept on the other side of the cabin. She liked the counselors, idolized them—they didn't judge, or bicker as much as she and her friends did. They respected each other, and Diana liked that about them.

This would be her final year at summer camp.

She planned to go for a swim, to help the younger visitors at meal times and take part in whatever activities were scratched on the chalkboards. Breakfast was in the dining room at eight. Large, wooden tables covered in toast and fruit. Diana played with her food and laughed when a slice of orange hit the cheek of a girl next to her. The culprit was nowhere to be seen. By nine o'clock she and the girls were in the canoes, life jackets around their necks. The girls talked about how cute the male counselor was. Twelve thirty rolled by and lunch disappeared down hungry mouths, boys made farting sounds, counselors huddled together and commented on the children. Their afternoon filled with artwork and swatting flies. Diana looked at the splashes of paint on her butcher paper, feeling the heaviness of the brush in her hand. Her work bore no shape, no form, just splashes of random color. Muddy. And this was weird, on account of her being very much a unicorns-and-flowerbeds kind of girl, despite her scuffed knees and willingness to play catch with the boys. Diana was unsettled. Insects on her easel.

The feeling passed by afternoon tea.

Back in her cabin the girls exchanged stories and told each other what they wanted to be when they grew up. Some wanted only to have children, which shocked her. Diana wanted to travel, to see places she never thought were real. The others laughed at her and she playfully wrestled them to the floor.

At six they sang songs in the Lodge, which smelled of old books and chimney smoke. People played with their homemade wooden nametags around their necks. Diana had painted hers with stars and glitter but some of it had fallen off, leaving behind dark glue stains.

When the music stopped, she heard the river over the hushed gossip of who-kissed-who and who-saw-a-scorpion-in-the-girl's-restroom. Then came the clanging of the courtyard bell. Dinnertime.

Halfway across the lawn, there came a gentle touch on her shoulder. Heather, the counselor who slept in her room at night. She asked Diana to come for a walk with her. They passed the Lodge and continued towards the Gate House, a building she hadn't visited since check-in. Heather looked awkwardly at her feet and silenced her walkie-talkie when it squawked, "Have you got her?"

Diana was a little excited to visit the management's quarters. Was she going to receive some kind of award? She couldn't help smiling, despite the violent rolling of her stomach and the return of that strange feeling from before, when the brush had trembled in her fingers and the painting stopped making sense.

Heather took her into a room, past a large and empty desk. It unnerved her to see it unmanned, the telephone receiver off the hook. They approached a door. It opened.

Her father was there, his eyes burnt out. Where they should have been were black and red scribbles. She felt two feet tall. Her dad wrapped his arms around her. He whispered in her ear how sorry he was.

"Why, Dad?"

She pulled away from him but he held her in a tight grip. Everyone else had disappeared.

Blood ran the lengths of the walls. Leaves danced about her feet.

She needed to pee.

Bad.

"Why are you sorry?" she asked again, noticing that her voice was different. Deeper. Womanly. She considered his face. Hollow. His eyes were no longer messy paint splashes. They simply were not there. His jaw swung wide and loose. Dislocated.

He trembled, scratched at her clothing. His cheekbone bulged like a leg under silk sheets. A thin stream of bile ran from his mouth, splattering her knees. From where his eye should have been there emerged a beak, black and strong. With a sickening tear, the head of a crow broke free of her father's face. The bird squawked, its feathers matted.

Her world imploded into color. Through the light she saw herself standing over a coffin, could see herself outrunning the tourist cart down the Astoria embankment because she thought she'd caught her mother among the faces and cameras, could see herself studying her dad's new girlfriend with predictable spite.

Diana fell through time and hatred and forgiveness until she landed—

TWENTY-SEVEN

—HARD AGAINST THE bus floor. Incredible pressure in her bladder.

Screams all about her. The old woman, whose name she couldn't remember, had her hands over her eyes and was kneeling in the aisle, rocking. She looked so sad, and Diana was scared for her, though not for herself.

The man with the big veins in his arms, the one with a goatee, ran past her in dreamy slow motion, and jumped into the stagnant air.

Jack landed hard on his feet. The faggot ran wildly around the back of the bus, thumping against the seats and windows. The faggot was everything wrong in the world. Sure, his eyes might look sympathetic and everything, but Jack saw him for what he really was: the conspirator in all things weak and lost. The faggot was the enemy, more than anything else. The faggot was the driver; the faggot was the dead kid, splattered on the road; the faggot was the driver's brother; the faggot was everyone but Jack, the only sane person left in this wasteland. The faggot was an actor and was in fact not really screaming at all. No, the faggot laughed.

Make a fist, the voice told him. *And smash it into the faggot's face.*

Jack knew the voice from somewhere. He wracked his brain.

Do it, Jack-o.

"I know you," he said aloud.

Yes, you do. Now do what I tell you. Do it and then maybe later you can use the scissors on him. You like the scissors, don't you, Jack-o?

Thoughts and memories flew like pieces of a shattered mirror.

"Where?"

The pieces fell to the ground in perfect alignment. His reflection.

The kid is to blame for all this. He's the devil. The faggot always is.

The voice was his own.

TWENTY-SIX

JACK DROVE HIS fist into Michael's face, watched the kid crumble to the floor and then jumped on him, arms thumping away. Michael kicked out in defense, one foot connecting with the base of his attacker's jaw. That he connected at all was luck alone.

The sound of a hundred busting soda cans under the heels of a hundred drunken men, followed by the tinkle of glass, exploded through Jack's head. He faltered, clutching at the already forming welt, and watched the faggot wriggling out from under his knees.

Jed stood on the hood of his destroyed pickup. In his hands, he held the hammer, ribbons of hair clotted on its head. He pulled himself up onto the roof of the bus, which was white and reflected what little light remained in the day. The clouds were at the point of breaking, weeping. Wind shook the trees through the valley. As Jed slid across the surface of the bus, he left a snail trail of gore in his wake. Dirt blew against his face, although it was no longer a face, rather a mask of gore. He scuttled, the hammer scraping as he moved towards the tail of the vehicle, towards the emergency exit hatch.

It was open a crack. If he could get the end of the hammer in, he might be able to lever it open. The bus rocked under him.

Jack preempted the brother's move overhead and leapt off Michael, squeezing a shout of pain from him as he bounded. He slammed a bloodied hand on a handrail to help himself up. Above, the roof creaked. Jack ran to the emergency exit, gray clouds through the gap, grabbed the handle and hefted it downwards with all his weight. The hatch snapped shut and he thumped to the floor.

"Fuck you!" Jed screamed at the now sealed emergency exit. The echo of its closing mocked him. Frantic, he tried to get his fingers into the divot but there was no leverage, not even the teeth of the hammer fit. He stood, bolts of energy filling his body. These murdering bastards had to die, and so help him God, Jed would be the one to do it.

Pain gave him power.

Jed snapped to his right, scooted to the lip of the roof, reached over and swung the hammer, aiming for the window.

Sarah watched it splinter in a web. Flashes of her husband in each impact.

Bill leaning in to kiss her.

SMASH.

Bill crying into her lap on the day he found out he was going to die.

SMASH.

Bill in a coffin, stuffed and stitched. This was the way she always imagined she would see him last. Only now it was her in the coffin, and he was beside it, crying.

SMASH.

After several blows, the laminate held the shattered pieces together like a frosted blanket. The hammer twisted in the mess and as the brother pulled the remains from the window bay, both glass and hammer dropped out of sight.

A hand reached inside, swung and clutched at nothing.

Jack dodged to the front of the bus, searching for what he knew must be there, his heartbeat so loud it hurt his ears. He found what he'd come for, so easy, as though someone left it there for him.

Me, said the voice. *You're welcome.*

Jack picked up the X-Acto utility knife and thumbed the blade, not pushing it too far, fearful it might snap off or chip.

Don't be too eager, cautioned the voice. *Hold it tight.*

Jack did as he was told.

Yep, that's it, my man. That's it.

He smiled. Flies landed on his face. He didn't shoo them away this time.

Now, Jack-o. That man on the roof is wondering what it feels like to be cut.

"Charles," he whispered aloud.

That's right, just like Charles.

Jack leapt at the intruding hand, screaming like a warrior going into battle, and stabbed. The blade slit through flesh with ease, striking the bone beneath. The tip of the blade snapped off and the man shrieked, just as Charles screamed that day. Only the man didn't run away as his cousin had done—the man held his ground and reached in again, swinging at him. Blood rained over his face, over the seats. Jack slashed again and again and again, and on the fourth stroke, the hand retreated.

Felt good, didn't it? inquired the voice.

Jack's grisly hands started to shake.

Michael sat up, and told himself to be brave, that he could do this. *This is it*, he thought. *It's all coming down. It's now or never. No, no, don't think of the ocean. No!*

But he did think of the ocean. Its heavy, cool waves crashed over him.

Diana stared into a world in which her father had scribbles for eyes, where her sister laughed next to her during a screening of some stupid movie called *Clueless*.

The windshield blew open. A single shot.

White noise and static filled their ears. The shape struggled with the smoking shotgun as it climbed over the nose of the bus.

When Wes wiped the tears from his eyes, he left streaks of his daughter on his face. His nose freckled with gunpowder.

Sarah ducked out of sight.

Diana barely flinched when the windshield blew out, even though diamonds of glass carved a game of tic-tac-toe into her face. She didn't feel Sarah's hand, nor hear her voice when her arm was grabbed.

"Move, baby," Sarah told her.

No reply.

Leave her, you got to. You tried to help the poor girl but you can't kill yourself saving her. You have a husband. You have children, grandchildren. They are supposed to be at home right now. They are waiting for you. You never should have left. It was wrong to go.

Sarah ran to the back of the bus.

Trying to move someone who's already dead is like trying to outsmart death itself. You always lose, honey. You always lose.

Jed's upturned face appeared in the empty windshield. Blood rushed to his head, filling his veins. He swung onto the dashboard just as his father pulled himself into the driver's hub, knocking the small, broken fan down the stairs. It clattered and broke into pieces. Jed landed, his knees threatening to give in. He held himself steady and espied the creatures scurrying about like frightened mice. He reached out to them, his hand bigger than them all. In his grip, he strangled them, crushed the vermin with wild eyes and sharp sister-killing teeth.

"Murderers!"

He hacked phlegm from the back of his throat and spat in their direction.

At the rear of the bus, Jack held the utility knife ready.

The survivors of route 243 backed into the corner. Jack hated them all. He hated them for making him so futile because it was so hard to fight against their terror. They should have fought while the going was good and attacked the driver on the road. He would never forgive them for this oversight. When he was free, Jack would tell the world what cowards they were and that it was he alone who saw the situation for what it really was: something that could have been prevented, if only they had come together under his wing.

Wes scanned them, shotgun in hand. Jed was on his right. They scoured the faces of those who had taken his daughter, his sister—the people who had robbed them of the opportunity to apologize for being a lousy father, a deadbeat brother.

Despising them was the most natural thing in the world.

Diana sat in a seat close to the father and son, unblinking.

Jed gagged. He knew it wasn't the time for flinching. "Jesus, Dad, the smell—" he said, gesturing towards the dead man in the aisle. The man covered in flies.

They're animals, Wes told himself. "We bury the bastard face first," he said. "The rest, chicken feed." A smile. "Bones for the birds."

Diana slipped from her seat. Her head cocked to one side.

Sarah yelled at her to sit down from the back of the bus. But she did not sit. Diana drew herself erect, the bones in her back snapping into place. A long strand of sweaty hair dove over her eyes.

"I really," she began, monotone, "need to go to the washroom."

Wes glared at the woman, surprised both by her accent and by how twisted it was: an inbred cousin of cultures. It upset him. And worse, somewhere deep down, he felt a tiny spark of pity for her. She was a skinny-minnie, just like his Liz had been.

Nothing but skin and bone. I've seen scarecrows with more stuffing.

The front of the woman's jeans grew dark. The smell of urine filled the air, yet another gut-churning odor here. Jed's stomach tightened again but he kept himself composed. A tingle went through his body, the blood-splashed hairs on his arms rising to attention. He laughed.

The pity in Wes disappeared at the sight of piss running down the woman's leg.

The weight in Diana slipped away, a space vacated, a place for her to be alone. Comfy. In some strange way, she'd almost come to trust the pressure, as though it were a constant hand on her stomach. The relief was sweeter and purer. No more fear here, no more. Her eyes eased shut and something materialized in the dark. She even grinned, the grin of someone far younger. A taste filled her mouth. Diana didn't know where it came from or why it should flitter over her tongue just then.

But there it was. Lovely.

Olives.

Her chest bloomed. A gigantic rose.

Wes watched her fly through the smoke; the shotgun recoiled. The stupid creatures at the back of the bus screamed. He deplored them for their predictability.

Diana slammed the floor, hands tossed above her head. Surrender.

Jed's mouth flapped open. Watching the woman die was like watching his sister die again. When he saw her body spitting blood into the air, he saw the stupid boy he'd shot earlier that day, too. He'd killed him near the Christmas cutouts, brains splattered against the angel's painted faces. Repulsed, Jed wanted the blood off his skin right that fucking second, so he wiped himself, but his cheeks were sticky. He caught a flash of distant movement in the corner of his eye and snapped his head to the driver's window.

It was his mother out there. She dragged his sister's remains over the doorstep and into their home. Jed bent over and vomited on his shoes.

Wes stepped forward, furious. "Into the fucking house, now!"

TWENTY-FIVE:
HOME

JED, WHO HAD run ahead of the rest, burst through the door, trembling and out of breath. The smell within hit him hard, offending and displacing his senses. Butcher shop stink. Blood. Raw meat. Shit. It wasn't just the room that smelled, but he, also.

Violent afternoon cartoons played too loud from the television. It was getting dark quick and the first hailstones were pelting the corrugated roofing, filling the house with hollow pot-and-pan rumblings.

Curtains billowed, signaling the arrival of rain.

Reggie cradled Liz between her legs by the kitchen door, hugged her from behind, an awkward bundle of limbs rocking to and fro.

She was conscious of the flesh in her hands, the sensation of her skin pressing against her daughter's dead weight, but her mind was mostly empty.

Once, she'd entertained the thought of being a teacher, only like most of her aspirations, it never eventuated. Instead, Reggie bounced between office work and retail, never quite happy. As a child, she dreamed of owning a horse, like every other girl her age. Some of her friends had horses—so why couldn't she? In the end, Reggie never got to ride her own Shetland or brush a mare that knew her by touch, and these days she hardly remembered the desire. Her one realized ambition was motherhood, though there had come a point somewhere along the line when Reggie forgot how to love the offspring she'd fought so hard for. This sadness was a wound that never healed because she'd never tried, ignorance turning it septic. So, Reggie looked at her daughter now, hoping against hope that it wasn't too late to be forgiven, and waited for an acknowledgement that would never come.

"I'm sorry, darlin'."

Sorry for what, Mum?

"I feel so bad I could go right ahead and jump off a cliff."

Don't say that.

Reggie held her daughter tight. "Then what should I say?"

Just tell me you love me and that everything will be okay. Liz smiled at her, so beautiful in the cloudy light with her glowing eyes.

A sharp pain in Reggie's chest. "I'm sorry, Elizabeth. I'm sorry for not being there for you. I don't know what happened to me. I knew you were alone and I saw it, plain as day. I don't think there's ever going to be a way for me to forgive myself for what I've gone and done to you. Darlin', you got such a sadness about you all the time. It scares me, always has. I don't know how to fix it. I should be able to. I'm your Mumma-Bear. I love you. Everything's going to be okay." Reggie kissed her on the cheek. "Maybe you can help me put the Christmas decorations up in a bit. You know, together? Take our minds off all this silly stuff."

But, Mum, it's not Christmas.

Reggie smiled. "Baby, that don't matter. As far as I'm concerned, I'm giving you a Christmas every day from here on in." They hugged once more. "I'll cook you up a meal, what you think?"

Jed watched his mother talking to a headless corpse.

Behind him, the rain and hail fell harder. The voices of his father and the three remaining passengers carried on the wind.

Reggie turned to him, her face covered in blood and brain matter from when she'd buried her chin in her daughter's open spine. "Liz, your brother just came in." She bent close to the body—the remains of the head swung heavily and thumped against its shoulder. "Jed, your sister is asking for you."

He screamed so loud he feared something in him would snap. His hip knocked over a vase and it shattered on the floor, dead flowers and soiled water splashing his feet. Gagging, he ran for the staircase, every step a struggle. Heat fired through him and his skin itched. Hurt, so much hurt everywhere. Blood poured from his gashed hands. He knocked family photos from the wall as he went.

Wes climbed out of the bus first and kept the shotgun on the passengers as they crawled through the windshield. They dropped onto the dirt one at a time. Jed, who had joined his father outside, followed, slipped and fell. He bounced back up, almost embarrassed. His boy was weakening, could see it in his face. Jed looked like he'd lost weight, even over the course of a day.

"Go ahead and tell your mother that I'm bringing them inside."

"Dad, I can't leave you alone."

Don't make me go back in there, please, he thought. *Mum's gone.*

"Appreciate that, son, but just go tell your fucking mother I'm bringing them in." Wes kept his eye on the passengers; especially on the broad-shouldered man with the goatee—that one had life in him.

"Go, now!"

Wes scowled and stepped forward with the gun. Jed ran from his sight, and he listened to the retreating footsteps.

"Get in a line," he told the passengers. "Lady first, then the boy." He studied the man. "You last. Got it?"

They acted immediately, hands on their heads.

"Now walk to the house. You run and I'll shoot you dead. Got that?"

None of them answered.

"You bet your fucking ass you got it. March."

Hail blanketed the valley. It crunched under their feet as they shuffled, it cracked and jabbed at their scalps. Wes followed them, watching their every movement for indications that one of them might dodge from the Indian-file and sprint for the trees. Rest assured, should one of them try, he—or she—would no longer be breathing for long. Zero chances. And if the others scattered, then they too would be shot to smithereens. Wes had a good aim, although there wasn't much to practice on in James Bridge. The nearest shooting gallery was miles away, and there was little worth hunting in this part of the state. Rabbits, mostly. He enjoyed shooting rabbits because they exploded when the bullet entered their fragile, disease-infected bodies. One minute a fuzzy bunny—and the next: a big old splatter on the ground.

I could just shoot them now. I'm in so far over my head anyway. What difference would it make? If I got in real close, a bullet might tear through two of them. Man, that'd be something to see.

His finger tensed the trigger. He moved in close behind the man with the goatee.

Jesus, Wes, what the hell are you thinking?

The sound coming from him wasn't quite a laugh, not quite a moan either. A girlish sound, excited and wavering.

I'm not thinking at all—and it feels fucking great. For the first time in my life, I feel alive.

The old woman with the short, spiked hair reached the first step leading up to the verandah. She turned to him, unsure of what to do ncxt.

"Yep, that's right," he said to her. "Up you go." Wes adored the sight of her dread. "One at a time. Quick."

TWENTY-FOUR

SARAH TRIPPED OVER the threshold and fell into the living room. Her glasses were back in the bus, and the heavy crucifix slapped against the side of her face. Though her vision blurred, the mother and daughter could be clearly viewed in their embrace across the room. It was like something from the Francis Bacon paintings her children had studied at school, the ones that upset her so much she'd written to the principal requesting the artist be removed from the curriculum. What she saw now was a grotesque knit-work of meats, impassioned and ungodly.

It made her sick.

As Sarah crawled across the musty carpet, Michael entered behind her, hands still on his head. Like Jed, the first thing he noticed was the smell. As a child, he'd talked his mother into buying him two pet mice for his birthday. This room smelled like the cage his pets called home—musty newspapers and urine and captivity and blood. Because unknown to his poor mother, one of the mice was cannibal, and it ate the other in the middle of the night.

This event schooled Michael in death.

A lesson he'd never forgotten.

He helped Sarah up. She was heavy, yet fragile under his touch, skin like rice paper. She held him close, hands turning into talons. Her sour breath against his lips.

They considered each other's eyes and knew they were going to die.

Sarah was grateful to him for giving her back some dignity. As foolish as it sounded, she would be ashamed to die on all fours.

Jack walked into the room, saturated from the rain. The front of his shirt had lifted to reveal the pad of his belly. A beat of quiet, just long enough for Jack to hear the flies. They zoomed past his ears, making him wince. Sudden cold on the back of his neck: the barrels of a shotgun pushing against his skin.

"Move forward," Wes said. And the passengers did as they were told.

Sarah, Michael, and Jack huddled close together. They saw the designs in the wallpaper, a crocheted rug of many colors flung over the arm of an overstuffed lounge. In the corner of the room, the television was playing. It seemed too bright as if the contrast was out of whack. Its images were distorted by the storm, jagged lines cut through cartoon characters as they leapt across the screen. A lamp in the shape of two kissing swans on top of a small round table.

The mother sat amongst these homely belongings, in a room that could have been anywhere in Australia, cradling the headless remains of the driver.

Wes stepped closer, trailing his aim on the group and kicked the door shut. It slammed hard, changing the airflow within the house. The curtains next to him reached out in ghostly grasps. Thunder shook the house again, making crockery dance in the kitchen. Wes saw his wife then and tried to speak. His face knotted, head shook, squinting.

What spilled from his mouth were softly spoken words.

"Reggie, what are you doing?"

Hailstones came down heavy and lightning tore the sky apart. Sheets of rain swept over the house, the drumming furnace-loud.

Reggie shifted the corpse in her lap and grabbed the loose, toothless jawbone. "Don't be scared, darl'. It's just Poppa-Bear. Time for us to have our grown-up talk."

Wes' face rolled red, the gun shaking in his hands. He heard his wedding ring tapping against the metal shaft—it sounded like Morse code.

"Merry Christmas," Reggie said to her husband.

"For Christ's sake, woman. Put her down!"

TWENTY-THREE

UPSTAIRS, JED THREW the bathroom door open and the handle smashed the wall. Almost slipped on the tiles. Panting hard, fast. Locked himself in. Scolding vomit threatened to rise in his throat again, so he grabbed the porcelain washbasin to steady himself. What he saw in the mirror made him recoil.

The reflected man couldn't be him.

This man's skin was covered in matted bits and pieces of other people.

A murderer.

Jed laughed. No, he wasn't a murderer. He was a youngish, fucked up, average guy. If anything, his worst crime was being a cliché, not a killer. He'd seen enough movies to know that murderers lurked in the dark, sharpening their knives; they danced in the moonlight wearing their mother's clothes and made lampshades from the skins of their victims.

He was just Jed.

History wouldn't remember him—he wasn't some future horror icon.

I'm as common as the cold.

The man in the mirror was someone *special.*

"So you can't be me."

Jed pulled his shirt over his head, revealing the eagle on his back. He forced his jeans around his ankles, kicked them hard against the wall, all the time repeating to himself, "not me, not me, not me."

He threw back the shower curtain.

Screech-screech-screech.

No, that was from that movie *Psycho*. That sound had nothing to do with Jed Frost, amateur boxer and so-so drug dealer.

He turned on the taps, not caring if it was hot or cold as long as it was running. Water splashed his face and poured down his chest in a gelatinous soup. The sight frightened him. So much blood pooled between his toes.

Blood, Mother! B-b-blood. Blood!

No, that was the character from the movie. *Norman Bates—the girly-boy.*

Balance failed him. Jed reached out, grabbed the curtain and slipped in the tub. Pinpricks of icy water danced through the air. The curtain tore off its rail, the oval brackets spinning. He thumped against the basin and pain exploded inside his head.

Jed's testicles drew up into his abdomen and he shifted his weight, squelching skin over porcelain until his buttocks covered the plughole. The tub started to fill.

"Not me," he continued to say. "Not me. Not me."

TWENTY-TWO

SARAH NUZZLED MICHAEL'S NECK.

He smells like Bill. Perhaps the two men even shared the same taste in cologne. Was it Old Spice, she wondered, or maybe Imperial Leather? Something with a ship on the bottle, sails unfurled and billowing in a breeze. It didn't matter either way in the end; this wasn't an attractive evocation. If anything, the familiarity startled her—and then it dawned why. These matching colognes were artificialities masking the natural, a musk to hide almost dead things, to hide fear.

Bill.

Thirty-nine years of marriage. While the majority of that time had been well spent, the skeleton of their relationship weathered dislocations more than once. In 1960, Bill, for some reason, thought it was okay to indulge in his newfound penchant for younger women. Caught in the act, he said that regardless of the error, his heart was hers forever, but owning it came with a caveat: he demanded she acquiesce and accept his flaws. Only human. Humans made mistakes. Bill compared himself to a stinger in the sea, floating around, purposeless, and explained the necessity of clinging to others so you don't go under. This hurt Sarah most, more than the affair itself. Above all else, he was loving and loyal. Just not always to her. Despite initial temptations, she didn't leave him. They persevered, and with time, those dislocated bones realigned.

The ache never left, however. *I'll never forget.*

They raised two children and together watched them breeze into adulthood. In a blink, the nest emptied, and Sarah and Bill stared down the barrel of retirement. The concept of buying an RV and heading inland to explore Australia's red center became a sudden possibility—the two of them gone in plume of dust to join all the other gray nomads on the open road, men and women like them who had worked hard and were now reaping what they had sown.

One. More. Blink.

Bill's diagnosis.

Sarah threw in the towel as an assistant at K-Mart, which hurt, because giving up one's job was *not* the same as retiring, her farewell cake frosted with pity, not sugar. They sold their Toyota to pay for medical supplies insurance wouldn't cover instead of contributing these funds to the RV she'd been eying off at Davenport's Used Dealership on Torrance Road. Sarah then dedicated her time to sweeping Bill's hair off the floor, mopping up his vomit. When he shat the bed, she starched the sheets until they grew brittle as crème brûlée toffee—Bill's favorite, though it didn't agree with his stomach anymore. Too rich.

That was love.

It petrified Sarah to think that she would outlive him. This thought plagued her on 'bad days'. On a 'good day', however, she sat back in her recliner and comfortably said, "Well done, girl. You haven't cried since yesterday!" A bitter victory if there ever was one.

Sarah distanced herself when she could, sitting alone, taking long walks. When Bill died on her, it would be she who was the stinger in the sea with nobody around to validate her purpose.

I don't want to be that person.

Not now, not ever.

On November 12th, 1995, Sarah caught the bus to Maitland because she wanted to escape her husband, even though it hurt to be apart. *Only that was the point.* She needed callouses on her emotional resolve. Being soft would be of no help to anyone—least of all herself—when the time came to bury Bill, when the sympathy casseroles stopped rolling in, and she was alone for good.

The plan had been to travel into town and walk streets that were just alien enough to distract her from reality. Maybe she'd swing by McDonalds Bookstore in the mall and browse through the titles. Afterward, maybe pick up an ice cream from the newsstand—something with nuts would be nice—and walk by the almost barren Hunter River. Coffee! There was a nice café near the bridge linking Maitland to Lorn, the adjoining suburb. Yeah, a big cup, black and with three saccharine spoonfuls, please. It would be nice to have strangers do something for her for a change, to pretend to care and fulfill her caffeine cravings, waving to her as she walked out the door.

Sarah told Bill that she had a doctor's appointment of her own, high blood pressure or something of the sort. A lame story and she knew it. In the privacy of her thoughts, she planned for it to sound false enough for him to know that she was lying. This way he would know how much his parting hurt her.

"Bill," she said.

The kid, Michael, looked at her, his eyes an echo of her husband's, her own, the father's, the insane mother's—all of them bar Jack, who appeared lively and prepared. That scared her.

Jack scared her.

"Let him go," the father said to her.

Sarah pulled away from Michael, and to her relief, he didn't cling on. Jack panted beside her.

The barrels of the shotgun pointed right at her.

Sarah experienced heaviness around her neck. Her crucifix, so thick and gaudy, faux jewels shimmering in the afternoon light. She'd often asked herself why she still wore the damn thing, the truth of the matter being that religion fought against her these days. That duel had been going on since the day that big RV in Davenport's Used Dealership set off into the sunset without Bill and her behind the wheel. Yet whenever Sarah took it off, she felt naked, and besides, as she told her grandchildren, *It's my bling*. That made them laugh, and that almost made her dedication worth it. What a fucking joke.

But right now, the crucifix was too heavy. Sarah alleviated some of that weight by caressing it in her hands, hands full of bones that never completely healed when broken. The years left her imperfect, proving that like her husband, Sarah was human after all. Love was arthritic.

Which meant she could die, too.

TWENTY-ONE

REGGIE CARESSED THE air where her daughter's cheeks should have been, were she to still possess a face. "Don't look, baby," she said, her voice syrupy with phlegm. "Daddy's got his gun. Who're these friends you've brought home? You should have told me so I could've had dinner cooked for them."

Wes stood over the remaining passengers as they dropped to their knees. He felt dissociated from what was happening, the gun a strange weight in his double grip—it teemed with energy he didn't think could be controlled. Comprehending what he had done proved a struggle, let alone what he knew he was about to do. That awareness sparked from a simple question, one he kept circling back around to: Who were these strangers, these people with their grotesque pantomimes and prayers? A shudder ripped through him, and Wes's mind re-entered his body. The answer didn't matter anymore. And he wanted it to stay that way.

He gripped the gun, sneered. It was he who couldn't be controlled, not it.

Sarah put her hands back behind her neck.

"That's right, that's right," Wes said, nodding.

Water dripped down his back and slipped into the cleft of his buttocks. Freezing. Small hailstones had stuck to his skin, mixed with the dirt blown in the storm, and turned into a thick, brown sludge. His hatred for them worsened now they were in his home; they polluted the carpet they kneeled against. Wes found it fitting that they would die in the living room of the family they tore apart. *Beg to die, fuckers. Beg and I'll give you what you need.*

How sweet that would be.

Power.

Wes gestured to his daughter's corpse. "Look at my girl."

Michael, Jack, and Sarah tilted their heads towards the kitchen doorway, though Michael's eyes remained pinched shut. Wes noticed this and stepped closer. He knew the kid could feel his shadow over his bruised and shaking form, knew he could smell the engine oil sweating from his pores. "Open your eyes, faggot."

In Michael's mind, waves crashed on white sand, the tide turning red. Limbs tumbled onto the shoreline and crabs scuttled from their burrows, danced sideways across the beach to feast. Ripping, tearing, nibbling.

"I said, open them." Wes lost his patience and pressed the end of the shotgun against the kid's lips.

Metal barrels banged against Michael's teeth. His ocean evaporated.

"That's better."

Michael's head spun. The gun tasted poisonous and his mouth hurt from where it pushed against his lips. Jaws ground open to make way for the barrels, though every instinct told him to do otherwise.

"That's it, put it in," Wes said. "As far as it'll go in your pussy mouth. Do it or I'll make a mess of you."

Michael's teeth chattered against iron. The gun was a dark highway before him, and on the horizon stood the father, a man surrounded by flowing clouds of curtain. "Now sing, faggot."

Silence except for the steady rain. Even the storm held its breath.

Michael cast a quiet wish. To whom, he didn't know.

I wish he would just pull the trigger. End it now. I've had enough. I'm already dead. In many ways, this is better.

I deserve this.

"Sing, faggot. You sing for my baby."

From the other side of the room, there came a voice. Thin and wavering, Reggie talking to the corpse. "Gee whiz, Liz. You need to wash your hair! You stink."

An atom bomb of anger dropped from the sky and landed in Wes's head. Detonated. His repulsion was an elixir he welcomed. He ripped the gun from the kid's mouth and turned it on his wife, flinging Michael to the floor in the process, the corner of his mouth torn open.

Sarah screamed.

"Woman," Wes yelled at his wife. "Let her go!"

Jack dug a hand into the pocket of his jeans now that the moment he'd been waiting for had come. Warm and wet inside. Fingers grabbed the handle of the utility knife he'd stashed in there before being led from the bus. Anxious to cut, he watched the father stagger across the room.

Wes eased the gun into his left hand, and slapped

Reggie across the face with his right, funneling all his weight into the blow. She slammed against the doorframe, hands shooting to her cheek. A bleat from her throat.

Gasping, Wes snatched his daughter's limp arm. The gun trailed the ceiling in abandon. With strength drawn from the last of his reserve, he dragged the corpse across the floor in three mighty tugs. He deposited her before the passengers. Skinny arms slapped the floor and the front of Liz's shirt drew open to expose a loose-fitting bra.

Blue skin.

Reggie slumped until her head brushed the ground—cool and inviting. She wanted to close her eyes and let the ringing in her ears usher her to sleep. It would be so easy to give in to the dark, to let it take her to a better place. Though disappointing, shock held her in a state of consciousness.

Jack peered at the father from within his bottom-of-the-well eye sockets. At his knees were the driver's remains; they reminded him of The Scarecrow from *The Wizard of Oz,* only after the winged monkeys tore him to shreds. The thought made him snigger.

Wes turned the gun towards Jack.

"You got a sorry for my baby girl, smiler?" The expression on his face changed. One moment he was serious and tortured, and the next he grinned. Lips ripped back, revealing the shine and polish of dentures. The loose skin around his mouth stretched taut. His eyes drew to thin slits surrounded by crow's feet. The laugh that seeped out of him was wheezy and full of spite. "Now *this* is a smile," he said.

TWENTY

JED HEARD EVERYTHING happening downstairs from the bathroom. Cringing, he stepped into his jeans. They slipped over his jagged hipbones with ease. He didn't bother with underwear or a shirt; they were in a wet, red pile in the corner. Water still ran from the showerhead. A single scarlet thread dribbled down the side of the tub.

Fingers formed a net in front of his face, a lattice between him and the mirror. His heartbeat raced as though he'd gotten "wet", but he was sure the drug was no longer in his system.

Pain and bleeding cuts and images of people flying apart in slow motion. His sister running at him with open arms.

He recalled how Liz came to him earlier that morning to say goodbye, as if she'd known these were her last hours. He'd seen a similar frightened and confused look on her face when they had gotten high together that one time in the shed, the day he'd lost control. He'd slammed her in the face with the heel of his foot. *She didn't bleed until after she hit the ground. The punching bag rocking on its chain. It swung at him—only it wasn't a punching bag anymore. It was the body of the boy he'd shot that afternoon hanging at the end of a noose. Swung back into shadow. A shape emerged from the shadows. Liz this time. She screamed, eyes rolling back into her skull. She disappeared and then there was just the man who looked like him, the man he'd seen beyond the lattice of interwoven fingers.*

Jed lashed out.

The mirror shattered under his knuckles. Slivers of reflection fell from sight.

NINETEEN

WES JABBED THE twin barrels of the gun against the side of Jack's head. "You want to kiss my daughter, you disgusting piece of shit?" he hissed. "You gonna marry her? Did you fuck my daughter?"

Each blow hurt but Jack resisted pulling the knife from his pocket. He wasn't going to risk blowing this bet until he was positive the timing was right. Chances didn't exist in this house, if indeed they ever did. The final smack of metal against scalp echoed loud and hollow. "Stop-stop it!" Jack said.

"Stop? You *dare* say stop to me?" Wes stared, incredulous. "Okay, you said it." Wes recoiled then spat a heavy wad of spit on the man kneeling before him. He pointed the gun at the old woman instead. She recoiled in shock, arching backwards, stopped her fall by slamming palms against the carpet. Her exposed throat.

"Why don't you tell me to stop, lady?" Wes inquired.

Sarah felt no pain, even though her body contorted into a position no woman her age should attempt, let alone accomplish. Her kneecaps, tight underneath her weight, popped off their hinges. She saw the window, the only source of light in the room. Through the curtains, she caught a come-and-go glimpse of green sky.

The silhouette of a man outside.

Lightning speared, so bright and final.

The man was gone.

"*Bill.*"

The father reached down and yanked the crucifix from the chain about her neck. Its weight left her body, and for the first time, Sarah didn't feel naked in its absence. If anything, it freed her. An unburdening.

The crucifix landed on the floor beside Wes's favorite chair.

His shotgun went off, welcoming fireworks of flesh. The recoil hurt Wes's arms. "Bugger," he said, a perfunctory word drowned by Michael and Jack's screaming.

Reggie called to her husband from the kitchen. "God damn it, Wes. You got mud all over the floor." She stepped into the adjoining room, grabbed the accordion door separating the two, and slammed it shut behind her. "You know how I hate it when you don't wipe your shoes on the mat."

Not that Michael heard the mother's tantrum over the ringing in his ears, a chime that gave way to rumbling, like that of an oncoming vehicle, one not too dissimilar to the bus that brought them to this innocuous two-story house in the middle of the Hunter Valley, the bus that homed the dead and flies. The rumbling was a kind of truth, a confirmation of cause and effect. Although it faded, its realities remained.

Sarah was dead.

The eyes of the shotgun slid into his vision with nightmarish slowness. Beyond the smoking tunnels issued the voice of the man with his finger on the trigger. “Look what you did, boy.”

Michael heard, *mmm-wahha-hhh-hhh-mwhh*.

An enormous sucking sound, like someone slurping liquid through a long straw. The ringing ended and sound engulfed Michael’s senses. The drum of rain against the corrugated roof *(so loud!)*. The father’s wedding ring as it tapped the shotgun *(make it stop!)*.

Shoot me now, Michael thought. *This is how it ends*.

I’m ready.

“Are you a faggot, boy?” the father asked. The question stabbed him. It hurt so much more to be asked than to be told.

Wes relished the terror in the boy’s eyes—but refused to be sidelined by it. He hadn’t forgotten the other man, and Wes reminded the bastard by gracing him with a quick, definitive wink.

“I asked you a question. I said, are you one of those faggots?”

“Kill me,” Michael said. “Please.”

“That’s not the answer to my question, boy.” He turned to the man with the goatee. “Was it, mate?”

Jack had been waiting for the right moment to pounce. All of his energy funneled into this calculation. The question shattered his train of thought, brow furrowing. “What?”

“Was it?”

“No.”

"Damn straight it wasn't." A mean twinkle in his eye. "So, boy. Is you, or ain't you?"

Huge, body-wracking tears erupted from Michael. "Please stop."

"IS YOU OR AIN'T YOU? *ANSWER THE FUCKING QUESTION*!"

"God, no. No! No, I'm not." It didn't even occur to Michael to tell the truth. He'd been lying to people for so long the deceit came naturally—even now.

"You're not, eh?"

"No!"

"You being straight up with me, boy?"

"Yes!"

"Then touch her pussy." Wes gestured to Sarah. The way the word—*pussy*—puffed within his cheeks and punched its way from his mouth satisfied him. A hateful birth of hot air.

Wes knew he could make them do anything. They could be parented.

Michael's skin tightened about his skeleton, making the flesh caught in between squeeze into cramps. Those words sunk in. *Then touch her pussy.* As best he knew, the human mind wasn't equipped to contemplate such commands—the sane mind, at least. His horror turned to despair that there were people like the father in the world at all, and in that very second, Michael overwhelmed with empathy for the driver who had rerouted their lives in the first place.

How did she grow up in this house without killing herself?

Numbness bathed him again, the ocean having returned. Michael let himself be lost to its brine, to its salt. The tsunami couldn't have come at a more opportune moment because his *empathy* had come so close to slipping into *sympathy*. That couldn't happen. Not now, not ever. There was strength in knowing the difference, of that Michael was certain.

Strength.

Some people were born tough, fighters through and through. He envied this lucky majority. And in contrast, there were the Michael Delaneys of the world, men raised to believe they were weak—and why *wouldn't* he take their judgment as gospel? As it had been pointed out to him over and over again, Michael didn't look or sound or walk as a man should. The mold was clearly set, a fact evidenced by Adonis-perfect statues filling museums across the planet; in photos reproduced in three-buck magazines as they bleached in shop front windows; paraded to viewers via the television set day after day, night after night.

The Great Underestimation.

However, in the end, Michael knew statues were only stone. Magazine photos were just clots of dots that didn't look like anything when you got up close. Television was cherry-picked illusion and electricity.

It paid to remember this when the world was against you.

As a child, Michael could have walked a different way home from school and avoided Mr. Maclachley's dog. But he didn't. Though it would have been hard, he could have kept on denying the parts of him that were easy to hate, and bubble-wrapped himself in lies and deposited the mess behind a picket fence. But he didn't. He could have done the easy thing and felt sympathy for the driver of route 243, a slope, which when tilted too far, slid the empathetic into a pool they ended up drowning in. But he didn't.

Some people stumbled into strength, and that was okay.

Because if it wasn't, the conspirators of The Great Underestimation won.

EIGHTEEN: JED BLEEDS

"DAD!"

Wes swung towards the staircase and the gun swung with him.

"Dad!"

Wes saw his eight-year-old son standing in the shadows of the hall, a line of paper dolls holding hands in a downward smile strung across the archway above. It seemed impossible that such a huge yell could issue from someone so tiny. Wes clutched the carving knife, watched Jed crouching low.

Anger danced with disgrace. These bloody kids had him wrapped around their little fingers. That wouldn't stand. A lesson had to be taught, and so a lesson they would receive—just as Wes's own father had taught him. One day his children would understand. Character was carved.

It paid to bleed out the bad if that was what it took.

A father had a right to discipline his children.

Liz sprawled on the ground at his feet. Shirt ripped open at the collar, one of the denim suspenders of her overalls unclipped.

Jed began to cry.

"Stop crying," Wes told his son, huddled at the top of the stairs, arms folded across his chest, hands pushed deep into the crotch of his blood-stained jeans. Tears rolled down Jed's cheeks. He looked freshly showered.

"I said stop!"

"Cut out the tears, boy."

The child's sobs did not end.

Blubbering like a little girl, Wes thought. *How did I spawn such soft, forgettable chickens? They both did wrong, so why do they fight me every time?*

Wes knew that on some level he enjoyed indulging in anger. He bathed in its brightness. Glorious. Pure.

The knife. It felt so powerful in his hand. He hoped they would never forget him like this, standing there in his prime.

He wondered why he should keep this rage locked away. Rage could be useful.

"You can't do this, Dad!"

Insolence. Wes stepped over his daughter, who

reached out at him but missed. Her hand landed beside a forgotten toy truck.

Am I invisible? Didn't I tell them to put their shit away hours ago?

He crossed the room, knife before him as though it were an extension of his arm.

The gun leveled at Jed.

Wes was alive with energy. Why had he resigned to living in the shadows of composure for so long? It had been years since he felt this good. He breathed new oxygen now.

My new life.

Every step towards his fatherly right to discipline and shape his children into what he wanted them to be was a step closer to a happiness he thought he would never have.

SEVENTEEN

WES RUSHED AT *the little boy framed by paper dolls.*

Which will rip easier? *he wondered. He laughed a little, even though a part of him was sad.*

He brought the knife up and before he knew what he was doing, lashed out to see his power enacted upon the world in the flesh of his son. Jed lifted up his hands to shield his face.

The wounds winked at Wes, and he stopped, lowering the gun.

Jed's slit wrists crisscrossed before his face.

"I'm sorry, Dad."

The arm holding the gun fell to Wes's side. He looked up the staircase. Along the walls, over the balustrade, were dark red smears and splashes.

Jed shied away from his father. He was getting dizzy. Incredible pain—he could never have anticipated such hurt. How long did it take for a person to die from such wounds? He hoped he'd snipped all the right veins; though he was sure he had.

When he slid the six-inch shard of broken mirror through his flesh, there had been an instant spray that freckled the ceiling. The thumping in his head came fast and grew constant, panic forcing his heartbeat on. He knew this was good. The quicker his heart forced blood through his body, the quicker he would bleed out.

Only then would the screaming stop.

Wes stood motionless, watching his son slowly dying right before his eyes. Thoughts shattered, he tried to form words. Only nothing came. The wires in his brain severed as effectively as Jed's wrists, and he was numb as a result.

He failed to hear the footsteps thudding across the room.

Jack plowed into the father, forcing him into a bookshelf—and not onto the floor, as intended. His aim was to get the man under his knees and then slash and slash and slash until there was nothing left to tear up.

The shotgun clattered against the carpet nearby.

With his left hand, Jack drove the extended blade of the utility knife into the father's upper torso. The blade slipped in easily.

Books rained about them.

A few yards away, Jed collapsed in a semi-faint. His head slammed the staircase railing on the way down.

Michael was still on his knees, mouth opened wide.

SIXTEEN

WES WATCHED HIS attacker raise a bloodied fist. It lingered. Descended, bringing the blade down with it, razoring the air, whistling as it went. Blood like red stars falling and exploding against his face. Wes didn't feel the square-ended knife slip inside his cheek, nor did he feel it snap against his gums. Almost casually, as though there was no such thing as agony, he reached past the splayed books for the shotgun. Fingers latched onto the barrel and wrapped around the trigger. He heaved it up, but the bastard on his stomach caught the blur of movement and halted his movement with a forearm block.

An explosion of light and sound; a hole opened in the ceiling. A huge cloud of plaster dust wafted over them.

The helix in-curve rim of Jack's external ear disappeared, the wound cauterized by the heat of the blast. His hand shot to the side of his face to touch the part of him that remained, and he shrieked.

Wes dropped the now useless, empty gun. Punches were all he had left.

Michael snapped from his reverie. The sound of the gunshot severed rationality from fear and fear from emotion, with only raw adrenalin left behind. *Go now,* screamed every instinct. And to this demand, Michael listened. He leapt to his feet.

Jack and the father rolled in the direction of the front door—not that there was any intent to do so, the tug and roll of their fight simply led them that way. Curtains billowed in the wind about them like impaled ghosts attempting escape. Lighting threw bursts of silver light through the house, shooting spidery shadows where there had been none before, and thunder followed almost immediately, so vicious and brutal it shook the valley. Though hail ceased hammering the corrugated roof, rain petered on.

Michael studied the front door, which wasn't a feasible escape because Jack and the father fought there. So he pivoted his focus to the one remaining exit in the room, excluding the staircase, of course: the accordion door separating this room from the next.

He spirited away, diving over scattered books. Slammed the sliding door, felt it heave against his weight. It tore from its runners and bent in the middle, a snapping sound amid the chaos and cartoon boings-and-donks of the television. His fingers grabbed at the handle and pulled. It wouldn't budge. Michael forced his fingers into the gap. It was a cruel parody of the bus door after the car slammed into it. Pulled hard. The door came clean away.

Light from the kitchen spilled into the living room, and in this pallid luminescence, Jack observed the wounds he'd inflicted upon the man. The sight of all that red sent a thrill through his body, made his cock twitch. As though jiving with that sexual power, he shot his index finger into a gash in father's cheek. It slid sideways, and when he yanked it free, the sun-spotted skin ripped like an opened envelope.

Storm fire bathed the kitchen a sickly green.

The mother stood near the oven with her back to Michael. Every cupboard was open. He'd gone to Taronga Zoo in Sydney on a school excursion once, and the kitchen smelled like the monkey house there—shitty and damp. The door of the refrigerator was ajar, broken jam containers and carrots spotting the floor.

The woman turned with a smile stretched tight across her face. In her hands, she held a raw chicken. Slimy in her grasp. Her words drew out, a record run at half speed. *"Bird's been ooooutt too long. Salmonellla in theee blood."*

Michael backed against the wall. Across the room was the closed door leading to the backyard.

Run, he told himself. *Now!*

FIFTEEN

THE OLD MAN attempted to grab Jack's hair but it was too closely cropped to hold on to. Instead, those thick fingers latched to his shirt, tearing it at the collar.

End this not because you have to, but because you want to, said the voice in Jack's head. The tone was sweet and low and comforting. *You have to end this because you were put on this earth to end it all.*

Jack had the father pinned underneath him once again. He smashed the face with a tightly clenched fist and heard the nose shatter.

Jed was on his side at the foot of the steps, bleeding to death. His world darkened, but not quick enough. It left him wondering how much longer he had to live. So silly—Jed assumed it would all blink out in an instant. Of course, he thought to himself almost wryly, a swift mercy would be denied. He'd never had the luck of the Irish. Not with girls, not with gambling, and not now when he needed it most, here in his final moments.

Though moving remained difficult, he could still see. Jed watched the passenger lean in close to his Dad's face as though he were going to kiss him.

Jack hefted himself upright and spat the lips he'd bitten off into the air.

FOURTEEN

MICHAEL PULLED THE door inwards as the mother's body pressed against him from behind, her heat on his skin. He grabbed her doughy face and forced her away with what remained of his strength. She flailed and an image crackled through his head: priests on late-night Evangelical commercials throwing the blessed to church floors. He dove outside, the contrast like a changed channel. Where there should be ground, there was a low step, just loose-packed bricks. One toppled under his heel. He slammed the earth. Instant pain. Rolled onto his back and saw static, saw lightning.

Jangling chains and panting.

Michael arched his head and took in the upside-down countryside. Between himself and the trees, which formed a fence at the back of the yard, there was a clothesline. Saturated sheets hung over its wires, flapping like wet skins.

A heaving blur ran straight at his face.

He was twelve and in his school uniform again, knees shaking. His face tattooed by the shadows of Mr. Maclachley's junkyard fence. On the other side, the mechanic's dog rushed at him, kicking dirt. The dog's maw the size of a dinner plate, breath hot through the wire as it tried to climb and attack and tear apart little boys who were far too inquisitive for their own good. Boys like Michael.

He didn't realize what was running at him until it was too late.

The Rottweiler sunk its teeth into his shoulder. Gasps, ripping.

Oh God, let that have been my shirt, he thought, frantic. But he knew better.

Long teeth snapped over his flesh—he could smell the blood already. Bitter foam splashed into his mouth. Two eyes buried in black fur. The dog pulled and dragged. It was bound to the clothesline by a thick chain, a trench in the lawn from where the Rottweiler had run back and forth. Michael punched at the dog, felt the bone under its slick muzzle, smelled saliva and grass.

Incomparable pain in his shoulder. Shock blunted it for a while, though not long enough.

Seventy-five pounds of dog bore down on him. He lashed out again, yelling.

It took three more punches for the dog to howl and release its jaws. The moment the teeth withdrew from his flesh, blood gushed.

Michael slipped in the newly churned mud, linked to the dog by strands of flesh and shirt. As he crawled away, every movement proved an agony. *I can't do this,* he said to himself, yet pushing on just the same. *I can't.*

He watched the dog shake its head, hindquarters squared. It ran again.

The dog's lips hauled back to reveal black gums. Blood dripped from its tongue. Overhead lightning haloed the animal.

Michael's eyes closed and he saw the junkyard fence. It saved him so many times in that no man's land between school and home. But not today.

The chain pulled taut, yanking the dog hard against its collar. It slipped sideways with a bark. Michael watched it howl, relief coming from some small, undamaged part of him. The dog continued its endless arc at the end of the chain.

Michael touched his shoulder, terrified at the *things* sticking up out of his skin. Again, realization snapped back at him and he understood: *that's my muscle*.

"FUCK!"

The yard was bigger than he'd first thought. Electricity landed in the valley, shaking the ground. He forced himself to his feet and swayed, body waltzing with the trees as they blew in the wind. Michael didn't have time to open his mouth and drink from what fell from the sky but he did so anyway. Drops ran down his throat, igniting a flare of life within.

More, I need more.

He licked his lips and shuffled from the house.

Daylight faded, sun swallowed by storm.

From somewhere behind him there came the sound of crashing glass, and a woman's scream.

Michael stared through the veils of rain to the back door. It slammed open. The mother fell onto the top step; another brick shifted and fell under her fingers. She hung over the threshold like a half-consumed mouse in the jaws of a snake, her lower half lost in the dark of the doorway. She scrambled, hands outstretched. Her teeth were stained red.

"Help!"

Her plea—and yes, that was what it was—was cut short as someone pulled her backward into the house by the ankles. As she disappeared, Michael felt a part of him go with her.

He dropped to his knees.

Leaves blew. Water pooled in the puncture wounds on his shoulder. His mind told him it was time to give up. Black dots painted the house and grass—only no, it was his vision starting to fail; there was no artist here, no controlled hand crafting beauty from chaos. Michael squinted. A shadow stood in the doorway.

I've come so far, I'm the last of them all and now it's my turn to go.

What did I do to deserve this?

I wish. I wish. I wish.

Only Michael didn't know what to wish for anymore. Perhaps that didn't matter, perhaps he didn't even *need* to. Because he wasn't alone; the crazy woman was gone now and he couldn't hear those crashing sounds from inside the house.

The shadow, his remaining company, stepped into light.

It held something in its hands.

The rain whispered lullabies to Michael as he kneeled in the grass. *Just put your head down and it will all be over*. Sleep.

Such a sweet, sweet idea.

Don't faint. Don't. Not. Now.

Michael collapsed anyway. As the world spun on its axis, lightning flashed, illuminating the doorway of the house. In the flickering light, a familiar man's face etched against the black. That face grinned from ear to ear.

THIRTEEN

THE MAN NAMED Jack stood in the doorway. Only it wasn't Jack. Sure, it looked like him, had the same muscular arms and tell-tale cheekbones as him; but this figure was *not* the same person who had been with Michael and the other passengers on the bus. Couldn't be. *This* man was covered in gore and held a pair of long-bladed sewing scissors. Though it would be easy to dismiss Michael's conclusion as pain warping perception, he believed—perhaps more than he'd believed anything—that the person emerging from the house wasn't even a 'he' anymore, rather a thing, a thing that had lost the most important parts of itself along the line, debris trying to piece itself back together again, only failing, always failing, and then becoming defined by that failure.

Maybe—

No. No maybe. Michael knew that he was seeing true.

This thing was an 'it'. A beast.

The Beast.

Michael pushed himself up off the ground, sluggish like someone coming out of hyper-sleep in the science fiction movies he got such a kick out of, despite the protestations of his parents who didn't have time for that silly stuff. They always wanted to watch gardening shows or grainy documentaries about wars in countries Michael couldn't for the life of him pinpoint on a map, places torn apart by violence he assumed he'd never be able to relate to.

So many hours spent fighting for television real estate.

Sometimes Michael won. Sometimes he lost.

However, on those evenings when he emerged victorious, he vicariously lived among stars where aliens prowled the hallways of flying cargo ships. In sewers accommodating cannibalistic clowns.

Here, he was most at home. Whilst in his own house, Mum and Dad shook their heads and *tsk-tsked* the interests that made him who he was.

Despite the self-consciousness they stoked in him, Michael hungered for their company more than ever. He'd happily take their judgements, welcome their weird ways of loving. And he would do all this with the enthusiasm of a freed prisoner desperate for the comfort of the cage again. Just one more day. Just one more chance to be with them.

Take me from this place.

Take me back.

The hyper-sleep sensation vanished. He was in the present. Awake. Those long-bladed scissors had stripped the fictions from his life, leaving behind the wet grass between his fingers as he drew himself upright, that icy rain, and The Beast, a thing that rolled all those silly science fiction and horror movie threats into one.

It took a step. Another. Closer.

Towards me?

"Oh, God. No."

Scissors slit beads of rain as it swung them through the air.

Pain was everything, but Michael forced himself to move anyway. He turned to run, his sense of direction as unfocused as his vision. Though it seemed so long ago, Michael's day began with a frantic dash from a stranger's bed, a simple act that severed his old life from the new. That same day lingered on, only now Michael's frantic dash was to save his skin. And he'd never felt so tender.

He headed for the trees. In their gnarled bulks faces laughed, like those he'd seen in Thailand when the ladyboys made fun of his jiggling man-breasts and stretch marks. The water splashing his face smelled of chlorine, of the pool. A flashback to his schoolmates and the way they stared at his body. Obvious, uncaring.

Michael's run started to slow, his fat dragging him down.

The trees continued to laugh as he disappeared amongst their branches.

TWELVE:
JACK

JACK WAS THE smallest kid in class. He hated being short, hated being so narrow shouldered. Everyone else was broad and tall. Some boys even had hair on their upper lips.

Though the runt of the pack, he emerged popular but never the ringleader he wanted to be. Time resigned him to their jokes about his size, and on some level, he hated himself for letting them get away with it.

Jack accepted that he wasn't extraordinary, or noticeable. In class, he raised his hand even if he didn't know the answer just so his teacher—whom he loved and often dreamed about–would look in his direction. She never did. He had no great aspirations and came from average blue-collar stock. Jack appeared destined to be forgotten, and worst of all, he knew it.

One recess, he slipped into the boy's restroom. In the farthest stall, he sat on the toilet seat and opened his backpack, dug through notebooks and lunch wrappers to fish out a pen. Nervous, he scribbled words against the back of the door. The tip against the paint squeaked like sneakers on the gymnasium floor.

Sat back. Looked at his handiwork. Proud.

He put the pen in his mouth and chewed on the end.

ur mother sucks coks in hell

It was a line from a movie he'd never seen and knew only by reputation. *The Exorcist*. He couldn't wait until he was old enough to watch it. He left the toilet stall just as a prefect rang the yard bell, signaling their return to class.

Later when the students were dismissed for the day, instead of going to the shelter under the school verandah where their bikes were kept, Jack returned to the restroom to admire his mark upon the world. Inside there was a photocopied note from the assistant principal above the rusted urinal.

Students caught destroying school
property (incl. graffiti of any kind)
will be suspended.

The room smelled worse than it had a moment before. Above him, the neon light flickered. He went to the far stall and pushed the door open. Where there should have been his scrawl there was nothing but a swirled, gray blur.

Jack lost his virginity five years later to a woman named Rena. She was two years his senior and had curves in all the right places. When she broke up with him, he did nothing. Just stared at his hands and accepted that he had, once again, been erased.

Anger came later.

He found her in the James Bridge Pub parking lot, alone and waiting for a taxi. *Stupid girl's asking for trouble*, he thought. It had never occurred to him before that *he* might be that trouble. He realized then that he had the potential to be heard and dictate to others as others had dictated to him. The urge rushed over him too quickly to think of risks and repercussions. He pulled the back of his shirt over his head and hooked it under his nose, upturned it into a piggish snout. The material was thin enough that even in the dark he could still see through.

Fast. Punched her in the back of the neck.

The cigarette she'd been smoking flew in twisting, red sparks through the air. She landed hard on her knees, skirt lifting in the back to expose panties with a cherry blossom print. Jack never looked back. Later that night in the quiet of his room he masturbated, guilty and afraid, but aroused nonetheless.

Rumor spread through town that he committed the crime. Unlike Rome, rumors *could* be built in a day, and they even sometimes outlived the people they involved. Jack still captivated crowds with his charm, but his unpunished crime was remembered by those who counted. There was an indelible black mark against him now. Small towns like James Bridge rarely forgot.

His anger. Hot. Burning.

There were ways to vent. He screamed into his pillow or stabbed his mattress with a knife. One night, a casual fuck found him darting around the living room, ripping at the furniture, tearing the curtains. She called him a psycho. He kicked her out and held himself back from wrapping his fingers around her neck and squeezing her throat so tight she turned blue. It terrified him that he liked the image so much.

He never saw her again and that was okay. *Cunt amongst cunts.*

Jack filled out, sculpted his muscles. He liked looking at himself in the mirror, flexing his chest so it appeared like the men in the sports magazines, in the pornos he watched. He wished his dick were bigger, liked the idea of punishing a woman with it, sliding it in so far it cut. Deep down, girls liked to be hurt. Of that he was sure.

Nothing hotter than watching a woman screaming through a smile, right, Jack-o? the voice would ask.

That voice got him out of trouble more than it got him into it. He came to respect and love it. Never questioned its presence. It was his friend.

But now that voice was gone.

"Talk to me," Jack asked as he ran through the backyard of the driver's house, choking on water and excitement. "Where are you?"

Only gray swirls of silence. Panic filled him. He felt alone for the first time since cutting his cousin's fingers with the scissors, the day the voice entered his life.

"Talk to me!"

Something had taken his friend away. Someone. He knew there had to be blame. Blame made his world go 'round, kept him sane. If there was nobody nearby to hate, there was no reason to be angry. Why exist *without* anger?

Everyone was dead except the one person he hated more than the rest.

Jack watched him run like a limp-wristed girl. Even through the sleet, he could see the flies swarming around him, could hear their buzzing over the dog's incessant bark. Jack knew why the swarm flocked to the kid: he was dying. It made perfect sense. The kid must be riddled with the gay plague slowly wiping the dirty fucks off the planet. How could he not have realized it before?

I will help the disease.

The scissors in his hands were the faggot's failing organs; every cut a Kaposi's sarcoma legion. In many ways, Jack respected, even admired the plague. It showed no mercy; it was almost enough to make him believe in God.

ELEVEN

THE UNEVEN GROUND beneath Michael's feet. Rocks jutted up through the earth with the sole purpose of tripping him over. He ran farther and farther into the trees. The sky was the color of a corpse—and Michael knew what a corpse looked like now. Heaven help him, he knew only too well.

Tunnel vision. Tugging branches. Twigs raked his skin.

The Beast pursued him.

Michael pushed himself harder than he ever had before. Every yard he put between him and The Beast was a yard closer to safety. He heard the monster crashing through branches behind him. Michael ran blind, praying for a road, or maybe to discover some half-buried weapon in the ground.

Lightning flashed. Trees in the strobe.

TEN

JACK SPRINTED THROUGH two places at once.

One was the dense Australian bush with its brambles and knots. The second was the room in which he'd killed the driver's father. He could see, clearer than the dwindling day itself, the ugly carpet lining the living room floor and the old man beneath him as he bent down to bite off his lips. They came off with such ease.

A scream. Coppery blood in his mouth.

Euphoric victory.

It was surprising how long it took to kill him. The human body was programmed to fight; a self-defeating trait, considering that in the end it was destined to give up the ghost. Given this, Jack found enjoyment in assisting someone fulfill his destiny.

The father had rolled around, grabbing where his lips should have been. Jack laughed. Damn funny! Power over another was a special kind of freedom.

A ceramic lamp in the shape of two swans kissing on a table near the television set. He picked it up, sneered at its tackiness, yanked the cord from the wall. Jack slammed it down on Wes's face, bulb shards impaling the eyes. They both heard them pop and *still,* he didn't die.

"Tough little fucker," Jack said.

He went into the kitchen with the hopes of finding something sharp. He found the fat old woman huddled on the floor. Once upon a time, he might have pitied her, but only disgust now. She scrambled for the open door, kicking a raw chicken in his direction. He laughed again as it skidded across the floor, featherless wings flapping. Absurd.

The mother didn't get far.

Jack went to the sink. Spoons and forks. He contemplated using the latter but shook the thought away. *Don't be a fool. A fork wouldn't kill her. Open the drawer and see what other goodies are inside.*

A long-bladed kitchen knife.

Ha. Happy birthday and all your Christmases rolled into one.

Jack grabbed the mother by the ankles and dragged her back inside. She shrieked louder than Rena had the day he punched her neck in the darkened parking lot. This was different, though. This time he was going all the way, baby. The knife found a home between her shoulder blades and the screaming stopped. Surprising. He watched her deflate like a pierced balloon, his head cocked with puppy dog curiosity. Blood didn't spurt as he thought it would. On some faraway level, it clicked that this was a fucked-up thing to think, his biting disappointment that she was a total non-event, but he didn't care.

Because—

"Hubby will make more noise," he told her, dismissive.

Jack snatched the knife from her back and stopped. His eyes caught a shimmer of silver to his left. What he saw erased the last good in him, and he knew he was brought here to do what *must* happen next. *My purpose.* Jack smiled. To think everyone thought he would amount to nothing, that he lacked ambition.

I might just end up remembered after all.

Next to the spice rack on the kitchen bench, a long-bladed pair of scissors hooked to the wall.

Jack followed his shadow through the living room, saw it creep over the old man, who by that point, had crawled to the couch where he pulled at the cushions in a laughable attempt at getting up. The curtains continued to billow. Cartoons in chaos.

"I'm blind! BLIND!"

Jack stood over him, scissors in hand. "Hey," he said. "Ever wondered what it feels like to be cut?"

NINE: PUNISHMENT

JACK ON HIS parents' bed from where he'd been thrown, face down, eyes closed. He waited for the unbuckling belt, a signal that his punishment was about to be enforced. And waited. Was his dad doing it slowly to prolong the torture? Or maybe he meant for it to be quiet—the element of surprise being the feature that distinguished this lashing from the others in the past.

Nothing. In the distance, his cousin's cries.

Jack opened his eyes.

The bulge of his father's stomach through the apron he wore. In his hands, he held the blood-streaked scissors Jack used to slit open Charles's hands and fingers.

"What you doing, Dad?"

"Don't speak, boy."

"What?"

"Don't you say a bloody word, you hear?"

Jack bit his tongue and pinched his lips together.

"Now," his father began, "you're going to learn a lesson. And it's a lesson I don't much like teaching. But I's got to do what I think's fair."

Jack was frightened. He breathed hot air into the

blanket. The fabric itched against his face. He couldn't bring himself to look his father in the eye; his focus was on the scissors instead.

"Now hold out your hand."

EIGHT

BACK IN THAT second reality, in the living room with the ugly carpet, Jack beheld the thin, white scars running the lengths of the two first fingers of his right hand. Surely all sons must hate their fathers for trying to make them stronger men. It was only natural to resent the teacher, the person who dealt cards no child wanted. But time passed and perspective drew things together. It made sense to him now. He didn't hate his father as he assumed he did—he respected the bastard. These scars were his old man's testament, and no doubt, they hadn't been etched with ease.

Those scars could never be undone. The carver and the carved had been united.

Forever.

The scissors from the kitchen weren't cold anymore. If anything, they burned with their own inner warmth.

He knelt beside another father—that of the driver who had brought him to this house—and wondered where to stick him. The stomach didn't seem vital enough. The chest plate would be difficult to puncture. The heart? No, that struck him as a wee bit clichéd. Jack wanted originality. He considered sliding the blade between two ribs and hoping for the best. That would not do.

Jack decided on the neck.

The twin points of the scissors punched through a thick layer of skin. An initial challenge. But they slid in with force. Like anything, a bit of effort, a bit of 'elbow grease' as his father used to say, went a long way. The blades snagged on something hard. The spine? It thrilled him to think so. When Jack pulled the scissors out, a gigantic spray of blood shot over his chest.

He smiled.

The father scrambled at the gash, trying to kick free.

"Don't you go anywhere," Jack whispered. "I'm not finished with you yet."

SEVEN

THE BUSH. The rain. The orgasmic scream escaping Jack's lungs.

"I'm gonna cut off your cock and stuff it down ya throat after I fuck ya, Charles!"

He didn't add that he planned to watch his eventual decay, planned to stand witness to the flies as they laid their eggs in his stab wounds. So much to see.

I won't be erased, he thought. *I'm not a blur on the back of a toilet door.*

He didn't need the voice in his head anymore.

Jack finally had his own.

Wiping rain and sap from his face, Michael burst through a blockade of trees and fell into a clearing. An uneven patch of ground with a fallen eucalyptus across its girth.

Two options.

Just keep on running and pray to God he shook The Beast off. It was getting darker by the minute and the bushlands were thick and knotted. True, this could be used to his advantage. But if he came across a road—what then? The chances of a car coming by at that *exact* moment were slim to none. So, alternatively, would he end up fleeing further into Nowhereville, Australia, population him and him alone? What if he chose left over right and ended deeper in the valley, away from James Bridge, and by that time it would be full dark, with visibility even lower. The Beast would have the upper hand in the open because it was faster, stronger.

One hell of a gamble.

Because the second option was to hide.

Michael glanced across the clearing. He hadn't realized it until then but he'd been running along a faint footpath, the grass thin and the rocks worn bald. He didn't know if the path was for people or a thoroughfare for livestock, but that didn't matter. *It's there.* His first instinct was to walk its winding length through the scrub, so it made sense that The Beast may also do the same. Perhaps this assumption could be used to his advantage.

Lightning blitzed, chased by thunder.

Michael decided to hide.

Wading through the knee-high grass, blades wrapping around his shins, dragging him back towards the house. *Don't fight me*, he thought. *Back the fuck off!* Michael spared a glance over his shoulder—the crashing had grown so loud he was sure The Beast was mere feet away. It wasn't. The scrub made sound tricky. It wouldn't surprise him to learn that the landscape itself had taken a similar toll on what once was Jack's mind—after all, he didn't strike Michael as the kind of man who only went *half* insane. The bush, a quiet conspirator. But to whom was it allegiant? Not knowing proved better.

Michael threw his foot onto the fallen tree—it groaned under his weight. His sneaker covered in mud and the green ink of crushed leaves.

Leapt over it. Landed on his knees. Out of sight.

The Beast stepped into the clearing.

The tree was long and bulky. A blackened crack ran its length from where a lightning bolt had likely struck it down. Because the clearing wasn't even, the tree propped up, creating a space between its bark and the ground, like a storage unit under a flight of stairs. With the branches and vines hanging along its sides, it made for the perfect hiding spot, a convenient tent for Michael to slide under.

It smelled of rot and mildew, eucalyptus, charcoal. Pain burst in his mangled shoulder. In the back of his head, he worried about blacking out—he'd come so close in the family's yard. That couldn't happen. Blacking out equated death, all his worth laid out on a platter for The Beast to eat. Michael clung to his alertness, used that pain to keep himself awake. He *owned* it.

I won't give in. I won't give in. I won't give in.

He pushed flat on his stomach and peered through the grass.

The Beast was in the center of the clearing, scanning its surroundings. It juggled the scissors from hand to hand, a move that spoke of anticipation.

Anticipation of the kill, Michael thought. To assume otherwise was naïve. And Michael had indulged in enough of that to last himself a lifetime.

He watched The Beast's barrel chest expand and deflate, saw the mangled cusp of his attacker's ear from where the father blew it away with the shotgun.

A paralyzing sight. Everything about The Beast was lethal, and the way it transcended its pain—in a manner Michael never could—terrified him. That transcendence went beyond ownership, deep into a realm he hadn't known existed, a place Michael had no desire to explore. Unless there was no other choice.

He feared that choice would soon be robbed of him.

At what point did Jack evolve from victim to murderer?

Michael clenched his fists. He understood.

We teeter on the brink of chaos every day, regardless of the tightly-wound control we think we have over our lives. Beneath everyone—himself included—there lurked the potential to do terrible things. This potential sometimes manifested itself, purged itself, stretched its spindly spidery legs, in a number of ways. And it wore many faces along the way. But most people hold true. They don't tap into the well.

This was different.

They were here in this tucked away corner of the valley, in the great property surrounding the family's house, because they had been *invited*, albeit against their will. The driver was their host, and in welcoming the passengers into her life, she unlocked that door within them all. This was what made that teetering control tip, sliding them into the murky waters where The Beast waited, where it eagerly grinned, a thing that was only too happy to rise to the occasion and fulfill its purpose in the world.

Come into my house, the driver said. *Be yourself here.*

Jack said yes and became The Beast. Now, as it scanned the trees, eyes black as a shark's, it invited Michael also. And even though he didn't want to go there, he could feel his teetering control giving way. Sliding, sliding, sliding towards the door as it creaked open, sighs escaping.

Could Michael hurt this thing to save himself?

Yes.

Yes, he could.

Just keep on walking, follow the path. Michael concentrated hard, as though attempting to send the message via telepathy. *I went THAT way.*

To his surprise, The Beast continued between the trees.

Michael nodded. *Yes-yes-yes.*

I can win this!

Michael let his head fall into the grass. So inviting, so cool.

Minutes passed, and still nothing.

What now? He parted the curtain of grass, slow and steady, careful to avoid drawing attention to his whereabouts. The eye of the storm passed above and the weather churned again, bringing first the howling wind. The trees, which ringed the clearing like a pack of wolves, shook and buckled under the rain. Freezing water welled underneath him, sloshing over his chest. *I'm going to die of pneumonia out here.* The cold penetrated deep, reaching into his throat and lungs until it hurt to breathe. A torrent of rain churned the soil, turned caked dirt into a foul-smelling sludge.

He lay there for another five minutes, shivering. At this point, he felt the crawling legs.

Lots of legs.

A foot-long centipede slithered out of the bark and onto his forearm. He was too shocked to recoil. It reared up to reveal a pair of fangs underneath its flat, brown head. Two twitching antennae waved.

You should be screaming. You should be flinging it off your arm, banging it against the wood—anything!

Move now. Run!

Only Michael couldn't move, didn't dare make a peep.

The centipede seemed to look at him. Did it understand the fear it evoked? He wondered if it were poisonous.

What? Are you kidding?

Michael, this is Australia. Everything here is fucking poisonous!

Its fangs protracted, clipped together. *Snip-snip.* Between them a triangular mouth homed rows of teeth. It inched closer, chattering.

The grass curtains spread in a V from the outside and The Beast's bloodied face stared in at him, roaring.

In a flash of ice-blue lightning, Michael saw chunks of stringy meat wedged between its teeth. He screamed, reached up, and with courage he didn't know he possessed, grabbed the centipede by its middle and flung it at The Beast's face. The wriggling insect landed on its cheek, legs dug into flesh. Jaws slammed shut as the insect's fanged head slipped into its mouth. A clean cut and the remainder fell onto the mud where it wormed and flipped, legs gnashing in silent applause. The Beast spat the head out.

Michael kneed his attacker in the chin, sending it

back through the veil of branches and into the long grass. The soles of clay-covered sneakers pointed at the sky and he dodged out the other side of the trunk.

"I got you! I got you!" Michael dove across the clearing. Spearheaded into the trees. Gone.

Taking the path he'd seen earlier didn't even cross his mind.

SIX

MICHAEL SPLASHED THROUGH running water and followed a fast-flowing stream to a narrow cliff face on his right. He couldn't tell how steep the drop was. Past the bluff, the valley writhed under the storm's onslaught.

His shoes slipped on mossy rocks. Behind him, The Beast jumped through the trees.

"I'm going to get you for that, you shit! I swear to God—"

Michael watched it twist its ankle on a loose boulder. The stumble gave Michael enough time to spirit into the thicket. Branches snagged his shirt, wrapped around his arms.

The Beast walked towards the trees, limping. Drool strung from its chin, its face a mask of blood and shit-smelling mud. "Don't you move, Charles," it whispered. "Got a lesson to teach you. You ain't going to like it."

The trees were its webs, and instead of fangs, the spider bore scissors. It crept closer and closer. It was as though The Beast *wanted* this to be drawn out, as if he was enjoying the thrill of the hunt.

"You're just too easy," it told Michael, who scrambled in the knot of thorny boughs. Strips of skin hung from finger-like branches.

He watched his to-be-murderer approach. So close he could smell him now. *This is it, I'm going to die, I've thought about it so many times today but this is it for real.*

Oh, sweet Jesus, I hope it doesn't hurt.

The Beast was within inches.

"Here we go," it said.

A burst of primal energy surged through Michael's body. He grabbed a tree branch and swung both legs up off the ground. The tree held his weight and Michael lashed out—feet slammed into The Beast's throat.

The branch gave way and snapped, sending Michael headfirst to the ground in a rain of leaves. Without looking to see where his enemy had fallen, he started to crawl.

The Beast fumbled. Its twisted ankle landed on a rotted log, shattered under its heel. It lost its footing and tumbled into the strong-flowing stream. Brilliant, cold water splashed over its face and up its nose, forcing its shirt up around its neck in a chokehold. It twisted, rocks jabbing at its stomach. The Beast's head emerged from the stream. The scissors were gone.

Michael slid under the branches, bugs crawling over his fingers and into his hair. The smell of soil and decay was rich. He kept on kicking with his legs, trying to pull away.

Jack looked around for his weapon. It was then that he realized how close he was to the narrow cliff face—ten feet at most.

"Oh, you bitch, you bitch," he yelled at the faggot.

Jack dragged himself out of the stream and collapsed in the mud. He glanced around. Nothing. "Oh, I'm going to cut you up so bad." Hope drained away as he said it. Loose packed earth fell under his grip and he shuffled away from the bluff's edge, but not before seeing the scissors in a flash of lightning. A thorny bush fifteen feet below had broken their fall. Water ran into darkened treetops.

"Fuck!" He threw rocks, kicked mud. Fury gave him a second wind. Losing the scissors equaled losing a limb; he sensed its phantom weight in his hands.

"I'm going to make you hurt, you faggot bitch. I don't need the fucking thing."

He followed the footprints Michael left behind in the soil. "I'll getchya with my hands."

FIVE

THE RAIN STOPPED as night fell over the valley. And still, Michael ran with The Beast close behind, clothed in shadow and craving meat.

Startled birds shot into the air.

I do exist, thought The Beast. *I'm not rumor or myth. I'm not a fairy tale told by parents to keep their children obedient. I'm not caged anymore. I shake off the clothing you keep in your closet where I was hiding. I wipe the dust from under your bed out of my hair. I will make you bleed and you will know how real I am. I will be heard. I'll lift up your skirt and see what lies beneath, teacher. My hand is raised and this time I know the answer. And there is only one answer.*

Don't turn back. Do not walk.

Run!

The trees cleared again. Moonlight across a field. At its far end, a steep incline, and at its very top, yellow streetlights shone through the grass.

The road leading to Flagman's Bridge, and the town beyond it.

Michael tried yelling for help but his voice was gone. Every step drew him closer to passing out again.

He was sixty-odd feet from the incline, which itself was as tall as a five-story building. This was the combined distance between him and the hope of survival.

The Beast thumped behind him. Michael broke through the tree line and began running across the field. He noticed something at the base of the hill: an old barbed wire fence divided private property from council land. He pushed himself farther, every step an agony.

Not quick enough, though.

Just a few feet from his target, sweaty hands grabbed his shoulders from behind. One finger slid inside the wound from the Rottweiler's bite. Michael screamed. He reached for the hill, even as he fell backwards, and landed on the ground. The sky stretched taut across the world above him where the clouds dissipated and the stars littered the dark. They were cold, distant, and beautiful.

The Beast blotted them out.

It grabbed his throat. Michael used his left leg to push himself onto his side, throwing The Beast over with him. He concentrated on his right hand, felt its weight and strength, and funneled every ounce of hatred into it. With a jolt so hard it almost dislocated his shoulder, Michael swung. The clenched fist sailed through the air and smashed The Beast's face. A crack echoed across the field. The Beast arched its spine, head slamming against the grass. Two teeth pinwheeled from its mouth.

Michael didn't savor this victory. He shuffled at the fence instead.

"That hurt, Charles," Jack yelled, voice deformed. Spat red. "OWWWWW!"

He dragged himself up again and shook his head. The chase had to go on; it could not end like this. He'd gone too far. Only the hunt existed—although as to what he hunted was beyond him.

The twisted ankle was forgotten now, even though ligaments must have been torn. Bone ground against bone with every leap. The only real slivers of pain existed in, of all places, his fingers.

In the burning white scars he'd carried since childhood.

You're doing it, you really are, Michael told himself as he reached the fence. *You're going to win this thing.*

He put his foot on the barbed wire. Weight pushed it into a crooked smile as he attempted to climb over. The fence post next to him snapped down the middle with a crack, termite-ridden splinters flying in every direction. He toppled to the ground in a mess of wire and wood rubble. Barbs latched to the left hem of his saturated jeans. He dragged wire along with him as he scrabbled up the incline. Fingers grabbed on to tufts of grass, on to jagged rocks. He used the outcroppings as leverage against the slope. Gravity was the third contestant in this fight for life.

Behind him, The Beast reached the remains of the fence. It leaned over and grabbed the barbed wire in its bare hands. Barbs stabbed into its flesh. It climbed the wire

---

The flies from inside the bus were back. They clotted the air around Jack's face. Before, they had been a source of annoyance. Now, their buzzing wings became music, singing a song he longed to dance to.

Michael's hands latched to a shard of rock embedded in the ground. As The Beast landed on his legs, it used its weight to force them both back down the incline. "Let me go", Michael shouted. The earth grated against him as he descended, splitting skin and raking grit into his eyes. Throughout, Michael held on to that rock, held onto it for dear life.

It dislodged itself from the soil, a souvenir just for him.

Flies crawled over Jack's body like a second skin of diamonded eyes and twitching arms rubbing themselves raw. They escaped his lungs and flew from his mouth when he screamed, lingering like a haze of black static.

Scissors of lightning split the sky. On the other side of that cut, Jack thought he saw something moving. Something big, and as familiar as a half-recalled dream come morning.

Michael cradled the shoebox-sized rock in his arms. Slate beetles crawled over his face; one even slipped inside his ear.

He kicked hard against The Beast's shoulder, forcing it farther down the slope. It would have skidded all the way to the busted fence, but it coat-hangered on the barbed wiring—the end of which was still wrapped around Michael's ankle. The Beast fought against it, throwing itself from side to side and cutting itself to the bone in the process. The tug of wire made the barbs dig into Michael's foot, dragging him off his keel like a steer in a lasso's pinch. The rock thudded soil as he slid into the ditch. Bugs scuttled. He spat dirt, wiped his face against the grass, and kicked in wild jerks to shake The Beast off his leg.

At the top of the incline, everything turned yellow. A car passed by.

Darkness swooped in again.

The Beast grabbed Michael's free ankle with his left hand. Even through the blood and grime, the scars of its father's discipline could be seen.

A crow sent out a lonely call. It sounded a little like a cry for he-eeeeellllppp.

The Beast sprung, a hound on a bone, and bit down on Michael's Achilles tendon. A snapping pop of flesh as teeth tore through skin, shooting salty-sweet blood into his attacker's mouth. A white-hot flame of heat coursed through Michael's system, and whilst he didn't feel pain in the traditional sense, a jet of vomit erupted from him. Bitter and bright green.

Michael's other foot, tangled in wire, smashed the top of The Beast's head, and he used its scalp like a ladder rung to heave up those crucial few inches. To what he wanted. To what he needed. His hand landed on the rock.

Hard and cold.

He lifted it, the muscles in his arms crying. It rolled against his chest. Michael forced himself onto his side as The Beast grabbed his crotch, pulling at his jeans. He grabbed the rock and held it tight.

Don't let go, please God, don't let go.

The crow landed at the top of the slope, spread its wings. It waited for one of them to become meat.

⸻•⸻

An old friend stopped by. Jack heard him whispering in his ear.

That's it, Jack-o.

That's it.

You don't have the scissors anymore so you might just have to fuck him yourself. It wouldn't be so bad, you know? You're already hard.

That's half the work done right there.

He smiled, happy to know he wasn't alone.

⸻•⸻

Michael used the rock to pull himself upright. He was as numb to emotion as he was to pain. This had to be right; he had to live.

He trundled onto his back and volleyed the rock in a direct line.

The Beast's jaw tore away from its face in a blistering crunch of cracking bone. The rock hit the ground, bone snapping in two underneath it. It fell down the remaining slope, and the back of its head fractured against a piece of broken fence post. Termites crawled into the short stubble of its hair.

Breathless, Michael crab-crawled to the rock as

though it were the only piece of floating debris in the ocean after the flight went down. He stole a breath from the night and exhaled hard against its even harder, blood slickened face. Reality. This had happened.

They were at the very bottom of the hill.

Stars.

They were all Jack could see now that he was on his back. That suggestion of movement through the scissor tear in the sky flickered again, and his heart seized in a great gasp of awe. Regardless of his disorientation, he knew he was witnessing something special, something most people weren't privileged enough to see in their lives. He reached out for the company of the voice to share this moment with, and if not it then the flies at the very least. But there was nobody here with him. Nobody at all.

Jack was alone.

And so he lay there observing the great shape unfurling from the cut. It moved like cloud shadows over the faces of mountains, slithering and worthy of its wonder. Jack watched this *thing* quicken, its ferocity making him as tiny and insignificant as an ant, and in the shade of that enormous comparison, he recognized it for what it was.

The Beast.

It drank the stars dry, one by one, until only darkness remained.

Michael brought the rock down a final time.

FOUR

A BULB SWITCHED on in the Frost home and a slice of light cut across the lawn. A silhouette moved past the living room window. The soft *shhhh-shhhh-shhhh* of its dragging feet could be heard from outside. It studied the landscape on the other side of the rain-speckled glass. It saw grass, the driveway, and the monolithic form of the bus wrapped in blue nightfall. These things didn't hold its attention. It focused on the trees near the verandah, at the fairy lights winking into life in its branches. It tilted its head and saw the Christmas cutouts. It was early November and yet it felt a chill. The silhouette noticed that the storm clouds were gone.

Something fell across Reggie's vision in gentle, downward swirls.

"I can't believe it," she said, blinking.

Snow.

She turned from the window and surveyed the living room. The tree decorated with stars and tinsel. It wasn't the plastic tree she usually put out every year. It was a Fraser Fir. At its peak, a crooked angel flanked by two plastic Santas, their faces no longer bent inwards. Their eyes were wide though, and donned eternal smiles.

Presents in wrapping of every conceivable color.

Warmth over Reggie's face. Her soul was light. For the first time in many years, she felt good. The record player started upstairs, the vinyl crackling through old speakers.

It *hisssssse*d.

Crackling wood.

But we don't have a fireplace, she thought.

She jumped at the sound of laughing children. Liz and Jed ran into the room, slapping each other with tennis rackets. They were young, their faces round and sunburnt, hands covered in orange pulp and play dirt. Sheepish, cute.

"We didn't mean to make so much noise," Jed said.

"It's all right, honey. Why don't you take your sister upstairs and wash yourselves good and clean. Okay?"

They nodded and ran, tagging each other all the way.

Reggie rubbed her hands over her face. Her palms smelled of herbs and stock. *That's right, I was getting dinner ready.* As she crossed the room, she caught her reflection in the framed photographs on the walls. She was thinner than she'd been in a long time, hair pulled up in a loose-fitting bun.

The kitchen was full of food—lettuce, tomatoes, mashed potatoes, stalks of fresh broccoli. Sauces and gravy and honeyed carrots in individual bowls. A pile of festive paper napkins near a chopping board. They peeled away from the stack and flew into the air. Reggie's gaze shot to the opened kitchen door. She ran to it, the wind blowing her bangs. She grabbed the doorknob and forced it shut. Just before it closed, she heard barking and rattling chains.

Stray maybe.

She turned to pick up the napkins but they were already back in the pile. Wes stood next to the table, returning the last to its rightful place. He glanced at her with kind eyes. Reggie smiled—so handsome. Her husband was well built, broad-shouldered, tanned. She liked that he was balding. There was something masculine about it. Her heart fluttered.

"Gee whiz that smells nice," he said. "Is that the roast cooking?"

This caught Reggie off guard. She had to think. Then it dawned on her—yes, it was the roast chicken in the oven that he could smell. How could she forget?

A bell rang in the room.

She ran to the oven, opened it and reached inside. Without the use of mitts, she took the tray and placed it on the chopping board. Juices pooled and sloshed. The aroma of white meat and rosemary filled her nostrils, breathed it in and a shiver climbed her back. A splash of liquid spilled when she transferred the chicken to the table. Took a tea towel. Bent to wipe it up. When she threw the soiled towel into the sink, it was covered in blood, though this she did not notice.

Husband and wife embraced in their kitchen. Wes pushed his nose into her collar. "You smell great, hon." He ran his huge hands over the small of her back. She arched her chest against his. A wave of ecstasy prickled her skin and made her dizzy.

"It's just me, I'm not wearing anything," she told him.

"You smell great, hon."

Reggie cocked an ear, thinking, *Didn't he just say that*? She dismissed it and kissed him. Their lips ground together. It had been a while since they kissed like movie stars. It surprised her how easily they fell back into the rhythm of it, their tongues flickering, tentative at first and then bold. His hardness against her leg.

Thumping upstairs.

"Hold your horses, Wes. The kids are coming."

They drew apart.

Studying him, Reggie realized how much she loved this man, regardless of his anger, his flaws. On nights like this when everything was perfect and he touched her just like he used to, she could forgive him for almost anything he did to her or their children.

Jed and Liz ran into the kitchen, panting. They were clean, as instructed. "Why don't we open a present or two while we're waiting for the chicken to cool," Wes said, turning to Reggie for affirmation. "That's okay, isn't it?"

"Yeah, of course!" She laughed but stopped. Had he just asked her in an accent? Reggie was positive he had. A thick, midday television, American accent. She shook her head, feeling stupid. *You're losin' it, Reg.*

They all went to the living room and kneeled before the tree and each took a present.

The record continued, only it played at half speed. The words drew out, pained. At first, she thought it was Christmas carols. But it wasn't. It was something from her younger days, or maybe from a movie she couldn't recall right now. The lyrics floated in her head, evading her, prodding at better days, until the moment they crystalized.

I Never Dreamed Someone Like You Could Love Someone Like Me by Katie Irving.

Reggie watched Jed open his gift. He tore the red cellophane away. She felt his expectation and smiled along. Revealed was a small, hardcover book on eagle breeds. It had been her husband's idea to get it. And of course, Jed loved it, flickering through the pages and coming to a double-page spread, an eagle's wings stretching from left to right. A beautiful illustration, she had to say. Very detailed.

"You must have behaved yourself this year," she told her son. "Santa's been good to you."

"I reckon so," he replied, holding the book to his chest.

Liz sat before the tree, its needles in her hair. She opened a gift. Reggie smiled. Part of the joy of being a parent was to live for and through the happiness of your child.

The box was empty.

"Oh, I love it," Liz squealed, holding the nothingness to her underdeveloped breasts. "Thanks so much, Mum, Dad."

Wes kissed her. "Don't thank us, thank Santa."

"Yeah." She winked. "That's right."

Liz hugged her mother then. "Gee, girl. God's stretching you like taffy. I'm going to have to put a brick on your head just to slow you down." Reggie ruffled her bangs. "Let's go eat, what do you think?"

Wes, Reggie, Liz, and Jed sat at the kitchen table. Wes cut the bird with her sewing scissors. The rib cage snapped with each brutal clench. Red meat dripped juices.

"Smells awesome, Mum, seriously it does," Liz told her.

"Thanks, darl'."

They helped themselves to food, eating in silence, with only the sound of clinking forks and scraping plates to punctuate the scene. After a few minutes, the back door started to rattle in the wind and blew open with a bang.

Reggie ran to it and looked into the backyard. Snow covered the grass and the trees beyond. Bound to the clothesline on a thick chain was a large Rottweiler. Its eyes glowed in the dark, its mouth wide and dripping foam.

From behind her, she heard Wes talking to Liz. Only his voice was slow and grating, like the record player. "You're nothing but skin and bone," he said. *"I'vvveeee ssseeeennn ssscccaaarrreecccrooowwwss wwwiiithhh mmoorrreee ssstuuffiinggg."*

Reggie threw her weight against the door, the wind blowing harder. She squinted as she stared back into the yard. Past the dog, on the ground near the trees, a stranger lay on his side facing the house.

Another gust of wind drove into her face. Gasping, Reggie saw her feet.

"I'm not wearing any shoes," she said aloud. She could have sworn she had been earlier. Reggie wore a thin, floral dress now. Her apron was gone. Bulbous knees, the beginnings of her cellulite-dimpled thighs.

The dog's barking grew more vicious.

The young man on the grass vanished. And so had the snow. Darkness outside.

The wind died. Her hair fell about her face, lifeless and spent.

Reggie turned. She felt heavier. There were pains in her body that had not been there before.

The kitchen was empty, food scraps on the table.

A noise escaped from the living room. Her heart skipped a beat.

Holding a hand to her chest, Reggie crossed the kitchen. As she walked, the wallpaper began to peel in thin, curling fingers. Her shadow long behind her.

She nudged an uncooked chicken with her foot. It slid across the linoleum.

Reggie entered the living room. Above, moths beat at the exposed bulb, burning themselves alive out of love for light. An ochre glow blanketed the room, the color of cigarette stains and tea bags. The Christmas tree: its branches had dwindled and died, a large pile of needles scattered over the floor.

The life bled out of her. Reggie searched for the photos on the walls, only they were gone now, shattered and destroyed on the stairs.

"What's happening?" she asked the room. "Where'd you all go?"

The two Santa ornaments at her feet. Faces bent inwards.

A quiet scratching from somewhere.

Reggie scanned for movement. The tree was gone. Where it had stood, there were only the remains of the reading lamp, dust balls.

The room came alive with the frenetic shadows thrown from the moths.

She saw the window overlooking the front yard.

And the face staring in at her.

Rabid eyes peered out from behind twisted locks of hair. Its mouth opened and its tongue lolled like a wet, blue steak. The face streaked with blood and brains and strips of flesh.

Reggie screamed.

The creature in the window screamed too, a high-pitched mewling—in its cry, one heard tortured cats.

Terrified, Reggie turned to run *and saw it turn too.* Then she saw what was in its back, sticking out from between its shoulder blades at a ninety-degree angle.

A carving knife.

A bolt of pain like nothing she'd ever experienced before, both blunt and sharp and hot and cold, exploded in her back. Reggie reached her arms around her sides until her fingers brushed against something hard. Like a dog chasing its tail, she spun and saw the kitchen door. And the long river of blood that stopped at her feet.

"Oh, God."

She prayed what she feared was not true.

It was.

The monster in the window was her reflection. It came back to her in a blinding flash: the man grabbing her by the ankles and pulling her into the kitchen. He had the knife in his hand and drove it into her. The sound of it puncturing flesh filled her mind and echoed.

It can't be true, she told herself. *If I've been stabbed, I should be dead.*

I'm alive, aren't I?

I'm alive.

Darkness clouded over—she dropped to her knees where her headless daughter sprawled. She recognized her distinctive jawbone, the remains of her uniform.

"My baby!"

Reggie felt the blade push in farther, as though seeking her soul, intent on tearing it to shreds. She caught sight of something large and red in her periphery vision.

Her son. The walls surrounding him near the bottom of the staircase were streaked in haphazard webs of blood. His wrists had been slit.

Agony filled her, burning hot. Everything fell away. The faster her heart beat, the darker it got.

Then she saw what was left of her husband lying on his side near the couch. His neck had been ripped open. False teeth shoved inside. Jeans around his ankles. Where his sphincter should have been, there was a red rose of meat. His genitalia were not in the room.

She wanted to scream at him: *You did this, you bastard. It was all you. You started this and now look what you have done to your family!* She was angry, ashamed. She regretted so much.

But above all, Reggie felt alone.

As she fell through the air she thought of the day they met. How Wes opened his umbrella to shield her from the rain. Such a charmer.

Reggie joined her family on the carpet.

Everything stilled in the Frost residence bar the television screen. Highlights from the Grand Prix. Footage of Formula One cars intercut with Bon Jovi singing to a screaming crowd, followed by shots of men in suits sitting at a bench table, sipping Gatorade. They smiled.

She looked up at the ceiling light. The moths continued to fly at it, as though within the glass something unobtainable, but forever desired, lurked and teased.

THREE

MICHAEL DELANEY WAS born December 23, 1976, with his umbilical cord around his neck. The doctors feared he might have suffered mild hypoxia; a depreciation in his heart caused by a lack of oxygen to the brain. Because of this, he was born by caesarean.

A fighter from the very beginning.

TWO

5:37 A.M.

A BLUE MORNING.

Birds sang along with the crickets. Trees patiently awaited yet another day's onslaught of heat. That would come later. It always did.

Michael opened his eyes.

While unconscious, the police arrived at the Frost residence. One officer threw up when he found the carnage in the living room. Detectives struggled to put the pieces together and wondered if they ever would. A troop of eager-faced police scouted the surrounding bushlands with sniffer dogs.

Michael's scent led the way.

A barricade at the top of the driveway held back coffee-toting reporters.

Word spread in town.

The nine o'clock church service filled with people praying for the lost. Mournful groups drew together.

At Michael's home, his parents wept with a counselor who prepared them for the news that their son might be dead. Every time the phone rang, their chests tightened. An officer unplugged it from the wall and was later reprimanded by his supervisor.

Pain pinned Michael to the ground.

The new day swam into focus.

There were shoes a few feet away from him. Beyond, two gargantuan legs in blood-streaked jeans, an exposed torso and the bloated stomach. A pulled-up shirt revealed twin nipples, hardened and speckled with morning dew. Above the neck was what looked like a busted pomegranate with a large rock growing up out of it.

'Jack'.

The body crawled with insects. Slugs crept over skin, beetles taking shelter under his fingernails. Ants searched his flesh for sugars, swam in his oils. In the middle of his torn-up hand, a spider had spun its web. A murder of crows squawked above his head. Their black beaks were shiny from the gore as they dove into the mess.

Michael forced himself upright.

As he stood, a car passed by up the incline, unseen. He spun to the sound, tried to scream. Still no voice.

Murderer.

He glanced at the sky. No clouds. Blood ran down his arms. A single black fly buzzed around him. The

Beast tried to swoop into his head. Michael squeezed his eyes shut, pressed his hands against his ears. Ground his teeth together.

Murderer, it said.

"No."

And then he heard it—soft at first but gaining power.

The ocean.

His head thumped in harmony with his heartbeat, bursting explosions of rhythmic pain.

Michael's feet were no longer on the rocky, blood-splattered ground. They were buried in sand. He had no shoes on; he wiggled his toes in the sparkling, gold grains. It felt so soft. The oncoming tide, cold and beautiful, washed over his shins.

Michael didn't remember wading out into the water, but the ocean was up to his waist now. He still wore his bloodied, torn clothes. Somewhere near the breakers, a new wave swelled. He smiled. The sound of the beach swallowed everything else. The wind kissed his lips. Michael tasted salt.

The wave drew closer, a rolling blessing rushing at him against a blue backdrop. He no longer just smiled. He laughed. And damn it, that felt sweet. Water exploded and all sound disappeared, safe in the sweet nothingness of it all. The ocean cleaned his wounds.

ONE

THE TOWN WAS never the same.

Funerals were conducted two at a time, and once the dead were buried in either Railway Street or Bowen Road cemeteries, a candlelit vigil was held on the town's Catholic School grounds. Memorial flames illuminated thousands of faces, and among them were the families of the victims, the media, and those who came out of curiosity and respect. Articles and books were written about what happened, each speculating about how the dominoes fell. No answers.

Michael didn't accept a single interview, despite handsome offers from both print and television tabloids. He moved away with his parents to a beachside town of similar proportions and prejudices as James Bridge. In their new house, a letter of sympathy from the newly elected prime minister, John Howard, and his wife, Janette, tucked away in a filing cabinet collecting dust.

A year after the James Bridge massacre, 28-year-old Martin Bryant murdered 35 people and injured a further 21 at the historic Port Arthur colony site in Tasmania. The human toll of both events prompted Howard to adopt gun law proposals initially developed from the 1988 National Report on Violence, and urged the states to accept said proposals under a National Firearms Agreement, necessary because the Australian Constitution didn't allow the government to enact gun laws.

Although there was never another James Bridge or Port Arthur to date, people still died in various creative and violent ways. In the year 2000, middle-aged housewife Katherine Knight murdered her husband 68 miles from James Bridge. She stabbed him 37 times in his sleep, then skinned and hung his remains on a meat hook in the architrave of a door to the lounge room. She decapitated him and cooked parts of his body with the intention of making her children consume the good bits.

The Australian Institute of Criminology released a study stating that 74 homicides in New South Wales alone, over a twenty-year period, were directly linked to gay hate crimes. Some of the weapons of choice included saws, spades, claw hammers, a car-wheel brace, fire extinguishers, crossbows and arrows. Most were simply beaten to death.

James Bridge became a footnote in Australian history and the town had no choice but move on. Shops opened, shops closed—just like the Pro-Choice foundation opened in Diana and Julia's memory. Throughout these streets, couples married and people separated. Trees were cut. Trees seeded. At one of the football ovals, a bench was erected to commemorate the Frost family. It sits forgotten, covered in graffiti.

On Combi-Chance-Road, a white crucifix is stabbed into the earth beside the footpath. Donna Marten replaces the flowers whenever she is in town.

Like many others, she relocated, but still works at the hospital. Around the crux of the crucifix, she places unread notes, birthday and Christmas cards in zip-lock bags. There is also a single ballerina slipper.

ZERO

MICHAEL CAME TO a road at the top of the hill.

Exhausted, he looked to the left. No cars coming in that direction. Nothing on the right either, just an endless stretch of black bitumen surrounded by fields and dancing flowers. On the horizon, James Bridge sat in a quicksilver haze. Helicopters swarmed above the town, their thudding blades lost on his ears. All Michael could hear was his pulse.

He wouldn't be found for another thirty-seven minutes. In that time, flies laid eggs in his wounds, in the corners of his eyes.

Michael Delaney felt a shadow on his face. He watched the crow swoop down to land upon a metal rectangle silhouetted against the sun. The bird spread its wings, claws scratching at the dented sign. Michael cupped a palm to his brow and read the words printed across its surface.

BUS STOPS HERE

THE SOUND OF HIS BONES BREAKING

Dedicated to Brian Edwards, a good egg.

“Of course, I’m not sure there is such a thing as a real self. You could ransack your innards looking for the real you and never find it—slice yourself open and all you’ll find is blood and muscle and bone.”
—Ryū Murakami, *In the Miso Soup*

“I was crying because I can’t get my shadow to stick on. Besides, I wasn’t crying.”
—J.M. Barrie, *Peter Pan*

PART ZERO

FORTY-EIGHT

NOT ALL WORLDS end in a crash of buildings and airplanes, in smoke and ruins and meteor showers. Some worlds come apart one humiliating crack at a time. And no matter how hard you fight, nothing can stop it. So, at the almost-end, you're left helpless, more exhausted than you've ever been, questioning how it came to this. These thoughts tightened the knot in Adrian Bonner's stomach. Some things he didn't *want* answered. He studied his reflection in the blank computer screen instead, and the sigh that followed came with an almost resigned expectancy. This was his new normal.

Christ, I look like death.

Looking back, the cracks were obvious. The unsealed medication bottle. That pulp of vomit in the toilet bowl the flush missed. Things which looked like they were flying but were falling in secret.

The smile that lasted too long. A touch that carried no weight.

None of it mattered anymore. Why would it, when it amounted to the same thing? He was, in essence, alone in a foreign country, trying with every ounce of his being to not let his grudges define him. Failing even that, on top of everything else, proved no easy pill to swallow.

If I sit here any longer, I'm going to go insane.

Aiden forced himself to his feet and slung the bag over his shoulder. Trembling fingers untangled his tie from the government-issued lanyard, patted trousers to ensure his wallet was there. His 'leaving work' routine, little acts that once signaled freedom but now meant it was time to journey back to the room where Danny sometimes was, and worse, where Danny sometimes wasn't.

The sick room.

Again, that awful coiling in his guts. The aches. His call to Country had never been stronger, only he couldn't go back to Australia. Not yet. To some, he was stubborn even anal-retentive. 'A dog with a bone', as his mother often said. Aiden, however, just saw it as not giving up. Danny was worth it—that he had to believe. He had no choice but let home wait.

Aiden strode out of the embassy and lost himself in the Bangkok crowd, a shadow among shadows, telling himself that despite not understanding how it came to this, he was doing the right thing. The cracks were still out there, though. Waiting and widening.

He just refused to see them.

FORTY-SEVEN

SCRATCH-SCRATCH-SCRATCH.

Danny Fletcher dragged himself into the shower—not because he wanted to be clean but on account of Aiden's impending return. He'd soon be exposed, and the shower, as best he knew, was the only place a man could cry without being noticed.

Naked. Footfalls against the tiles, a sad clap for one.

He came here to be alone. To beat off without his partner knowing. To laugh at jokes nobody else found amusing. To wrestle memories of the prick who bullied him at school thirty years ago, all those painful twinges he couldn't quite untie; and then, after this, to weep like the pussy everyone made him out to be. The shower was where men of Danny's breed haunted themselves.

Over the thrum of water, he heard skeletal branches clattering at the window trying to get in and toy with his animosity and hurt. He knew what must be done. Oh, the freedom blame brings.

Blood pooled pink between his toes.

Scratch-scratch-scratch.

FORTY-SIX

THE FERRY.

Some of the people around Aiden stood, some sat, but all watched the water and the fish snatching low-flying dragonflies from the air. They swam amid the bags, those plastic river ghosts. Next to him a boy wore headphones; the two of them swayed with the ebb and flow of the Chao Phraya's current. Aiden broke down against this young man's shoulder, buckling, despite this being his weight to carry. After all, Bangkok hadn't called to Aiden alone, though it may have seemed that way at first. Aiden came to Thailand for his boyfriend.

Even after all he's done, I still love the bastard.

What a crime it is to think Danny's worth saving. Well, fuck me then. Fuck it all.

No stop, mate. Thinking that way will do you in, too.

The boy with the headphones was, of course, awkward about Aiden's tears but relented. He patted the older man's arm, kind and tender and non-judgmental. In English, the boy lied and said everything would be okay. "Tell me what is wrong."

They drew nearer to the riverbank.

"I'm scared." Aiden faux-laughed the honesty

away. "Sorry. I'm being a dick. Thank you." He pressed his palms together and bowed, paying the kid the respect he deserved.

The boat kept rocking. Carp swam toward hooks in waiting, shimmers in the dark like recent memories. Their barbs were sharp, not that the fish knew that. No, not yet.

Aiden disembarked into the street, cats skittering between his feet to hiss at a hog tethered to a pole near the toll booths. Sweat coursed. Questions probed again, not letting him be.

How about we ask ourselves where things went wrong, hey? Ask again. And again.

I used to be happy.

Looking back, Aiden thought his world started falling apart four months earlier, the night he and Danny were at the Lismore pub with the wind warming their faces and the pounding music at their backs. The night the taxi pulled up out front.

Shattering glass. The moon.

Aiden thought wrong. He just didn't know it. No, not yet.

PART ONE

FORTY-FIVE

DECEMBER 29, 2017

THE TAXI SCREECHED into a U-turn as today teetered into tomorrow, slowing at the last possible second. It mounted the curb in a scrape of metal against cement. The two men in the pub's open bar across the street glanced up from the matching pints of ale they were downing.

Neither Aiden nor Danny realized how drunk he was until they leapt from their stools. The small Australian city spun around them.

"Woah. What's going on over there, you reckon?" Aiden said.

"No idea, babe."

It was unusual for them to have imbibed quite so much—they were lightweights, after all. Hangovers in your early forties were harder to wrestle than those in your early twenties. "But it's Christmas," they said, a free-for-all excuse if there ever was one. They didn't have to show their faces at their respective workplaces until after the New Year shutdown period. As far as they were concerned, whatever hangovers they accrued between now and then were *more* than well earned. Besides, they were holidaying in style—albeit at one of Lismore's less than graceful establishments. The Duck's Nuts: a pub where the floors were sticky and the automatic teller machines never functioned as they should. The pay-as-you-go cigarette dispensers, on the other hand? Now that was a different story.

Beers—hoppy and golden-hued—blunted some of their senses. Not all. The two men caught the whiff of danger on the balmy summer breeze as distinct as downwind road kill and felt themselves chill over.

"Dude's drunk as a skunk," Danny said, pointing to the taxi with one hand and rubbing his chest through the button gaps of his plaid shirt with the other, one of his many absentminded habits. Like a few of the other patrons in the outdoor area, he staggered onto the footpath and into the glow of orange halogen lamps.

"Hold up, Danny."

"But those girls just leapt into the guy's backseat."

"Wait a tic, alright? Something's—"A broad-shouldered man trundled by, clipping Aiden's shoulder on the way. "Jesus, watch it, mate."

Of course, the man didn't listen. He took one look at the color of Aiden's skin, tossed a dismissive "Bugger off, abo," his way, and crossed the street to where the intoxicated women and their young, willowy male friend had loaded themselves into the back of the taxi, which was yet to drive off—thank God. Aiden noticed the bottles left behind on the curb, glass catching the light and glowing as if candles burned within, as if this was a memorial to tragedy and not the place where partiers had been waiting for a ride.

"Check out Batman over there," said an older woman by Danny's side, a cigarette dangling from her mouth. Her voice was a rough, country drawl. "Off to save the day."

Seagulls fought over a dropped pie on the road, white feathered blurs turning against one another in a desperate fight for food. Beaks stabbed. Eyes stared. Screeching. Through it all, the hoot of a distant vehicle somewhere, a drawn-out sound that showed no signs of stopping, incessant as the warning bells in Danny's brain.

Something's not right. Something's not right. Something's not right.

Batman pulled the rear taxi door open and leaned inside, muffled voices Aiden had to strain to hear escaping. He caught bits and pieces. That was enough.

"—get out—"

"—what you on about, mate—"

"—he's smashed—"

"—fuck off—"

Aiden stepped beside his partner, shoulders brushing, which was about as far as they allowed their public displays of affection go in this part of northern New South Wales. Sydney or Melbourne, this place was not. Neither man liked that they had to live this way, but this was their reality. Not liking a situation wasn't enough to make it untrue. As of recently, yes, they could legally marry; however, it wasn't like that particular social progression had scraped every barnacle of bigotry off every person nation-wide. A black and white gay couple: it paid to be careful. As ever-cautious-Aiden often said, "Don't we have enough shit to deal with, babe? Yeah, let's keep our pants on."

"Jesus, here we go," Danny whispered under his breath.

Drunken passengers spilled out the back door. Two women in white dresses better suited for the races emerged from the side facing an adjoining building. Vintage murals of mill employees watched them stumble and laugh. The willowy man climbed out of the taxi on the pub's side. Danny squinted: movement in the front seat.

"The driver's off chops," they heard Batman say. "Didn't you see the way he came tearing in here like there's no tomorrow."

"What you on about? Back off, will ya."

The group came around to the rear of the vehicle, all bathed in red from the taillights. "Stop it guys," said one of the girls. "We'll get an Uber. Go away, mate. We can look after ourselves."

The driver came out from behind the wheel.

He was tall and dressed in black, the Johnny Cash type, sans swagger. Hair an unkempt mop. No shoes. There was no mistaking it. Aiden's initial assumption, as shared by Batman himself, was correct. This guy was driving blind.

Wind swept dirt, plastic bags, and cigarette stubs their way. Grit slapped Danny's face. He didn't blink, didn't shy away.

If anything, it sobered him up.

The interaction between Batman and the drunk escalated faster than anyone could have imagined, which was saying a lot. For those who frequented the Duck's Nuts at that time of the night, a street brawl came as little surprise. Aiden, however, was a public servant, and Danny a social worker from right here in town. They were lovers who rarely drank unless they were on holidays, when Christmas excuses paved the way for greasy breakfasts with aspirin chasers. Fights became a foreign concept to them long ago.

This one started, as most brawls do, with a single push.

"Oh, shit," Aiden said. "Someone call the cops!" He shouted this to anyone who would listen, even though he was pulling out his phone himself. In the time it took for him to scan the screen for bars of reception, the man he loved spirited from his side and onto the road.

"Babe, stop," Aiden yelled, not caring that the 'b' word slipped out, here on the Lismore street in front of men and women who didn't just sit in this part of the pub to smoke, but who claimed these stools because they wanted front-row seats to the fights that always came, without fail, weekend after bloody weekend.

Babe. From a blackfella, no less.

There were a couple of laughs.

Unperturbed, he watched Danny go, noted the slight swish of his buttocks. A silly thought popped into his head, a thought that made no sense considering what was happening. *Oh, he's wearing my shirt.* It was the striped one Aiden often wore to the office beneath his blazer, only now the sleeves were rolled up to show off Danny's slender arms as he slipped into silhouette.

No. Not slipped.

Rushed.

A man with a death wish.

Batman and the drunk from the backseat started throwing punches at each other. One of the two girls rushed forward and tried to pull them apart, handbag flying, knocking over empty beer bottles. The other girl scrambled for her phone as the driver attempted to stumble away—almost forgotten—until he tripped and landed on his ass.

Gulls took to the air, passing over a quarter moon.

Aiden's heart raced as he chased his partner of six years, a man who was inserting himself into a brawl in which he had no stakes, all in the apparent hope of pulling these strangers apart. Aiden pushed his phone into his pocket, not wanting it to fall to the ground and smash—the fate of his last Samsung Galaxy three months ago. Only on that occasion, he'd been running late for a meeting with the first assistant secretary of his division.

Thirst hit him like one of those wayward punches, sudden and crushing, and he wished he and Danny were back at their rental by the beach, sipping tea, scanning the horizon for whales. Something herbal in the mugs, something soothing. Jasmine, maybe. That was how they liked to end their nights when they were here on the coast, away from family and work and the year that was.

That was Christmas to them.

Batman hit the ground. Arms flailed.

"Leave him," screamed the woman on the phone as she ran in confused circles. "He's only trying to help. GET OFF HIM!"

Aiden watched Danny thrust the backseat passenger away from Batman, who was on the bitumen like a beetle on its back, peddling the air. Twirls of scarlet-lit plumes from the taxi's exhaust pipe. A rain of gull shit. The passenger lost his footing and swooped to the curb.

Oh, Christ, Aiden thought. *Don't crack your head—*

His concern was for the wrong person.

The passenger snatched one of the forgotten bottles and bounded to his feet, nimble as a dancer and not someone who'd spent the evening downing booze like there was no tomorrow. Like a man who was completely unaware that for every action there was a reaction.

Crashing glass in slow motion. Terror gripped Aiden.

Pin-wheeling shards.

The passenger smashed the bottle against Danny's face, sending him twirling to the ground by Batman's side. It didn't end there. The broken neck of the bottle came down again, the force of its descent speeding time up to catch the present, a moment that couldn't be erased, no matter how anyone on the street soon wished otherwise.

Glass stabbed into Danny's neck. Withdrew.

Came down again.

Imbedded in his upper arm.

A tide of patrons followed Aiden across the road. The play had gone too far. There was blood on the stage now. Danny's blood.

Babe's blood.

Aiden tackled the attacker with force he hadn't needed to exhibit since his days on the Lismore under 22s football team, a time when the stink of churned dirt and menthol creams were as much a part of his life as his scholarship-funded studies. He used to think he missed that kind of action.

Not anymore.

Police wouldn't turn up for another ten minutes, followed soon by an ambulance. The warm midnight wind blew and blew, shooting dust and debris along the street and up into the pub. Bags rolled through the smoking area to wrap around bar stool legs, the plastic flapping, rippling. Christmas tinsel draped from the awning came loose and waved.

A cigarette stub landed in Danny's half empty glass.

Flashing red and blue lights through the beer.

FORTY-FOUR

FEBRUARY 30, 2018

"YOU OKAY IN THERE?" called Sue, the receptionist, over torrents of pounding rain.

Her voice filtered from the door leading to the men's bathroom. Danny didn't think she would come any further but she did. He lifted his head from the toilet bowl, listening to her tip-toe approach, reminded then of the billy goats Gruff in the old tale from his childhood, as one by one, they journeyed up the hillside to make themselves fat, disrupting a troll in the process. Clip-clop. Clip-clop. Clip-clop. *Who's that trapping over my bridge?*

"I'm f-f-f-fine," he said.

Only Danny wasn't fine. Sue's shoes emerged under his door; flats, sensible and comfortable looking. Perfume crept into the cubicle with him. Such a foreign smell in this place.

"Maybe it was too soon to come back to work, Danny."

He shifted around to sit on the porcelain seat, face in hands that refused to stop shaking. Danny contemplated using one of the mindfulness apps on his phone, breathing prompters for people with anxiety, the kind of aides he recommended for his clients, and in what he considered an embarrassing act of self-defeat, he'd downloaded for himself. Danny abstained this time.

The phone remained in his spit-covered trousers, which were damp from having purged. Danny had been food binging again and put on weight—not weight Aiden or others had pointed out, rather weight he could feel. Post-vomit lightness helped, though only for a short while. Soon, as always, the familiar heaviness crept on his bones, heavy guilt.

When the panic attack struck him in the consultation room of the community services organization he worked for, he'd excused himself from the weeping man opposite him and rushed to the bathroom, convinced the barbs itching out of his thoughts were going to spear up through his skull. Fingers slipped down his throat on automatic. Nothing came up because Danny hadn't eaten anything. Just coffee. Without coffee, he wasn't convinced he could function at all.

Sue's feet didn't move.

The sound of rain reminded Danny of fly wings brushing together.

He was glad he hadn't let the app guide him into calmness, ushering those barbs back into his brain. If he had, he might not have said what he did next, and to Sue of all people. She was a new employee, one he hadn't taken the time to get to know, yet she cared enough to chase him into the men's toilets. To force him to say what he didn't want to admit. Sue: good people.

"I think I n-n-need some—" Danny started, those fingers reaching up to touch the scar under the collar of his shirt. The rippled, sewn-together flesh that had been a part of his life for the past two months. He fingered it as a child tongues an aching tooth, or like an adult lifting a Band Aid to sniff the stink beneath—curious, but nope, still not better.

"—help."

Not better at all.

FORTY-THREE

THEY WERE IN bed together that afternoon, still wearing their work shirts, trousers intertwined on the carpet. Aiden spooned Danny this time. He exhaled, soft tummy pressing against his partner's spine. Summer sun on his back from the window as he studied the rear of Danny's head—heat from behind, chill in front—wondering what it must be like to exist within it.

That thought retreated, a little afraid.

Squeezed. "Endolphins," Aiden said, coy and cutesy. Their old joke. A play on endorphins, the rush their touch once evoked. No laugh this time.

A thick sludge of hush.

"I've got something to tell you," Aiden said. Lips against Danny's neck now, stubble scratching skin. "Well, something I want to run by you, more like it."

"Y-yeah?"

"I've been offered a posting. An embassy consulate position."

"O-o-o-okay."

Danny's stutter was awful today. He hated seeing him trip over words that used to come with ease. It was hard to listen to and even harder to watch, sentences turning into invisible hands clutching at Danny's throat. Aiden was patient, of course—he had to be. This wasn't like those irks in all relationships, or at least in the relationships he'd experienced thus far. Such as the annoying way Danny wiped his mouth after every bite of food; that for some reason he insisted on pissing sitting down; or worst of all, his approach to the domestic landmine known as The Dishwasher, which on account of Danny being such an unabashed Harry Potter fan, Aiden pronounced with a Voldemort-inspired intonation.

Dissshhhhh-wwwassshhhhaaaaaa.

Aiden would be the first to say that he wasn't perfect, either.

He was a bit OCD and often overbearing, especially when it came to bookkeeping. Watching their joint finance account was a sport to him, stalking those sneaky bank fees, and worse, quizzing Danny on purchases. "Babe, did we *really* need a new set of audio speakers for the living room? Sure, the old ones are kinda tinny, but we should be saving for our next trip." Still, Aiden couldn't help it. The irks.

This was different.

Danny's stutter grated him because it was obvious it grated Danny himself. Though quiet, it shouted of hurts his lover would have otherwise denied, a verbal tattoo for everyone to see, one that read: "Well, maybe I'm *not* doing as well as I'm letting on." Danny had made references to a previous bout of stuttering when he was younger, and given what happened then, Aiden hated to think that the attack in Lismore carried similar weight.

Of course, it did. He was human.

Still—and that was a big, bold STILL—Danny had

got through it. Healing was hard, but rock-bottom proved harder. This conclusion, his partner came to on his own. Aiden knew those past resiliencies would have to be rediscovered again if they were going to get through this, and sooner rather than later.

I know you'll beat this, too.

Don't forget I'm here. As hard as this is, I'm not going anywhere.

Aiden adjusted the way his shoulder rested against the mattress and chewed the inner lining of his cheek. Danny tensed beneath his touch. Damn it, his timing was way off. The empty hush waited to be filled.

"The position is for four months," Aiden answered.

"W-where's the eh-ehhhh-e-embassy?"

Aiden exhaled and kissed the spot he'd been scratching. "It's in Bangkok." No reply. No reaction. "I'm not going to take it."

"Yu-yu-yu-yu-you have t-to. D-don't be s-stupid."

"I'm not going to leave you. Not when you're like this."

"W-what do you me-me-me-me-mean like 'this'?"

"You're hurting."

"Then why'd you tell me?" Danny said all at once, the words flowing in a rush, as though the bottleneck had passed. "W-why'd you even bring it up? Now I f-feel gu-gu-gu-guilty on t-top."

Aiden drew his partner close. "Don't do this, babe. I didn't mean it. I didn't think." He felt him resist the embrace and relent after a minute of silence. It was so like Danny to tip from okay to *really* not okay on a dime, a mood that swung hard and at dizzying speeds. Over the years, Aiden had witnessed far too many leapt-to conclusions, from pans and into fires aplenty. Nobel intentions could only carry you so far.

A twisted nerve of memory:

Danny's blood had appeared black in the moonlight as they waited for the ambulance. Aiden's fists pushing against the wound to stop the hot spurts, gristle and flesh poking through his fingers like weeds through concrete. Shouts. Seagulls. Wind blowing. Tears plopping against Danny's shirt. *No, my shirt. He'd looked so good in it, too*. Drunk men and women with their phones out, recording everything—something that infuriated him at the time yet he was thankful for once the trial rolled around.

Three weeks ago, Batman, the man who stabbed Danny, the man whose real name was George Prescott, had been sentenced to four years and two months' imprisonment for one charge of recklessly causing serious injury with a non-parole period of two years and four months. The taxi driver, Paul Dee, pled guilty to driving under the influence; his license was suspended, the fine a hefty $3,300. He was ordered to undergo drug and alcohol counselling.

It wasn't fucking fair, none of it.

When all distractions faded, in moments just like this, an awful fact crawled into Aiden's mind, a kind of monster from deep down under the bed, its claws reaching out to snatch him by the ankles. Trauma had teeth. Big sharp ones, too. And all the jail time and fines in the world couldn't satisfy its hunger. Trauma always came back for seconds.

"S-sorry," Danny said. "I'm nervy is all. Th-the p-p-pills the psych' gave me aren't w-worth shit. Feels l-like th-there's a st-st-st-st-st-strain in my h-head."

"I'm sorry." Aiden wasn't apologizing for the emotions he'd stirred, but for everything. Even though he didn't have to. Even though, like Danny's medications, it offered no relief. "You know, you *could* come with me."

"W-what?"

"For the four-month stint," Aiden said, excited. "Take leave from work. You'd be my spouse. The government would provide you with a stipend. It'll be birdseed, but hey, better than nothing. It'd give you time to get better. Space. Away from all this shit."

"In B-bangkok?"

"In Bangkok." Aiden thrust his hips against Danny's ass, two firm pounds. "Love you long-time."

Danny half-laughed and pushed back on his boyfriend's crotch. The monster retreated to feast again another day. "I haven't been to T-thailand in over t-twenty years."

They breathed in the hot February air flooding their townhouse in Casino, an hour's drive from the places they didn't want to be: Evans Head, where Danny's parents lived and fretted; from Lismore, the city in which they both worked, where the stabbing occurred and Aiden's family connections stemmed from. Far away, all of it, just as it needed to be. This dwelling was their safe zone, one they even had a nickname for.

The Panic Room.

"I'm Jodie Foster-ing," Danny would say, pretending to fight against forces pushing against the door from the other side. Forces that took the form of answering machine messages from Danny's parents. "Hide, babe. Duck and cover! They're on to us."

Where was that man now, the one who made Aiden laugh? Well, he wasn't here in The Panic Room today. Or yesterday. Or the day before that.

Aiden glanced at the walls where photographs were hung.

Happy snaps from their travels, kisses in the shadows of monuments. Danny's folks, a couple whose down-to-earth affability never translated to film; they glared at Aiden from within their frames with stoic, forced smiles. Seeing them there like that, he couldn't blame Danny for assuming The Fletchers wouldn't be okay with the 'whole gay thing'. They had been. Surprise of surprises, they had *also* been okay with a black boyfriend. Aiden had the Christmas cards with the little x's and o's to prove it.

His own family situation was somewhat more complicated, and the fact that he even *thought* this way stoked the embers of his still-burning remorse. Aiden traced his bloodlines from photograph to photograph this time.

Brothers and sisters. Cousins and aunties and uncles.

These were his people, people of the Bundjalung, who identified amongst themselves and other Aboriginal men and women in the Richmond Valley as Gooris. However, were you white, you referred to them as Gubbers, the word for government, the true custodians of the land; a single word intended to be an acknowledgement from the invaders who took their earth and children, which even after all these years, was rarely given.

Bam-smack in the middle of the wall was a picture of a skinnier Aiden on his graduation day, mother by his side. She beamed a cheeky smile, trying to yank the four-pointed hat off his head and toss it into the second-growth bushes of the university grounds behind them. He, in turn, thumped her with his rolled-up degree in International Policy Making. *Click*.

Mother and son: blurs of pride and disbelief. Aiden had accomplished what nobody in his upbringing said he could. He'd made it. It felt good to not be underestimated.

Things had strained since then.

Yes, his mother knew he was gay but the rest of the family didn't. Maybe the absence of her cheeky smile eight years ago, back when he explained why he hadn't had a girlfriend since the ninth grade, implied it should remain that way.

This was one of the reasons he'd moved to Casino in the first place. The city was close enough to dart home for Sorry Business, yet just far away to maintain his sanity.

The Panic Room.

Their safe place.

It was small—and Aiden knew it would only get smaller without him in it, walls inching in day by day, constricting until positive thoughts spilled from Danny like pus from a bursting blister. Aiden didn't want any of those notorious mood swings happening whilst he was out of the country, not when Danny's scars were still—and that was another big, bold STILL—this raw.

"Just think about it," Aiden said, blood rushing from his head and into his groin. He wanted to fuck but didn't push it. Though Danny's medications refused to work, the side-effects persisted, a mocking reminder of how long the path to recovery would be, if indeed it would ever be reached. On and off again impotence was one such side-effect.

"It's o-okay," Danny said, easing against the tent in Aiden's trousers. "I d-don't mind."

"Nah, babe. Not if—"

A pause between them. "I w-w-want you to feel close t-to me."

"Are you sure?"

Danny nodded and reached around to touch the small of Aiden's sweaty back. That caress spoke so much without saying anything at all; it put both men at ease because where there were no words there was no stutter.

Go easy, implied the touch. *It's been a while.*

"Endolphins?" Aiden said, just as coy. Just as cute.

"Endolphins."

FORTY-TWO

APRIL 2, 2018

A CLOUDLESS DAY. Towns resembled spilled salt on a checkered tablecloth of green and ochre. It was beautiful down there through the Boeing's window, and it didn't seem real, and as they flew over the gulf into the great wide blue, it was soon all of it gone.

The journey to Thailand began, fates sealed airtight as their breaths within the plane.

Spilled salt, as Aiden's mother used to say, brought with it bad luck. Later, when their lives came unsewn, he would hate himself for not heeding such warnings sooner.

Aiden flicked through the old movies on offer, settling on *It's A Wonderful Life*. He'd never seen it before and didn't realize it was a Christmas story until it began. He sat through the whole thing though, almost in defiance. It was an okay flick, sentimental and very, very white. He did, however, enjoy the scene where Jimmy Stewart offered to lasso the moon for the girl he was crushing on, the ultimate gift. Yeah, that made him smile. Given the chance, Aiden would do the same for Danny.

In a heartbeat.

The food was good in business class, which Danny, being on a social worker's salary, had never flown before. Each time they ordered a drink they toasted the Australian government. Diplomacy: tiring and often thankless work, yet it had its perks here and there.

No turbulence.

Aiden dove in and out of dreams he couldn't remember, waking to reach across the armrest and take his partner's hand. Squeeze-squeeze. Danny always seemed to be alert, sometimes watching a movie, sometimes staring out the window. But never sleeping.

PART TWO

FORTY-ONE

JUNE 1, 2018

BASKETS OF FRUIT and meat in the hulls of canoes, manned by proprietors tapping wares with fresh Baht notes, shouted, 'First sale of the day!' They did this because tried-and-*maybe*-true tradition implied it brought good luck. In places like these, where the skillful prospered and the lazy went hungry, good luck was a currency that mattered.

Men and women, buyers and sellers both, contorted themselves to reach for that perfect durian, to shoo away flies. Tourists laid down their earnings after a volley of intense and often inappropriate bartering. Back, forth, back, forth, relent, feast.

This was Damnoen Saduak, the famous floating market west of Bangkok, a spattering of colors spanning the river's girth from bank to bank.

Or to be more precise, this was a photograph of those markets, one clipped and mounted within a nice bamboo frame, purchased by the Australian government with taxpayer coin. The remnants of the price tag could still be seen.

This photograph adorned one of the four walls of

Danny and Aiden's bedroom on the third floor of their building on Soi 9 between Krung Thon Buri BTS Station and the Chao Phraya waterfront. With the windows shuttered, it felt more like a prison than a diplomat's sleeping quarters. Danny liked it this way.

A ceiling fan cut the humid air—*whomp, whomp, whomp*.

He sprawled on the mattress in his underwear and only pulled on a shirt when his computer beeped to life. The Skype tune sang a song that made his ears hurt.

"Shit." Danny had forgotten about the appointment. "Bugger-shit-shit-shit."

Half clothed, he walked the laptop into the living room opposite the kitchen, passing their bathroom where dirty clothes waited to be herded and taken to the laundromat down the street. The blinds were drawn out here, too.

Shadows everywhere.

He drew out a chair and plonked himself at the table in the middle of the room. Hit the accept button on the call. A mug of coffee on the bamboo placemat; Aiden must have brewed it for him before heading off to work a couple of hours ago. The drink would be cold. He was thankful nonetheless. Aiden was good to him, despite the shit he put him through.

Chilly caffeine danced across Danny's tongue. Good.

In the two seconds between the Skype tune ending and the caller's face beeping onto the screen, their cameras struggling to catch up with Bangkok's temperamental Internet connection, Danny enjoyed a moment of silence.

Yes, he thought. *This.*

Nothing.

Static snarled. He winced.

"Hi, Danny," said his psychologist from her office in Brisbane. "Can you see me okay?"

"S-sure can."

The pain in his shoulder flared.

"Great. Well, let's get started. Tell me how you've been since our conversation at the end of last month."

Danny twiddled his fingers as he recited all that had been happening. Adjusting to life in Thailand; strategies to cope with isolation; mindfulness exercises; the way his stutter was receding—thank god—and of course, his relationship.

"How have things been on that end, Danny?"

Jesus, he hated the way she pronounced his name. It was a punctuation to drive home an agenda—here's my question, Patient X, and I'm using your name to let you know I already know the answer.

Well, sorry, but I don't want to be one of your outcomes, Doc.

I do not consent.

He picked up on this because it was something he himself had done with many of his clients. This depressed him further.

Hip-hip hooray. I've become one of them.

A mental health worker in need of a mental health worker.

"Things are g-g-going fine with Aiden and me," Danny lied, rubbing the scar beneath his shirt, scars existing on already existing scars. Through the screen, across the thousands of miles separating him here in this dingy room from the psychologist in her office, he saw her eyes zooming in on his hand.

To where he scratched.

Danny dropped his arm, caught doing something he didn't want anyone—let alone her—to see.

Keep the wall up. Keep it. Jesus Christ keep it up.

Brick after brick aligned with well-trained precision, only something was changing. A slipping. Cracks. He could feel them.

Scratch-scratch-scratch.

Danny forced himself into the shower once the scheduled session was up. Pipes groaned behind the walls as he stood there, hands against the tiles, lukewarm water coursing down his back. Bed was easier than this, than any of it. Dried off, he brushed his teeth with bottled water in front of the mirror, a towel around his torso. His phone rang—again that shrieking static, headache booming. Danny spat into the basin and noticed scarlet threads in the foam.

How long did I scrub for?

Time was slippery in the apartment, and more so with each passing day. This blurring, however, wasn't altogether unwelcome. His focus was rough-edged and sharp. It cut.

He strode into the bedroom and answered Aiden's call. "Hey b-babe."

"Sawasdee Krab! How'd the psych' session go?"

"Yeah, fine. She k-kuh-kunk-knows her stuff."

"Good. Want to debrief?"

"Nah. I'll walk it off."

"Good idea. Hey, why don't you catch a ferry down to Thon Buri and pop into the embassy to visit me. It's only a ten minute walk down Sathon Tai Road. There's not much happening over here. All those Aussie tourists are behaving themselves."

"For n-now. Wait u-u-until after dark."

"Ain't that the truth. So what do you say? Come visit me. There's coffee."

"We'll see, babe. I'm feeling a b-b-b-bit blah."

"Fair enough," Aiden said. "Up for tonight still?"

"What's happening t-tonight again?"

"Danny, I've told you, like, five times. It's the department dinner. Partners are invited. The Minister's in town. A bit of western food for your tummy." Another one of those beats, emptiness that was full of something neither one of them wanted to acknowledge. Like the psychologist's pronunciation of Danny's name: a quiet agenda. "There's free drinks."

Whomp, whomp, whomp, went the fan.

"I'll s-see how I go," Danny said, gripping the phone. "I had a rough night."

"I know, babe. I heard you talking in your sleep."

"Really? W-what was I saying? W-w-w-waffle, as usual?"

"You, waffle? Never!" Aiden laughed, a kind sound that made Danny feel loved. How on earth had he managed to find someone as patient as Aiden? This question elicited a deep, rumbling sigh. Danny hated that he couldn't remember how to love right, that his affection—like his voice—caught in stuttered knots. The love was there, but he saw it through bars he couldn't widen.

"I'd n-never waffle," Danny said. "I'm eloquent as f-f-fuck."

"Not last night you weren't."

"Huh?"

"I don't envy whatever dream you were having. It sounded like you were being chased. Kind of scary. You were semi-awake and I remember touching your shoulder. You jumped like I was electric. Then you looked at me like you'd never laid eyes on me before. 'Who's after you, babe?' I asked. You said peep, rolled over. Still as a bub."

The itch in Danny's shoulder increased. "Oh."

"You sure you're alright?"

"Yep. G-got to go."

Danny dressed, and poured himself the day's first drink, *Chang* beer from the 7-11 down the street poured straight into a glass he kept frosted in the refrigerator. He liked the cool on his fingers, the chill against his lower lip as he sipped. It was one o'clock in the afternoon.

He opened the walk-in wardrobe and rifled through the clothes to find something appropriate to wear that night. Like everything in the apartment, it was musty, swampy despite the chug of the air conditioning unit built into the far wall.

Another glass poured, another sip. It went down easier—hell, it always did.

The numbing wrapped around him nice and slow.

FORTY

DANNY MARCHED THROUGH Bangkok's crooked street-veins like a bubble of oxygen seeking out a heart to stop, listening to a playlist on his phone as he went. He wasn't moved by what he saw and gained pleasure only in those moments when the world tripped into rhythm with one of his songs. These little synchronicities turned everything Technicolor. Streets came to life, clouds parted. Now there were smiles on the faces passing him by, food smells that cut through the humid sewer fog.

These moments didn't last.

Either the world shrugged off the song or the song shrugged off the world, and then all that Technicolor bled to black and white again, leaving Danny to settle into his strides and walk those uneven streets alone, dodging cars and tuk-tuks, sky spitting. He didn't know where he was going or why he'd left the apartment in the first place. He never did.

Dogs scurried between buildings, each minute of their lives spent fearful of beatings. Food scraps everywhere. Meat-stripped skewers poked out of trash cans. Cats scrutinized him from rooftops, from shadowy awnings, their eyes catching the afternoon light. Bubbling oil in street-cart vats. Telephone and electricity wires gnarled from building to building like masses of hair pulled from a drain. Bangkok may be singing, but Danny only heard its shrieks.

The numbness wore off.

His scars began to itch.

He stepped into a bar where backpackers played Connect Four with one of the hostesses. This was a place of laughter and fairy lights and easy-appeasement, and it would have to do. He ordered a beer. Fifteen minutes later, the numbness returned and that improved things.

He twisted his glass so the condensation made Olympic rings on the wooden table, and watched the backpackers from where he sat. *I was one of them once.*

I don't even remember who that person was.

Or he didn't want to.

No. That wasn't true.

Danny longed for his past, could feel it tickling as an amputee must feel a phantom limb. The truth was he didn't *let* himself remember. Going backwards wasn't healthy; this bubble coursed a one-way vein, a rule he'd set for himself.

Connect Four tiles dropped. Lights flickered.

Why am I not happy?

Danny yanked off his earbuds, startled. His mouth was dry, despite the drink. He thought he'd heard dry, bony branches clattering right behind him. But there were only flies.

THIRTY-NINE

AIDEN CAME HOME to find their apartment empty. This would happen many times over in the months to come.

"Babe?"

A faint echo off the walls.

The dial tone as he called, and called, and called.

Aiden sat on the edge of the bed he shared with a man he'd dragged across the world because he thought 'getting away' might be healing. Sure, healing may very well be a part of what was happening here, but he couldn't help questioning why it had to hurt so damn much along the way.

Danny's suit was laid out on the mattress, a shadow freed of its master.

THIRTY-EIGHT

JULY 3, 2018

"YOU'VE LOST WEIGHT," Aiden said.

"Yeah."

"Must be all those long walks."

"M-maybe," Danny replied, staring at his food. He scooped Pad Thai into his mouth with chopsticks, their wooden ends clicking. This sound—crab claws, carrion-feeders—made Aiden's skin crawl.

Silence again within the apartment, while outside Bangkok exploded with evening activity. There was always a festival of some sort happening, or night markets with a multitude of foods to try, temples to explore.

Yet here they sat at their table for two.

Aiden held his fork a little harder than he needed to; he'd never mastered chopsticks. Knuckles rolled white, bones rising through the skin.

I want to throttle some sense into him.

Look where we are, Aiden longed to scream.

There are people all over the world who would kill to be here.

He did no such thing, of course. Danny would only

withdraw if confronted. This was their emotional tango now: one step forward, two steps back, and if the moves were blundered they both went down.

It takes time to get better, Aiden had to assure himself. The grip on his fork loosened. *I've got that time to spare, and if I don't, well, I'll make time.*

I brought him here after all.

Things weren't always bad. The fleeting laughs over the past few weeks, a handful of Netflix binges interrupted by the buffer wheel as they waited for the Internet to catch up with their desperate need to know what was going to happen on the next episode of *Game of Thrones*. The show itself wasn't Aiden's cup of tea but he knew Danny enjoyed it, so he'd gone along because that's what healthy couples do, he figured, the yield and tug of interests going this way and that. These times spent together, taking turns to rest the laptop on their chests, were lightening to Aiden.

Did the few good moments make up for the bad ones?

Aiden couldn't, in all honesty, say that they did. This may be why his knuckles often rolled white, why the urge to shake and throttle his partner surged.

He'd also received an email from Danny's parents in Evans Head, forty kilometres away from The Panic Room, an email addressed to Aiden because, "We never hear back from Danny these days. Do you know if he's changed his contacts?"

"Are you sure he's okay?"

That question was a stain. Aiden saw it when he was at work. He saw it as he waited in the café near his office on his lunch break for Danny to join him as planned, and where he eventually ate alone. Every forced smile since then, every 'It'll be okay, he just needs time' pep-talk Aiden delivered to the man in the mirror was an attempt to scrub that stain away. Only sometimes it felt like he was spreading it in the process.

His reply to The Fletchers was short, loving.

"We miss you both. Danny's just been snowed under with some side projects he's working on—you know what he's like once he's got his mind set on something. That's no excuse. I'll crack the whip on him and be sure to get him to contact you ASAP. Let's all do a Skype session next week? Does Thursday night work for you? xxAiden."

Side projects? What a joke.

After hitting the send icon, he'd gone to The Sick Room, as he now thought of it as, and found Danny sprawled across the mattress, snoring. The shutters were drawn, lending the room its cell-like appearance again, one with bars he couldn't see, each erected by a prisoner who gave no indication of wanting to leave. Aiden eased the door shut, wood wisping over carpet.

Tip-toed to the bathroom.

Opened the cupboard beneath the hand basin.

Drew out the box of medical and First Aid supplies, and rifled through the contents. Fingers latched onto one of Danny's prescribed antidepressants. The seal was broken, as expected. He flipped the bottle face up to read the printing.

LEXAPRO: SEROTONIN REUPTAKE INHIBITOR.
TAKE ONCE DAILY IN THE MORNING WITH WATER.

Aiden twisted off the child-proof lid and upended the contents onto his palm. Nine round pills stared up at him. He funneled the medication back in and slid it into the box beside seven other identical bottles.

The following evening, Aiden came home late again. He'd been anchored to work filling in reports after receiving a call from a distraught mother who'd been informed her son was being held in Bang Kwang Central Prison on drug possession charges. 'People never fucking learn!' were the closing remarks Aiden longed to write in his summary.

He bit his tongue.

This wasn't Monopoly. When it came to being caught with drugs in this part of Southeast Asia—even MDMA pills, a small grace if there ever was one—there was no get out of jail card the Embassy could toss onto the board. Were that the case, all seventy-two Australians held in Thai prisons for similar crimes, including those on death row, would find themselves on the next comfy Qantas flight home.

Still, Aiden did his work as he was paid to do. He did it with a smile.

The distraught phone calls were over for now, though they would come again tomorrow. Those briefings weren't going to write themselves. The concept was draining, and coming home on the ferry, his day took its toll.

Who helps those who help others?

This question often robbed him of sleep. His drive to fix any situation, to be the peacemaker, a diplomat to the bitter end, was to fight smoke. Now he was doing the same thing at home. No wonder he was exhausted.

Who helps those who help others?

Who *try* to help others?

Try.

No answers waited for him in the empty apartment that day.

Aiden took himself straight to the bathroom, the walls funneling by as those nine pills funneled back into their child-proof bottle the night before. He slammed the lights, fluorescents blink-blink-blinking, and crouched before the cupboard. Aiden snatched up the opened Lexapro. This was something from a suspense movie, he thought: amateur sleuth goes through suspect's house searching for evidence, that kind of thing. Only Danny wasn't guilty of any crime. He just was a man worthy of love who'd gone through some really tough shit he didn't deserve.

That's why I'm being a prissy snoop: because I think I'm here to help.

Or maybe I just want to know I'm right.

In a coincidence that served no real point, yet which unnerved Aiden to his core, the young man spending that night in prison had been caught by Thai police with the same number of pills Aiden held in his hand right now. In his shaking hand.

Nine.

THIRTY-SEVEN

AIDEN BOLTED UPRIGHT, shock slamming him awake. It was still dark in their bedroom, the ceiling fan whipping the air. Danny screamed in his sleep.

"Wake up, babe," Aiden said, rolling over to touch his partner's back. He stilled his hand instead. Heat beamed off Danny's pale flesh through the weave of his cotton shirt. Feverish. Sickly. The sheets were wet with perspiration.

"Stop!" Aiden cried, not sure what to do. He couldn't have been more surprised if he'd woken in the night to find himself spooning a crocodile. Danny thrashed the mattress, beating at it in blind swipes. Jaws clenched so tight the grinding of teeth could be heard above the shrieks.

"Jesus fucking Christ."

This couldn't go on.

Aiden ignored the thoughts ricocheting through his mind as to whether night terrors were like a sleepwalker's trek—and if they were, was premature waking a bad idea?—and shook his partner as hard as he could. Danny flipped over, scream cut short, and snatched Aiden by the neck.

Fingers curled around his throat. A semi-strong grip.

Moments before, Aiden had been dreaming of Australia, as he so often did, memories and fantasies mixing together like tree breeds in the bush. Now here he was in his Bangkok bedroom, strangled by a man strangled by night terrors.

It didn't seem real. Couldn't be.

But the fingers dropping from his throat weren't imaginary, nor were the coughs that followed. Not a dream. This shit was actually happening.

Aiden stole a gulp of air. "What the fuck?" He gripped the flesh under his chin, which now burned as Danny's had before, as though the fever were passed via touch.

Danny sat up, bedsprings crying.

Aiden could see his silhouette detailed against the glow from the venetian blinds, and watched, angry and hurt, as that silhouette drew him into a hug. Sweaty skins clapped. Aiden tried to push his partner off, but Danny clung to him, not with apology as best as he could tell, but desperation.

Save me, this hug implied—no, screamed.

SAVE ME.

Aiden eased his fury aside and didn't shy away when Danny started crying.

"It's okay," he said. "I know you didn't mean it."

They remained like this for some time, until fatigue drew them onto the damp, twisted sheets again. Danny refused to let go. It felt good to be wanted like this, Aiden realized. This was what partners were for.

"I'm here for you, babe. Always."

Danny's kiss came from nowhere. Rough lips. Stubble. Aiden kissed back, drew away, and then asked in a whisper, "What's happening to you? I'm worried you're not well. I don't know what to do. I—I just don't."

Another kiss.

Aiden feared this tender sequel was fuelled by the need to silence him, as opposed to affection. Still, he let it come and their tongues intertwined. Aiden didn't worry about his bed breath; they were too far gone for that.

Soon, Danny's hands were running down his chest, past his bellybutton. They slipped beneath the waistband of his boxer shorts. Aiden gasped again, not out of fear this time. This gasp was different, albeit unexpected.

Heat continued to radiate off Danny's skin as they made love for the last time.

THIRTY-SIX

JULY 11, 2018

"What in the buggery is going on over there?" asked Danny's mother. She leaned close enough to the camera for her face to fill the entire Skype screen, which sometimes froze and kaleidoscoped into squares. "You've lost so much weight!"

"It's t-t-the he-heat, Mum."

"Humidity's a killer over here, Bev," Aiden added. "All you do is sweat day in, day out."

"Don't go getting heatstroke, boys," Danny's father said, fighting for airtime. "It happened to me once on Chinaman's Beach. Thought my head was going to explode. I came over all shivery, too. It knocks you about, for sure."

"I'm b-b-be-being s-safe," Danny said, the last annunciation coming out pained. His words were more barbed than usual today, not that Aiden blamed him. There was something about these two old people that churned their anxieties. It was odd, too, Aiden thought, that he considered them as being more advanced in years than they were. Something about the way they fussed and contorted their concerns into agonized efforts aged them. For many people, love was hard, and it always took a toll.

Aiden related to that.

"I'm just being a worry wort," Bev Fletcher said. Her husband, Saul, nodded. "I can't help it, you know. People lose that much weight, you get worried. Jenny down the street dropped five dress sizes in two months and it turned out she had cancer."

"Mum, I d-duh-duh-don't have c—"

"This is the last thing I need right now, Danny. Doctor Benson has changed my medication and I'm up half the night these days with my worries. Are you sure you don't need bloodwork done? What kind of medical facilities do you have over there? You hear awful things about Bali."

"We're in Thailand," Aiden said, trying not to let his annoyance show.

"Oh, you know what I mean. Don't go getting any tattoos or anything. They don't change the needles. I've read about it in the magazines."

"We won't, Bev," Aiden said, desperate to change the subject. The very idea of having to go through this entire routine again with his own mother in about twenty minutes was in and of itself fatiguing. "How are things back home?"

"Well," Saul said with a kind smile.

It took no time for Bev to correct him. "The weather's dreadful. Everyone's getting sick around town. Lucy, next door, her little bub got the pneumonia. Poor chicken. I made them a casserole and took it over. It's the least I can do. God only knows I've got the time. You know how they say it takes a village to raise a child? They weren't wrong."

Aiden tensed.

Bev had a habit of turning conversations around to other people's children and grandchildren, she not having any of the latter to flaunt herself. It was no secret that she ached to be a part of the knitted booties and bibs club. Aiden knew how much this upset Danny. Why wouldn't it? Neither of them had a womb. It upset him, too. He was confident they would be wonderful fathers.

Aiden reached under the kitchen table to caress his partner's thigh. A little squeeze to let Danny know he was there.

Still.

Once the conversation wrapped, Danny went to the kitchen sink. He started doing the dishes. Steam clouded the window above the bench, Bangkok twinkling beyond like a galaxy viewed through clouds; whatever lives were lived out there were far away, and enviable.

Aiden joined him. Those plates weren't being washed. They were punished.

Arms slipped around Danny's waist. "Her heart's in the right place, but holy-fuck sticks, she's too much sometimes." No reply. Shifting muscle beneath the shirt. A splash of suds on the floor. "Ready for round two? My mum will be calling soon, if she can figure out how to work the computer."

"I-I-I can't."

Aiden exhaled into Danny's neck. This revelation piggybacked annoyance but carried with it no real shock. Of course, it would go like this. He let his hands drop, where they hung heavy by his sides. The drain glugged and slurped when Danny pulled the plug and turned sideways to avoid his eyes.

Danny shuffled to the refrigerator and pulled out a bottle of *Chang*, because that was easier than acknowledging how unfair this all was.

"I've got family, too, you know," Aiden said to the man slipping towards their room. This coincided with the Skype account's delightful chirp. There was something in the melody that reminded him of morning birdsong in the northern river region, the kookaburra trying to laugh but not quite getting it right as it hunted for snakes, the blue kingfisher as it sought a mate. Hissing trees when the wind blew.

The art of the earth.

I need to go to Country, Aiden thought. This ping of homesickness caught him off guard. *I need my home real bad right now.*

Needing something didn't make it so. Aiden went to the computer and spoke with his mother, her brown face framed by silver hair. He longed for her hugs.

Finished, he passed their room on his left to see Danny on the bed with the beer tucked between his legs, phone in hand, fan spinning loud and fast above. Aiden didn't join him. He went to the bathroom and slid the door shut behind him instead.

Drops of water grew fat at the end of the faucet before plopping into the hand-basin. The whir of those two bulbs as they shed their unnatural light over this cramped, damp space. A cockroach scuttled across the mirror and slipped into a crack in the wall.

Caught you in the act, fucker.

Aiden didn't drop to his knees, didn't open the cupboard, didn't shuffle through the box of medications. He didn't need to. Those nine pills would still be there, clustered together in a bottle that was, yes, child-proof, but not *fool*-proof. So, it was with another sigh that Aiden went to the toilet bowl to lift the lid. The ring clattered against the cistern loud enough to make his heart skip a beat.

It was like a gunshot.

Panting and weak-kneed, Aiden shrugged down the front of his shorts and freed his penis. Unlike Danny, he was circumcised. Back when they first started dating, this difference proved a bit of a novelty, as Aiden had never been with an uncut white guy before—and only one since, a Grindr hook-up they invited over to The Panic Room and had a threesome with last year.

That was a distant memory. Not the act itself, rather the mutual hunger that drove them to it. Sure, Aiden was horny as ever, but the same couldn't be said for Danny. Excluding their lovemaking the week before, his partner had neither initiated sex nor accepted his invitations in over two months.

Maybe I'm not pissed about him avoiding Mum.

Jesus. Maybe I've just got blue balls.

That was what happened with people who had been hurt, said every one of Aiden's Google searches. A search that was always followed by a prompt deletion of his browser history.

This is what happens.

Head swimming, Aiden propped one arm against the wall and let his bladder loose. Keeping his balance was important, because love Danny as he did, he couldn't count on him to help him were he to fall. However, their situation wasn't without hope. Those Google searches also suggested most people bounced back from tragedy.

Most people.

This train of thought snapped in two. A yelp escaped his throat.

It felt like he was pissing razor blades.

THIRTY-FIVE

AIDEN DIDN'T TELL Danny about that stabbing sensation.

Not then.

He kept this information to himself and crawled into bed fifteen minutes later, shame-faced, clutching the novel he'd been attempting to get through since arriving in Thailand. Not that he was reading it, mind you. His thoughts were a jumble of diagnoses and rationalizations.

If it's a urinary tract infection, I'll bloody scream.

Wait 'til tomorrow. It could be a one-off kind of thing. That happens.

What if it's a kidney stone?

Mate, just stop.

Aiden placed the book down on the bedside table and rolled over to spoon Danny, who was still playing on his phone with his back to him. "Tell me how much I should be worrying about you," Aiden whispered. "Please, just tell me."

The phone clicked off.

"I'm j-just guh-going through a r-rough patch is all." Danny's stutter, as was always the case post-beer, was less pronounced.

"I want to keep you safe."

“I know. I ap-preciate it.” A gecko sounded from somewhere in the room. “Even if I d-don’t show it.”

“Tell me what you’re thinking. Please. It’s driving me barney not knowing.”

Aiden could feel Danny’s pulse through his back. It quickened. “I-I—”

“You can tell me, babe.”

“I-I feel—” Danny stumbled, and then tried again. “Empty.”

Aiden linked his hands across Danny’s chest, locking the man in.

“I w-wish I was a dad.”

Aiden had no reply for this. There never was because there was nothing he could do to change it. So many times, he’d thought about how much easier it was for straight people whose relationships were on the rocks. ‘We’ve got to make it work for the kids,’ they often said—or so, Aiden had been told by his cousins after a beer or two. This was the great ache of being a gay man; you were haunted by the ghosts of those who had never been.

Please don’t leave me, he thought. *Please*.

Night wound on.

I wish I was a dad. Dad. Dad.

The gecko chimed a few more times. Aiden’s arms remained linked across Danny’s chest, even though it started to hurt. He put his ear to the middle of his partner’s back and the sound beneath the skin was like something groaning just before it breaks.

THIRTY-FOUR

JULY 19, 2018

"SIR, YOU HAVE tested positive to chlamydia," said the nurse on the phone.

Aiden imagined her face glancing up from her clipboard, the curve of her cheek catching the afternoon light seeping through the windows of the sexual health clinic he'd been sitting in eight days earlier, a place the doctor at the hospital referred him to, 'just in case it's not a UTI'. Aiden couldn't tell if the woman on the phone was the same person who had run the procedure, although she sounded familiar.

Green eyes. A deadpan tone.

He sat back in his office chair, the imitation leather creaking. Aiden blinked, leaned forward again, volume dropping. "I don't really know how that could be."

"Excuse me, sir? I don't—"

"I mean, are *you* sure?"

Aiden laughed.

"Sure? Yes, sir."

"Right then."

"Treatment is easy. I'll prescribe you a course of antibiotics. Take two pills a day for three weeks. It's a bigger course because you have tested positive in your penis and in your throat. I'll need you to come back to the clinic to pick everything up. You can do this?"

"Yeah, yeah, fine. I guess I'll be there in an hour-and-a-half. Jesus, I'll duck over on my lunch break."

"Good. But it is not all bad news. You have tested negative to everything else. No traces of HIV in your blood."

Later in the day with the antibiotics tucked into his bag, enough sweat pouring down his back to make his business shirt almost transparent, Aiden tried hailing down a cab. Cars and tuk-tuks scooted by, not stopping. Horns blared. People swept trash into the drains all around him, an act which at any other time would have been jarring, only he was too distracted to be bothered now. Smog snatched the breath from his mouth.

Aiden coughed and thought yes, he could vomit right there and then.

Keep your cool.

Times like this, with all the chaos around him, Aiden struggled to tell if he loved or hated this city. His call to Country reached out once more.

Come back to me.

This place, all of it, it's just not worth it.

He couldn't go. Aiden had a job to do—in fact, his presence was required at the prison within the hour. If his personal life was going to keep falling apart, it was imperative that work remain healthy at least.

Without that, what the fuck do I have here anymore?

"You fucking prick," Aiden said as a cab stopped in front of him.

Panic swooped in.

He hesitated to get inside. He imagined Paul Dee, the drunk driver from Lismore greeting him, bringing with him the stink of booze, and then, as always, the coppery tang of blood.

Pull your head in, Aiden.

Time to man up.

Listening to the best version of himself, Aiden clenched his fists and sidestepped into the backseat. Paul Dee, who in his mind set this awful wheel in motion, wasn't the person in the driver's seat, the person reaching for the meter, the person throwing a delightful, "Sawadee krup" Aiden's way.

Just a stranger.

Aiden pulled out his phone and showed the driver where he wanted to go. Settled. Foot jiggled against the floor. Reached for a seatbelt that wasn't there.

THIRTY-THREE

DANNY, TOO, WAS in transit.

He took a swig from a water bottle that didn't contain water.

Fiery gin. Its safe warmth.

The tuk-tuk pulled up by the curb, engine purring. Danny stepped onto the street. Hot sunshine against his neck. Nausea thrummed as he paid the driver. He didn't bother with the change, nor did he care that he'd been overcharged. The cart puttered away, merged with traffic rocketing by at three times its pace, motorcycles swarming, some toting four people to a seat. That was Thailand for you, he thought and almost immediately forgot.

He spun around and faced Wat Pho, the Buddhist temple complex in the Phra Nakhon District on Rattanakosin Island, just south of the Grand Palace. Danny had come here on his first trip to Bangkok over twenty years ago, and dressed now in a pair of culturally appropriate trousers, he entered the grounds again, this time at the age of forty-two.

Pigeons took to the air. Twirling feathers. Stray dogs lounged in the shadows of the trees. Barking. Incense filled the air; it smelled of powdery jasmine.

Danny walked to the chapel of the reclining Buddha, a forty-six meter gold statue with lazy eyes that gleamed from a head propped up by a giant hand as it lounged, so casual and indifferent. *Draw me like one of your Thai girls.* Danny came close to laughing.

Close, but didn't.

Before getting any nearer to the attraction, the visage of which was said to be the gateway to Nirvana, he approached a string of vendors selling street food. There, roti was flipped, jellyfish deep-fried, noodles spun from mess and into meals topped with peanuts and coriander stems. It was the first time he'd felt hungry in far too long.

Danny slipped off his headphones, killing the music that made the outside world tolerable, as he came to the last stall. Two women, one of whom it turned out spoke decent English, cooked bones in a broth.

The younger woman wanted to know where he was from. He told her. She laughed, saying "Aussie-Aussie-Aussie-Oi-Oi-Oi!" He asked her what they were cooking, and the older woman leaned in close.

Too close

"These are knuckles," she whispered. Danny smelled something on her breath. Something familiar. What was it? Yes, licorice. "Do you have arthritis?"

"No."

"Too bad," the woman replied. "Eating knuckles helps sore hands." She smiled at him once more, showing off the spaces between her missing teeth, tongue pushing up to fill the gaps. "Eat the part that hurts. Where do you hurt?"

THIRTY-TWO

DANNY EXPLORED THE temple grounds. He hadn't eaten in the end.

The old woman's licorice-scented words followed him down every avenue, into every gold-gilded tabernacle.

Eat the part that hurts.

His nausea returned as he looped around to stand before the reclining Buddha, surrounded by twenty tourists taking photographs, a tangle of selfie-sticks and shawls given to them at the front gate to cover the parts of their bodies considered undignified to reveal in such a place. Languages volleyed back and forth.

Snapping camera lenses.

Wailing children.

They're like seagulls, Danny thought with a dash of contemptuousness. Their feathers bristled against him as he tried to wiggle free, beaks stabbing. Not around him. At him. He couldn't tell if it was the gin or the heat or the fact that he was a wreck of his former self, but something was wrong.

The temple began to revolve. Colors greased together. Earbuds slipped free and squawks and bell chimes slipped through. The air turned reedy, thin.

Through the great turning, he caught glimpses of that night in Lismore. There were feathers flying there, too. Gulls feeding on a dropped pie, ratty eyes twitching. A cab slamming up over the curb. The lanky man falling to the ground. Smashing glass. A man blocking out the moon as he stabbed, and stabbed, and stabbed.

Terrible lightning spears of pain.

Where do you hurt?

Danny shoved his earbuds back in and fumbled with his phone, turning the volume up as loud as it would go, humming along. He didn't know the words. No matter. All he needed was the beat and for his surroundings to trip into musical alignment.

It wouldn't fit.

The heady aroma of incense again. Dog shit. Heat, so hot and blinding.

I'm going to faint.

This revelation was clear, as matter of fact as someone pointing out the weather. He dropped to his knees. It didn't hurt. If anything, the collapse offered release. Danny's phone and bottle hit the ground, bouncing out of reach, coins leapfrogging across cobblestones.

He lowered his head. All sound vanished except for the tinny song from the earbuds around his neck. Forced air into his lungs like breathing through a straw. Danny lifted his chin and studied his surroundings.

Everyone had vanished.

The temple was empty, as were the greater grounds. The untended vendor carts. Dignity shawls billowed in wind carrying brine, as though this place were closer to the ocean than it was. Come to think of it, Danny thought he could almost hear the rhythmic thud and shchooooo of faraway waves.

He stood. So easy now.

Wandered onto the street.

The city was vacant. Not a car, bus, or tuk-tuk to be seen in either direction. No pedestrians, either. Even those stray cats and dogs were gone. There were no bubbles in the food stall oil vats.

"Hello?" Danny asked of the day.

To no answer.

For the first time since the night he'd been glassed in Lismore, Danny experienced a flicker of happiness, the flash illuminating carved and unmoving smiles like petroglyphs on a cave wall. Something historic and distant, yet related to the person he was today somehow, here on this empty street, in this evacuated city.

The last man on earth.

Yeah. This is where I need to be. It only hurts when other people are around.

This reprieve didn't last long.

Danny heard the wicker-crack of bark against bark and flung his head to the right. He saw an alleyway between two buildings across the street. It made no sense that there should be so many dead trees wedged within that cramped space, knotted like skeletons atop of skeletons.

They clattered at him now, they clicked. The straw through which he breathed tightened further, a pained whistle that brought splotches to his eyes. *No*, he had the time to think, panicked. *No, not this.*

A thing he couldn't see stirred in the crisscross

shadows of the branches and thorny vine. Danny heard it murmuring from all the way over here.

Terrified, his hand rose to touch—

THIRTY-ONE

"NO! NO! NO! NO!" screamed the stranger.

Danny's unfocussed eyes bounced from face to face. They were crowded over him. A woman fanned him with a map. Another person offered water from a plastic drink bottle. He noticed his reflection distorted and pale in the curve of their sunglasses as they bent to help. Anxiety twisted, chest tightening.

"No," shouted the stranger again, this time slapping Danny's hand away.

"G-get o-ooooff m-me," he said. "DON'T."

Danny glanced at his fingers almost by accident, still reeling from having been touched in such a way by someone he didn't know, and saw the bloody gum of torn skin under his nails. He stopped, still as the city that no longer was. In that part of him where the light flickered to reveal smiles before, there now issued a second spark, only the light was blue this time. Cold, and burning.

The light was pain.

Danny had been scratching at his scars.

THIRTY

AIDEN STOOD WHEN keys turned in the door, as ready as he imagined he ever could be for the confrontation to come. He'd played the scene in his head of course, knew how it might go down, maybe even mustering a bit of self-pride along the way as his under-the-breath rehearsals hatched into realities. A man could hope, after all—even if Aiden didn't recognize said man in the end.

Bloody hell, here we go.

The door unhinged from the lock, painted wood catching the light. Opening slow, the quiet entry of someone who didn't want to be seen. *Well, too bad, mate. I'm here. Waiting.*

Always fucking waiting.

Danny stumbled into the room.

Aiden's anger derailed at the sight of bandages protruding from beneath the collar of his partner's loose-fitting shirt. Red splotches on the fabric between his breasts.

"What happened?" Aiden asked.

He was desperate to hug the man—he was hurt, damn it—but knew he had to stand his ground. For a bit longer, at least. Long enough for Danny to know that a serious conversation was on the horizon. Actually, scratch that. It wasn't on the horizon.

The horizon was here.

"I fainted."

"You what?"

"Y-you heard me."

Aiden chewed on his thoughts. Yielding to sympathy would be the uncomplicated way out. Sighed. For months, he'd been walking across a tightrope with an elephant on his back, and below was a landscape of razors ready to cut him to shreds. Down there, the more you thrashed, the more your skin slit open, flesh carving free of your bones. Down there, you writhed. Down there, you screeched. Down there, nobody saved you.

Danny is that elephant.

Aiden wasn't satisfied with this crushing—and most importantly—unsustainable pressure. Was this how he wanted to continue living his life?

No.

Well, don't back down.

"Maybe you fainted because it's hot as hell out there and you're drunk. I can smell you from all the way over here."

"S-s-sorry."

"Don't 'sorry' me. I don't want a bar of it. I just—I just can't." Aiden rubbed his temples, a headache forming. "How did you hurt yourself?"

"Don't kn-o-ow."

"This has got to stop," Aiden said. "You know that, right?"

Danny bowed his head, wounded as a scolded puppy, and went to the kitchen. He threw the refrigerator open and drank milk straight from the bottle, rivulets streaming over his chin and down his neck.

Aiden stepped close behind him.

I don't want to do this, he thought, *but I've got to. Self-respect, remember?*

"We need to talk."

"N-no. Y-you need to talk."

"Just stop, okay?"

"Please d-don't yell at me. I don't like it w-w-when you yell at me."

"When do I yell at you? When have I *ever* in all these years?"

"You do it all the t-time."

"I do not, Danny. I really don't. It's all in your head."

"Well, m-m-maybe I'm a nutcase then!"

"Enough," Aiden said, palms raised. "Go to the doctor tomorrow. You've got chlamydia." With that, he left the kitchen and stormed into their bedroom, slamming the door with enough force to rattle the walls. He panted, perched on the edge of the mattress. Cupped hot cheeks. Eyes shut.

In his private dark, Aiden saw Danny on the day they met.

A windy Tuesday in Casino. They had decided on a pub in case either one of them ended up being a psycho. Both men lined up a 'just in case bail-out call' from a friend should things go pear shaped—not that either admitted this up front, though later that night, when it became apparent things were going well, they spilled their secret and switched off their phones.

Danny: the skinny white dude with the crooked smile, who came across as vulnerable whilst acting tough, with shadows in the edges of his jokes, a wounded-quality Aiden found really, really hot.

Danny: the Manhunt.com hook-up who never went away, slowly revealing himself in wonderful ways. The kind of guy who called Australia Day what it really was. 'Invasion Day'. Big tick in Aiden's book. A guy who wasn't afraid of being the kid he used to be.

Danny: who now opened the bedroom door and stood there with tears in his eyes.

Caught.

It was perhaps the first real emotion Aiden had witnessed from him since things soured. Aiden found that nothing short of tragic.

The tightrope frayed. Those razors had never been sharper.

"I don't know how to help you anymore," was what Aiden wanted to say, but didn't. Instead, he swept his anger aside as he did the dust on the blanket beside him. He gestured for Danny to sit.

Danny did.

"I'm s-so s-s-s-s-sorry," he said into Aiden's shoulder. "So, so s-sorry."

"Why'd you do it, babe? *Why?* We could've worked something out. I get it. We've been together for yonks. You've been struggling. People who struggle—oh, I don't know—they act out."

"Suh-suh-sorry."

"Stop fucking saying that. I don't want to hear it. I want to hear you tell me why."

"I don't—I w-wish. God. I-I was drunk."

"That's no excuse and you fucking know it. Fuck. FUCK. I can't fucking believe this is happening to us."

"I'm s-so sorry."

The tears were full and flowing. They dripped down Aiden's shirt.

Danny's hands draped around his shoulders, clinging to him like a shipwrecked sailor on a piece of debris. Aiden suspected that were he to shrug his lover off, the Manhunt.com hook-up who never went away would slip below the tide. Never to resurface. Aiden didn't want that. Even after all that had happened.

But he *was* tired of being hurt.

"Was it a random here in the city?" Aiden asked, voice clipped and edgy. He focused on the doorway in front of him. Through the architrave, the bathroom. Another one of those cockroaches scuttled over the wood. His questions were directed at the bug. At its antennae. The glimmer of light on its hide.

This was easier.

He fucked you, right? I know you sucked him off because I tested positive in my throat as well as my urethra.

Did you look for it, or did it just happen?

So, what were you doing at the ladyboy show?

What do you mean, you'd been there before?

Right. What did he look like?

Was he a white-fella?

Was his cock bigger than mine?

Did it feel good?

Better than me?

Did you make love to me the other night because you felt guilty?

Did you, Danny?

Did you?

Did you?

The cockroach scuttled into the dark bathroom. No food here.

TWENTY-NINE

DANNY LISTENED TO Aiden's breathing change some hours later.

Asleep at last.

He was certain, if given a choice, Aiden would have remained awake to spite him, as though to say, 'Look at the toll this is taking on me—I've got to work tomorrow!' This was one of his partner's most passive-aggressive traits. Still, Danny couldn't blame him. Not now. Not on this particular night.

Not after what he'd done.

The snores came just the same.

Danny contemplated slipping out of the apartment altogether. Running. It would be so easy. As to where he would end up, there was no way to know. Or maybe he didn't care. Were Bangkok's jaws to part and swallow him alive, who would notice?

I'm not worth it.

He thought back to the vision of the empty city. It had been good to be alone. Invisible. Assimilate with that nothingness. This was his challenge. Where there was nothingness there was no aching.

I can't go on this way. It's not—

Danny deliberated. It was important he get the next word right.

—Natural.

The bathroom door creaked shut. He contemplated sitting in the dark and decided against it. Harsh light illuminated harsh truths, but the only hope of redemption came with flicking the switch in the first place.

Click.

At least I did that.

This sliver of self-respect recoiled. It was imperative every step forward be followed by two steps back. He was acquiescent to it now.

What a piece of shit I am.

Danny plonked down on the toilet, hugged his chest. He could feel all the weight he'd lost in his younger years creeping over his skeleton again the way vines do a tree. Like those vines, he could feel the old haunts strangling him as well. Guilt squeezed through the web, bursting and spilling. Spilling what though, Danny wasn't sure. As best he knew there was nothing left in him. Nothing to purge.

His scar tingled. A tingle that turned into a scold.

He forced himself to his feet and faced the mirror. Danny pulled down the collar of his shirt to expose the blood-splotched bandage he'd applied after ducking into a 7-11 store on the way home. The register jockey hadn't even blinked when Danny handed over the packages for price scanning; if anything, the woman appeared bored.

He touched the bandage now and winced.

Something stirred in his scars. Something beneath the skin.

Next to the shower stall, there was a small window at eye level. His and Aiden's toiletries lined the sill, their toothbrushes, hairbrushes, toenail clippers. The glass was grimy from the smog. Danny had stared through it too many times to number. From this vantage point on the third floor, normally all that could be seen were powerlines crisscrossing clouds reflecting the city's orange lights. Not now.

Danny's hands dropped from the burning wound on his neck. It hurt to swallow. Breaths came quick and short. Something shifted under the wound.

Leafless branches clawed at the window, trying to get in.

TWENTY-EIGHT

TIE KNOTTED. Or strangled. Shirt tucked in. Or forced. Suit blazer slipped on, and this Aiden did with a sigh.

Morning had finally come and he strode out of the bedroom to find Danny at the kitchen table, sitting on one of the chairs that came with the apartment, staring into nowhere. He stole a breath and found the air clammy with the richness of unwashed, sweaty skin. The smell of yesterday.

“Enough is enough,” Aiden said and walked to the living room window. “I’m sick and tired of this place being in complete bloody lock-down.”

He yanked the shutters open and slid the window into its recess. The fly screen mesh gasped as humid, but at least fresher, oxygen rushed into the space. Light cast their shadows over the opposite wall; Aiden’s stretched from floor to ceiling, whilst Danny’s doubled over.

No response from the breeze, from the sun, or from his words. This didn’t surprise Aiden much. That wouldn’t stop him—it couldn’t. After waking to find the bed empty, he’d spent the morning wondering why he was even fighting to keep this—whatever this was. The answer, however, came through clear.

Despite everything. Despite it all.

Love.

Aiden stood in front of his partner. "I hate that you're making me into this person. It isn't me."

Instead of standing with his hands on his hips, looking like a half-assed school teacher trying to lecture a class that refused to listen let alone learn, Aiden curled his fingers around the neck of the chair opposite Danny and sat. He leaned forward, purposeful. The warm tabletop under his laced hands.

"I know you want me to give up. That'd be easier, but I'm not letting this bone go. Do you hear me? I'm not."

The noises of the city droned on outside. Blaring horns. Bells.

Smashing glass.

"So here's what I'm asking you to do. No, scratch that. This is what you *need* to do. Go to the hospital and get checked. Get the fucking treatment. After that, do something good for yourself. Get a massage or eat something decent—but don't you dare drink. Okay? Do you hear me on that one, Danny? Don't you dare drink. Once you're done, I want you to come back here and pack."

Another pregnant pause.

"I want you to pack enough clothes to last you four days," Aiden said, a huge rock of emotion in the hollow of his throat. "We're going to go away and work through this. We're going to see some of this country. Remember how we used to travel, Danny? Remember our trip to Tasmania? You were so pissed at me for not booking us a cabin on the boat out of Melbourne, and you had every right to be, too. The Bass Straight was so damn rocky. Even though you were angry as hell and green around the gills to boot, you still rubbed my back and got me water when I hurled up my guts from seasickness. It was worth it though, right? All of it, worth it.

"We got ourselves a hire car and went right around the island. Remember that car? Big black thing, super shiny. You called it the Batmobile. We stayed at that cabin near Cradle Mountain. We near froze our balls off. It was so rainy we couldn't see three feet in front of us, let alone that big bloody rock. Still, we had a kick-ass time because I had that bottle of Dewars your dad gave me for my birthday. The smoky one.

"Or what about when we were in Bernie. We parked the Batmobile in this shit-heel of a town and we were sure it'd be gone by the time we got back. All that worry for nothing though. We went into the paper mill. Remember that chick who took us on the tour? Funny as shit. Turns out, yes, you *can* be too excited about paper. But look at us, after all this time, still talking about her. Who would've figured, huh?

"Things have been tough, Danny. I know that. It feels like all we've been doing is going backwards. We need new memories, yeah?" Aiden sculpted the air between them with his hands. "Now, I'm not going to sit here and apologize for you. Fuck that. I'm still pissed—but I'm not dumb. I understand why people reach the point you've found yourself at. It's not your fault. Let's get out of town and do this right. Only the right things from here on out."

Silence.

"Do you hear me, Danny? It's not—your—fault."

Nothing.

"Danny?" he said again. Irritation dislodged that rock of emotion. Aiden didn't want the anger beneath to come out but he could feel it slipping, slipping, and the heat at his core breathed out on his next word. It was a name, the one Danny had been born with. The name that was never mentioned. It burned.

"Michael?"

TWENTY-SEVEN

"MICHAEL?"

They sat on kitchen chairs, only there was no table. No kitchen, either. No apartment. The clearing was surrounded by trees, a mesh of branches curving up and sideways like the miss-matched teeth of wolves; and as a wolf howls, so too did the wind. It blew and the trees applauded, perhaps amused by this tableau, their bone-dry clapping making Michael chill all over. It was an awful, dead sound, both there and not there, here, in this place of unease and hush. Rain petered, cool against Michael's skin. The clouds bloated, almost infected looking swirls of grey and green that admitted little in the way of light.

He lifted his head.

It wasn't Aiden sitting across from him. It was her.

This failed to shock him. Of course, it was going to end like this. All those days and months and years of mending. Even the toughest threads fray, given time.

It's. Not. Your. Fault.

Yes, he'd heard Aiden, but it didn't make sense until he saw the woman. She was propped up in the chair, a play thing, twitching on the breeze in a perfect imitation of life. Her face titled his way.

Blank eyes stared. Flies crawled over her cheeks.

Every delicate thread he'd sewn over the years had been to keep her out. Michael wanted her deep in his dark, because hatred—the kind of hatred that didn't dissipate with sleep, or therapy, or denial—wasn't in his constitution. Or so he hoped.

The wind picked her up. He noticed her bloodstained uniform, the shirt dangling over charcoal shorts. Skinny legs. Bow-knees. Hair dangled down in a lifeless tent beneath a bus driver's cap too big for her. The woman's name was Liz Frost. That he had no trouble recalling because he'd never been able to forget.

She jittered his way. The clunk of popping joints beneath her flesh.

Shoes dragged through grass. Flies swarmed.

Michael wanted to run but remained rooted in place, as though the rain had crisped into a layer of ice and trapped him. He wanted to be Danny again, only Danny didn't exist in this familiar clearing. This was happening in a time and place before Danny.

It's not your fault.

Michael knew that, always had, but it was hard to heal without someone to blame.

Dominoes in reverse up-righting back and back and back.

A stranger's cock inside him, thrusting hard—too hard. Aiden proposing they go to Thailand. The good and bad times spent together. The lanky man who glassed him. Dewars in Tasmania drunk from plastic cups. Laughter and more than a few tears along the way. His clients. His lies. Those drifting times before 'Danny'. His first round of wounds. Pain. The man named Jack coming for him through these very trees, armed with a glimmering pair of scissors. The bus. The blood. Gunfire and screaming. At the end of it all, the last domino was also his first: her.

It.

The Beast.

"You," Michael said.

Liz's palsied fingers wilted as they reached out and latched onto his shoulder, dragging him home.

TWENTY-SIX

AIDEN JOLTED. Danny screamed at his touch.

He felt his partner quivering. Fear through and through. Primal. All Aiden could think to do was hold him tighter than ever before.

Wrong move.

Danny snapped around and drove his fist into Aiden's throat. Winded, he stumbled backwards, ass thudding the couch a few yards from the table. He couldn't tell if it was shock or anger or a hurricane of both but Aiden charged. It was like he was on the football field in the Lismore Under 22s again. *Earth churning beneath his boots. Ball in hand.*

He tackled Danny to the ground, chair clapping the floorboards.

TWENTY-FIVE

IT WASN'T LIZ *on top of him anymore.*

Lightning recollection struck and burned: Jack, the man who tried to kill him, the man who wielded scissors, a feral opportunist with short-cropped hair and hatred in his heart. Crests of dead trees grew out of his back like angel wings. That hateful face perched at its center, eyes weeping blood.

Lips parted to spit a severed centipede at Michael's face.

"Ever wondered what it's like to be cut?" asked The Beast inside his attacker. No, not inside. This was Jack. Its voice undulated, hummed, the brushing of fly wings over rotting road kill.

TWENTY-FOUR

"STOP FIGHTING ME, DANNY!"

Aiden deflected punches until those punches ran out of steam. His partner deflated beneath his weight, folding in on himself. This sight saddened him more than anything, and Aiden found himself saying Danny's name over and over again.

Willing him back. Willing, willing.

Aiden shuffled off and crouched on the floor near the overturned chair, tie over his shoulder, beads of sweat rolling under his shirt. He watched Danny crawl to his feet and swan down the hallway, listened to their bedroom door opening and then closing—not in a rush, not in anger, but with a spider's precision.

"Don't make me come after you," Aiden whispered. It wasn't a threat. This was pleading. Begging. "Don't make me come after you."

In that moment, after so much fighting, Aiden felt his heart crack in two. The hurt was equal to every bone in his body breaking, hurts of relief. You could only take so much bending, so much straining, before things snapped.

Aiden picked up his bag, went to the mirror by the door and forced the trim of his shirt back into his trousers. He did this with tears in his eyes. He didn't go after Danny.

The front door clicked shut behind him as he left.

TWENTY-THREE

INTOLERABLE BURNING IN Michael's shoulder.

All he wanted to do was turn to one of the strangers around him and ask for help, for someone to please—please!—put him out of his misery. Someone swish a magic wand and take it all away; and whilst they're at it, strip the planet of its populace to let him wander the streets alone. Only there were no magicians here, no quick fix hocus-pocus.

Just the ticket in his hand and fire in his scars.

He studied the veins in the back of his hands.

Boom-boom. Boom-boom.

Fingers strangled the air. Now there was the headache, too, as if those dry, dead branches were growing within his head now, twigs gouging at his grey matter, pinching nerves until there was no sense among his senses. The urge to vomit doused him again. Prickling flesh.

Walk. Don't run.

He strode up the long white corridor, bored faces warped by fatigue gliding past him. He could see the toilet ahead and continued towards it as the walls inched in.

Boom-boom. Boom-boom.

The roar of overlapping voices and engines diffused once Michael entered the bathroom. At least here muzak chimed, heavy on the synthesized violins: an instrumental cover of The Carpenter's *Top of the World.*

There was nobody around except for whoever sat in the last stall on the right. He dodged to the sinks and steadied himself, breathing in the stink of piss. Michael drew back the collar of his shirt to reveal the bandage on his skin. The gauze splotched red, and even though it couldn't be the case, Michael could have sworn he saw it rise and fall, just as his veins had done. Something under the weave tried to force its way out.

"Oh, God," he said, though, to the best of his knowledge, there was no higher being around to confirm its existence. Only Karen Carpenter looking down on creation.

Michael picked at the bottom corner of the bandage, drew it back. The adhesive came away with a squish. Old wound smells floated up to his nostrils; the odor wasn't unwelcome. He leaned forward, groin against the basin, and studied the inflamed scratches on his scars. That heat was so intense and bright Michael was shocked the mirror didn't blacken right before his eyes.

Flesh puckered in a kiss, convulsing, rising.

Don't touch it, he told himself, knowing of course that he had to. *Don't!*

The urge overcame him.

Pain was a song you had no choice but to dance along with.

And this song, the person who used to be Danny knew, was just for him.

He touched the wound. Skin ruptured. Infected pus and blood glopped down his shirt. A blowfly skittered out of the mess. Its large head flicked back and forth, forearms rubbing in an insectile imitation of prayer. Wings beat the air as it flew in circles. It settled on the mirror and crawled across the glass, leaving behind a gory string of calligraphy.

Michael stumbled, hand over his mouth, and bumped against a man coming into the room. This stranger held a briefcase—though not for long. In the knot of limbs and quick-fire apologies, the case dropped. Papers soared in every direction.

Sorrys turned to accusations. A flushing toilet at the end of the room. Its sound was thunder. Music blared.

Michael didn't flinch; there was numbing relief after the purge, which neither sound nor feeling penetrated. He knew he was making the right decision. This had to happen. There had to be somebody to blame.

The maggots had been feasting on the rot *they* left behind.

Her. Him. Them.

It.

So much of what Michael did for work was keep his clients moving forward on a road to recovery. *What a load of shit,* whispered a voice in his ear, the voice of the insect. *Sometimes you just have to hate. Why fight it?*

Because I—

who am I?

—didn't ask for this.

help

Hundreds of flies crawled over the mirror.

Michael pushed the angry man aside and marched out of the bathroom. He eased into the crowd. Dead eyes glaring. Mouth open. He gripped his ticket and walked to the terminal at the far end of Suvarnabhumi airport.

PART THREE

TWENTY-TWO

JULY 21, 2018

HE MADE HIS way northbound along Australia's M1 Pacific Motorway from Newcastle, skirting towns without stopping, not present enough to notice the winter rain coming and going. A passing truck flashed its blinders, a reminder to switch on the headlights. Sure, Michael did this, but everything remained peripheral.

The road, its white lines sometimes solid and sometimes broken, yet always there to guide him. Not that he needed guiding, mind you. Michael had traveled this stretch many times over, though not for years.

He'd picked up the rental Hyundai Elantra at seven p.m. after catching a taxi from the bus station, the bus which brought him into Newcastle. His flight had been to Sydney, one-hundred-and-fifty kilometres south. Michael's destination, however, was deep in the Hunter Valley, about an hour's drive from the Avis rental office. Doing this last leg should have been a breeze, though fatigue ran deep.

Michael kept the radio on.

Voices bled together like ghosts competing for attention, songs about the country coming and going. Songs about religion. Songs about kissing the person you loved, and about losing the things that made you who you were. These songs were soap operas with melodies hiding mayhem that would have moved him in his other life, back when he was 'Danny', but which were decoration now. Michael registered this as a loss; music had been so important to him once. Even this melancholy was distant, remnants bleached by blurring stations and hymns.

Flies crawled around the inside of the windows.

Every so often, he glanced in the rear-vision mirror to see the silhouettes of passengers. *Peekaboo, I see you*, Michael would think as he caught them between the passing glow of streetlights. These were the only moments he was alert on the journey, when he saw Liz Frost's face, when he saw Jack with his scissors asking if he'd ever wondered what if felt like to be cut. These people were his history whether he wanted them to be or not.

"Don't go," Michael said. "Don't leave me."

They always did.

Alone again on that long highway. The flies remained; the buzzing of their wings a lullaby. Michael pulled the car into a rest-stop about fifteen minutes from where he was heading, though where he intended to stay once he got there, he had no idea. His eyes were just too heavy. He killed the headlights, reclined his seat and rolled onto his side.

I'll nap for a bit and then keep going.

The parking lot overlooked a farmer's property where, by the light of the moon, Michael noticed a scarecrow propped above a field of wheat. He experienced a strange empathy for the stitchling. All men are scarecrows stuffed with regrets and trauma they are not allowed to speak of. Mouths sewn tight.

No. Not empathy.

Sympathy.

Michael was free now. His stitches were undone.

Soon he slept and saw a long chain-link fence. Fingers curled through the mesh as he watched Mr. Maclachley's dog crawl out of its kennel in slow-motion. Black fur caught the light as the wheat had the moon's radiance, and almost appeared blue. Michael knew that he should be afraid, that this should be a nightmare. The sight of the dog brought comfort instead, and when it pressed its mouth to the fence, it licked his fingers.

Good boy. Good boy.

Michael dreamed a smile.

He woke with the sun, the coming of crows.

TWENTY-ONE

"WHAT THE ACTUAL FUCK?"

Aiden scuttled from the computer. His cheeks were hot, a weird contrast to the icy disbelief rippling down his neck. The hairs on his arms stood upright as a wave of goosebumps pebbled his flesh.

"What are *you* doing?" he said to the screen. Without warning the tears were back. What he was reading couldn't be correct. But he knew it was.

Danny wasn't home when he returned from work last night, and hadn't been seen since. Six hours had passed. Aiden was almost at the point of calling the police.

A word taunted him.

Suicide.

Even though every fiber of his being screamed to do otherwise, Aiden didn't act. Not yet. *One more hour*, he told himself. *One more to be sure.* If he made a report and set those wheels in motion, and Danny wasn't in danger but had gone on another bender, then there was every chance this straw may break the camel's back. And then Aiden would lose everything.

Assuming, of course, he hadn't lost it already.

His email chimed. The correspondence came from

his bank, notifying him of suspicious activity on their joint account.

Danny wasn't coming home. He was in Australia, as evidenced by the $400 booking fee at Avis car hire in Broadmeadow, New South Wales.

"Broadmeadow?" He didn't even know where that was. He opened another tab on the screen and embarked on a quick Google search. Broadmeadow was a suburb of Newcastle in the Hunter Valley, New South Wales.

That makes no sense.

Aiden logged into his online bank profile and confirmed the amount had, in fact, been withdrawn. "Son of a bitch," he said, followed again by another volley of what the actual fucks. Scrambled thoughts branched into two paths.

One: This had to be a mistake. After all, it wouldn't be the first time his bank had made a blunder on their account.

Then there was option number two.

Aiden glanced around the empty Bangkok apartment where Danny was nowhere to be seen and watched this emptiness dissolve into a memory of the doorway to his local bank in Casino where he'd had an international travel alert placed on their profiles—and for this exact reason. Aiden could still see the cashier's over-friendly face, the way her smile was etched with the blunt blade of employer threats and potential commissions.

Aiden scrolled up the computer screen to reveal the $990.98 payment to Qantas airlines from thirteen hours ago. It was just a number, of course, and bore no additional information—which was frustrating, because he had no way of telling what the destination was. It made sense that if Danny were bailing out and heading back to their apartment in Lismore that he would fly in to Brisbane and then bus it the rest of the way.

Why the car hire in Newcastle then? Newcastle of all places. That was an eight-hour drive from The Panic Room. What business would Danny have that far south?

Aiden rubbed his temples, trying to massage the thoughts beneath. He stopped. That terrible chill came over him again.

No. There was no mistake at play here, excluding the oversights he'd made himself.

I should've seen this coming.

Danny was headed for his old stomping grounds, which to the best of Aiden's knowledge, were about an hour's drive away from Newcastle, further down the coast in the middle of the wine region. He'd never been to that part of the state before, although he'd been tempted, just to get a better understanding of what Danny had been through.

For the life of him, Aiden couldn't remember the name of the town where it all happened. That part of Danny's life was never spoken of, not even by The Fletchers. If any one of them, Aiden included, veered too close to that flame, the reaction was always the same snake-strike brush off.

"We're not going to talk about it, okay?"

The venomous manner in which Danny delivered that word, *okay*, terrified him.

Aiden clicked open one last tab, typed Danny's birthname into the search bar, and article extracts about That Which Must Never Ever Be Spoken Of, one of the most bizarre crimes in Australia's history, filled the screen. Fingers shook. He felt guilty for peering into Danny's past like this but what choice did he have? Aiden clicked on the top article and scanned individual words, which when strung together spoke of horror to which Aiden had no comparison.

WHATEVER HAPPENED TO MICHAEL DELANEY, SOLE SURVIVOR OF THE JAMES BRIDGE MASSACRE?

Next to this text was the classic black-and-white photograph he'd seen all over the Internet: an eighteen-year-old Danny—*his Danny*—in the back of an ambulance, surrounded by police officers, a heat-reflective space blanket draped over his shoulders to cover wounds that would, with time, become scars, a coffee cup in hand, his snowman's face with eyes of coal. The young man's t-shirt.

Everyone who had seen this photograph remembered that shirt.

It was as iconic as Aurora Chamberlain's gory jumpsuit after the dingo had its way with her, or a gun-toting Martin Bryant at Port Arthur. Who hadn't seen it more than once, really? Every few years a story about what happened in 1995 cycled through one of those tacky crime retrospective programs. Aiden had even seen the photograph appear on Buzzfeed lists about Australia's most significant historical images.

Everyone remembered that shirt because it wasn't just the kid's blood all over it. That kid killed the man who had tried to murder him.

Aiden considered the same hands which had, in defense, crushed an attacker's skull with a rock cupping his face with a tenderness he'd never experienced before. Fingers that had linked with his own, which he'd kissed, which had been inside his body. No wonder Danny's family moved away and changed their identities.

Thirteen dead bodies found in and around a small two-story house on the outskirts of James Bridge, New South Wales. Some had been shot. Some mutilated. One had been strewn on the floor of the public bus that brought them to that house, driven by someone who for a while there, became a household name, a bogeywoman whispered to children to keep them safe.

Go and play, kids. Just make sure you're back in time for dinner, otherwise, Liz Frost will come along in her bus and take you home to meet the family.

Slammed the laptop shut. Leaned forward in the chair. Put his head to his knees.

Never in all his life had Aiden been this alone. He was in a foreign country without friends or family to call and ask to come with hugs and wine, left high and dry by the one person he'd trusted with his raw and previously battered affection. Footed, in the most literal sense, with the bill.

I should've done more.

Aiden leapt to his feet and paced. At one point, he snatched a pillow off the lounge and tossed it at the wall. It spun across the floorboards, stirring dust bunnies.

"You absolute dickhead!" He wasn't sure who this was directed at. Danny? Himself? Were it the latter, Aiden had to ask why was he *worthy* of the offence.

Was it because he'd let things slip so far from his control?

Or was it because of what he was about to do?

You're crazy, he thought, decided now. *Damn it, you're as crazy as him.*

TWENTY

JULY 22, 2018

MICHAEL PARKED THE car by the side of the road and walked the rest of the way. It hadn't even gone six in the morning and the fog was thick and bright.

He traced footsteps through the memory of a dream. Fingers curled around tufts of grass as he slid down the slope leading off the main road and onto Crown land. The scents of wet, earthy loam and animal shit. At the bottom of the decline he sat, rocking. This was where he once killed a man to save himself.

The bush woke around him. Birds sang. Crickets droned. Wind churned the fog and made the trees hiss the truths they had witnessed and kept secret.

Until today.

Michael walked across the clearing. Soon the cuffs of his jeans were wet with dew. He passed through a net of trees, wearing a mask of cobwebs. The further he went, the darker it got, as though normal timelines didn't exist anymore. Continued. Ducking under branches, turning sideways to shimmy between lightning struck trees that were collapsed together like hands in prayer. All the while, spiders ran back and forth across a face that didn't flinch.

Not once.

Soon he arrived at a running stream, followed its glittery flow to the edge of a ravine. He couldn't tell how deep it dropped; the fog erased everything. It wouldn't pay to stay here. The ground didn't strike him as settled. Memories here, too.

After another stretch, the bush spat him into a clearing without canopy. Morning light scythed the dim. Closer now. He kept on, twigs crunching under his weight, often stopping to remind himself to breathe.

Dead trees grew out of the gray.

Here, he walked with ghosts.

Michael kept thinking there was something just out of sight. A shadow against shadows trying to move with deliberate quietness—but failing. Skeletal branches rasped as it skittered. Michael wasn't afraid; his pulse didn't climb. There was nobody out here but him.

These were *his* echoes.

He arrived at their yard.

Long strides over hickory grass. Recollections of a barking dog. Flies swarmed around his head. He chased the fog and expected to see the house emerge from the wash.

It didn't come.

The only hint that there had ever been a domicile on this open land was the occasional brick, a pole spearing from a cement base—the remains of a clothesline and planks of wood, which may or may not have come from the shed where the girl whose name he couldn't remember had gone to find weapons. There was limited grass here, as though the ground were too sour for a second life.

Michael tired. He sat where the bus must have been. Legs crossed, head tilted. He didn't know why he was here but understood that coming was worth a try. Whatever unfocused outcome he'd traveled halfway across the planet to find evaded him. The land hadn't only been robbed of the Frost residence but of its charge.

He left.

Kangaroos watched him go. Crows cawed through fog that refused to retreat with the oncoming day. He slipped into the trees, their bony fingers embracing him.

NINETEEN

THE LOT WHERE the Frost house once stood was on the outskirts of town, and it didn't appear that the surrounding landscape had increased in population very much in the years since Michael's last visit. This may have been for the best. It didn't take a genius to realize the town had been bleached raw by tragedy, with this area suffering the worst. Some marks never went away.

Scars.

He passed over Flagman's Bridge, wooden boards clattering under the tires. It was only a matter of time before the whole thing fell apart and tumbled into the Hunter River. Liz Frost had taken them across this exact same bridge in 1995—going the opposite way, of course. Towards her home. Her's was a one-way ticket. She'd wanted to make a new family to call her own, one pieced together from them, her passengers.

Hostages.

Memories stirred as he drove into the dense hollow on the other side of the bridge, into the dark. He didn't let them stop him. Flies crawled around the inside of the windows. That was good. They made memories easier to handle.

Fifteen minutes later, he entered the main part of town. The old sign was still there, paint chipped and blistered.

WELCOME TO JAMES BRIDGE—WE HAVE TWO CEMETERIES AND NO HOSPITALS, SO DRIVE CAREFULLY!

The day was young, the streets empty.

Odd.

What day is it?

Saturday? No. Sunday.

He wondered if religion was as important here as it used to be or if the Royal Commission into sexual assaults in the Hunter Valley had stripped these parishioners of their priests too. *I guess I'll find out when the nine o'clock church bells ring in an hour-and-a-half. If the flock lumbers up the hill, it'll be obvious.* Thoughts of Father Mason. It struck Michael weird that the image of this old man, one always viewed through a confessional gauze, remained clear in his mind yet he struggled to remember the last time he ate. If there ever was a pedophile waiting to be caught, it had to be Mason. He had that look about him. Shifty eyes, wine-stained teeth. Breath like dead mice. A sad man. So sad.

Run-down, neglected buildings. Almost non-existent traffic. The money in the mines must have dried up, taking with it the town's primary means of employment. Something in the back of Michael's head nudged him to feel depressed about this, but that something wasn't loud enough to be heard over them, the flies.

His flies.

Every muscle ached. There used to be accommodation on Maitland Street, up past the Federal pub. He drove nice and slow. Not a soul anywhere. Unlike the Frost residence, the James Bridge Motor Motel had withstood the test of time.

Just.

Michael turned into the driveway, hoping the place was open. Check-in would be a few hours off, but he'd wait in the car if need be, maybe even nod off again. Were luck erring his way, the rooms would be equipped with a kitchenette, somewhere to whip together a makeshift meal. He didn't need much; a few slices of toast and a pot of dirty coffee would see him through. Surely there was somewhere around here to score bread.

Parked. Killed the engine.

He caught his reflection in the rear-vision mirror. The caul of webs still covered his face. Wiped, wiped, wiped it all away, smearing the mess on the underside of the seat. Spiders scuttled. He instructed himself to breathe again.

So he did.

Exhaled. Good.

He unclicked the belt and turned to see if Liz or Jack rode with him. No trace that they had ever been there. That didn't mean anything. Some people were tricky that way.

Michael slammed the car door and tilted his head in the direction of the main drag. From here he could see the main intersection where the only set of traffic lights in James Bridge was erected. The red eye of the stop cue beamed through the fog, and past it, waiting for the inevitable green to come, peered two headlights. He heard the engine growling. The lights changed and a bus lurched across the road into a right-hand turn, heading up the highway.

A thud in the pit of his stomach. Flies swarmed in.

He saw shapes in the windows. Were there screams, too, he wondered? Had those passengers been stolen against their will, a gun trailing their every move? Maybe—as the case had been with him—those aboard were 'this close' to getting their shit together only to have the rug yanked out from underneath them all. And had some been waiting for this to happen so they could become who they always wanted to be? Men like Jack?

The bus faded from view, fog folding in like origami. Michael crossed his arms, fingers kneading the pudge beneath his foul-smelling shirt, and turned his back on a road that would be waiting for him later. As it always was.

OFFICE OPENS AT 9, read the sign on the door. Movement through the glass. Michael gave a curt wave. "H-hey in there. Any chance of an e-e-e-early check-in?"

A silhouette limped over to let him in.

"Come on, squirt," said the old man with the manager's tag pinned to his lapel. "You'll catch your death out there. Once the damp gets into your bones you're a goner. Trust me. Do yourself a favor and don't get arthritis. Actually, avoid gettin' on in years altogether, you hear?"

Michael nodded, and waited for the manager to round the desk and lean over the register. The lines in his face were accentuated by mine grit that would never wash away. "Looking for a room?"

"Yeah." Michael drew out his wallet. "I know it's e-early."

"No worries. Not too many people coming through these days. It's no bother. Are you paying with cash or card?"

"Ughh. Card. C-cool?"

"Yeah, just let me get this fandangled computer all booted up. This thing's about as old and slow to start as me. Where are you trekking from, squirt?"

Michael went through the motions, the whole time thinking to himself, *Wait a minute—I know this guy.* His mind hopscotched, seeking a name that aligned with the face, which Michael suspected had always appeared old, though perhaps none the wiser. It clicked.

"Hey, you d-didn't used to be the puh-puh-postman around here, did you?"

The manager glanced from the computer as the screen bloomed to life, casting the caught-off-guard expression in a tint of green. Those caterpillar eyebrows arched. "Do I know you, squirt?"

Michael crossed his arms again. "I'm o-o-originally from M-Maitland but I used to spend some time here. Way b-back though."

"Right. This place ain't like she used to be. Life's bled right out of this part of the valley since they put in the Expressway. The mines are closing and we're not close enough to the wine region to draw in the crowds. We're up shit creek without a paddle, to tell you the God's honest truth. Got some I.D. you can flick my way, squirt?"

Michael handed over his license.

"Can't say I recognize the name, Daniel, but Hell, I

can't hardly remember to put my trousers on the right way these days." The clickedy-clack of arthritic though nimble fingers dancing across the keyboard to rework the identity he'd built into data and invoices-to-be. "Then again, who cares?"

"Yeah," Michael said. He snapped his fingers. "Your name's Deakins, right? You d-delivered mail on a mo-mo-motorcycle."

"Jesus, I haven't saddled up the bike in quite a few years. That's me, alright."

"You had a suh-son. Marshall?"

"You knew my boy, then?"

"Everyone kind of knew everyone back then, didn't thhhh-they?"

"Nobody really knows anyone, squirt. That I'll swear 'til I'm blue in the face, and sometimes you don't *want* to know anyone. I guess that's why I gave up my old position at Australia Post and bought this place when the opportunity came along. Locals don't have a reason to step inside this door. That's the way I like it."

The manager flicked Michael's I.D. his way with a dismissive jolt of the hand, an apathetic card dealer who didn't care if you bet on the farm or not, because in the end, The House always won. It didn't matter that Michael hadn't walked these streets in years; you could take the boy out of James Bridge but you couldn't take James Bridge out of the boy—and for some reason, this made him worthy of the old man's contempt.

"Here's your key. Room'll be a wee bit stuffy or account of the early check-in. No maid today. Open the windows or crank the air-con. She groans like a bitch but gets the job done."

Michael stuffed the credit card back into his wallet. "Th-thanks. All the best to your son."

"Marshall's dead, squirt."

The man, who according to his I.D. answered to Daniel, watched the old timer watching him from the other side of the desk. Mr. Deakins's cataracted eyes were the color of the fog outside. Those lines in his face, a roadmap down which nobody traveled anymore. This was the face of James Bridge: damaged yet perseverant, ignored but not quite forgotten. It wasn't altogether benevolent. The once-upon-a-time postman had bitterness in his blood, no doubt tainted from journeying these streets for years on end, gaining glimpses into private lives that should never be understood. You could only see so much before things turned on you. Maybe Michael knew that better than most. It wasn't surprising that Mr. Deakins cut and run. When Michael peered into the old man's face he saw the town's cancer boiling beneath, and in turn, feared his own truths were scrutinized.

Time to leave this room. Now.

Perhaps Mr. Deakins was right. You didn't know anyone, not even in small towns like this, places where there were two cemeteries and no hospitals so you better drive carefully. Or maybe it was that people didn't want to know their neighbors, because door to door, we weren't all that different. Just mirrors within mirrors. The funhouse you never left, not really. And if you were lucky enough to escape, you were about as easy to forget as your own reflection.

"You're him?" asked Mr. Deakins. "Aint you?"

EIGHTEEN

AIDEN TOUCHED DOWN in Sydney at four in the afternoon. Busting, he took a painful piss in the terminal toilets and then downed his meds with a cup of coffee from the Gloria Jean's stand. He switched the sim card in his phone, a task that should have been simple but proved otherwise due to the trembling of his hands. He fiddled with the chip, noticing he'd bitten his nails down to the quick on the long, overpriced flight.

"Get in there you—"

Snap.

The sim clicked into place. Waited for the reception bars to bloom. Pounded Danny's Australian number. Aiden killed the call before it had a chance to connect and sat on one of the airport benches whilst waiting for his rental car to be brought around.

Maybe I shouldn't tell him I'm coming just yet.

What if he runs?

Per Google Earth's not always accurate calculations, James Bridge was a two-hour drive north, assuming Sydney's traffic proved merciful. If everything were to go to plan—if a plan this even was—Aiden should get to the small New South Wales town by eight-thirty. He felt like a dog chasing a car, unsure as to what he was going to do once he got there. But Aiden remained certain this was worth pursuing. That he must believe.

That more than anything.

Danny had checked himself into the James Bridge Motor Motel earlier that morning, evidenced by a pending payment on their account. Right there, clear as day, deceits in dollar signs and decimal points. He chewed his lower lip, tense. The paper trail was a little too obvious for Aiden's liking.

In fact, it made him sick to his stomach.

Either Danny's spiral was so impulsive he wasn't taking the time to consider the blatant crumbs left in his wake, or worse, those crumbs had been laid with a deliberate hand. As though Danny *wanted* to be followed. *Wanted* to be found way back there in the boondocks. At ground zero.

But why?

Stop thinking, Aiden.

Doubt was a vampire; it threatened to suck the inertia right out of you. That couldn't happen. He'd come too far.

Aiden snatched up his luggage. It wasn't too heavy. There hadn't been time to pack properly before leaving; and besides, he would have to go back to Thailand regardless of how things panned out. It was important a man finish what he started, or at the very least bail with his head held high, knowing a limited mess was being left for someone else to sweep up. There were people at work who would only be too happy to see him fall flat on his face, screwing the pooch on an opportunity others had fought for and lost. Aiden wouldn't have a bar of it; nor would he let Danny sabotage any of his potential career advancements, either. Naïveté got you nowhere. Word on the grapevine was that there were less-than-delightful colleagues in the department who said—or worse, *implied*—he'd only been deployed to South-East Asia because he was Aboriginal. His success or failure would be for the benefit or detriment of the Minister.

What a laugh.

Casual racism was part and parcel of Aiden's day-to-day life, always had been. Learning that he was spoken about in half-whispers didn't evoke much in the way of surprise. Who was more naïve, he wondered: those willing to spit vinegar in the faces of disbelievers everywhere, or the entitled majority who'd convinced themselves that entitlement was quantified by skin color and stereotypes? *Get fucked.*

Aiden huffed, gripped his luggage.

Maybe he *did* have something to prove after all. Not to them, not to the men and women whose prejudices lurked behind handshakes and Outlook calendar invites. No. As arch as it sounded, Aiden had something to prove to himself.

I'm not a statistic. I got to where I am because I'm good at my job.

The old uphill climb. Yeah, Aiden knew its gravity well.

Get it done, mate.

Get it done.

As he waited for the Holden SV6 he'd paid for on his individual account to come around, Aiden wondered if Danny would do all this for him in return? Once, and without thinking twice, he would have said yes. Today, though? Right now?

He just didn't know.

To think they had spent so much time talking about their crushing desire to be fathers, to build a family, something strong and downright envy-inducing. Throw in a dog, too—because *why not*? Instead of down payments on that long-standing dream—the great 'Aussie dream', really—all Aiden had were hurts. *Fathers,* he thought, vindictive as Hell and hating himself for it. *Ha*. As best he knew, there were no antivenoms to antitrust.

He watched people dodging around him, their movements jaunty as marionettes on strings, all rushing to get somewhere. Aiden could see hunger in their faces, the hunger for home. Keep moving. Faster and faster. He knew it must be in his expression, too. In fact, he'd seen it in the mirror for months now. His call to Country had been so loud. Just being on Australian soil gave him ease. The strings on his own limbs tightened nonetheless, pulling him back to the northern rivers where family, cousins, and his people waited for him.

But he couldn't go. His mission drew him in the opposite direction.

The rental was handed over, luggage loaded into the trunk. He clicked himself into the front seat and smiled when the dashboard lit up, reverse sensors blaring, GPS binging instructions. His mother, hardly tactful at the best of times, called such vehicles White Dickhead Carriers. "Because even the bloody car tells you what to do!"

Christ, he missed her.

Aiden drove those Sydney streets. He longed to pull over and find a patch of land to stretch out on, for only ten minutes perhaps. To run his fingers through the grass. Be with the land, be whole. He didn't award himself this small necessity, pushing on instead, taking the sharp Newcastle Exit. At no point did he feel sorry for himself.

I'm not going to give up.

Why? He knew the answer to this. He knew it too well.

When your heart breaks, your world fissures and a desperate craziness escapes. It clouds your sense of reason, fleecing you of dignity along the way. The cloud is blinding. It turns you into someone you are not: the most desperate version of yourself who ever lived, someone stripped of flesh so all the nerves are revealed. *This is who I am and this is all I have left*—take it or leave it. So, you keep on going, going always in the hope that on the other side of the cloud your heartbreaker waits with arms wide open, and praying, always praying, that they have changed. Whatever is left, you break yourself.

Sunday evening. There wasn't much traffic.

Aiden expected to arrive on time.

SEVENTEEN

THERE WAS NO way to tell if the fog had dissipated throughout the day because, by the time Michael woke, the town beyond his window hazed again. Blue light from the halogen lamp in the carpark dueled with the neon pink MOTEL sign, dousing everything in slicks of color that refused to merge. Their glows seeped into the room, reflecting off his phone, burning in the dusty television screen.

It itched to look at, all that arcade lighting. Dreams were easier.

Flies crawled the walls and across the bathroom mirror. Every time he scrubbed the webs from his face they came back twice as thick. Michael gave up, breath pressing against the caul. In. Out. In. Out.

Readied himself in the kitchenette opposite the bed. Slipped on his shoes. Didn't bother to take his phone with him. Key slid into the pocket of his jeans.

A closing door. *Click*.

His room was on the second floor of the wraparound balcony and he inched down the stairs at a deliberate pace. The last thing he wanted to do was trip and break his neck. That blue and pink light was brighter out here; it probed at his headache, its prickly touch refusing to ease until he reached the dim main drag.

The flies came with him.

An occasional car greased by but the streets remained more-or-less empty. At one point, Michael thought he saw someone standing on a corner. No. Just the tricky alignment of tree stump and water main, dark conspirators to keep his heart rate up. A basketball bounced into the halo of a streetlamp, its rubbery boink-boink-boink distorted by fog. No child chased after it.

To Michael, James Bridge had always been the type of place where every family had a dog, where evenings thrummed with happy barks and howls. This night was silent. At what point, he wondered, had this become a cat town? Even the shadows were feline, so slinky and secretive.

Memory nudged him in a direction that didn't make sense until he got there.

"Here," he said. This was where it started.

This was where he'd boarded.

Hawthorn trees flanked Antis Street. It struck him odd how much larger they were now, whereas the rest of the town seemed smaller. Coming home was like that, though; the pull of what was and what is, what you want and what will never be again.

Something pattered on his scalp and shoulders. Twigs fell from the tree above his head. Michael studied the twenty or so white cockatoos chewing on the seedlings. The snip-snip of their beaks shearing as they leapt from branch to branch, some of the birds suspended upside down like fruit bats as they feasted. Michael watched one of their feathers see-saw through the air and land on the debris-coated bench below.

For the first time since arriving back in Australia, Michael experienced a flutter of emotion. Not fear. If anything, it was exhilaration. At this exact spot, he found the energy he'd sought at the abandoned Frost property.

Here, things buzzed.

This was where Michael had stepped inside the bus to Maitland at the age of nineteen, the bus driven by a skinny young woman with a gun in her handbag. He'd been one of her nine infamous passengers, among whom there was also Jack Barker, the man who had fallen into the ebb of the driver's madness and tried to end Michael's life for reasons no detective ever discovered. How could they? How could anyone?

He closed his eyes and the clipping of branches turned into the ticking blades of the fan above Liz Frost's seat on the bus. Glimmering sunlight off chrome handlebars. Sweat beads. Blood.

His eyes opened. Without realizing it, he'd brushed aside the chewed seeds and twigs to sit on the bench. That energy hummed around him. He was close, but not quite there yet.

The blame was not in the bench.

Memory's invisible hands heaved him off those hard wooden planks to push him further along the footpath. Towards the house he'd run from.

SIXTEEN

AIDEN CAUGHT HIS warped reflection in the surface of the Hyundai Elantra, the only other vehicle in the James Bridge Motor Motel carpark. The AVIS hire sticker was right there in its rear window.

"Jesus." It was real now.

All of it.

He walked to an office tucked into the corner of the building on the first floor facing the street. Aiden pushed the door and heard an old-fashioned bell cry. A man with bushy white eyebrows slept behind the desk, mouth open—'catching flies', as his father used to say in those days before becoming a big cliché, one of history's many bastards who went out for a slab of beer and never came back—and a tattered Louis Lamour western cracked across his chest.

Aiden approached the counter, noticed the antiquated hook board on the wall where keys were hung. Like everything else in this sleepy town, nothing about the motel interior had been dragged into the twenty-first century. Even the computer was old. Aiden remembered using a similar such type at school, the kind with a black screen and green text. He'd been so charmed by the technology then. However, time moves on. It has to. If it doesn't, things calcify and then fall apart. He knew that now.

From the twenty hooks on the board, nineteen numbered keys were suspended. Room eleven was missing. It wasn't rocket science.

"Gotchya."

The old man snapped awake. "Christ, don't you make a noise when you walk?" He inched out of his chair and laid the western face-down on the countertop.

"Sorry, mate. Didn't mean to sneak up on you."

He grumbled and relented. "Yeah, well, you've got to catch shut-eye when you can once you reach my age." The man, whose name-tag read Mr. Deakins—MANAGER, rubbed his stubble-covered chin. "I hope you don't mind me saying it, but it looks like you haven't had much in the way of sleep lately, either."

"You could say that again, mate."

"Room for one then?"

"Yeah." Aiden opened his wallet and handed over his driver's license.

"Crikey," said Mr. Deakins. "Another bloody person from Casino. What are they doing up that way, evacuating or something?"

"What do you mean?"

"Well, you're the second fella I've had check in today from there. First guy flew in from Sydney, but the town on his I.D. was the same. Go figure. That's a mighty weird batting average. Could be good luck. Maybe I ought to pop on down to the newsagent's in the morning and snag myself a lottery ticket."

"Could be. Is this dude on the first or second floor?"

The manager pointed to the ceiling.

Aiden took back his license and tapped its edge against the counter. "Chuck me up there as well. Hopefully I'll cross paths with him. You're right, Casino is a small place. For all I know, we could be related."

Deakins gave a laugh. "I guess it's no skin off my nose if you want to top-and-tail the whole damn state only to crack a beer with a fella who lives a stone's throw away. Me? I see a cousin or an old neighbor, I high-tail it out of dodge lickedy-split. I don't think he's your kin, if you don't mind me saying. Fella's white as a ghost."

"Still," Aiden said, forcing his hands into his pockets to avoid fiddling. "Put me upstairs. I'm a glutton for punishment."

FIFTEEN

AIDEN'S SHOES CLUNKED the metal staircase. He stepped onto a veranda overlooking the carpark where the two rentals sat near one another. *Strange bedfellows,* he thought.

Or maybe not so strange after all.

He gripped his bag in one hand, steeled himself before progressing, heart pounding, mouth parched. If this had been a mistake it was a mistake he was about to own. Aiden wasn't going to stand there all night, deliberating as to whether this was the right thing to do; he'd crossed the Pacific Ocean to get to this spot, damn it.

No backing out now.

Aiden stopped before room eleven.

The big windows were closed but at least the curtains had been drawn back. However, he couldn't see into the dark interior on account of the blue and pink lights outside. The glass reflected his neon-coated reflection like a mirror. And as it turned out, yes, the old manager had been correct. His fatigue was obvious, cheekbones gaunt from not having been able to keep meals down, hair fanned up on one side from where he'd rested against the Qantas jet's cattle class seat. Aiden watched the man in the window lift a phone to his face.

Condensation beaded on his unshaven skin as he waited for the line to connect. A gust of wind churned the air about him, ruffling the collar of his shirt. He'd only been in James Bridge twenty minutes and already disliked the place.

As superstitious as it sounded, there was something sickly in that wind—a mildewy rot that reminded him of the public laundry in the high-density government building in which he and his mother lived in his younger years. God, he hated that room, with its gritty tiles and the stink of wet dog and the used syringes behind the washing machines. Were anyone to come along and tell that eleven-year-old that one day he would go from living in a government property to working for the government, he would have told them they were dreamin', mate.

Things *had* changed. He *was* different. Yet the dampness followed, followed. That same nauseating sense of wrongness was with him again like the clingy nudge of an unwanted hug. All he could do now was push these sensations aside and keep calling, keep waiting.

A screen lit up in the darkness of room eleven.

Danny's ringtone through the wall.

A tear slipped down his cheek. "Come on, babe. Come back to me."

That green screen on the other side of the window remained where it lay. Room eleven of the James Bridge Motor Motel was soulless.

Aiden killed the call and put his phone away. Danny must be out getting something to eat. The car was downstairs where the blue and pink glow beamed brightest, so it stood to reason that he would be back soon. After all, everybody must eat—though Aiden wouldn't have included himself in that number just yet.

His guts churned, regardless. The motel flyer tucked under his arm said all the rooms came with a kitchenette stocked with cutlery, plates, and tea and coffee—THE COMFORTS OF HOME FOR THE FAMILY ON THE GO. He had no intention of using any of it. The toilet was a different story.

Aiden went to his room two doors down. The light fixture was full of dead bugs cast in silhouette; he stood in their oversized shadows, patient as can be. Waiting, at least, was something. It occupied the air. He knew, beyond doubt, that he was here for the correct reason. When you weren't busy loving, you were busy hating—which was fine, too. It was apathy, that terrible emptiness, which you had to worry about. Nothing killed you like nothingness. Depression lurked at its worst there. Beyond anxiety, beyond sadness so intense you think it will end you.

I'm doing the right thing.

And Aiden's plan was to reach into that nothingness to pull out what remained. If, come dawn, he came back empty-handed, if all that eventuated tonight was a goodbye, well, Aiden felt he was *worth* that. If nothing else.

His thoughts turned fierce.

So long as he lived, nobody would abandon him without explanation ever again.

FOURTEEN

"Can I help you?"

The man in the doorway to the one-story house glared at Michael with cautious curiosity, head tilted in an almost puppyish manner. This parallel extended to the man's eyes, which were big and brown and hadn't changed over the years. They still clung to the vulnerability that attracted Michael to him in the first place. Clive had always elicited an air of melancholy.

However, the rest of him had aged. Like the hawthorn trees on the street, the man with whom Michael spent the evening and following morning prior to boarding Liz Frost's bus to town, had also filled out. Young pudge turned an older gent's fat; the cute moustache now a full-blown beard.

"I said, can I help you?"

Michael recalled looking back at the house before striding off into the day. No, not strode. Ran. He'd wanted to stay longer. Clive had looked at him from the shadowy window, too. The curtain *had* shifted. Michael was sure of it.

You know it did, said the voice of the flies.

"Clive."

Their kiss.

The virginity the older man took. Initial pain and a kind of wonderful fullness once it was all over with and done.

Used condoms in a flower of toilet paper.

Michael brushing his teeth with minty paste squirted on his index finger.

"Clive, it's me."

It only occurred to Michael then just how lucky he was that the man still lived here. But he knew what people were like in James Bridge. They were snug and complacent within their familiarities, and very few found a need to move on. Had a stranger answered the door, Michael would have shuffled away throwing apologies and excuses, taking with him the swarm of flies that kept him safe—even when he wasn't.

Those flies cartwheeled now, riding waves of electric energy Michael couldn't see, but felt. Oh, boy, did he ever. This was where he was meant to be. This was where it began. If Clive hadn't lured him in, then Michael never would have become one of Liz Frost's infamous nine.

If.

If.

IF.

He drew in excited gulps of air through the webs, which Michael suspected the man couldn't see for some reason. The energy about them made him feel more alive than he had in years, and when one of his flies landed on Clive's face and crawled inside his mouth, he laughed.

"I don't know you," Clive said. "Bugger off, mate."

With those words, the door closed.

The verandah light flicked off and Michael stood in

the foggy dark. Though Clive was gone, the energy thrummed. This rejection wasn't unexpected, but the fury coursing Michael's system came on strong nonetheless. It rocketed up his innards, zig-zagged to his brain, a strike of lightning in reverse.

Flies in riot. Their buzzing drowned all noise, except that now familiar voice, the whisperer. *Bastard didn't even say sorry. What a cunt.*

Michael knocked louder than before. Three firm blows against the wood. Wind blew at his back, shaking the trees and dead leaves. Spiders scuttled across his webbed face.

Overhead, the veranda bulb clicked back to life.

The door opened a second time—in anger, not curiosity—and Clive leaned out. Fire burned in those eyes; this puppy had gone rabid. "You can't *fucking* be here, Michael," the man said, spit flying. "Go away or—"

"Who is it, honey?" came a female voice from within the house.

All the flies died.

THIRTEEN

ROWENA WEBB SAT upright at the sound of the three knocks against their door.

She was in the living room after yet another draining day, watching MasterChef, her favorite program. A glass of Shiraz clamped tight in her hand. It wasn't often she cracked a bottle to have on her own. Clive never drank on a work night, but the idea had been percolating in her head since about ten-thirty that morning.

Pfft. Who cares?

Some of the toughest women she knew needed an occasional carrot on a stick to see them through—her mother on the opposite side of town sprang to mind. Now that everything was settled, now that the contestants were prepping for a surprise elimination, now that her socks were off and her feet up on the couch, things at long last felt in their place. Yes. This was where all busy weeks should end: with cooking shows paired with a well-earned red.

A dollop of wine leapt from the glass as she righted herself. Splotched a cushion.

"Damn it."

Rowena placed her drink on the dog-eared copy of

her new work enterprise agreement spread across the coffee table she hated but Clive refused to get rid of because it belonged to his long-dead grandfather. Sometimes that man could be such a sap—but that was why she loved him. Rowena was a part of the union, privileged enough to have seen the upcoming draft prior to voting in two weeks' time. It wasn't just her own job that she wanted to see advanced, rather all aged care workers across all states and territories. It paid to fight. Even when the administrators of the world brushed you off and said, *Nup, there's not a snowball's chance in hell this thing will get drafted.*

Let alone pass.

But it *had* been drafted. And if Rowena and the other members of the union yelled loud enough, and if they didn't give in to all the men on the board who said they were silly for even trying in the first place, then maybe—just maybe—it would pass, too.

Of course, this was only one factor contributing to her fatigue. One factor which made the taste of that Shiraz so damn sweet.

Rowena stood. The drink went straight to her head.

Good.

She heard the front door opening. Frigid air swooped through the house to stir the beaded Mona Lisa curtain separating the living room from the hallway. Her hand slit the clittery-clattery strings. Lingering heat from the kitchen across her face. Clive had taken one for the team earlier, having recognized her exhaustion, and offered to whip together his tried-and-true signature dish: curried sausages. He stewed a diced apple in the mix, a nice addition to the way she'd grown up having it. That was the way things were with Clive. Everything he did was a wee bit different, and after four years of her second marriage, a wee bit of difference went a long, long way.

Rowena was younger than him by almost twelve years. People still talked about that.

"Who is it, honey?" she said, stepping onto the floorboards.

They creaked.

She stared up the hallway and saw her husband at the threshold. He twisted around on the spot, bouncing from one wall to the other like a ball-bearing in a pinball machine, hands thumping plaster and knocking photos off their hooks.

Frames hit the floor. Glass shattered.

Harsh sounds issues from his mouth, glugging and sputtering. Clive danced onto his back with a knife buried in his throat.

TWELVE

THE BEAST SPILLED into the house, quick as running water, inky and filthy water from deep within a well. It had teetered for too long, poured out now, something glorious in its release. When it opened its mouth to roar, it did so not with anger, but ecstasy. The sound it made was akin to dead branches clattering together.

It didn't walk. It surfed the hallway on electric waves of energy, fingers curling about the handle of a knife thieved from the kitchenette in room eleven of the James Bridge Motor Motel. The blade came away clean from the throat and a ribbon of blood jetted across the adjoining wall, red against white. The man it stabbed started to kick; hands lashed out, gripping its shirt, trying to punch and fight. Laughable. When something was funny, it was only natural to let loose.

So it did.

Why be apologetic to those who were not, in essence, willing to apologize.

It brought the knife down again. Into the cheek, where the flesh was soft. Into the eye, which popped like bubble-wrap, blade bending on the skull socket. Heaved the knife out. Stabbed the man in the chest.

When the knife withdrew, air cooed through flesh from the deflating lung beneath.

Blood ran down its face. War paint.

It lurched to its feet, slipping in the gore but steadying itself against the wall and knocking more photos from their hooks. Glass tinkered across floorboards. Moments spliced from history escaping broken frames.

A woman stood at the end of the hall.

She appeared small, though her shrieks were huge. Her pain was part of that secret, unseen energy. Electricity crackled through it once again, making its cock stiffen inside its bloodied jeans, a response without sexuality of any kind, as natural as flesh blackening under flame.

ELEVEN

THE MAN CAME for Rowena and instinct forced her into the kitchen, feet slamming the tiles as she ran. That same instinct screamed at her to snatch the nearest available weapon. Anything would do.

Anything.

Her fingers curled around a long-bladed kitchen knife housed in the chopping block—yet another antique Clive hadn't been able to let go of. Grief was like taffy, it was sticky as hell, and the longer you played in its snare the sweeter it became. Even though it frustrated her, Rowena couldn't begrudge her husband that. No, not one bit. Some messes, people must escape alone.

She drew the knife and spun. "CLIVE!"

Their intruder thundered down the hall.

Rowena sped out of the kitchen with the blade in both hands. She didn't know what she was doing. Fight instinct with instinct, that was the extent of her thoughts. She was armed and ready, if it was possible to be ready under such circumstances. Rowena prayed that she would never have to be this ready ever again. Her Clive was hurt, his wounds severe. As crazy as it sounded, it was *his* blood splashed over the walls up there. She had to help, and that first meant helping herself.

The knife was heavy, as though weighted by the ferocity of her intent. Her desire to live.

She met the man at the kitchen corner. His heat on her skin.

He brought the fog with him, twirling at his back.

Rowena arched sideways and his knife tore through her flimsy tracksuit pants—the pair she loved wearing on a Sunday night because they were the epitome of 'winding down'. Her thigh slit open, and if she yelped, she didn't realize it. Just a flicker of discomfort. Were Rowena to have not glanced down, she may have not noticed she'd been cut.

The incomparable power of adrenalin. All nurses knew about it.

However, the man's weapon wasn't the only one swishing through the air. Her own came in fast. It embedded in his left upper forearm with a dull *thwok!* He flinched and clambered backwards a few steps, granting Rowena enough space to swing her leg and plant the heel of her foot in his chest.

PUSH.

The man pitched onto his back, the knife deep in his flesh.

Rowena saw his shirt lift to reveal the gaunt whiteness of his belly. A flicker of ribs accordioned through tight skin. The jut of an erection tenting his jeans. Despite the chaos, repulsion sang loud and true: "You sick fuck!"

She leapt through the Mona Lisa curtain. On the other side of the living room, there was another corridor where the landline had been mounted to the wall. They hardly used it these days, but she had no idea where her mobile phone was. It didn't matter. What mattered was that the entry to the corridor had a door hinged to its frame.

A door with a lock.

The latch, which she couldn't remember ever having had the need to flick, wouldn't hold up to an aggressive assault. But it might buy her thirty seconds or so—and when your life was on the line, thirty seconds was a lot of time.

Beaded threads wrapped her like boas, curling about her throat, crossing her breasts. She pivoted and heaved her weight without thinking. The rod holding the curtain to the architrave snapped free of its brackets and they all came down together, her fall broken by the coffee table she hated so much.

Wind dove free of her lungs, and if Rowena could have reached out to catch it and gulp it down again, she would have. Only that wasn't how things went, and this wasn't a place for wishes. She saw the overturned glass spilling wine across the enterprise agreement she'd fought for, and beyond it, the blur of MasterChef contestants running to ovens in dramatic cross-cuts.

Movement in the corner of her eye.

The man's bloodied hand curled around the doorframe one finger at a time. His nails turned white under the pressure. The sick fuck was getting up. Air, which she'd spent so much effort drawing into her lungs, expelled in a flash again, this time on a scream so loud it cracked the inner lining of her throat.

Rowena soared to her feet, still caught in the tangle of beads. Everything moved slow. Too slow. She ripped free of the curtain and limped through the door, into the far corridor where the remaining suites, second bathroom, and rear exit from the house were situated. Rowena flung the door shut behind her and pushed the lock into the latch. Light from the television beamed through the gap between the floor and the bottom of the door.

No shadows. Yet.

Thirty seconds. Give me thirty seconds! That's all I need.

In the dark hallway, Rowena found the phone. She gripped it with the ferocity she had the knife; and in many ways, it was a weapon, too. Rowena wanted the man who had hurt Clive either killed or caught. If she fled without calling the police and an ambulance first, her husband might die. No. Correct that. Not might.

Would.

And the man might get away, too.

No. Correct that. Not might.

Would.

Her eyes attuned to the dim to make out the numerical touchpad. Zero. Pounded it three times, just as the intruder knocked at their door three times.

BANG

Beep.

BANG

Beep.

BANG

Beep.

Shadows slinked under the door. Him. The man rmed with both knives, sharp and bloodied xtensions of his arms. How could she have been so areless to have let her own blade go? Regret would only slow her down. Rowena backed into the corridor as far as the coiled landline allowed.

A click in her ear.

"Triple zero," said a woman's voice. She sounded bored. "What is your emergency?"

"15 Queen Street, James Bridge," Rowena shouted. The first throb of pain played catch-up with her senses and her legs buckled. Knees slammed the floorboards. The man squared his shoulder against the door and it heaved within its frame but held true. For now. His shadows were in frenzy.

"What's your name?" asked the emergency dispatch officer, concerned now. "What's happen—"

"My husband's been stabbed. The killer's coming for me. KNIVES! KNIVES! SEND HELP NOW!"

Another crash against the door. Rowena dropped the phone and let it pinwheel to the ground, the clatter of its casing rapping the wood.

She knew the back door was unlocked four yards away, but couldn't escape yet. There was still one more thing to do. The most important thing.

TEN

IT TOOK SIXTEEN minutes for the police to arrive, and considering how long it took for the authorities to respond the day of the James Bridge massacre, this wasn't too bad a turnaround. Some things *had* improved in this part of the world after all.

Units dispatched from Maitland, further up the valley, their journey quickened by the expressway killing the town, skidding off the exit, kicking dust, their red and blue blinders like fireworks in the fog. They sped down the main drag and took a sharp turn, not bothering to stop at the traffic lights. Cockatoos feasting in the tree above the bus bench were startled into flight, feathers twirling and the branches tumbling into the gutter as they took to the air, screeching as though they were the chased ones.

Units mounted the curb out the front of 15 Queen Street. One by one, lights bloomed within the surrounding houses. Rubberneckers took to their windows, clutching nightgowns, cupping faces to the glass.

Officer Kaaron Brennan hit the ground first, her partner, Officer Jeffro Null, hot on her heels. Their counterparts flanked in close, and by the time Brennan noticed the open door and the figure doubled in its arch, all guns were drawn.

Wind blew leaves across the bloodied threshold. Their shadows were huge against the face of the house. Brennan smelled the shit, the metallic essence of the male victim, her heart punching against the pull of her bullet-proof vest.

The man moved.

He sat upright against the wall in an enormous pool that extended to both sides like ruby angel wings. One shaking finger inched off the ground and pointed down the hall.

That way.

The man's puppy-dog eyes locked with her own, a magnetic pull as strong as it was doomed. His mouth blew a single bubble of blood, and then he slipped into death, a journey carved out for him against his will. With KNIVES, as the caller had said. No, screamed.

KNIVES!

NINE

AIDEN THOUGHT HE'D dreamed the coming and going of sirens. He lifted his head from the pillow, muscles giving a kick. The musty motel air made his eyes itch.

The television was on, evening soap operas playing out their inevitable dramas.

Those sirens sounded so real.

He fumbled for the remote and switched the old unit off. Beautiful faces shrunk down to a dot, bleeping into oblivion.

Aiden propped himself up with one arm and looked to the window across from him, brow furrowed with concerned tension lines. He strained his ears, blinked his quiet shock away, and registered the fading screech of police cars. Or maybe an ambulance.

Legs swung around to touch the carpet.

He licked his lips. Dry.

Aiden was at the point of crawling off the mattress and taking himself over to the kitchenette to drink water straight from the tap like he used to when he was a kid, but he stopped in his tracks. And he stopped because of a fresh sound, one that couldn't be confused with another.

The clunk of feet coming up the metal staircase at the end of the veranda.

Fingers dug into the ugly flower-printed bedspread, drawing fabric into his clutch. His nerves prickled and that hollow feeling twisted in his stomach again. If the stress of all this didn't give him an ulcer, Aiden didn't think anything would.

Clunk-cuck.

He knew what that sound was, too. A nearby door opening. It did not close.

Breaths stalled in Aiden's throat as he stood, and in the hold of that choke, he considered something that had never occurred to him until this moment. All things considered, why would Danny *willingly* go into social work as a profession? And even more awful than this question was its kindred answer prancing along close behind, flippant as children singing Ring a Ring o' Rosie as people died from the plague in the streets all about them. It crushed and it mocked Aiden, even as it affirmed his reason for being here in the first place.

I guess working to save others is easier than working at saving yourself.

EIGHT

AN AMBULANCE PULLED up as Kaaron Brennan entered the house. Never once in her six years on the force had she ever drawn her gun with the intent to shoot; she was more terrified now than she'd ever been. Null was by her side, covering blind corners. Every door she kicked open revealed empty rooms, rooms of unfinished business. The paperback on the bedside table with the bookmark tucked within, the mobile phone blinking messages received, a scented candle that had never been lit.

Death in the details.

Blood caked thick where the hallway branched into a T intersection, kitchen on her left and living room on her right. There was no mistaking which way the action had progressed; gore led to weeping MasterChef contestants.

The door hung off its hinges on the other side of the room. Darkness beyond. Null shone his flashlight to reveal handprints on the architraves, swipes of blood resembling red, drooling smiles.

Footsteps and flashing beams outside the window, past the television.

"This is the police," Brennan called into the dark.

"We've got this place surrounded. If you're in there, drop your weapon and come out now."

Only nobody came out. No shame-faced perp' with hands raised.

"I'm doin' it," Brennan informed her partner, gesturing with a tilt of her head. Her words were spoken through grinding jaws.

"Don't," Null replied. In his voice you could hear their history, one stretching back to year three at the Catholic school here in James Bridge.

Brennan fortified herself. She switched the safety off her loaded gun.

"Yes," she said. "Yes."

SEVEN

BLUE AND PINK neon light illuminated Aiden's way.

He listened to the buzz of electricity from the MOTEL sign at the carpark's entrance; it sounded like a hive, bee stingers rasping together. Another gust of wind blew through town to rustle his fringe, to stir the foggy cauldron obscuring the sky, stretching it thin in places to reveal the quarter moon beneath. He sweated. And he was scared.

Aiden stopped.

He thought of his flight from Brisbane to Bangkok and the black-and-white movie he'd watched on the way. *It's A Wonderful Life,* it had been called, and while it featured numerous set-pieces, one particular scene returned to him now. In it, Jimmy Stewart's character said he would lasso the moon and gift it to his gal to win her affection.

And earn her love.

The fog rolled in. Everything turned blue and pink once more.

To think that he—or any man—had ever set their sights on the moon and thought it a three-dimensional thing worth dragging to Earth for the sake of someone special struck him as cruel and naïve. It was a fantasy, of course—but still. Most fictions were spun to mask the truths within, and at the center of most truths there lay a hurt. Were Aiden to swing a lasso and toss it around that moon, he knew the rope would sever on its scythe edge, the remainders uncoiling from the sky to thud against the ground. Because without someone to admire it with, the moon was flat. And so very, very sharp.

Fuck Jimmy Stewart.

Aiden pushed on, even though his feet were heavy, regardless of how he ached. As suspected, the door to room eleven was open. Danny would be in there waiting for him. As to how their conversation would pan out, Aiden just couldn't predict. At this point, there was nothing to do but hope.

He rounded the corner and stepped inside. No. No endolphins here.

SIX

NULL RELENTED AND nodded, stepping up to his partner's side as they inched to that doorway. Brennan smelled blood in there, in the pit of nothingness.

They forced themselves through the arch, the quaking beam of Null's flashlight revealing an upended phone on the floor, and farther ahead, the soles of two pale bare feet.

Brennan didn't want to see. Yet it was her job to see.

It wasn't that the woman's clothes had been torn away. The comfy looking Sunday garments had bloomed off the slippery corpse, shed like the scrim of a cocoon. There was no beautiful butterfly here, not here in this dark house on Queen Street. Only cuts on top of cuts.

For all Brennan knew, she stared at eighty stab wounds. Or more.

"Good God in Heaven," whispered Null. These were the quivering tones of that boy in the third grade, the one who feared his teacher's yells because he hadn't done his homework again.

If only there was a way to wind back the clock and erase this sight from her mind, to go back to a time when they were young and things like this didn't exist. While the image of the corpse would live with Brennan for years to come, it was what she saw next that would follow her to the grave.

Always with her. Stalking.

FIVE

SNEAKERS WISPED OVER CARPET. Aiden was tempted to reach into the dark, but he held off for the time being, letting his eyes adjust instead. The room sketched into form one shade of blue and pink at a time.

Aiden found his partner sitting on the bed with his back to him, lit in neon glow.

The quiet hotel room. Quiet, except for a curious suckling sound.

"Danny?" Aiden said and took another step. His chest seized when he saw a shape on the far wall near the kitchenette, where the drawers had been opened.

Just his shadow.

You bloody fool, he could almost hear his mother say, leaning over to scold him as she did when he was a kid, bringing with her a wave of scented lady sweat and bush smoke. *Pull your shit together*.

Aiden longed to have her here with him now, even f only to condemn him. That, at least, would be omething. He felt so disconnected from his people, rom his land. He couldn't wait, one way or another, or this Hell to be over. Besides, he *did* need to pull his hit together. Indulging in all this was insanity. bsolute fucking insanity.

I'm not far away, Mum.

I promise.

"Danny?" No reply. Aiden tried again, concentrating on the word in his mouth, the ugly way it sat on his tongue. Greasy. He spat it out. "Michael?"

Nothing.

That twisting in his gut itsy-bitsy-spidered up to Aiden's lungs, and then further, into his throat. It choked him. As he came closer, he noticed Danny held something.

FOUR

THE WOMAN WHO'D made the emergency call had collapsed at the entrance to another room on Kaaron Brennan's right. Long, red hand streaks also palmed the door there. Blood lathered the handle, grew fat at the bottom of the knob, dropped to the puddle by the woman's severed ear.

Ploink.

Ploink.

Ploink.

Brennan wanted to cry. She didn't, and kept her pain inside.

Stenciled across the ajar door were two words. It must have taken a caring, steady hand to inscribe that lavender printing so well, even going to the effort to put a little heart above the 'I'. A mother's touch, if there ever was one.

"Timmy's room," Kaaron, who had two kids of her own, read aloud.

Later, there would be time for weeping. That time was not now.

THREE

AIDEN CAME AROUND to face his partner head on, Danny's silhouette outlined in blue and pink. He could see every hair on his head, the fine peach fuzz along his arms, all of it highlighted in vibrant detail. Seeing him, Aiden thought, was to observe a painting, an oil on canvas titled 'Man on Bed Holding Baby'.

The itsy-bitsy-spider within Aiden's throat bit down. Muscles tensed. Terror filled him and froze, painful cracks appearing in the ice as he brought his hands to his face. Things like this didn't happen to people like him. This was something from a horror movie, or maybe, tomorrow's headlines.

I'm a good person, Aiden wanted to scream. *I—we—don't deserve this. It's gone too far. Take it back Take it back!*

Too late for that now. Aiden Bonner was in room eleven of the James Bridge Motor Motel, with the carpet beneath his feet and the stink of copper tainting the air. He was in room eleven with Danny as he brought the child to his face to plant a kiss on its cheek Reality.

A strange memory shot at Aiden.

He was at the airport waiting for his rental to b

brought around. His legs, still cramped from the flight, grounded the concrete between tired-looking ferns and cigarette butts. People had been coming and going in a rush. He recalled how they looked like marionets on strings, limbs jerking as they ran, heads bobbing along, all controlled by a desperate need to get somewhere fast or get away from something even faster. It was time that these people chased or were chased by. *Time*. And Aiden, too, had been caught in their strings and drawn along, hurried to this shitty town and the little room at its heart, to an ending which, deep down, he suspected had been coming. A moment in which all time stopped.

Its absence petrified.

He wanted—no, needed—to be caught up again and taken from this place. Fast. Their strings had been clipped. No inertia. It was so still in here, a stagnant, almost festering diorama. As if to prove this point, Aiden watched with mounting horror as the child's hand slipped loose and dangled by Danny's side. Lifeless. A puppet without a puppeteer, all strings cut free.

"Babe," Aiden said. He reached for the kitchenette wall. "What have you done?"

His jittery fingers found the toggle and flicked the switch into the ON position. There was a plastic clap, followed by the fly-like buzz of the fluorescent bulb above the sink blinking into brightness.

Aiden watched the blood-coated man he loved upright himself, the sound of bones snapping into realignment. The baby was dead, mutilated beyond recognition. He couldn't even tell if it was a boy or a girl. What Aiden had mistaken for a kiss in the dark was, by light, just Danny swallowing the last of his meal. The child's exposed skull glimmered through shreds of cartilage and gristle. An eye dangled from its socket on a thread of sinew. Teeth scythes along its throat like bites in apple skin.

Danny glanced up at Aiden. Into him. Through him. He'd never looked so sad.

TWO

EAT THE PART *that hurts,* said the voice of the flies.
Eat the part that hurts.

ONE

OUTSIDE, FOG YIELDED to the winter wind and moonlight beamed through. That same rush of air swept over the James Bridge Motor Motel to rattle its eaves, blowing dirt against its windows. The night's breath, so very much like a sigh, eased the door on the second floor shut. Ungreased hinges creaked, creaked, and trapped the new fathers within.

Somewhere out there, time moved on. But not here. Not inside room eleven.

ABOUT THE AUTHOR

Author, artist, and filmmaker Aaron Dries was born and raised in New South Wales, Australia. His novels include *House of Sighs, The Fallen Boys, A Place for Sinners*, and *Where the Dead Go to Die*, which he co-wrote with Mark Allan Gunnells. His short fiction and illustration work has been published world-wide. Feel free to drop him a line at aarondries.com. He won't bite. Much.

THE END?

Not quite . . .

Dive into more Tales from the Darkest Depths:

Novels:

Beyond Night by Eric S. Brown and Steven L. Shrewsbury

The Third Twin: A Dark Psychological Thriller by Darren Speegle

Aletheia: A Supernatural Thriller by J.S. Breukelaar

Beatrice Beecham's Cryptic Crypt: A Supernatural Adventure/Mystery Novel by Dave Jeffery

Where the Dead Go to Die by Mark Allan Gunnells and Aaron Dries

*Sarah Killian: Serial Killer (For Hire!)*by Mark Sheldon

The Final Cut by Jasper Bark

Blackwater Val by William Gorman

Pretty Little Dead Girls: A Novel of Murder and Whimsy by Mercedes M. Yardley

Nameless: The Darkness Comes by Mercedes M. Yardley

Novellas:

Quiet Places: A Novella of Cosmic Folk Horror by Jasper Bark

The Final Reconciliation by Todd Keisling

Run to Ground by Jasper Bark

Devourer of Souls by Kevin Lucia

Apocalyptic Montessa and Nuclear Lulu: A Tale of Atomic Love by Mercedes M. Yardley

Wind Chill by Patrick Rutigliano

Little Dead Red by Mercedes M. Yardley

Sleeper(s) by Paul Kane

Stuck On You by Jasper Bark

Anthologies:

C.H.U.D. Lives!

Tales from The Lake Vol.4: The Horror Anthology, edited by Ben Eads

Behold! Oddities, Curiosities and Undefinable Wonders, edited by Doug Murano

Twice Upon an Apocalypse: Lovecraftian Fairy Tales, edited by Rachel Kenley and Scott T. Goudsward

Tales from The Lake Vol.3, edited by Monique Snyman

Gutted: Beautiful Horror Stories, edited by Doug Murano and D. Alexander Ward

Tales from The Lake Vol.2, edited by Joe Mynhardt, Emma Audsley, and RJ Cavender

Children of the Grave

The Outsiders

Tales from The Lake Vol.1, edited by Joe Mynhardt

Fear the Reaper, edited by Joe Mynhardt

For the Night is Dark, edited by Ross Warren

Short story collections:

Frozen Shadows and Other Chilling Stories by Gene O'Neill

Ugly Little Things: Collected Horrors by Todd Keisling

Whispered Echoes by Paul F. Olson

Embers: A Collection of Dark Fiction by Kenneth W. Cain

Visions of the Mutant Rain Forest, by Bruce Boston and Robert Frazier

Tribulations by Richard Thomas

Eidolon Avenue: The First Feast by Jonathan Winn

Flowers in a Dumpster by Mark Allan Gunnells

The Dark at the End of the Tunnel by Taylor Grant

Through a Mirror, Darkly by Kevin Lucia

Things Slip Through by Kevin Lucia

Where You Live by Gary McMahon

Tricks, Mischief and Mayhem by Daniel I. Russell

Samurai and Other Stories by William Meikle

Stuck On You and Other Prime Cuts by Jasper Bark

Poetry collections:

Brief Encounters with My Third Eye by Bruce Boston

No Mercy: Dark Poems by Alessandro Manzetti

Eden Underground: Poetry of Darkness by Alessandro Manzetti

If you've ever thought of becoming an author, we'd also like to recommend these non-fiction titles:

Where Nightmares Come From: The Art of Storytelling in the Horror Genre, edited by Joe Mynhardt and Eugene Johnson

Horror 101: The Way Forward, edited by Joe Mynhardt and Emma Audsley

Horror 201: The Silver Scream Vol.1 and *Vol.2*, edited by Joe Mynhardt and Emma Audsley

Modern Mythmakers: 35 interviews with Horror and Science Fiction Writers and Filmmakers by Michael McCarty

Writers On Writing: An Author's Guide Volumes 1,2,3, and 4, edited by Joe Mynhardt. Now also available in a Kindle and paperback omnibus.

Or check out other Crystal Lake Publishing books for more Tales from the Darkest Depths.

Hi, readers. It makes our day to know you reached the end of our book. Thank you so much. This is why we do what we do every single day.

Whether you found the book good or great, we'd love to hear what you thought. Please take a moment to leave a review on Amazon, Goodreads, or anywhere else readers visit. Reviews go a long way to helping a book sell, and will help us to continue publishing quality books. You can also share a photo of yourself holding this book with the hashtag #IGotMyCLPBook!

Thank you again for taking the time to journey with Crystal Lake Publishing.

We are also on . . .

Website:
www.crystallakepub.com

Be sure to sign up for our newsletter and receive two free eBooks: http://eepurl.com/xfuKP

Books:
http://www.crystallakepub.com/book-table/

Twitter:
https://twitter.com/crystallakepub

Facebook:
https://www.facebook.com/Crystallakepublishing/
https://www.facebook.com/Talesfromthelake/
https://www.facebook.com/WritersOnWritingSeries/

Pinterest:
https://za.pinterest.com/crystallakepub/

Instagram:
https://www.instagram.com/crystal_lake_publishing/

Patreon:
https://www.patreon.com/CLP

YouTube:
https://www.youtube.com/c/CrystalLakePublishing

We'd love to hear from you.

Or check out other Crystal Lake Publishing books for your Dark Fiction, Horror, Suspense, and Thriller needs.

With unmatched success since 2012, Crystal Lake Publishing has quickly become one of the world's leading indie publishers of Mystery, Thriller, and Suspense books with a Dark Fiction edge.

Crystal Lake Publishing puts integrity, honor and respect at the forefront of our operations.

We strive for each book and outreach program that's launched to not only entertain and touch or comment on issues that affect our readers, but also to strengthen and support the Dark Fiction field and its authors.

Not only do we publish authors who are legends in the field and as hardworking as us, but we look for men and women who care about their readers and fellow human beings. We only publish the very best Dark Fiction, and look forward to launching many new careers.

We strive to know each and every one of our readers, while building personal relationships with our authors, reviewers, bloggers, pod-casters, bookstores and libraries.

Crystal Lake Publishing is and will always be a beacon of what passion and dedication, combined with overwhelming teamwork and respect, can accomplish: Unique fiction you can't find anywhere else.

We do not just publish books, we present you worlds within your world, doors within your mind, from talented authors who sacrifice so much for a moment of your time.

This is what we believe in. What we stand for. This will be our legacy.

Welcome to Crystal Lake Publishing—Tales from the Darkest Depths

Printed in Australia
AUOW01n1338200918
302994AU00003B/3

9 781643 16